THE DEAD EFFECT

Terry L. Vinson

THE DEAD EFFECT

GRAVESTONE PRESS

Prologue

Ladies and gentleman, my name is Jamison. Phillip Jamison. I have been duly chosen to serve as your host and guide this evening, and I warmly welcome all fourteen of you back into modern society (clear throat), for want of a better term. Rest assured, the medical staff states that the disorientation you feel is natural, and the associated dizziness, nausea, and blurred vision will indeed vanish within a twenty-four to thirty-six hour period.

Please feel free to sip the water from the plastic containers provided. There are also packets of saltines if you feel the urge to indulge. The medical staff also says to expect your normal appetite to return within a day or so, at which time you will more than likely experience a ravenous hunger like no other. Whoops, not too much water, Mister Vincent. It's liable to increase your nausea unless taken in minute increments. Yes, that's better. Miss Conners sitting to your left has the right idea. Sip- don't gulp.

Good people, I cannot even begin to fathom the levels of mental confusion and physical jet lag you must be enduring.

While you nibble and sip, allow me to fill you in on the planned itinerary. To allow you proper... decompression, again for want of a better term, you will remain here for another two to three hours. From what we understand about Cryogenics, the system requires at least this much time to properly recharge its eternal clock. Currently, your blood pressure and pulse rates are dangerously low.

You've each been injected with B-1 and B-12 shots, as well as a multi- vitamin booster with enhanced Beta-Carotene.

Questions?

Yes, Misses. Jackson I believe?

A fair question, indeed. We are a freelance agency not directly affiliated with but hired by your corporation, pre-plague, to search out, rescue, and revive its former staff heads and associates. We are also tasked to relocate you for reintroduction into present day society, or what we refer to as 'The Colony'.

Mister Bowen?

Affirmative, sir. This site has been cleared and duly secured. Fortunately, the isolated location of this particular facility keeps the population of infested at a relatively low number. You'll be relieved to know they've long since abandoned this area due to the lack of a fresh food source.

Misses...Clarke, please proceed with your inquiry.

Why no, you're perfectly entitled to an answer concerning our uniforms.

These are a variation of the military chemical suit, though tweaked somewhat as to better protect us from germ and bacterial invaders. You people are presently in what we term 'Code Blue Quarantine', meaning you present a minimal threat to those around you. Do not be alarmed by this, as it is simply a precaution we are forced to take by regulation. Once we get to the in-processing station, a series of more advanced testing will take place that will clear you to move about freely within the colony population. Again, this is just a precaution. In the meantime, please excuse our rather ominous appearance.

Mister Caldwell?

Yes, well, I shall soon discuss in great detail the duration of your downtime. For now, please continue to ingest the liquids and settle back into a comfortable consciousness. Once the medical staff is convinced you're stable enough, you will be bused to a safe house for continued observation. The safe house in question is a former five-star hotel located approximately forty-five miles from this location. Having been properly reinforced and secured, the hotel presently serves as 'in-processing' headquarters for all new arrivals. In the meantime, I will provide an in-depth de-briefing as to fill in the blanks. Let me initially state that in terms of what you've missed during your period of downtime inside the Cyro canisters, consider yourself extremely... fortunate. It must be noted that the company showed a great deal of hindsight and intelligence by placing its top people in suspended animation just as the plague hit its peak.

Unfortunately, your president and CEO did not survive the ordeal. It appears he suffered a massive coronary sometime during the incubation period, more than likely from the chemical treatment. In addition, the vice-president and operations chief also expired under similar circumstances. I'm...sorry to have to pass on such tragic news so soon following your reawakening, folks.

Mister Caldwell, I believe by following the company chain of command, that you are next in line to succeed your former superiors. I'm sure such matters can and will be discussed in length following the conclusion of the in-processing phase.

For now, please relax, breathe deeply and continue to ingest the provided nourishment. I'll return in approximately twenty to thirty minutes to begin the main thrust of this in-briefing. And again, allow me to be the first to welcome you good people back from oblivion.

THIRTY-SIX MINUTES LATER

Okay, people. I hope you're feeling a bit more chipper. I see you've all managed to finish off the refreshments. I know it wasn't much, but there'll be a more substantial, not to mention tasty, meal awaiting you at the in-processing station.

For now, allow me to get to the heart of this in-brief and begin answering the questions I know must be burning holes into each of your collective psyches.

First off, there is the subject of just how long each of you has been incommunicado since the day you were placed in the Cryogenic chambers on September 23rd of the year two-thousand fourteen. Utilizing Old World calendars, the present date is now the sixteenth of April in the year...two-thousand thirty-five.

Please people, please. I know it must be extremely difficult to accept, but try to control your emotions. Your immune systems are still very weak at this point, and such self-induced stress might well affect your overall cardiovascular well-being.

Mister Caldwell, please sit and calm yourself, sir. I...we as a company have no reason to be *untruthful. I understand the shock you must be experiencing, but we'd rather not be forced to use sedatives at this point. I'm...going to break now to allow our medical staff sufficient time to counsel and/or treat each of you on a one-to-one basis.*

SIXTEEN MINUTES LATER

I'm glad to see everyone back in their seats and looking a bit more subdued. Again, I truly sympathize with the shock and disbelief you must feel. From what I've gathered from the counselors, most of you figured to have been in suspended animation for less than a decade. Twenty-one years spent in limbo is quite a span, no argument, but please bear with me as I unequivocally state, without even a tint of irony, that you folks definitely picked the right two decades to skip I know, I know, many of you shake your heads and wonder how I could possibly verbalize such an outlandish remark. Please, at least give me the chance to back it up with cold, hard fact. Fair warning, folks; what I have to say is less than uplifting. Keep in mind, however, that the planet you are now re- entering is a dramatic improvement over the one you so secretly exited all those years ago.

The plague that came to be known as the 'ER, or Exterminator Re- animator Virus' had just begun its Earthly sweep in the days preceding your decision to be reborn into a different time via chemical comas. By late summer of two-thousand fourteen, an estimated three billion had fallen victim Worldwide, and that's not counting the countless million others who were...completely consumed by those previously re-animated by the virus. The medical and scientific community, what small portion remained, had more questions than answers as precious time ticked by and nation after nation was overtaken by roving legions of its own dead.

By the fall of two-thousand sixteen, a state of martial law was declared by default on a planet-wide basis, as all world leaders were assumed dead or hiding out, and governments and armies disbanded without fanfare. By the time spring rolled around the following year, all major lines of communication were severed, and the actual number of known survivors impossible to tally, though it was estimated at less than one-hundred thousand world-wide. Those left manning the torch for mankind were basically relegated to an existence more appropriate for moles or similar nocturnal beasts, hiding out in underground facilities or holed up in concrete and steel prisons of their own making. To label it simply a 'dark age' would be to woefully underestimate its place in history.

Stories, such as the ones I'm tasked to regale to you now, were later discarded as simple myth or legend, since the majority of those involved did not survive to verify their authenticity. Nonetheless, the powers that be insist these tales be told to all new arrivals as an abbreviated history lesson of sorts.

Let me begin by saying there have been hints of a similar plague long before the big one hit in twenty-fourteen, beginning with an incident that supposedly took place in the mid-eastern and southern U.S. in the late nineteen sixties; an incident allegedly covered up by a Government unwilling to share its horrific details with the general public.

Again, let me issue a fair warning before initiation; unlike history lessons of old, there will be no editing of content nor sidestepping the grisly details. The last two decades have been anything but tranquil. It has been a period filled with suffering, anguish, and agony unparalleled. Prepare yourselves, people, for this is your legacy...

1 - WORM DIRT

Bakerstown, West Virginia (Population 596)
Circa 1968

Part One: Unnatural Happenstance

"Come on back, Margie. That last transmission was a mite garbled. Over," Sheriff Masterson had said, holdin' that radio mike tight up to his lips. We was ridin' back from Knotts Valley, where he'd just picked me up for transportin' several hundred liters of JW Dant's finest Kentucky rot-gut to the Watts brothers. I'd been slumped over in the back seat' a his Ford Galaxy, sweatin' like a rented mule an' tryin' to figure out how many nights I'd be hold up in the county lock up this time. I'd just got out on a similar charge a few months past, havin' spent almost six weeks as a guest of Lauders County, but had the feelin' that Judge '*Iron Balls*' Wilkes wasn't gonna be near as easy on me this time around. Besides which, the wife was gonna be beside herself. She'd laid down the law just a few weeks prior about my secret 'side job' activities, sayin' she'd have nothin' more to do with it if'n I got caught again. Figured she'd already stashed away a packed bag or three just in case, and would be headin' off to her mama's in Wheeling once this latest case of bad news came down.

Little did I know at the time, but such matters was gonna be the least of my troubles once early morning gave way to late afternoon.

Masterson had trailed me down Little Bear Creek Road 'til I'd ditched my pick-up, then chased me through Dickerson's woods on foot. Man ain't a thing if not persistent...I'll give 'im that much. Caught up with me whilst I was hidin' inside the old barn next to the Forrester's abandoned farm, but not 'fore a couple'a stray dogs had caught up with me first. Damned knee finally stopped bleedin' from the fall I took outta that hayloft, but it ain't quit smartin'. Wasn't real sure of my bearings after that pop on the noggin, least not 'til I was already takin' up space in the back of the patrol unit.

"Ya need to get back here lickitty split, sheriff. We got some serious going's on...plum crazy going's on...a-all over...all around town, I mean to say...over," came the woman's reply from the other end of that talk box, soundin' like someone had just goosed her titty.

"Could ya be a mite more specific, Marge? What kinda trouble? Bane McBride beatin' up on his wife and kids again? Over."

"No...no...nothing like that, Sheriff. You...it's just...you'll have to see for yourself. I've been hearin' about all kinds of strangeness. Phone ain't stopped ringin' since nigh on seven AM...from Pearl Jacks down atLake Meyers to Merle Dean up at Dry Creek Manor Over."

Masterson steered the vehicle (pronounced *vee-hick-ul')* through a steep series of curves that leads into Mill's Valley, then turned about and shot me a grave look, still holdin' that mike to his mouth. Wyatt Masterson had been the law in and around

Bakerstownsince I was knee-high to a Blue Tick pup, a genuine straight arrow who didn't take bribes nor lip from no man. Big as an ox and twice as ornery, old '*WEarp*', as everyone called 'im, had no patience for my kind, and in truth, I can't say I really blame 'im. No doubt if I had to spend most'a my day runnin' down no count bootleggers, cow thieves and wife beaters, I reckon I'd have a similar disposition.

"I'm a good eleven miles out, Marge. Got Pete Van Zant in tow for haulin' fire water. I'll petal her down and be there as quick as I can. Have ya heard from Perry? Over."

"Not since 'bout ten AM. I'd got a call of a break-in down at Childer's Seed 'n Feed. Can't reach 'im on the radio and I can't get no answer at Childers. That's been pert near an hour ago, Wyatt. Over."

"Tell ya what, Marge…I'll head on over to the seed 'n feed from here and radio in once I get there. Over." Perry Finch was Masterson's only deputy As tall as a valley pine but built like a bean pole, Finch was one sour, stone-faced SOB that took his job way too serious. Man wasn't much on brains but damned high on cockiness. Rumor had it he'd only got the deputy job 'cause he'd married Masterson's sister, and couldn't hold down a job doin' nothin' else.

The sheriff turned back to me just as we'd drove out of the western edge of Mills Valley, passin' the Wilbery farm on the left hand side. The man was sweatin' more bullets than his gunbelt could'a ever held Even that thick, gray mustache of

14

his was soppin' wet. Thinkin' back, I don't believe it was just the boilin' heat inside that patrol unit causin' such a meltdown. Can't help but recall my own gut was rollin' a bit from a spell of nerves. Didn't know why at the time, just had a bad feelin' somethin' wasn't right.

"We gotta take a little detour, Pete. You just hang tight. I'll get ya to the lockup soon enough," he'd said, his breathin' kinda huffy, like he'd just got done sprintin' up a steep grade in his stockin' feet.

"I'm in no particular hurry, Sheriff, By all means, take yore time."

It took us another fifteen minutes or so to wind our way down Old Hickory road towards Childers feed store. Funny thing was, I don't recall meetin' or even seein' a single vehicle along the way, despite the fact that farms littered Old Hickory like ants on a picnic trail.

"Unit B, you copy?" The sheriff had yakked into that mike as we'd got 'bout halfway. "Perry, are you hearin' me, boy? Come back, over…"

"Maybe his battery petered out, Sheriff. That unit ain't near as slick as this one. I'll bet th-"

"Shut your pie-hole, Van Zant. When I need the opinion of a two-bit bootleggin' rat bastard like yourself, I'll *pound* it outta you," he'd growled in response, tossin' that mike into the passenger seat and cursin' under his breath. I'd decided to heed the man's words, havin' seen up close and personal he wasn't one to mince 'em when dolin' out physical threats.

He'd parked out front of the seed 'n feed, which

was deserted 'cept for old man Childer's delivery van, Lloyd Gordon's rusted old Chrysler and Deputy Perry Finch's patrol unit.

"Unit A to dispatch Marge, you receiving? Over" he'd asked, standing with a boot still propped inside the unit and that mike cord pulled taunt.

"I…Wyatt? Y-yes, I'm still here. But…I've had t-to…this is…this ain't…things ain't right here, Wyatt…not right at'tal…o-o-over," Marge had replied, soundin' more scart than ever. The conversation that followed 'tween those two sent cold chills up my back despite the swelterin' heat inside the tin box I was occupyin'.

"Marge, what's goin' on? What's happenin' there?"

"I've had to…barricade the courthouse door, Sheriff. Locked it…t-tight and then managed to…push two of the filin' cabinets and Deputy Perry's desk be-behind her. Otherwise…th-they would'a got to me already. O-over…"

"Bar…barricade? Marge, what in blue blazes is goin…"

"Waitaminnit, Sheriff. I…somebody's poundin' on the door (*loud crashing noise*).Can…can't you hear that? Oh Lawd…oh lawdy…Wyatt, the-they breakin' through (*another loud crash, followed by the sound of multiple footsteps*)!

They…oh dear *GAAAAWDDDD*!! (radio squelches, then goes silent)" "Marge? MARGIE??"

Quick as a flash, the sheriff leaned into the front seat then reached back and slapped cuffs over both my wrists.

"Back in a wink. You stay glued to that seat,

16

boy."

I don't mind confessin' that at that point and time, I'd swallowed a heapin' helping of panic, and wasn't ashamed to show it.

"But sheriff, wh-…don'cha think we outta get back to town? Is it a joke or somethin'? I mean, what was them noises in the courthouse? Shouldn't ya get ba-"

"I said, back in a wink. Just settle down, Van Zant. I'll get to the bottom of all of it. Just…settle…down."

I watched 'im climb the wooden steps leadin' up into the feed n' seed's loadin' dock, then vanish inside. It was about that time that the morning sun fell behind some fierce cloud cover. I'm talkin' some real low-hangin' thunder- bummers, and it didn't take no time for things to grow real dark over the valley. Tragedy was, things were about to grow a helluva lot bleaker.

Part Two: Reality Takes A Powder

Now, I ain't gonna lie. I'd smoked some real fine rabbit tobacco in my day, not to mention made a bad habit outta suckin' down a sample of my main transport from time to time, that bein' *Evan Williams, Jack Black* or *JW Dant* brand hooch. Hell, I'd even munched on a wild 'shroom every moon or three when I wanted a different sorta buzz. That said, I was never one to get so gassed or stoned that I startin' seein' things that simply weren't there. Had a buddy or two who'd see flyin' saucers or bats with human faces sailin' about after a few choice swigs of my Uncle Gerard's homemade 'shine. Not me. No siree. I was always what'cha might call 'grounded into reality' at all times, no matter the quantity or quality of consumption on any particular evening. The old lady's influence had a lot to do with that, I reckon. She kept me on the straight and narrow more oft than not.

Yep, it was always said that ol' Pete Van Z could manage to keep a cool head, no matter the level of hell breakin' loose. Like the old sayin' goes, I guess all things do come to an end, 'cause at around eleven AM on that fine West Virginny morn, the head in question was anything but cool.

First off, I heard a single shot go off inside the store. Duckin' down into the seat 'til my head was propped agin one window and my feet pushin' hard agin the other, I then heard two more ring out, followed by a pair of screams timed 'bout three seconds apart The wailin' had come from the same mouth, no doubt about it, though I'd have never bet a silver dollar on Sheriff Wyatt 'Earp' Masterson bein' capable of soundin' so damn...lady-like under *any* circumstance.

Secondly, the sheriff leapt off'n the edge of that dock like a cliff-diver, twistin' his body around and firin' off another round just 'fore hittin' that hard-graveled drive in a balled up roll.

Thirdly, well...this is when things *really* got squirrelly. The next couple'a minutes was kinda hazy, I mean, at that time it was only natural to doubt what I thought I'd seen. Lookin' back, and sad as it might sound, it just don't seem so all-fired strange anymore.

After he jumped back behind the wheel, the sheriff had spun outta there so fast it was like we was ridin' through a dust cloud. I did manage to get in one clear look at the seed store dock through a break in that murky funnel just as he'd spun the vehicle back onto black top. I saw two figures amble their way to the edge. I believe the first had been old man Childers, though I couldn't swear to it. He wore an apron that looked like it'd been dipped in fresh barn paint. Couldn't really make out the face, 'cause it was similarly splattered in dark red...I mean, even the man's *hair* was matted up into the shape of an arrow tip.

The second figure was one Deputy Perry Finch, minus his left arm past the elbow and with a mangled pile of his innards hangin' free from his gut like a freshly gutted sow. Man had been holdin' what looked like the slashin' end of a sling blade in the only hand he still owned, and his face and head were just as drenched as old man Childers'.

"Jesus…Jesus…Jesus…" the sheriff kept mutterin', pullin' the mike to his mouth but not really sayin' nothing, like the words just wouldn't come. After the glimpse I'd gotten from the backseat, I couldn't rightly say I could'a performed any better.

"Ma-…(clears throat)…Marge, this is Wyatt. You there, Marge? Come in, over. MARGE! Come IN! *Damn* you, woman…"

I'd straightened up a bit by then, havin' crawled up from the floorboard where I'd been scrunched like a stink bug in a pea patch.

"This is Sheriff Wyatt Masterson of Lauders County, am I reaching anyone (clears throat)? Repeatin', this is Sheriff Masterson of Lauders County…is anyone there?"

We took the steep curve in front of Bellwood bridge doin' about sixty, and I recall feelin' my sweet meats crawlin' up inside my belly for temporary refuge. Looked down and noticed my left knee was seepin' again. Figured I'd opened it back up rollin' around in the floorboard. By the time we crossed that rickety pile of loose boards and hit Highway Six headin' towards main street Bakerstown, the sheriff had discarded the mike and was diggin' on the radio like a teenager searchin' for just the right rock 'n roll tune to cruise by.

Despite my better judgment screamin' otherwise, I was about to inquire about the madness we'd just left at the Feed 'n Seed when he stumbled upon AM one-oh-seven in Jonesboro Flats. For the next several minutes, we both sat back and listened to a Halloween spook story come to life.

The announcer was spoutin' some nonsense bout reports in Marion and Jelks counties of people attackin' one another for no concrete reason other than to spill blood. Said the governor hisself had called on National Guard units to set up shop as near as West Bayonet, which sits just eight or nine miles from the Bakerstown city limits. Another report said all the trouble had started inSouthern Pennsylvania, and was just now spreadin' to the east and south like a wind-blown flu virus. Accordin' to official (pronounced 'o-fi-shal') reports outta Washington (pronounced 'Warsh-in-ton') DC, everythin' from contaminated water to a meteor from outer space was bein' blamed for all the craziness.

"Lord…help us. Gotta get to a phone, that's all. Make a couple'a calls and find out what the real story is. The *true* story," the sheriff had whispered more to hisself than to me, I reckon.

"Was…was that deputy Finch back there, Sheriff?" I finally found the courage to ask once we'd ridden to within a few miles of the Stratford Boardin' House and the north entrance to main street. He didn't answer for a few seconds, and I figured I was in for still another butt-chewin' Meanwhile, a light rain had started to fall, and the clouds overhead seemed to be growin' blacker the closer we got to town.

"Y-yeah. Him and old man Childers. When I walked in, they was…was…fightin' over a slab of…rib meat…r-raw…it was bloody raw…they were like…rabid animals they was. I ain't never…I thought for a minute I'd blown a fuse 'til…*Holy MOSES*!" he yelped, causing me to flinch back like

21

he'd nailed me in the forehead with his billy-club. The unit swerved, and I ain't talkin' a harmless little skid neither. By the time he'd straightened her out, my front end was jammed into the floorboard with my feet mashed up against the back glass.

I'd heard 'im cursin' and raisin' Cain as we'd left the pavement for dirt and rock, but was too busy rollin' around to really understand any of his wild jammerin'. By the time I'd pushed myself upright, we'd just passed Hoyt Vincent's Lumberyard, only a hop, skip an' jump to the courthouse.

"Did ya...did ya see that, Van Zant?" Masterson had asked, starin' at me through the rear view.

"Naw...didn't see a damn thing, Sheriff," I'd shot back, and not in the best of moods,"I was a too busy floppin' about like a banked catfish. Got the knots on my noggin' to prove it.

"What happened anyhow? Thought I heard ya cussin' up a storm."

"It...it was Larry and Dot Romero. Just standin' in the middle of the blamed road, hand in hand like school kids playin' ring around the blessed rosey. I only saw 'em for a flash and had to jerk the wheel to keep from pancakin' 'em, but they both looked kinda glassy eyed. Perr-...deputy Finch and old man Childers had that same exact look, like they was in some kind'a trance."

The man's voice had turned all gravelly and low, like a chunk of stale bread stuck in his throat.

"Plus which, both of 'em were shirtless. Dot's tit-...breasts were all smeared an' bloodied. Looked...like one of 'em had even been...torn

22

off…just…just like P-Perry's arm.

"I could'a swore Larry grinned at me just 'fore we swerved around 'em. The man had…stuff hangin' from his teeth. I dunno, m-might explain the hole in Dot's chest."

"What in hell's goin' on, Sheriff? How's about let-…uh…releasin' me on good faith? I…I'm kinda worried 'bout the wife…" I finally asked, no longer able to hide the fact that I was basically scared shitless, and not just for yours truly. Sad to admit, but Pete Van Z looks out for number one on a regular basis, as priority one normally, but this day wasn't normal. Couldn't help but think 'bout Trudy all alone in our cabin. A cabin so far back in the sticks we might well be *hard* to find, but damn far from *impossible* if somebody puts forth the effort.

Truly, it was like livin' a daytime nightmare…one of them real freaky corkers that wakes you in the middle of a hot, humid summer night. Ya bellow like a whipped dog and sit up, soaked to the marrow and your chest poundin' like a jackhammer. My wounded knee was screamin' with all the sweat pourin' into her. Felt like somebody was curin' my upper leg with bacon salt.

"I…can't say I know any more than you, Van Zant. Just…we gotta stay calm, that's all. Stay calm and get to town. We'll find some answers there, by god. By hook or crook, we'll get us some answers."

Have to admit, at that point I really didn't give a god damn 'bout answers. Fact is, if I'd been behind the wheel of that black and white Galaxy, Bakerstown would'a been pretty damned low in terms of priorities for this kid. More than likely I would'a turned that bad boy around, retrieved the wife and a suitcase or two, then drove straight past the Florida line, not stopping 'lessen the tank was drained dry or I saw ocean waves dead ahead.

Can't say for sure, but I do know for a cold hard fact that the yellow streak up my back was surely glowin' bright.

Part Three: HELL in a Hand-Basket

"Holy   sweet   Jo-ho-sa-phat…mother of…god…" I heard Masterson cry out; cry out like a frightened little girl instead of the twenty-plus year law enforcement vet he was. Took me a sec to get a clear look at what caused such an embarrassin' whine from a man I'd always feared from both a mental and physical standpoint, but once I did, let's just say I both understood an' forgave 'im without hesitation.

Main Street Bakerstown was a war zone. Don't know how else to describe it. Sayin' it any other way would be to short-change its impact. No shit, it was straight outta one of Duke Wayne's WWII movies, only instead of gun and canon shots rattlin' off in the middle of the pacific (pronounced '*po-ca-fic*') ocean or some far off Eu-ro-pean shore, the settin' was a rural township in the middle of the southeastern U.S A. A quiet, peaceful township whose main law breakers were the local bootleggers, maybe a wife-beater or two, and perhaps the occasional (pronounced '*o-kay-sio-nail*') jay walker.

The sky had opened up right fore we hit the main drag, comin' down in buckets like every angel in heaven was cryin' down on us, then clearin' up just as quick. Damnest thing I ever saw, least until we turned that last curve at Crowley's bait shop and swerved directly onto Main Street, Bakerstown.

As the sheriff managed to steer around (or in

one case, *through*) the majority of the mayhem, I managed to accomplish two things simul- …simultinos-

…two things at once. One was to maintain a wide-eyed view of all the craziness we passed, and the other was a dirty little deed I'd hadn't experienced since grade-school; wettin' my pants like a spooked toddler and totally unawares of it 'til minutes later.

Funny thing was, and I'm talkin' funny strange and not funny *ha-ha*, the sheriff kept that patrol unit's gasoline pedal mashed to the floorboard, 'cause I doubt we ever got under fifty in a marked twenty-five mile per hour zone.

Weirdest thing, but all the craziness streamed by real gradual-like. It was like everybody and everythin' was movin' on a slow-motion picture reel, 'cause I was catchin' details that should'a been impossible the way we was hummin'.

Anyhow, much as I'd like to forget, those details stick with me in order of how they transpired:

Craziness number one:
Luke Comstock chasin' his old lady, Maggie I believe her name to be, down the main drag towards Elm. Truth be told, Ol' Luke was more like 'stalkin' than runnin' since he was missin' most of his left leg. The reason for the chase was pretty damn simple once I put two and two together. Wish like hell I hadn't, actually. Maggie, all two-hundred plus pounds of West Virginy Farm Wife and built like an ice-house, had her old man's foot an' calf stuffed

26

in her mouth, sprintin' down the street just a gnawin' and chompin' like she'd won the turkey drumstick contest on Founders Day. No sense guessin' if old Luke ever retrieved that missin' appendage, but he sure 'nuff left one hell of a slug trail along the way. Somebody was shootin' at the both of 'em from a second floor window of the Bakerstown 'Sleepwell' Motel, but a car explosion just a few yards away distracted me just as I was about to identify the mystery shooter.

Craziness number two:

Wendy Jacobs, local Bakerstown grade school teacher, sittin' on the corner of Main and Oak with her hands an' head buried inside some poor bastard's gut. Just as we swerved by, I swear she looked up and right into my eyes, a string of half-gnawed innards hangin' outta her mouth like a stringin' of raw sausages.

Craziness number three:

The Sprague brothers; Al, Howie, and Roy, thunderin' down main street in the back of Wilber Danley's old Chevy truck, all armed with twelve gauges and blastin' everything that moved One of 'em even managed to nail the passenger side of the patrol unit as they whizzed by us doin' at least fifty-five. The sheriff had his siren wailin' at full blast, but the boys just plum ignored it and kept on reloadin' and firin' away as I saw 'em disappear into an alley behind the Rexall drug store. You would'a thought they was out in the middle of a field some where's shootin' at quail.

Craziness number four:

Main street was not only caked in smoke and fumes from at least a half dozen burnin' cars and almost as many buildings, it was also littered in bodies, some sprawled out in the middle of the street and others curled up on the sidewalks. I noticed a few of 'em burnin' like somebody had doused 'em with kerosene and threw on a lit match. Hell of it was, even the ones laid out wasn't stayin' that way for very long. I saw at least four or five roll over and back up, like one of them kid's toys that ya hit and knock over but it just keeps boucin' back upright. Swear I saw Wilma Parker, a hairdresser over at Macie's salon and one helluva looker, joggin' towards First Avenue with half her head missin' above the eyebrows.

Damned if it hadn't looked like she'd had the top half sheared off by a circular saw. Truth be told, I could only properly ID her by those jigglin' jugs and that wide, bouncy rear end. Never forget a well-shaped caboose, no sir.

Even saw Clint Carpenter, the local postman, tryin' to beat down the front door of Lamar Dante's hardware store with both fists. Thought for a second he was just tryin' to find a safe place to hide, you know, to escape all the madness. That is, 'til he turned around and I saw his lower jaw was gone and 'bout half his throat had been ripped out. Man's tongue was floppin' about like a big ol' creek eel.

Couldn't swear to it, but I think his eyes was missin' too, cause all I seen was two black pits surrounded by bloody rings.

28

By the time Masterson pulled behind the courthouse and into a fenced-in parkin' lot totally empty 'ceptin' for us and Marge Bolton's beat up old Ford jalopy, I felt numb, like I'd gulped down a pint of Evan and then taken one humdinger of a shot to the back of my skull.

"Let's go, Pete. Sure can't be leavin' you out here," the Sheriff said, pullin' me by the elbows outta the back seat. I must'a been 'bout half dazed, 'cause I don't clearly recall departin' the patrol unit at all, much less runnin' through the back entrance of the courthouse.

On the other hand, my mind was clear as a bell once we'd both made our way inside. Truth be told, I wish to the good lord above it hadn't. Guess I should'a been spendin' more time in church and less sittin' around gettin' gassed on my own wares.

The power must'a been out, 'cause it was pretty dim inside the rear of that lock-up. Hadn't been for a couple'a small windows allowin' some daylight to sneak in, we would'a been blind as owls.

"Wyatt! Sheriff...oh thank...thank heavens," Marge Beasley yelled out from just to my left. A fluffy-haired, heavyset but not altogether unattractive woman in her late thirties, Marge had locked herself in the last of three holdin' cells, and was grippin' a nightstick in one hand and a heavy duty flashlight in the other.

"What the...somebody lock you inside?" the sheriff asked, frontin' the cell door with his revolver facin' towards the lone entrance from the front of the courthouse.

"No...no! I...they chased me back here.

Cornered me like a rabid...like wolves on the hunt for...fresh meat. Everybody's gone crazy as a loon out there! Off their gourds! Outta their goddamned trees, sheriff! Didn't ya...didn't ya see? It's...I ain't never seen anything like it..."

While those two co-workers had commenced jabberin' away 'bout how's, why's and when's, I'd walked over a few feet and stopped dead center at cell number two, a rancid-smellin' eight by ten I'd spent my fair share of nights in, normally in ten to twenty day increments (pronounced 'in-cra-mints').

For a couple'a seconds, all the yellin' and gunfire noises comin' from outside had let up, just long enough for me to hear the sounds leakin' out from the back of that cell.First the sounds, then the sight, then the *odor*. Gotta say, the sounds were bad enough...moist suckin' noises, like kids slurpin' on melon rind. Then there was the sight; pretty damn horrifyin', of one man bent down over another, his head buried so far into the other's open chest that I could hardly see the lobes of his ears pointing towards the ceilin'. Man's ribcage was pulled apart like a butchered buck...I could even see rays of light breakin' through the spread bones.

But it was the stench, like perforated gut, easily the worst of the lot.

Could'a gagged the *Queen* maggot, I'm bettin'. Guess I'd somehow drawn the matter to the sheriff's attention, though I'll be damned if I recall bein' able to speak or even point at the time. Found myself plopped against a cool stone wall with shakin' legs and tremblin' lips. Ain't no doubt I probably looked as dead as the man layin' inside that cell with his

30

innards hangin' out. My ears were goin' numb from the poundin' at my temples, and my knee wound stung and throbbed like a rotted tooth. Also had a bad case of the cool shivers, a nasty little symptom added to the sickenin' mix sometime 'tween witnessin' all the crazy shit along main street and enterin' the 'dungeon of doom' known as the Bakerstown courthouse and county lock-up.

"But that's...that's Elroy Hutchins and...and Willie Mac Myerson...locked 'em up j-just last night for drunk...drunk drivin'..." the sheriff had said, I figured talkin' more to Marge than me, though Margie was still babblin' a mile a minute just a few feet away, somethin' about her daughter bein' up at the lake with friends.

I saw the sheriff jump back like a mule had just planted both hooves in his gut, then saw what had caused it. Elroy Hutchins had his face plastered directly 'tween those steel bars, resembling a man what had dipped his face inside an oil drum. Only everybody present knew it weren't no oil drippin' off'n his nose and chin. Nor was it honey baked ham hangin' from his bared teeth. He was growlin' and groanin' like a fox with its hind leg caught in a steel trap.

The sheriff fired a single shot, I reckon on instinct alone, and I swear to all that's holy that I saw that slug punch into the front side of Hutchins' neck, drillin' a sizeable hole, then exit out the back in a messy spray. The man never budged.

Oh, he reached up and stuck a forefinger into a quarter-sized hole just below his chin, but the way he was actin' it might as well have been an itchy skeeter bite.

Kept on groanin' too, though the damaged air pipe made 'im sound a might wheezy.

"Som...bitch...he didn't even...like I didn't even...did you...right through the back of his..." the sheriff was ramblin' just as the front entrance flew open and a pile of bodies came streamin' through. None of 'em were exactly runnin' or even walkin' very fast...no, as I recall, they all moved kinda sluggish-like, almost as if they was injured in some way. They was all moanin', growlin' and hummin', same as Hutchins. Sheriff Masterson fired a few shots into the masses, then turned and grabbed me by the arm, pullin' me back the way we came. After shovin' me almost flush with the exit door, he stopped and began diggin' a set of keys from his belt. I realized what the man was tryin' to do, and I did and *still do* understand his train'a thought. Then again, that didn't make it neither smart nor practical. Sure, he wanted to free his co-worker and friend and get her the hell outta that feedin' pit. Then again, Masterson wasn't a dense man by any means. He had to know there weren't near time enough to pull those keys free, find the right one, then unlock, go inside and pull her out. By then, ya see, Marge wasn't comin' out on her own. She was crazy as a bed bug with swamp fever, and he would'a had to wrestle her all the way to the patrol unit.

"Get...get outta here, Van Zant!" I heard 'im scream just as the first wave of bodies got to within a few feet of 'im. He'd managed to find the right key, even had the lock turned while emptyin' that blue steel gat into the crowd.

"Get, dammit! G-get help! GO!!!"

He'd been tryin' to shut the cell door behind 'im, to at least lock himself in with Marge, but by then three or four of...them *things* had squeezed 'tween the door and the lockin' mechanism. By that time, enough light had leaked through for me to recognize at least two outta that rabid mob. One was a local auto mechanic named Jeremy Fowler, minus a large chunk'a flesh from his left cheek. The other was Bonnie Peterson, who was missin' an eye and whose left ear was hangin' by a thread onto her shoulder. Hell, it was a true shock to see ol' Bonnie, who all the guys had referred to as 'Boner Bonnie' durin' our high school days together. Last I'd heard, she'd been turnin' tricks 'round Mobile and was bein' pimped by one mean-ass, gun-totin', gold-toothed Ace'a Spades.

I'd like to say I considered jumpin' back into the mix to save 'em, that I'd at least *tried* to push a few of 'em away so's the sheriff and his girl Friday could find a safe space. Then again, I ain't fibbed 'bout nothing up to this point, so I figure (pronounced '*figger*'), why start now?

The last thing I saw 'fore high-tailin' it outta there like a man with his ass- cheeks ablaze was the image of Sheriff Wyatt Masterson standin' over Marge Beasley like a Mama bear protectin' her cub, kickin', punchin' and head-buttin' his way through at least ten or twelve of those damned things. Looked like Marge had already taken the high road and passed out, and I saw one of *them* had bent down onto the cell floor and proceedin' to bite into the calf meat of her left leg.

The door slammed behind me as I'd heard Masterson holler out one last time. This time it weren't instructions he was barkin'…or any brave battlefield cry. It was the scream of a man fixin' to die…and die badly.

I hopped into that unit and fired her up in record time, havin' never given a thought that the sheriff might'a taken the keys with 'im. With the siren blastin' and the blue lights flashin', I peeled out of that lot with my cuffed hands at ten and two, takin' the back alley onto Pine Street, then took a sharp right onto the east edge of route two-forty seven.Even with the pedal shoved securely to the medal, I still figured to be a good twenty minutes from the homestead, barin' any further craziness along the way.

Part Four: Bone-Yard Road

As it turned out, it took me less than fifteen minutes to reach the one-lane dirt leadin' to the Van Zant hideout Bein' that the highway had been pretty much deserted 'ceptin for a slew of abandoned vehicles, I was able to keep the unit movin' at a brisk pace all the way outta town. There'd been a few stragglers along that paved path, most of 'em limpin' down the center of the highway with droolin' lips or missin' limbs, or both. I dodged a few an' nicked a few, makin' damn sure I didn't wreck my ride as a result.

The plan, as I'd mapped her out, was fairly simple. Me an' the wife would stock the fruit cellar out back with enough water, grub and sour mash to hold up a week to ten days, while also armin' ourselves to the teeth with every piece of live ammo and fire arm I owned.

I parked the unit a dozen feet from the start of our driveway. Had to make sure the place hadn't been overrun already. Hated that I was dwellin' on the possibility, but I'd already seen enough crazy shit in the previous hour not to take chances. Bein' as quiet as I could manage, I pulled a double-barrel shotgun from the unit's trunk, checked to make sure she had a load in her (she did), and left that trunk door hangin' in the wind as I crept toward the drive. I'd already searched the unit for the keys to my cuffs, but couldn't find hide nor hair. Figured they was still attached to the sheriff's belt, which meant they might'a already been somebody's lunch.

The homestead an' barn sat 'bout two hundred

paces from where the drive started, hidden by a thick line of head-high shrubs an' tall elms just eaten up with kudzu. Yeah, me and the little lady loved our privacy, even though most would say it weren't necessary to hide at all. See, not a single soul 'cept for the Van Zant clan ever dare lived down what the townsfolk called '*Bone-Yard Road*', labeled as such for a civil war era graveyard that lies a stone's throw from the back of our barn. Story goes that a lost Yankee patrol met their maker there, and was buried on site. Bein' that none of the dozen or so scattered graves are marked by a single blessed name or date, I never bought that cock-and-bull story myself. Always figured it to be nothin' more than some old coot's pet cemetery, where the bones of a pack of faithful coon dogs was laid to rest.

By the time I'd crept up to the front porch, my knee felt like it was comin' unhinged like an old shutter. I was holdin' that shotgun tight in against my midsection, bein' that I couldn't properly separate my hands to aim her correctly.

I leaned against the front screen door with my ears cocked for any sign of either trouble or the wife herself movin' about inside. All I heard was a passel of crows in the growed-up cornfield to the left of the barn and a few croakin' bullfrogs near a small pond out back.

Gettin' a might worried, I finally built up the nerve to bolt inside with the gun's barrel leadin' the way.

The livin' room was unusually dark, and it took my peepers a few seconds to adjust to why. Seems

Trudy had strung up blankets over every damned window in the house; tacked 'em up with twenty-penny nails. The hammer she'd used was still layin' on the couch, along with a handful of scattered nails.

As I walked by the kitchen, I could hear the radio playin' low from the bedroom.

The local news folks were pleadin' for everyone to 'stay inside their home' and 'lock all doors, windows and basement entrances', while also advisin' to board, cover up, and barricade the same. I strolled into that room expectin' (hopin' against hope, in truth) to see Trudy sittin' on the edge of the mattress, dressed to the nines in her finest blue cotton dress and her hair tied up in a ball atop her head.

"Where you been, Peter Van Zant?" she'd say, the corners of her mouth curled up just so as to make me wanna plant a big ol' wet kiss on those ruby lips of hers, "your supper's getting cold...and so am I. Better hop on while we're both still warm, mister."

The devilish specter who'd been placed in charge of *cold hard reality* had a different notion, it seemed. One more in line with the rest of that day's occurrences.

The bed was neat and unwrinkled, as Trudy was always one to tidy up after a night's sleep.

Stumblin' through to the back deck, it didn't hit me 'til I was standin' at the railin' peerin' over into those dense woods that the back door had been wide open. In retracin' my steps, I then noticed the overturned chair and busted night stand layin' beneath the oak table we took dinner from each night.

Leanin' up from where I'd knelt, I came to near passin' out from a sudden spell of lightheadedness. 'Bout the time I reached up with one hand and felt the heat radiatin' off my own forehead like a lit stovetop, I also heard the shuffling noises comin' from the livin' room.

I kicked the oak table over and took up a crouched position behind her, strugglin' mightily with my bound hands to get the damn shotgun lined up to fire straight.

The first of 'em waddled into my sights a second later, and I ain't recalled takin' a relaxed breath since. Whatever the hell it was, the bony stalks it was walkin' on cracked and snapped with every damn step. I recall seein' one of them laboratory (pronounced *'lab-I-ra-tory'*) skeletal men in the biology classroom back in school. Well, if this rotted som'bitch wasn't completely striped'a fresh, he was damned close. Another one joined 'im a second later, both of 'em dancin' a jerky jig into the kitchen entrance. The second one had a strand of cloth hangin' from its rib cage. A faded *blue* cloth strip with some kinda insignia that weren't familiar 'til I gave it some hard thought a bit later. Yankee blue…Yankee *insignia.* Seems the myth and legend surroundin' that lost platoon hadn't been as much rumor as fact. Bein' worm dirt for a hundred (pronounced *'hunnerd'*) years or so hadn't stopped 'em from wantin' to join the party, it seemed. In fact, I had a sinkin' feelin' they might even be behind the whole ordeal, though there was no findin' out the why's or how's of such a wild notion.

Damned if my whole body didn't break out in gooseflesh from head to toe at that very moment in time, fever be damned.

It don't really seem possible I know, but I'd swear both of them stinkin', rotted demons from hell were starin' me directly in the eye, despite the fact that neither of 'em owned a pair.

I was about to let 'em both have it some where's near the chest or neck bone areas when I heard a new noise directly behind me.

Turnin' with the gun barrel leadin' the way, I slapped the first one right across his forehead, sendin' a busted skull flyin' across the wood floorin' like a split melon. The rest of the thing's body just fell apart right at my feet, like some damned skeleton puppet with cut strings. Sailin' forward and usin' the gun like a ball bat, I wasn't about to let myself get cornered by the masses. I'd decided to make a run for the cellar, hopin' (but not really expectin') that Trudy had already done the same.

I managed to kick one of the skinless bastards down the wood stairway leadin' off the deck, and was windin' up the rifle for another strike when the newest target of my aggression came clearly into view.

As I recall, I'd only cried two times in my entire thirty-five years up to that point; once when my mama passed from a sudden heart attack when I was in grade school, and the day Grandpappy Van Zant breathed his last just a few short years ago.

Seein' my wife of pert near fifteen years standin' on those stairs with her arms stretched wide to give me a hug, I felt my eyes welt up and grow moist like somebody had tossed Cheyenne pepper into both of 'em. I dropped the gun, hearin' but not seein' it dribble down the steps and into the grass.

It weren't 'til she shambled closer that my throat hitched up and I felt a cold chill race the length of my spine. I ain't about to lie; wouldn't serve no purpose whatsoever to do so. Seein' the love of my life, a woman I'd first dated as a bony, pimply-faced teenager and married right outta high school, haul herself up those rickety stairs with hands missing all the fingers but the thumb on the left and a single pinky on the right, just about shredded this poor old boy's heart.

Worse yet, it looked like her upper lip had been gnawed off, 'cause she was in a state of perpetual grin with her top plate suckin' wind for all to see.

I heard my sweet thang moan just 'fore she reached forward with those jagged nubs; a soft, kinda mournful cry, remindin' me of the day we buried her papa up at Whitestone cemetery Just 'fore I snapped outta my fog and found the strength to leap over that top railin', I'd felt my partner's touch at the base of my throat. Only thing I can rightly compare it to was a shavin' of ice meltin' against my flesh.

Landin' fairly smooth a good ten feet below, I rolled to my feet and made tracks for the cellar door. I looked back only once, and saw my sweetie-pie desendin' with all the speed she could muster, which wasn't much considerin' her right leg was all gnarled up and shaped kinda funny, like one of them sea-farin' birds you see whose knees bend backwards. There was at least a dozen of them skeleton Yankees trailin' behind her. Hell, one of 'em was even wearin' a faded blue cap that was their trademark, and grippin' what looked like the end of a bayonet blade, probably pulled offin' his very own rifle.

I just about dove into that cellar, slammin' the door shut and shoving the plank bar in place just about in the same movement. I'd dug the cellar mainly for twister season, but also to hide a few select jugs of happy water for special occasions.

Not sure how long I was in there 'fore figurin' enough was enough.

Might'a been as long as three or four days, or as short as twelve or fourteen hours. Weren't much to eat 'cept a few raw taters and a barrel of rotted carrots. No water neither, so I ended up sippin' on a quart jar of aged moonshine that I'd stashed away a few months before. Can't recall much 'tween the naps, 'cept for cryin' a lot. It was a shameful kinda cry, more for myself than my poor, dear soulless wife, who fate had cursed to walk with the damned; side by side with an army of corpses 'til whatever cruel God had seen enough and saw fit to end the whole miserable shootin' match.

I recall wakin' more than once and it bein' dark as a coal miner's asshole, then passin' out and wakin' to bright sunrays sneakin' through narrow spaces in the planks. The fever had really took hold by then. Not even the shine helped. Didn't seem to matter, really. Lost my taste for it after half a jar.

Woke up heavin' my guts up a bit later; rotted veggies an' all. Smelt 'bout as appealin' as gopher guts bakin' on hot pavement. 'Least it served to numb the pain in my knee. Come to think of it, it weren't but a few minutes 'fore I crawled outta that cellar when I noticed my whole damn body felt more'n a little strange, like I could'a fell on a box of fishhooks and never felt the sting.

The sky was a dark shade'a black as I'd shoved that heavy oak door open and stumbled out, clouds as thick as a heavy fog hangin' down to cover the nearby hilltops settlin' over Kelsey's woods.

At first I thought maybe all them walkin' skeletons had skedaddled, but soon I noticed a half dozen or more of 'em ramblin' my way. It weren't like I had the strength to fight 'em off at that point. My head was crazy with fever and my body had long since taken the high road to a better place.

Not sure why I gave up the way I did. Never had been one to surrender without a scrap. Somehow, someway, I just knew it weren't necessary. As it turns out, my reasons sure as hell weren't a mystery to no one else present.

The first wave passed me by without so much as a nod to show they even knew I was standin' there.

A second later a different trio shuffled by, and one of 'em kinda leaned over and sniffed me. Least I think it did....hard to tell really when the damn thing's nose had long since been eaten away. I cringed back a bit, but again, it weren't at all necessary as things progressed.

I recall fallin' to one knee, no longer havin' the

stamina to stand for more'n a few minutes at a time. Next thing I knew, an arm wrapped itself around my neck, then reached down to rub my chest with a hand that held only a single digit; a pasty lookin' pinkie finger that was the color of sealin' dap. Kinda looked like a well-fed maggot, wrigglin' an squirmin' along my neck bone and then down to my bare nipples. My darlin' Trudy always loved teasin' me with her touch. Guess there's some things even death don't change. I guess in some ways I was expectin' the worse, like maybe she'd lean down and bite a healthy plug out of my neck or start gnawin' on my nose. When she finally did lean down, allowin' me to fall into her lap like we was on a Sunday picnic, she tilted her head just so, puckerin' her lips, which by then looked more like dried slugs. A part of me knew such a couplin' weren't right…just plain unnatural it was. Then again, that was a real *small* part. True love endures all, I've heard it said. Guess that ain't just a sayin' after all…

Epilogue: A Permanent Hunger...

Not long after, Trudy and I departed the old homestead for the last time, trudgin' down the dirt road towards town. Not sure what town, mind you...maybe Kingston Springs or Wellington. Headed east we were, along with seven or eight of what I've come to think of as The '*Van Zant Brigade.*' Destinations ain't hard to choose. The condition itself warrants the direction (pronounced '*di-rac-tion*') really. Basically, it's where the smell of meat carries the stoutest.

Warm, *unspoiled* meat.

Ya see, I'd been fightin' it for hours, ever since that dog had bit my knee inside the old Forrester barn. I'd been kiddin' myself, thinking it was the fall that'd opened my flesh and invited the fever in.

Guess the incubation period from animal to human ain't quite as fast, though it's just as damning. I can surely vouch for that.

Regardless, I can't put much true heart into complainin' about it. World's change.People just have to learn to adapt. No choice in the matter. Sides, it ain't so bad really. Got my loved one by my side, walkin' hand in hand. Now, if it just weren't for this dad-blamed gnawin' at my gut...

...and this cursed *hunger* that just won't let up...

***

Please take into account folks, that the validity of events such as these are virtually impossible to prove and thereby are highly questionable. That said, I myself have witnessed similar horrors up-

close and personal in the past several years. I'm sure many of the staff present here today would attest to the same. It's been said that soon after the previous events took place, the government took it upon themselves to cover them up with a rather wide, sweeping broom, even to the point of ensuring local townships such as Bakerstown could never again be found on any Atlas.

Question, Miss Jackson?

Well, you have to keep in mind, madam; we were born and raised during this rather dark period. Personally, I had just turned six when the plague occurred. The majority of Colony citizens have little or no memory of what you deem a 'normal existence' I can only attempt to relate via the historical data we've been privy to.

What's that, Mister Vincent?

Yes, I'm sure our parents experienced quite the dilemma in deciding to conceive and raise children in this era, just as my generation is now facing the same. I guess the ultimate question becomes: do we allow the species as a whole to fall prey to extinction due to our own inner fears? A very hard question, indeed, the answer to which depends on the individual being asked. Personally, though happily married, my wife and I have decided to remain childless for now.

To continue then...we still have a few hours remaining before loading the bus. We'll go the democratic route, put it to a vote. Shall I continue with this rather grisly history lesson or would you folks prefer some extended 'quiet time' before departure?

All right then. Looks like a landslide. Story-time shall continue. Please feel free to interrupt at any time. Believe me, I would more than understand. There have been groups in the past who grew weary of my prattling tone. Is anyone having difficulty comprehending? I realize this face plate makes me sound as if I'm speaking underwater. I do appreciate your patience and understanding.

To proceed, this next entry is a tad more personal, as it involves a close- knit family torn asunder by the horrors of the plague.

2 - BLOOD KIN

Ah, Gerald, my favorite nephew, he was. My dear sweet sister Rachel's boy, always so energetic; so chock full of vinegar and vigor, a Barton male all the way. Boy had Ivy League potential written all over him.

Through the years, I dare say I favored young Gerald over my other nieces and nephews. Showered him with extravagant gifts. Went out of my way for thrice-yearly visits from as far as six states away. Anything for '*Little Gerry*'', as I so lovingly referred to him. Oh, how Rachel used to scold me so, as did that Neanderthal husband of hers, though it never seemed to faze me in the least, nor alter my plans in terms of spoiling the boy rotten. He so reminded me of myself as he grew into a man: athletic, intelligent, and just a wee bit ruthless in matters of personal gratification. That young man not only wanted to grasp the brass ring, but to store it away in his personal vault. Such a *healthy* attitude for one so youthful and inexperienced, I must say.

Following the catastrophic collapse of their family business due to Rachel's fool of a spouse and his gambling *slash* drug problems, I saw a gradual change in my nephew that frightened me somewhat, though at the time I simply chalked it up to the dramatic change in lifestyle he'd been forced to endure. Offer as I might, Rachel simply would not accept charity. It seemed the deuced Barton pride wasn't limited to the male side of the family after all. The louse she'd married left them in a lurch, though rumors were rampant that he'd later met with a rather grisly fate at the hands of one of his many debtors. Over six hundred thousand dollars in debt, Rachel had been forced to sell off her portion of the family estate to secure funds to move her and Gerald to what she'd deemed a more 'stable' environment. Oh, I'd offered to pay off a sizeable chunk of her debt, but dear Rachel, stubborn as ever, had declined.

The last I saw of my older sister and favorite nephew, he having just turned nineteen with the physique of an Olympian and the sharp, handsome features that are the Barton curse, had been at the airport as they'd boarded a commercial airliner bound for the West Coast.

Hard to fathom that almost four full winters have come and gone since that fateful fall day.

Tragically, sweet Rachel passed on some twenty-one months ago at the still youthful age of forty-four. The coroner concluded she'd died of a skull fracture after an accidental fall from a winding staircase within her beachfront home. At the time, I thought nothing suspicious at such a finding. Rachel had always been a bit of a klutz, even as a child.She'd left behind little but the astronomical debt her worthless husband had so casually constructed, though it was later revealed through my younger brother Steven that Gerald had received nearly a quarter of a million dollars from a life insurance policy Rachel had taken out some years previous.

I'd spoken to her grieving son but briefly at the funeral. True, his behavior had been understandably

48

solemn under the circumstances, but there had also been an aloofness present; an underlying layer of off-putting coolness toward family that seemed downright cruel. It was as if he were...purposely avoiding us in lieu of seeking out the support only blood kin can provide in such perilous times.

Now that I've had ample time to dwell upon it, I have serious reservations that my dear sister's fatal tumble was accidental at all. Less than two years following Rachel's untimely death, my favorite nephew showed up at my door practically demanding a handout. His once handsome features and athletic build had been replaced by the hollow, guileless eyes, sunken cheekbones and emasculated features of a stereotypical drug user. I had been forced to kick him off my estate just three days following his arrival once he was caught attempting to pawn the family silver.

Driven away from the estate by my personal bodyguards, my favorite nephew vowed to 'pay me back in spades'. Have to confess, not one of my happier memories.

I must give the boy credit, however. Like all Barton males, he isn't one to dole out meaningless threats.

The hill that looms just past the estate's front gates is quite steep, with perhaps a sixty foot drop from either shoulder, where all manner of jagged rock formations and wrecking-ball sized boulders await.

I must have been doing at least forty-five or fifty when I footed the brakes on my newly purchased Jaguar, only to discover they no longer responded. I clearly recall seeing an image just before crashing into the rocks at the bottom of that dark ravine. The image was of my favorite nephew's grinning visage. It had been a snapshot not of youthful innocence and exuberance, as with the boyish version of Gerald that I had so loved and cherished, but of pure, predatory evil; the merciless, heartless man-child that he had become and that I had never truly known. Darkness ensued; an all-consuming blackness that bathes me still.

Oh, how the world has changed since my abrupt demise. Changed in ways that man could have never envisioned, even in his darkest, most desolate nightmares. Strange how the freshly deceased can continue to monitor the voices of those around them. I would have never dreamed such a queer phenomenon possible, having long been taught that the soul, once detached from its physical shell, is magically transported to some faraway purgatory outpost to await permanent placement. Alas, as I lay across this cool stone slab and feel my outer flesh grow equally chilly as minutes and hours pass, the vocalizations of those around me reverberate like mixed radio transmissions.

"*It's gotta be a joke, right? A sick practical joke, that's all,*" one says.

"*TV says it's spreading like wildfire,*" blurts another, clearly on the edge of hysterical panic.

"*They've got army and national guardsmen shooting them down in the street.*"

"*Hell on Earth, man...I'm telling you. This is it...they're crawling outta their graves. Hell on Earth, man,*" screams still another, followed by a plethora of mangled verbiage that, when properly edited for content, actually began to make sense in an admittedly warped sort of way:

"Saw the first batch of 'em in Williamsport, just outside of Philly..." *"Attacked a busload of school kids in Altoona, I heard..."* *"Scientists on TV are calling it some type of mass hysteria..."* *"I heard one say it's a rabies outbreak turning everybody into ghouls...started in West Virginia and swept east like a runaway virus."* *"Devouring the living...I swear, that's what they just said...devouring the living..."*

"Everybody's leaving. Civil Defense is saying to get home and lock your doors..."

"The hell with this waiting shit, I'm out of here!"

"They can't really be dead. That's crazy...no damn way...I mean, how...h- how is that even...possible?"

"I'm going home to my family. I suggest you all do the same..." *"...lock the doors? Why, somebody gonna steal 'em?"*

"We can't just leave 'em here, damn it! What if they...wake up...you know...like the others?"

"Don't know about the rest of you, but I'm hopping the next tub to the Pacific and finding me a deserted island..."

Funny, I never would have thought a mausoleum so bustling with activity, but then, the family crypt wasn't a place I'd frequented for meaningful conversation or otherwise. Stranger still, I didn't recognize a single voice as that of a relative.

How ironic, in a *Vincent Price* double-feature

sort of way. The dead rise to find nourishment amongst the living. An epidemic of sheer lunacy right out of a Stephen King novel. Stephen King with a sizeable helping of *George Romero* tossed in for good measure, that is.

It is only a matter of time, then. Unless I've misjudged the level of greed involved. Surely my dear nephew hasn't forgotten the priceless family heirloom I'd long sworn to be buried with. A combination timepiece/stopwatch that was passed onto me by my father and his father before him. Last apprised in the early nineties, its value was then listed at just under seventy-five thousand dollars, and has surely doubled by then. Since I'd recently, although not without a touch of sadness and regret, written dear Gerald out of my will, he will undoubtedly seek financial gain by playing the part of graveyard ghoul. Why do I seem *so* cock- sure of such a dastardly crime, you may ask? Being that the young man is surely responsible for my current condition, that being a soon-to-be revived member of the newly christened '*dead-alive*' masses, it's only logical that he isn't beyond stealing from the very same.

The crypt is eerily quiet now, all voices having been quieted as only the occasional thumping or faint dragging noise permeates the blanket of darkness.

My own damnable reincarnation is already underway, it seems. My entire body is ablaze, every fiber tingling like mad as what began as a dull sensation slowly mutates into something akin to high voltage electricity surging through my veins.

Similarly, a dim light pierces the pupil of each eye, the initial blurriness slowly giving way to a more defined outline, though the lids themselves still feel quite heavy and unnaturally cumbersome.

I feel my fingers and toes begin to twitch with new life even as my scalp and the flesh of my face burns as if dipped in acid.

Even as the tingling subsides somewhat and I feel quite capable of rising and joining my undead brethren, I know the urge must be, *has* to be controlled.

For soon, my favorite nephew will come to claim his gold-plated, diamond filled prize, only to discover the cadaver of his loving uncle quite unwilling to part with same.

Despite what others might think of the admittedly vile and unmerciful act I plan to execute this night, personally I feel not a semblance of shame. The once adorable child I so cherished is now the same spoiled, evil brat no doubt responsible for both my sister's demise, and my own. There will be no hesitation on my part. If there *must* be an initial taste of warm, human flesh...it may as well be that of a once revered family member.

The dragging, shuffling noises grow louder as the mausoleums uninvited visitors draw near. Damned scavenger must have brought a buddy or two with him to 'share' in the moment. Not a problem...I've always had a healthy appetite, another mark of the Barton clan.

Despite an overwhelming desire to leap from this concrete slab and face my desecraters on an even playing field, I manage to remain as still as the rotting corpse I'm supposed to be. After all, it's a proven fact that the element of surprise is vital in such a scenario.

They seem to stumble toward me, like drunkards on the verge of collapse. The shambling footsteps end, replaced by a barrage of guttural, animalistic grunts. All at once, the arid aroma of rotted poultry fills my nostrils. If I still possessed a working gag reflex, it would most certainly have activated.

Unable to maintain my guise a moment longer, I open my eyes and prepare to rise into a sitting position even as twin shadows loom overhead.

A thick, white sheet is torn away, revealing a single bright bulb shining overhead, its intrusive glare temporarily blinding me from those who stand posed on either side of my still prone form.

As I'm able to prop myself up onto shaky elbows and my vision begins to adjust, I find the simple act of breathing akin to swallowing a mouthful of powdered cayenne pepper.

Wait! Breathing? But, why would the dead need...require such a useless act when...

I peer downward to analyze my condition, only to discover myself not adorned in my best blue suit, but instead my limbs and torso utterly bare save the thick wrapping of bandages wound around my left knee, right ankle and ribcage. A series of IV's run into my right elbow just above the crock and two separate pouches hang from a nearby stand.

A glowing monitor sits to my left, humming incisively while displaying a current blood pressure reading of one-thirty over eighty-five. The scent of freshly applied antiseptic quickly overpowers that of reeking entrails.

My god! This means....I'm...I'm not dead after all! I was never...j-just heavily medicated!

Even better, the table I lay across isn't stone, but a well-padded mattress! A mattress located not within the Barton family crypt but...but where? A hospital! A hospital of course, where my injuries are being properly treated! Praise be! I've been spared...somehow....someway...I've been spared!

My joyful elation lasts but a scant few seconds, cut off as I twist about and the true identities of my surprise 'visitors' swim to horrifying light.

Oh, such a grave mistake I've made! The blunder of a lifetime as it were; a miscalculation of epic proportions. Alas, the last mistake I'm ever fated to make, at least in this lifetime or present incarnation.

Hands that are inhumanly strong, each finger like an individual vice forged from steel, force me back onto the mattress, my struggles as futile as the girlish screams that accompany them.

The first of my 'visitors' swoops down in a wide arc from the right, removing a rather sizeable chunk from my left shoulder. I see the tendons beneath the flesh stretch and snap like overextended rubber bands. If there is a bright spot to be noted here, it is the pain medication that still serves to numb what I'm sure would otherwise be a rather agonizing experience.

The second 'visitor' places a hand on my forehead and shoves back, pinning my skull flat while leaving my bulging neck an open plain from which to feed. I feel the sticky warmth coat my upper chest in a gushing torrent I reach up to punch and jab with what little of my fast-ebbing strength remains. Thrashing from side to side as my vision again grows gray and spotty, I manage to wrestle my way into a sitting position at the center of the bed.

Though their eye sockets are hollow and soulless, it's the *way* in which they feed that brings the most shocking of realizations home.

There is a subtle gentleness to their grip, a *suckling* in their bites that hints at something deeper than merely the instinctual acts of a predatory beast.

As bodily fluids and consciousness escape me in equal measure, I find just enough time, and the mental faculties, for a final, totally unexpected, and rather *touching* observation.

One eats away the fingers of my left hand, nodding in sad acknowledgement as it tilts its horribly misshapen skull to one side.

The other has chewed away the majority of my right forearm, but manages to pause and shoot me the briefest of winks, despite the fact that no actual pupil exists within the blackened pit below its sagging lid.

Ah yes, they do what they must do…what they are *reborn* to do, for they know no other way. But I think, they also recognize. They also recall. They also…love.

I cease my struggles, laying back as the ritual hits its grisly crescendo.

As it is, I have but one thing to offer, and what better, more noble sacrifice than to those who matter the most?

Similarly, I have but one final thought as my dear *sister* and favorite *nephew* reach with greedy, blood-soaked hands toward my midsection and begin to rend and tear with gleeful relish.

To… forgive is indeed…divine…and…*The only thing that…truly matters…* in this…or the damnable life that awaits…is the tried and true…kinship…blood kinship…of…family.

* * *

Again, I feel the need to apologize for the gruesomeness of the story content, though omitting such details would both undermine and detract from the point being made. These are indeed the same tales we were told as children, as our parents and guardians had no choice but use the element of fear to emphasize the very same point. I'm afraid the graphic nature of this briefing is a necessary evil. Trust me, people, it's preferable you learn in here before seeing for yourself…out there.

Are we sufficiently comfortable or does anyone require a lavatory break? Fine, allow me to continue with the next entry. It supposedly took place near one of the U.S.'s most popular vacation spots a few months after the plague had really taken hold. Seems the trip was less than tranquil, and anything but relaxing…

3 - The GRAVE Canyon

Leaning his ample bulk against a truck-sized boulder, Vito spoke only after a labored series of noisy huffs. If one were to utilize the pinnacle of politeness, they would refer to a man Vito's size as 'big boned' or 'hefty'. On the other hand, one prone to overt rudeness might well choose from such terms as 'fat and/or lard ass', 'chunky-cheeks', or possibly even the old stand-by 'tub 'a guts'. More scientifically edged descriptions might include 'immensely obese' or perhaps even 'elephantine'.

"Shit, I'm wiped. How's about we don't go no further, Gino? I wasn't built for this kinda *roughin' it* bullshit."

"Ya ain't exactly built for Olympic wind sprints either, Vito, so do me a favor and shut the fuck up."

In stark contrast, Gino was rail thin; a human 'waking stick' with knobby knees and matching elbows. With his slicked-back, greasy black hair (with just a tint of gray at the temples), pointed noise and close-set, piercing blue eyes, he was the stereotypical Italian mob boss come to flamboyant life. Legendary amongst his peers for possessing the temper of a rabid pit-bull, he wasn't one to either mince words or regret an impulsive act, no matter the level of cruelty utilized.

"How far in ya think we are, Gino? Seems like we been ridin' those nags for weeks."

Gino shrugged his narrow shoulders, scanning what little of the dusty terrain that remained visible in the murky gloom.

"I dunno. Been a couple of hours since we

58

passed through the North Rim. At least the breathin's easier down here. Where'd you park the mules?"

"Tied 'em to a couple of rocks about twenty yards down the hill. Tough little bastards, I gotta say."

"They would have to be to haul that train-sized caboose of yours around." "You're a real *Scassacazzo*, Gino. Always breakin' my balls."

"And you, my friend, are a super-sized *Frocio*. Now, grab your gear and start hammerin' in stakes already. It'll be light in a few hours."

"Shit, Gino, that's woman's work. I'm beat to the socks, man. Let Vanessa do-…"

Turning on his rotund cohort like a predatory beast prepping to feed, spittle flew from the corners of Gino's mouth like car wash foam.

"WRONG, shit-stack! Cookin', cleanin', and fuckin' are a woman's job. Construction work is all male, *all* the time, that is, less your lookin' to sack down in my tent tonight with those cheesy-fat thighs spread wide and those poutin' lips painted ruby red."

Sauntering into their midst from between a spattering of gnarled, shoulder-high shrubbery, Vanessa struck a seductive pose while simultaneously shooting Vito a wicked glare.

"Don't even think (pronounced '*tink*') about it, fat man. I ain't about to share Big G's lovin' with nobody."

Despite the light banter, Vanessa's high-pitched tone was laced with nervous apprehension.

A frail-looking little boy of perhaps seven or

eight ran to her side, ducking beneath her left arm and hugging her tight. The boy's eyes were moist and huge with fright as he scanned the surrounding darkness.

"Are—are we safe from the monsters here, Auntie V?"

Vanessa reached down and rubbed the boy's sweat-soaked head while staring at Gino with a look of grave concern. In silent response, Gino met her searing gaze for only a brief moment before averting his eyes.

"Sure…sure we are, honey. We're just gonna set up camp and sleep out under the stars tonight. Sounds like fun, doesn't it?"

The boy nodded weakly and sprinted away.

"Don't…go too far, Nick, you understand (pronounced 'unnerstand')?" Gino blurted a bit more sternly than he'd intended.

"Yes, Uncle G," the boy replied, scooping up a handful of rocks and playfully tossing them into the cool, crisp night air.

"Lover, you sure we don't need to cover a little more ground? I mean, those damn things might be right on our heels."

"Calm down, Sweet Cheeks. We didn't see any coming through the rim.

They must figure (pronounced 'figger') they got nothin' to feed on out here. Probably stickin' to the cities and leavin' the wide open spaces be."

"But…how long are we…safe here? Where do we go from he-…" "How the fuck am I supposed to know? Ya think I've done this before?'

Gino barked, tossing his arms about as if

60

shadow boxing some unseen opponent while pacing atop the desert sand like an expectant father, "This shit is new to me too, woman! Rival gangs I can handle. Family members turned traitor? No fucking problem. No instructions or blue print needed. You plug the motherfuckers (pronounced '*mudder fuckers*'), they die...period! On the other hand, an army of rotten cadavers who can take a half-dozen slugs from a nine mil and keep on truckin'? Gotta admit Darlin'...I ain't got a fuckin' CLUE!"

"Well, you better *ACQUIRE* a fuckin' clue, lover-boy, 'cause this girl ain't breathin' her last in the middle of this...this fuckin' dust bowl!" Vanessa shrieked in response, performing a stutter-step 'jig' while pumping both her clinched fists airborne.

Rising from his self-imposed coma with all the speed of a sloth on amphetamines, Vito strolled over as to provide a buffer between the two.

"C-calm down, you two. I mean, shit, we've got this far, right?" he pleaded, his sagging jowls jigging like unsettled Jell-O, "we got outta Vegas with our skin intact, right? Drove over and around their shuffling asses 'til we crossed the Arizona line. Ain't seen any since...since Boulder City, am I right?"

Pulling Vanessa to his slender chest, Gino hugged her close in an attempt to quell her shaking.

"That's right...you come to pappa now. Shit-stack's...um, Vito's right, Sweet Cheeks," he whispered in a much calmer, subdued tone, "once we cross the Colorado River at that Phantom Ranch place, it's just a hip, skip and jump to Quedo's

61

hacienda in Mexico City. We'll be safe there. You've seen Quedo's set- up, remember? Man has a trained militia that makes the U.S. Marines look absolutely pussy-fied. Meanwhile, ya can't ask for a bigger or better safe haven than the fuckin' Grand Canyon, right?"

"Lord," she sobbed, burrowing her head into his chest, "I always wanted to see this place, y'know? Ever since I was a…kid. But…shit…not like…like *this*.

"Damn Gino, I never thought I could ever miss *Queens* this much."

"I hear ya, girl, but the last radio report outta Vegas said both Coney and Long Island were overrun. Big Apple ain't nothin' but one big-ass graveyard by now."

With that, the girl's sobs grew ever louder, her upper body wracked with spasms Increasing the pressure of his hold, Gino positioned his lips over her left ear and whispered in his best reassuring tone, the effect of which was pathetically insincere.

"We'll make it, Vanes. I swear to ya. We'll make it. Come to pappa…ssshhh…pappa's got you now."

Gently pushing her away, Gino took her face into his hands and stared into her tear-filled hazel eyes.

"You really think I'm gonna let any harm come to my best girl?" "I'll…um…uh..get the gear, boss," Vito mumbled awkwardly, whirling about with newfound fervor.

"You do that, V. Gonna be light soon. Least we can grab a couple Z's. 'Sides, believe those Jackasses need a breather as bad as we do. Another mile or two and I would'a needed a fuckin' wheelchair. I do believe I'm carryin' around hemorrhoids the size of bowling balls."

Minutes later, a piercing shriek forced Vito to freeze in mid-swing while attempting to hammer a thick wooden tent stake into the cracked terrain with a small rubber mallet.

"Gino! Gino! I c-can't find Nickolaus! H-he...he was...I thought he walked o-ver. ..that way...h-...he's..." Vanessa wailed, frantically waiving her arms while dashing by Vito at full gallop.

Walking back from the mules with a trio of rolled sleeping bags balanced atop his bony shoulders, Gino quickly tossed them aside and met her near the makeshift campfire he'd lit a half-hour earlier.

"Calm down, woman. We'll find 'im. I mean, Jesus, he couldn't 'a got very far."

"I...it's so...dark. I couldn't see. I kept sayin' his name over and over.

Didn't..h-hear nothin'. Not...not even a fuckin' bird chirpin'..."

"It's all right, Sweet Cheeks. We'll get 'im, dammit," he spat sternly, gripping her by the shoulders as he turned towards Vito. "V, grab a flashlight and start walkin' the perimeter. I'll circle around and meet you halfway."

"Check, G. I'll grab the sawed off while I'm at it, just in case."

Upon departing Vegas amid a swirl of frenzied panic as untold legions of the undead swarmed over the city in massive waves, they had stolen a Yellow Cab (the cabbie having been dispatched with the butt of Gino's Glock Three-fifty Seven Magnum) and packed the trunk with what Gino considered only 'the bare necessities' These included the aforementioned camping supplies (flashlights, mini-tents, canned foods and bottled water) and also a varied collection of revolvers, shotguns and combat cutlery copped from a local Sin City gun shop.

"You need extra hardware, boss?"

With a devilish smirk, Gino lifted his leather vest to reveal the shoulder holster tucked inside.

"Got all the firepower I need right here, V. Get goin'. Vanessa, you stay put in case Little Nickie wanders back into camp, and get strapped while you're at it."

Shaking her head weakly, Vanessa wiped her tears with a raised forearm and watched the two men vanish into the darkness. After a short pause and several deep breaths, she strolled over and pulled a twenty-two revolver from one of several backpacks.

Tucking the revolver inside her belt, she had just began warming her trembling hands over the fire when the sharp retort of snapping twigs echoed to her left.

She spun about to see a small figure jogging toward her in a lumbering gait, the child's facial features masked in swirling shadows.

"Nickie! Sweet Lord, boy...where have you been?" she blurted sternly, attempting to mask the relief in her tone as she fell to one knee to embrace the youngster as he approached, "Vito and Uncle

Gino are out lookin' for y-.."

It wasn't until the boy dived head-first into her waiting arms and the tiny, pubescent teeth tore into her throat with ravenous glee that Vanessa realized that the price to pay for such blatant carelessness was apt to be *horribly* steep.

***

"Hoooly shiiit, Gino. Fuckin' things l-look like they was run through a fuckin' blender."

Standing over the pulped, shredded remains of the three mules they'd rode into the canyon, each man sprayed their flashlight beam wildly from side to side, essentially covering the same ground repeatedly even as they side-stepped the carnage as if treading atop quicksand.

"The heads are gone, Vito. I'm talkin'....*just...not...there.*"

"J-Jesus, Gino. They…they gotta be nearby, am I right? Had to be…them that did…*that*, right?"

"Sure as hell wasn't a sand-crab, dumb ass…" Gino replied flippantly after temporarily concentrating the light at the center of Vito's face.

"H-hey, Gino…Vanessa…" Vito blurted, his bloated face grotesquely contorted from the light's blaring intrusion.

"Oh, fuuuuuck…" Gino cried, his light bobbling spastically in all directions as he took off in a rambling gallop back toward the camp clearing.

***

"Oh fuck…fuck… fuck…FUUUCK!" Gino screamed, hoisting the Glock airborne and firing several shots straight into the clear Canyon sky, which was just beginning to lighten as the sun crept

65

over a distant mountain range.

The blood had already coagulated somewhat, resembling half-settled pudding, and was spread around the campfire in thick pools, littered with the occasional shred of torn flesh or jagged chunk of pulped tissue.

"Jesus Crow, G-Gino…c-could that b-be…but, we didn't hear no screamin' or…" Vito whimpered between labored swallows, leaning over the dwindling fire and pointing inside the few remaining flames, where a severed finger popped and sizzled like a ballpark frank cooking on an open grille. A severed finger adorned by a meticulously manicured nail and accompanied by a gold-banded, three and a half- karat diamond ring.

"Mother fuc…" Gino whined, tossing his flashlight to the ground and reaching down as to somehow salvage what little remained of his fiancé of over five years before jerking his hand back in disgust.

Having discarded his own light, Vito tucked a sawed-off thirty-gauge snugly against his sagging breasts while scanning the dusty plains around them as the dawn gradually broke.

"Let's get the fuck outta here, G…this ain't no place for us…"

Gripping the Glock in one hand and a Smith & Wesson forty-four magnum revolver in the other, Gino's sniveling subsided as shock and self-pity quickly gave way to burning rage. Having mercilessly dispatched many a target in his meteoric rise to the top of one of New York's largest crime families, it took practically no effort on his part to surrender to the dark side, especially when it involved the death of a loved one.

"Fuck that flight over fight *bullshit,* Vito," he snarled, twirling the Glock around his forefinger like an old west gunslinger of old, "I'm gonna find me some dead-head mother fuckers and play firing range on their rotten asses."

"B-but boss…"

"I'm through runnin', lard ass. Quit kiddin' yourself. You saw all that crazy shit on the tube before we skipped outta Sin City."

Tilting his wrecking-ball sized head to one side, Vito studied his boss and mentor with an expression of comical befuddlement.

"Don't you get it, you miserable *Mook*? In the two days we've been wanderin' around the canyon seein' the sights, the entire planet's probably been infested by those fuckin' things."

"But, what about Quedo's place?" Vito pleaded in obvious desperation. After a moment's hesitation, in which his anger abated somewhat in lieu of sympathy for his longtime ally and loyal underling, Gino stared into the overcast desert sky and sighed.

"Okay, Vito, Okay. We'll shoot our way through the fuckers, what say? All the way to Meh-E-ko fuckin' city!"

The larger man flashed a warped smile, propping the shotgun's stubby barrel atop his left shoulder.

"Fuckin'-A, Gino. We may go down, but we don't go easy, right?" "Yeah. Besides," Gino replied somberly as they turned to face a steep grade just to the left of the camp, "maybe…maybe Vanes and the kid are still alive out there... somewhere."

Breaking eye contact with the smaller man, Vito leaned down with his free hand to retrieve a snub-nose thirty eight from a holster attached to his right ankle.

"It's...it's possible, boss. I mean...it's worth a shot, right?"

Gino silently nodded before stepping slowly forward with the twin handguns resting against his upper thighs.

"Let me just...I'll...go get the backpacks and canteens, Gino."

Whirling clumsily about, Vito froze in mid-step and slung the shotgun forward while simultaneously raising the thirty-eight chest-high.

The trio of figures shambled past the smoldering campfire like drunken ballroom dancers, displaying equal portions of astonishing grace and comical clumsiness, the former made all the more amazing considering the shattered or missing limbs involved.

"Gino! I got three..." Vito blurted, his first shot sheering off the right ear of a large African-American woman with a grotesquely bloated head.

"Gino...I got t-three over h-here...GINO!" he repeated, having successfully blasted away the lower jaw of perhaps what had once been a middle-aged Hispanic male missing a sizeable portion of his right arm and whose eyes were empty, plum shaded pits.

"FUCK! Need s-some...help here, boss! You know I can't... aim worth a shit!" he bellowed, using the thirty-gauge to blow a softball-sized hole into and through the chest cavity of a stick-thin white female whose face was little more than a scab-coated skull.

Vito turned around only after plugging the black female (the closest of the three) with a shot to the center of the neck that had practically decapitated her.

"Shit boss…what're ya do-.."

Like a recently erected statue, Gino stood at the crest of the shrub- infested hill, resembling a messiah-like figure preparing to deliver a mountaintop sermon. The handguns lay on either side of his dust-coated boots, having apparently tumbled uselessly from each hand.

"Gino! Gino, what the HELL?" Vito screeched, scampering up the jagged terrain as rapidly as his bulky frame would allow.

"Check it out, Vito. Ain't that a fuckin' site? Ain't that a beautiful (pronounced 'boo-ta-full') fuckin' site to behold now?" he heard Gino babble as he neared.

With both his throat and chest burning from the effort, Vito stumbled forward and almost directly into his superior's frightfully prone form.

"JESUS, boss," he huffed, regaining his balance while standing directly to Gino's left, "…what the fuck's got into ya? Didn't ya hear me screa-"

The remaining words stuck in Vito's parched throat like a chuck of stale garlic bread. Even as his legs and arms began to go numb, he felt the flesh of his face start to sting and itch as if it were being pelted by tiny shards of jagged ice.

"I gotta tell ya, Vito, the brochures and videos

just don't do this place justice," Gino announced cheerily, his eyes pulled inhumanly wide and unblinking, a thin trail of frothy drool coating his lips like beer foam. His once coal-black bangs had turned the color of a fresh mountain snow.

"Hell's Bell's, Gino…get a grip, boss. We got a big fuckin' problem.

Those things are-…."

He was abruptly cut off as Gino suddenly pointed straight out with both hands, holding his palms out like some ancient carnival barker introducing the show's star attraction.

"Check it out, V. Check out all the tourists. Man, this place sure packs 'em in, don't it? Like Coney Isle on Fourth of July weekend."

Vito followed his superior's gaze into a wide, majestic valley. A concave shaped valley framed on all sides by picturesque mountain formations that literally seemed drawn into the picture by some Hollywood CGI artist.

"Oh…shit…" Vito managed, instinctively backing a few steps down the hill. "Now I remember…" Gino ranted, reaching up to playfully slap his own forehead, "…brochure said that most visitors enter the canyon through the South Rim.

The *South* rim, Vito, not the North. My fault, man. Shiiiit, I sure fumbled that one away."

Vito shot his boss a final frantic glance before dashing back down the hill, all the while releasing a shrill, rather feminine wail.

Gino paid no mind to the shots that echoed in the background, nor the panicked cries of his loyal servant, or finally the anguished screams drowned

70

out by a plethora of animalistic growls and grunts.

Like a curious bystander observing the aftermath of a particularly grisly auto accident, he found it virtually impossible to tear either his gaze or concentration from the scene ahead.

They ambled forward like an army of worker ants to a designated picnic area, though their marching cadence was horribly out of step; comically so in most cases.

As with the millions upon millions who had made the trek to the canyon through decades of spring and summer vacation seasons, most wore clothing, however tattered, easily associated with the stereotypical tourist. Women donned light-colored sneakers, sundresses and matching hats, while the men and boys were decked out in baseball caps, khaki shorts and leather-soled sandals.

"Damn, must've been the peak season all right," Gino concluded with a pathetic grin as the first wave ambled up the hill toward him.

It was then he spotted Little Nicky, void a sizeable portion of his scalp and missing his left hand, crawling forward with something resembling a deflated soccer ball tucked under one arm. "Well, I'll be damned. Nicky my boy...come to Uncle G," Gino blabbered as an impossibly strong hand gripped his left ankle, sending him tumbling into the masses like a punk rocker diving head first into a mosh-pit.

As greedy fingers began to poke, prod, and eventually dig through his clothes to the fleshy reward waiting beneath, a former mob boss and soon to be main course for a canyon full of carnivorous canyon tourists was allowed a final peak at the origin of his own demise.

Little Nicky had squatted onto his chest and removed the mystery object from beneath his arm. The boy cackled in apparent glee between coughing gurgles while balancing the object directly in front of Gino's face.

"Well, h-hello there…sweet c-cheeks…" Gino screamed hysterically while staring into the lid-less eyes of his fiancé's severed head.

"C-come to…p-poppaaaaaaahhhhhhhh…"

The head rolled forward like a slithering snake, its teeth chattering together on pure instinct as it burrowed through flesh, sinew and bone until the Grand Canyon was filled with still another round of echoing shrieks.

***

It wasn't at all uncommon for the diseased and deceased masses to congregate at places that were familiar to them. Malls, athletic arenas and concert halls supposedly became quite the rage; that is until fresh food sources became scarce. It was simply a matter of returning to ones roots or attempting to re-live a particular memory.

Unlike the majority of these segments, the authenticity of this next chapter is not in question. It took place, in fact, less than three years ago almost to the day. A rescue team, much like the one I am currently so proud to be a part of, stumbled upon the scene while on a rescue mission similar to our own.

Unfortunately, those they had come to rescue weren't quite as lucky as you good folks…

4 - Old Stomping Grounds

Tendons stretch. Ligaments tear. Bones creak as hairline cracks spread like a freshly spun spider's web. Regardless, The THING shambles forward, driven by an unrelenting urge; a gnawing hunger that refuses to abate. The hunger is all The THING knows-all it understands-all it answers to. It is The THING'S universal reason for being. It is the sole priority in a world once littered with a million separate agendas. The precious life source it seeks is a rare find indeed, much like an ancient relic buried within a rocky mountainside. Time has dwindled this precious resource to an almost nonexistent commodity, forcing those damned souls driven by the unstoppable urge to feed to seek out nourishment atop not only unfamiliar terrain, but also old haunts long since dismissed.

Still, regardless of such overwhelming, insurmountable odds, the search will not-*cannot* be abandoned, for The THING exists only to search out, discover and consume this elusive rarity.

The heart of the city has long-since emptied, leaving little behind save an army of lifeless husks and a landscape littered with hollowed out structures that paint the horizon like an apocalyptic mural.

The metal gate is spread wide, allowing just enough room for The THING to squeeze through. Its right forearm scrapes across a hanging strand of razor wire, peeling away jagged strips of decayed, mummified flesh. The THING glances back briefly but feels neither physical nor emotional pain over such a superficial loss. Being that its limbs, torso and exposed organs have long since hardened, fossilized, or simply dropped off, this doesn't exactly fall under the category of dire straits.

It knows not what drives it toward its mystery destination. Acting on primal instinct is not a chosen behavior, but simply the lone option available since its pulse faded and its battered mind lost the power of independent thought. The THING ambles through a caged sally port, past several abandoned ton-and a-half trucks and scattered piles of jagged bone and tattered clothing. As The THING makes its way down a winding catwalk toward a gray, two-story concrete building with smooth, window-less walls, it peers upward at a metal overhang which reads 'BOLEN Cryogenics INC – Main Building'. Reaching up to scratch it's bald, scab-infested dome, The THING pauses in mid-stumble and tilts its misshapen head to one side, as if struck by a sudden thought or impulse. As is normally the case in such a rare occurrence, the faint vibe fades almost instantly. There is no time for such nonsensical drivel, its hollowed-out gut relays, not when there is still the hunger to feed.

The glass double-door entrance stands ajar and smeared with the aged residue of spilled bodily fluids. The THING sniffs one of the metal handles as if to officially eliminate it as a drawing source, even giving it the obligatory lick before spitting a dark brown splotch onto the dusty tile flooring below.

Passing a circular, marble-based console littered with soiled computer monitors, keypads and assorted blown trash, The THING soon finds itself posed at the cusp of separate elevators, centered by a tiny numerical keyboard.

Initially, The THING attempts to pry elevator one's doors apart by wedging its skeletal fingers into the sparse space provided between creases, but quickly realizes the futility of such efforts.

Stepping forward, it peers at the keypad through one blackened eye, the pupil of which is plum red and shrouded in slug-like tumors the color of coal.

After a short pause, The THING reveals a hideous grin while slapping its palms together in drunken glee.

Reaching forward with one bony forefinger, it expertly pokes out a six- digit code before backing away as if expecting an impending explosion.

Elevator one immediately begins to sputter and hum as the single door slides back as if slightly off-track.

The THING steps through just as the door slides securely back into place behind it, narrowly missing trapping its jagged left heel in the process.

Without prompting of any kind, The THING is automatically transported downward at warp speed, grinding to a screeching halt innumerable levels later.

Following its less-than-speedy departure, The THING follows a curved hall past several offices and conference rooms until it dead ends at still another elevator. As before, there is but a short pause before The THING taps in the appropriate code and is allowed access.

It exits several moments later, stepping through a glass-walled sally port housing the skeletal remains of a figure still adorned in faded green khakis. A silver badge hanging lopsided from the tattered chest cavity reads '*BOWEN Security – CHIEF OIC*'. The bones, as is universally the case it seems, are sucked clean, like some invaluable archeological find that's been acid-brushed and subsequently bleached to sparkling perfection.

The THING trudges past several unmarked doors, pausing momentarily in front of each as if following a mental map to its ultimate destination.

It stops in front of a black paneled entranceway with an engraved metallic sign reading:

-CYRO-LAB ECHO-2444
ONLY   AUTHORIZED   PERSONNEL BEYOND THIS POINT –
DEADLY FORCE AUTHORIZED

This time, The THING is forced to utilize two separate keypads, one numerical and one letter-only, punching in separate five digit codes for each. It does this as a thick stream of greenish drool leaks from the corners of its opened mouth, which serves as an impromptu landing pad for a swarm of bloated blow- flies. A strained humming sound ensues as the panel slides gradually to the left, pausing several times as if to halt altogether before resuming its sloth-like movement.

If The THING still possessed an operational heartbeat, it would have most assuredly pounded like a jackhammer upon entry into the dark, cool space beyond. As it was, it lumbered forward rather hesitantly, as if unsure if it truly belonged. Though such emotionally driven states as Déjà vu were no longer possible from a medical or scientific standpoint, the creature's cautious movements and fearfully scanning eyes seem to indicate otherwise.

A single emergency light provides the sole illumination as The THING descends farther and farther into the spacious enclosure.

Bypassing several communications consoles and conference tables, the creature shambles onward as if fueled by a sudden revelation. Its speed increases with each rickety step, a low moan escaping its leathery lips as its tongue protrudes from the side of its mouth like birthing larva.

Standing at the center of octagon-shaped double-doors encased in matching one-way mirrors, The THING cocks its head and briefly studies the shadowy figure staring back through the dim reflection. Unable to clearly visualize its own blurred image, it quickly dismisses the effect and reaches up and over to grip an L-shaped handle attached to door number one The THING pulls the handle upward in a clock-wise motion, then backs away several steps from a loud hissing sound, like air brakes from a fleet of semi-trucks. The handle rolls down and out, rotating like a motorized piston, followed by a series of low clicks just before the doors slide back in perfectly synchronized unison.

The THING stands at the threshold for a full thirty seconds, rubbing its flaky palms in anticipation.

As its ruined stub of a right foot makes contact with the cool marble floor and the entrance door automatically closes behind it, the room is immediately lit ablaze from at least a dozen security lights built into the concrete ceiling.

Groaning ever louder, The THING practically sprints forward toward the first of several glass cylinders, its chin, neck and upper chest now coated in slimy froth.

It places its hands on either side of the slick, circular dome, leaning forward as to closely analyze the content within.

The creature's movements grow increasingly jittery. It salivates like a starving canine whose nostrils are filled with the coppery aroma of bloodied, raw meat. Whirling about in desperation, it scoops up a metal-framed desk chair by the legs and swings it around in a frenzied blur, striking the cylinder dead center. It takes three additional blows, each delivered with increased ferocity, in order to obtain the desired result.

An explosion of glass and metal fragments shower the room, accompanied by virtual tidal wave of bluish fluid that hisses and smokes as it strikes the marbled flooring.

Before the first is even able to completely purge its contents, the creature waddles over and smashes three additional domes in a similar fashion, then tosses the shattered chair aside and steps back to survey its handy-work.

The THING then waddles into the spilled mix without trepidation, squatting down over the freed content of the first cylinder with clutching hands that better resemble the scaled claws of some mythological sea creature.

Sniffing the thawed but still cool- to-the-touch

flesh, The THING nibbles cautiously at first before indulging in larger bites that rip sinew, severe tendons and snap bones with equal efficiency.

Several minutes of ravenous feasting follows, that is until the creature realizes there are other delicacies to sample. Crawling over the gutted remains of course number one, it leans down with chattering teeth and tears a meaty portion from the contents of spilled cylinder number two. Leaning its head back and grinning like a food critic grading cuisine from a five-star restaurant, The THING then scampers forward on its hands and knees toward the third and final course. Its teeth and nostrils are packed with chunks of pulped tissue, its scalp coated in reddish/yellow fluid that resembles a blood/anti-freeze cocktail.

Flipping the slime-covered corpse over as to take its initial bite from the more pliable neck region, The THING freezes in mid-lunge, it's jaws dripping fragmented gore onto the bare chest of its intended meal.

Cocking its head quizzically, The THING studies the facial features with great curiosity. Lodging its hands beneath the stiffening corpses' armpits, the creature drags it past the wreckage of the shattered cylinders and toward the entrance/exit door.

Propping the corpse into a standing position until they stand practically side-by-side, The THING is instantly taken back at the eerie resemblance. Although the one-way mirror provides a slightly skewed reflection, much like the 'funhouse' variety in carnival days, the similarity is plainly obvious.

The THING hasn't nearly the amount of hair atop his peeled, scaly dome, and its own face is horribly gaunt as opposed to plump and fleshed-out. That said, the drooping eyes, oversized ears and long, pointy noses are strikingly similar In addition, their height and body frames are a perfect match, give or take ten or so pounds that the creature has shed from the effects of gradual decomposition.

After an additional few moments of intense scrutiny, The THING shrugs its bony shoulders and releases the corpse, which instantly collapses like a house of cards at his feet.

Pounding its chest like a bull Gorilla on the warpath, The THING pounces onto its deceased look-a-like with renewed vigor, having already felt the energy- replenishing effects from the earlier consumptions.

The creature will remain tucked comfortably inside the locked chamber for three days and three nights, snacking between hour-long feeding frenzies until every edible morsel is heartily consumed and every cartilage and bone sucked clean. During this time, the remaining three chambers within the room are shattered and their meaty contents added to the menu.

Without the power of either deductive reasoning or logical thought, The THING is unable to unravel a mystery whose solution would have otherwise been labeled simplicity in itself. The THING pays no heed to the words engraved at the top of each domed cylinder. Engravings marked *C-A1* through *C-A7*. Nor is the creature able to correlate these markings with a coded inscription attached to metal bands at the bottom of each dome. Inscriptions that clearly identify six adult males and one adult female as clones of not only the CEO, but also six individual Company heads for *BOWEN Cryogenics INC.* Clones manufactured in top-secret fashion once it became apparent the plague was indeed a viable threat to the modern world. Clones created and placed within cryogenic domes with automatic timers set for reanimation ten years later, but whose system's shutdown prematurely due to an internal wiring malfunction.

Departing the premises with a bloated belly and enough stored energy to keep it upright for at least another month to six weeks, The THING is blissfully ignorant of one final clue; easily the most vital, *telling* clue of them all.

A clue that might explain why the creature was initially drawn to the lab, or how it instinctively knew the numerical entry codes.

More importantly, it is a clue providing solid evidence of its former identity. The clue in question? A gold band practically fused to the bone around THE THING'S left hand ring finger.

A ring with an inner inscription of its own, which simply reads:

'B.Bowen – CEO'

***

Sad to report, but there were quite a few such blatant breeches of security in locations all over the globe. Breeches with outcomes equally grisly as the one I've just described. I know...as I bore witness to several such scenarios myself. In almost every case, it was a former employee responsible, as only they would be privy to the required entry codes to such well-secured locations. Obviously, the benefits of a powerful long-term memory aren't just limited to the living.

To continue, I consider this one of the more educational within the canon, as it covers the rather chilling aspects of the much-dreaded 'turning'...

5 - The TURNING

Gina glares at me like I'm some psyche patient three days off her meds.

You'd think she'd exhibit more compassion. After all, what if the shoe were on the other foot, Miss *'Self-Preservation and Logic' of the year 2014*? Would she leave her dear, sweet Matthew in such a situation? Just walk out and discard him as if their marriage vows never really meant squat? I seriously doubt it, though Gina does have quite the cool streak in her. Saw it on many occasions, even more so of late. I'm certain dear Matthew could tell me some stories, yes sir.

"This could be our last shot, Leah. I mean, like, I...understand your loyalty but..."

"No, no you *don't* understand, Gina. Nobody in this room ...in this building understands but me. Just...me."

Rolling her eyes, Gina props her hands on her hips and sighs, looking every bit the spoiled socialite, despite her recent, rather drastic lifestyle makeover.

"Is it better that you *both* die, then? Like, I know it's hard, but girl, you gotta like, think about yourself now."

Why is it that ninety percent of all females under the age of twenty-five have a tendency to sprinkle every other sentence with the word 'like'? Mental causalities of the MTV generation, perhaps? More than likely victims of the public school system. At thirty-four, I'm barely nine years older than her, but you'd think we were hatched from different galaxies.

"Gina, the man's my husband. We've been married for over thirteen years; most of them damn good ones. I won't leave him here like…like *that*. If roles were reversed, he'd do the same for me.

I wish you, Matt and the group all the best in getting out of this hell-hole, but I won't be with you."

Matthew lurches into the room at full bore. I swear the man has lost twenty pounds and roughly half his hair since this nightmare started. He wasn't exactly the picture of health to begin with. Looking waaaay too much like a 21st Century version of Ichabod Crane these days.

"She won't listen, Matt," Gina says with weary conviction at best, as if she were announcing I'd decided to skip the Senior Prom, "Like, I don't know what else to do."

"Nothing more to be said, Gina. My decision's made, and it's final." "Leah, listen. It's commendable, but there isn't..," Matt begins, squatting down next to me and placing a hand on my shoulder. Normally clean shaven and meticulously manicured, the man has cultivated a rather grubby looking beard and reeks like a room full of peeled onions. Much like myself, I'm sure. After all, I'm smack dab in the middle of my monthly menstrual cycle and haven't bothered to even search out the proper padding in order to quell the leaks, using rolled toilet paper instead.

Such mundane rituals as bathing and proper grooming have fallen by the wayside in terms of priority. Funny how a simple little word like *survival* supersedes all that came before it during such madness.

"Would you abandon *her*, Matt?" I interrupt, pointing toward Gina and locking eyes with a man I've known to be nothing less than the pinnacle of honesty.

"What?" he replies in obvious shock, glancing briefly toward his wife, whose own expression is comically clueless.

"If Gina were in Gerry's state, would you just pack a bag and leave her lying in your apartment on the same bed you've shared as lovers? Talk to me, Matthew Be honest. Don't say what you *think* you need to say to convince me otherwise."

"Leah, I...um...'

"You were my husband's best friend, Matthew, butI was his wife. I don't blame you or anybody else for trying to escape this complex. Good luck and God speed. But I won't leave him here. Period."

"He's going to turn, Leah. They...everybody does that contracts..." "Understood. Then again, there's a first time for everything, right?" "Not likely. Speaking bluntly, I'm of the belief that the age of miracles is over. When he does turn, and he *will*...he...well, he'll..."

"He won't recognize me and he'll attack on instinct. Again, understood." Never mistaken for the most animated or overly emotional of individuals, hence the nickname '*Data*' of *Star Trek: Generations* fame, Matthew nonetheless begins to pace the room, waving his arms about like a politician on the election circuit The apartment smells of stale urine and rotten poultry, which I assume is pretty much the aroma of the entire city, or World for that matter.

"Leah, be reasonable. I can't *allow* you to stay here If Gerry were able, I'm positive he'd insist you go with us. I worked side by side with the man for almost a decade. Pretty damned confident he'd allow me to vote by proxy."

"Matthew," I mumble, surprising myself in that I didn't physically attack the smug jackass for such an inane, thoughtless comment, "don't make me keep repeating myself. Though I appreciate your concern as a friend, I won't leave my husband. All I ask is two days provisions"

"Jesus, Leah, even if Gerry…makes it somehow, the masses are growing thicker by the minute out there. They'll have the whole complex blocked in by dawn. This is our only chan…"

"End of conversation, Matt. I'm… staying."

They stood there for a few seconds, shaking their heads in apparent disbelief. Guess I got my answer concerning whether or not they'd do the same for each other. Not really fair to jump to such conclusions, really. Honesty, it was downright mean. People never know what they'll do unless they're actually faced with such a decision Gina opens her mouth to apparently begin a new series of verbal volleys when Burke bounds into the room like a raiding storm trooper. Guy's a former Corrections Officer who has the annoying tendency of treating everyone like an ex-con. Being that he stands about six-eight and has arms the size of sequoias, it's no wonder such rude treatment is essentially accepted without complaint.

Gerry had secretly referred to him as 'Sergeant Rock-*Head*'. "Pack it up, folks. We load up in T-minus five minutes. Buses are warming as we speak. As discussed, I'll be taking point in the van. Got that bad boy reinforced like a tank."

Matt and Gina shoot me a final, desperate glance.

"Leah's decided to stay," Gina blurts, her tone similar to that of a grade school tattletale.

Rock-head Burke barely bats an eye, never even bothering to make eye contact with me. I'd met his kind before, unfortunately. Uptight, bossy blockheads who were used to being in charge and who made such words as 'protocol' and 'organization' their sole priorities, no matter the situation.

"Her choice. Let's go, you two. Jenkins just reported from the rooftop that the natives are definitely getting restless out there. To quote the King of Rock & Roll, it's now or never."

"B-but Burke, we can't just leave the Martins here, t-they-..." Matt stuttered to no avail as the 'Sarge' dashed out of the room even faster than he'd arrived.

"Forget it, Matt. Man's got a schedule to keep," I say with my best manufactured grin. With just under a decade of route sales under my belt, it takes little to no effort, "You guys better hurry. Don't want to miss the bus. Man like ol' Rock-head there won't think twice about pulling away without you."

Gina walks over and gives me the consolatory hug I'm sure she deems mandatory from a 'drama class' perspective while Matt simply shambles away with his shoulders sagging, for all the world resembling the very beings which threaten our existence as a race.

"Take care, Gina," I manage with still another forced smile. "You too, girl. I…hope it does work out. I really do."

"Oh, it will. One way… or another," I conclude with just a hint of biting sarcasm, reaching down to pat the pearl handled revolver tucked inside my belt.

Her eyes grow wide with shock as the meaning of my remark hits home.

Mercifully, she departs without further dialogue.

It isn't until the building is completely vacated that the finality of it all hits home like a fifty pound sledge, and the tears begin to flow fast and furious.

***

After checking Gerry's condition (unchanged), I take a casual stroll through the building, then up onto the roof, which has served as 'lookout point' for the past several weeks.

Scanning the city's east side, I can see several fires burning in the distance, one of which looks to be coming from the downtown EPCORP Chemical Plant. If that baby blows, it'll take at least three city blocks with it. No matter. Gerry and I are at least two miles away. A part of me wishes we were closer. Hard to believe such vile thoughts not only occur, but actually hold merit. Then again, *oh my,* how times have indeed changed.Peering downward (vertigo not withstanding), I see a dozen or so shufflers manning the building's front entrance. The way they pace aimlessly back and forth always brings to mind striking picketers. Guess those nasty boogers are always on '*hunger*' strike, so to speak. Checking the view from the west side, I can see the head and taillights of the buses trailing off in the distance, more than likely less than five or ten minutes from the interstate, depending on blockades and the like. Funny, I don't see the lead van's lights. Guess it drove further ahead to play 'scout' Good Ol' Rock- head strikes again, no doubt. Have to admit, the man covers every possible base. Regardless, he'll always be a self-important prick in this girl's mind. It's a true relief no longer being under his dictatorial 'command'.

I wish them all nothing but the best, though we had all conceded weeks ago that the term *safe haven* was no longer relevant within the grand scheme of things. The underground garage door stands wipe open, and I can see the occasional straggler stumble inside from the street. You'd think the least they could've done was close the damn thing behind them. I'm certain the interior barricades will hold, but still, there is no need for such blatant carelessness. No doubt the Sarge convinced the group that Gerry and I were as good as doomed anyhow. Like I said-selfish *jack-ass*.

With a gut-full of apprehension and more reluctance than I care to admit, I reenter the building in order to perform the 'every-half-hour' check on my better half.

Despite the foolishness of such malarkey, and for at least the thousandth time in the past forty-six hours, I pray (plead, beg, et al) for a miracle.

***

God, how we had loved this apartment building. The day our mail slot officially read '*THE MARTINS*' was indeed a joyous one. We'd been renting an aged two-story ranch outside the city for almost three years, waiting for an opening we had begun to think would never come. Signed up on a rather exclusive waiting list before finally getting the green light to move in almost two years later. Not only was the location infinitely more convenient, being that it cut both our commutes in half, but the amenities were rated as some of the best in the entire city, including the suburbs. Sadly, it seems like little more than an empty tomb now.

I take up position at Gerry's bedside and gently stroke his forehead. His flesh is red-hot and moist with sour-smelling sweat. The fever seems to gain strength by the hour, as do both his shivers and seizures. My sweet lover seems horribly emaciated after less than two days. His cheeks are pasty and gaunt, his eyes shaded by blackish raccoon circles. No doubt all the familiar symptoms are present. Regardless, I won't lose hope. Simply put, it's all I have left. I give him an injection of B-12 and force a few sips of water into his mouth, which he mostly coughs up. I've seen incubation periods stretch anywhere from forty-eight to seventy-two hours. That said, a conclusion should be forthcoming. To understate the obvious, the building tension is damn near unbearable.

Even from the fifth floor, I can hear the moans of the dead from ground level. I can't help but wonder how many within their ranks are former friends, co- workers or possibly even family members. Gerry's folks lived in the Green Hills Suburbs just six or seven miles west of here. My older sister and her family are a five-minute drive away. Once all the craziness came down and the main lines of communication fell, we were unable to contact any of them. As grisly a thought as it is, one can't help but ponder the horrible possibility that all or many of them are now lost among the wondering masses. *

I can't believe...how little I've cried. This man was all I had. Hell on earth continues to evolve and I now face it alone. Tried for ten minutes to find a pulse; to detect breathing, however weak. I heard him release a low moan just as he...passed. Even tried CPR, though I'm fairly positive my less than expert techniques resulted in blunt trauma to his chest cavity.

Strange how quickly sadness mutates into a numb acceptance. One might think the self-pity factor alone would trigger enough tears to float a luxury cruise-liner. I...guess I'd already cried myself out in the days following the incident. I saw it in Gerry's eyes that day...the very *moment* he got bit. He'd leaned his hand out the van window for less than a millisecond and drawn it back with bloodied teeth imprints on both the topside and palm. I...we both knew...instantly realized, that his life had ended. As with all the others, it was just a matter of time. True, I'd hoped his case would be different, some miraculous medical milestone that would soon translate into a World revival, as the human body would surely build an immunity to their poisonous touch.

I began the obligatory anti-biotic treatments almost immediately, injecting him hourly while shoving anti-inflammatory and pain medications down his throat by the handful. I'd already witnessed dozens of similar attempts fail miserably, true, but admitting defeat was never an option. A devout Methodist, I've done more praying in the last two days than a convent full of nuns. No surprise it's all been for naught. It isn't as if I had a choice, morally or spiritually. Now comes the part I've dreaded even more than my own lover's inevitable death.

Now comes... the *waiting*. Since this Hellish scenario began, there has yet to be a report of someone passing via scratch or bite that hasn't eventually turned. Again, all I can do is hope for the best while expecting the very worst. There's always a first time for everything, I repeat ad nauseam while checking my pistol's chamber for at least the tenth time in as many minutes.

I've locked Gerry inside the bedroom while I sit in the kitchen and nurse a glass of J&W scotch. Never one to hold my alcohol very well, I feel the effects almost immediately. Nevertheless, I desperately need the booster shot of liquid courage it supplies. There's simply no way I'll be able to deliver on the promise otherwise. The promise we as a couple made weeks ago.

More of a pledge really; a sacred vow.

I have no intention of breaking such a vow.

Tragically, '*Til death do us part*' is only the beginning these days.

The praying ritual begins anew, and if possible,

with increased fervor.

***

No way to properly gauge when the noises began, or how long I'd been passed out with my head pressed against the kitchen table. A loud crash woke me, and in my unique clumsiness I managed to not only knock the revolver off the table, but tumble onto the tile floor face first, mashing my nose like a ripe tomato in the process. *Damn*, I always was a klutz. High levels of stress and distress just seem to enhance the effect.

I stumble to my feet, retrieving the weapon while using my shirtsleeve to wipe away the blood pouring from both nostrils.

The pounding at the bedroom door rings in my ears like the chiming of a giant cathedral bell. I hear his frantic grunting, his predatory growls. My lover urges to feed, his craving made ever stronger by the fresh blood coating my face, hands and clothing, and no doubt the menstrual cycle flowing full-bore.

For several moments, I seriously consider whirling about and leaving, even to the point of physically turning to face the front door. A voice stops me; freezes me in my tracks. A deep, husky baritone that permanently wipes the yellow streak from my backbone as I reach to remove the wooden chair propped against the bedroom door A voice whose words reverberate like a mountain echo as I shove the chair away and leap back with the cocked revolver held straight out in both hands.

The exact words that drive my actions: "if it comes to that, we know what we *have* to do."

The door swings inward just as my trigger

93

finger tightens.

***

I…couldn't do it. When the moment of truth arrived, it just… wasn't in me. It isn't as if I hadn't blown away my share of…their kind in the last few weeks. On the contrary, Gerry had pegged me 'Deadeye Dee', Dee being my middle name, for my deadly accuracy with various hand and shotguns. What stopped me was the look in my lover's eyes. A bit cold and glazed over, which is the norm following the turning process, but I swear there was still evidence of basic human emotion dwelling just below the surface. Maybe that's simply what I…what I *wanted* to see.

I'd shoved the gun's shiny silver barrel flush with his temple even as he'd forced me against a far wall- increased the pressure of my trigger finger even as he'd tugged at my free hand and pulled it toward his open mouth. My lover had bitten down just as my finger slid free. I watched three digits from my left hand vanish inside his grinding jaws like Lego building blocks. May sound like an ancient cliché, but it was truly like watching it all happen to someone else.

Strange thing was, or perhaps surreal is a better word, it wasn't *I* who broke contact, but Gerry. Instead of pressing the attack, he backed away with a section of my forefinger hanging from his lower lip. Backed away and…I swear on my deceased mother's soul…turned as to *allow* clearance for me to dash into the same bedroom he'd just exited. I did so, locking myself in collapsing onto the mattress.

As things presently stand, I'm losing blood by

the quart, from both a crushed nose and the trio of jagged nubs on my left hand. Getting weaker...by the second. Vision is... getting bleary. I swear the room grows a shade...darker with every...blink. Gerry doesn't....bother pounding...on the door. He knows that eventually....I'll emerge...on my own. He knows...he can...wait it out.

God help me...I still...*cherish* ...that man. He could've...easily...so easily...finished me...feasting on my...corpse. Why...why did he so c- casually....refuse what comes so...natural for...their kind? I have...but one guess...insane as it sounds. Natural law...applies.

Love...is...indeed blind...after...all. Even...through...the eyes of...the dead...

***

Burke sips quietly from a metal canteen, careful to maintain total silence even as the jagged edges of the van's inner wall dig into his side like a dozen separate sewing needles.

He isn't sure how long he's been stowed away in the back of the crippled vehicle, since he'd lost consciousness when it had overturned upon departing the complex. The buses had obviously made it, a wide path cleared for them once the van had taken the brunt of the mysterious explosion that had flipped it onto one side after traveling less than three full blocks. He hadn't heard a peep from the cab, more than likely meaning Williams had long since expired or been pulled from the wreckage and consumed. Though he had volunteered to drive in lieu of playing armed gunner from the van's rear, Williams had insisted on taking the wheel. In hindsight, Burke hoped Lady Luck had seen fit to intervene for a reason.

Since coming to, he'd heard countless shufflers pass by, at least one of which had paused just outside the upturned vehicle, possibly in an attempt to 'sniff' him out. Once that threat had passed, he could safely assume he possessed no bleeding wounds, otherwise the passing masses would've piled atop the wreckage like maggots on a rotted carcass. Thick sheets of stainless steel had been welded to the outside shell of the vehicle, thus providing not only added protection from impact, but also an extra layer, which disallowed easy detection by the creatures' amazing sense of smell. The disadvantage of the added walls was the pitch blackness of the interior, which made it virtually impossible to speculate the time of day. He'd hoped to use the cloak of darkness in order to remain undetected upon escape, but was unable to even guess if it were dark or light outside the metallic tomb.

Just gonna have to take your chances. It's eat or be eaten, anyway you look at it.Can't lay here like canned tuna forever.

Taking a deep breath, he plants the butt of the sawed-off thirty-gauge against his left shoulder and proceeds to kick the rear door ajar with the heels of his steel-toed boots.

He combat-rolls through the open space and onto the street, the blaring sunlight piercing his pupils and causing temporarily blindness.

Upon rising from a shooter's crouch, his vision begins to clear just as the shotgun is jerked from his grip and he is subsequently shoved backwards, landing on his back with a resounding thud.

Rolling onto one side, Burke pulls a serrated combat knife from his right boot but watches it fly from his grip as the first wave of bodies pin him to the cool, moist pavement.

Having once been revered for bench-pressing upwards of five-hundred pounds, the former college wrestling champion and Corrections Officer for the great state of Texas struggles and strains in futility as the steely grip holds him securely in place. He attempts an alligator 'roll' to possibly toss his attackers aside, but is unable to garner sufficient leverage. In the midst of the melee, Burke realizes something isn't quite right about the situation; something vital, though in the mad frenzy he isn't able to decipher exactly what.

It isn't until his assailants inexplicably release him and back away that the answer becomes clear.

His attackers did not possess the putrid, sickening smell of the long- deceased, though their touch had held the same cold, clammy feel.

"What th-? You? Oh…hell…no…h-hell noooo…" Burke mutters as his eyes lock with those of his assailants, pushing himself back with the heels of his boots until he has virtually pinned himself against a concrete wall.

The couple poses less than a dozen feet away, the male having embraced the female and hugged her tightly to his chest. They each look away from Burke just long enough to exchange a warm, loving glance.

They nod knowingly before retraining their

focus on Burkes' badly shaking frame.

"Get...get the hell away f-from me, damn it! We...we were...t- teammates...remember? We...we're...on the same side, DAMN IT!" he screams just seconds before they lunge toward him with clawed hands and bared teeth.

Following the feast, the loving couple share a passionate kiss, pausing only long enough to lick streams of blood and shredded gore from each other's faces.

As the shuffling hordes soon move in to claim the spoils, the Martins exchange a satisfied grin and clasp hands, departing the scene with a spring in their step rarely seen among the legion of the dead.

***

Though recent breakthroughs in medication have seen the incubation period extended somewhat, I regret to inform that a cure has yet to be found. Obviously, research has been hampered by somewhat primitive conditions in the past several decades On a brighter note, I am privy to the knowledge that the Colony's newly formed government does have a crack team of scientists and physicians working around the clock on a serum designed to further slow the effects of the disease following bodily fluid transfer with an infected host You will receive a more in-depth briefing on this matter once we reach the in-processing station.

By now I'm sure you'd all welcome a break to stretch or visit the lavatory.

See you back here in about...ten minutes. (ELEVEN MINUTES LATER)

Welcome back, folks. I've been reminded to tell

you that frequent urination is a normal side-effect of the 'reawakening' phase you are now undergoing. Please don't hesitate to interrupt me during this briefing if Mother Nature calls. Also, the medical staff will be drawing a small amount of blood from each of you before we arrive at the in-processing station. Again, this is just a precaution which will speed your release from quarantine.

Next, we cover another short-lived trend that became all the rage just as the plague hit its stride, at least among those fortunate few with the financial means to swing it. Many with the required transportation attempted 'escapism' once the death tolls began to rise, flying to distant lands or sailing the World's oceans in order to procure a suitable safe-haven. As they were soon to discover, however, the old adage 'easier said than done' was never so appropriate…

6 - Next Stop... DELUSION ISLAND

"Yep. Those are bones. No doubt about it B..o..n..e..s I whole-heartedly confer. Anything else?"

"They're human, Jack-O. That's a human femur. That's a human pelvic.

Over there's a hum-"

"Quiet down, Einstein! You want the girls to hear?"

"Well shit, Jack. I really don't think this is something we need to keep from them."

"Clark my man, this means nothing Whoever these remains belong to could've fallen offa boat two hundred miles from this island. Probably been floating around collecting algae for years.

"No reason to panic the wives over it. As far as I'm concerned, we're still in condition Yellow. Now, what say we collect 'em, stash 'em, and forget 'em?

"C'mon, we still got time for a game of hoops before chow, whatdaya say?"

"I *say* we better monitor this closely, Jack. I *say* we've grown a damn site too lazy for our own good. I *say*...(sighed)...come on then, let's get these hid so I can kick your ass again before they blow the lunch whistle."

It had been sixteen months since the couples had fled the Carolina coast aboard Jack's yacht in search of a suitable haven. The island had floated into view at mid-afternoon of day ninety-one of what Jack had referred to as '*Atlantic Seaboard Tour 2014*", a two-mile long, mile and a half wide dune with little in edible vegetation but an ample supply of fresh water and just enough shade to suffice.

Jack and Clark had been best friends since junior high. Each had served as the other's best man. Each served as godfather to the other's children. Now nearing their forty-fifth birthdays, neither could have envisioned such an existence in their wildest nightmares. Men of substantial wealth and stature (Jack a highly respected psychologist and Clark the vice-president of a nationwide freight company), the simple loss of *control* within their daily lives had easily been the most difficult and frightening aspect of the entire ordeal.

It had taken them less than a full week from the time initial reports of the plague had streaked across TV screens to organize and plot a plan of escape to parts unknown. Casting off around midnight of day eight, they'd watched in wide- eyed horror as CNN had reported world-wide casualties at nearly three-hundred million and climbing. By day three of trolling the North Atlantic for suitable island refuge, that number had nearly doubled. By day six, around the time they'd attempted to dock on an uncharted island in the Bahamas, all radio and TV transmissions had ceased altogether. The bodies of the diseased had littered the Bahamian islands like fruit-flies after a pesticide spraying, after which Jack had turned the yacht north once again, where they eventually discovered an uncharted island approximately sixty miles south of Bermuda The fifty-foot Dyna Motor Yacht, christened the "*Jack-A-Roo*' had been well-stocked upon departing the

Carolina's, and subsequent supply runs into the as-of-yet disease free Cayman islands had seen three of the six staterooms packed with canned foods, bottled water and equal amounts over-the-counter and prescription medication.

"Grub is served, you two!" Jessica yelled through cupped hands as Sonya set the table behind her.

"On our way, Mon Capitan!" Jack retorted, whirling about just as Clark tossed in a six-foot hook shot that essentially ended the contest.

"Let's see now," Clark spewed gleefully, wiping the fop sweat from his tanned forehead with a white rag, "that makes the official count six-oh-seven for me...and three for you."

"Keep talking, smart ass. Don't think for a minute I'm not capable of putting together a six-hundred game winning streak. Just a matter of time, pal."

"Uh-huh. You, my good doctor, are a genuine glutton for punishment."

The men departed the matted down sand of their makeshift basketball court, which was shaded in coconut and juniper trees, and headed for home base, all thoughts of beached bones having vanished from their collective subconscious as if they'd never existed.

Up ahead, Jack's ten year old son, Chad, was playing a casual game of catch with Clark's six-year old daughter Christie, who managed to mishandle even the gentlest of tosses.

"Kid has her father's hands," Jack quipped, "mitts of stone."

102

As was the daily ritual, lunch was consumed between peacefully swaying palms on a meticulously constructed picnic table Jack had built on only their fourth day on the island. Jessica, or 'Jessie', as was her nickname, jokingly referred to her husband of fourteen years as 'Doctor Jack Villa' for his prowess with hand and electrical tools. Jack had taken no chances as they'd departed the marina, packing one of the yacht's below-deck storage rooms with a plethora of tools. All remaining space had been earmarked for food, water, and first-aid supplies, an initial six-month supply that had been stretched out to nine before an emergency run back to the mainland was deemed necessary.

"How many packs we have left, son?" Jack asked Chad, who sat atop a large boulder, placing a fresh set of batteries into his I-Pod.

"A whole bunch, dad. At least a dozen of the six packs." "Even so, limit it to two hours a day like we talked about."

"Yes, sir," the boy replied, shooting his father a mock salute before sprinting toward the beach, where his mother sat beneath an umbrella stand as waves cascaded over her bare feet. After a moment, Jack reached over and retrieved two chilled bottles of beer from a nearby cooler before joining his family for an afternoon of tranquil frolic.

Meanwhile, inside the largest of two man-made huts, constructed solely of palm leaves and bamboo poles, Clark playfully nibbled at his wife's neck after a brief but intense bout of lovemaking.

"Beast," Sonya chided with a barely concealed grin, reaching around to gently slap his bare, golden brown tanned right shoulder, "one of these days your daughter is going to walk right in on us. Going to be a little late for the 'facts of life' speech then, big boy."

Dwarfing his Chinese-born bride of twelve years by a foot in height and nearly seventy pounds in body weight, Clark clasped an arm around her slim waist and hoisted her airborne with minimal effort.

"I'll just tell her it's all mommy's fault for being so damned irresistible." "I'm serious, Clark. Didn't you tell Jack to attach a lock of some kind?" "I'll remind him already," he replied in mock annoyance, "I'm busy now, woman! A man has to have his priorities."

She slid back into his waiting arms and they kissed deeply, and passionately.

"I've said it before and I'll say it again,' he said as they fell back onto the bed and locked eyes, 'as far as this boy is concerned, paradise is found."

As dusk broke, the families took up their usual positions on what Clark had long since dubbed 'The Overlook', stretched out on lawn chairs and sipping cool beverages as the sun gradually sank beyond the distant horizon. A light, soothing breeze was evident as the night set in, though the seas remained steady and calm.

A short time later, they trudged slowly back to camp. Soon, the children were fast asleep inside the huts as the adults picked sides for their nightly bridge tournament. As midnight approached, they all slept deeply and without concern for whatever horrors still faced the outside world. Without a doubt, they had found their asylum, and had no plans, immediate or otherwise, to tread the potentially treacherous waters beyond its serene perimeters.

***

"What are they pointing *at*?" Jack shrieked, huffing between words as he and Clark sprinted up the spongy dune in bare feet.

It was barely six AM, and each had been jarred from a deep slumber by the high-pitched wails of their children.

By the time they reached the top of the hill, where Chad and Christie stood pointing out into the open sea like posed statues, each felt the air in their lungs grow frigid even as their limbs slowly went numb.

"Oh god....oh my g-god..." Clark whimpered through trembling lips while reaching down to scoop his daughter into his arms. "Shit...shit, is that really a....what I think it...shiiiit," Jack replied in shock- shelled awe, unconsciously gripping his young son's shoulders and turning him about as if posing a ceramic doll.

"Let's grab the girls and get the hell outta here, Jack!" Clark bellowed, having already taken off toward camp with Christine bouncing wildly in his grip. Jack nodded without reply, having hoisted young Chad across his shoulder like a GI duffel bag. Fueled by equal portions of adrenaline and stark fear, the men made it back to base camp in roughly half the time it had initially taken them to reach the children.

***

"Stop it, Jack! Just…stop it! Tell me why we're doing this, damn it! TELL ME!"

"Because, Jes, the island wasn't…isn't safe anymore."

"Wasn't safe from…what? Why won't you tell us?" Jessica pleaded, using her slim form to block the stairway leading to below deck. Holding a five-gallon water jug in each arm, Jack frantically scanned the surrounding beach for movement.

"We'll…I'll fill you in as soon as we're launched, Jes, I promise. Now, get out of my way so I can stow these jugs."

"Jack, I'm not moving until you…"

"Damn it, woman…MOVE!" he bellowed angrily as they locked eyes.

Stuttering incoherently, Jessie turned sideways and watched her husband rush by.

"You'll understand. It was all for you," he whispered a few moments later, hugging her close as they both ascended topside, "I…I just pray you'll…understand."

The yacht sailed away from the eastern edge of the island less than twelve full minutes after the mysterious 'viewing' at the opposite side, penetrating a thin, grayish fog that only seemed to grow thicker and increasingly ominous the farther they traveled. "Where to, doc?" Clark inquired barely five minutes out, failing miserably in his attempt to inject much-needed levity.

"Anywhere but there, old buddy," Jack responded in a weary, bone-tired rasp, gripping the wheel as if they were treading swirling, stormy seas instead of the dead calmness that prevailed.

"The girls are…really scared, Jack-O. I heard Sonya grilling Chrissy about what they saw."

"And?"

"Damned strange. Chrissy just shrugged and clamed up, like she was purposely avoiding the subject or had…somehow completely forgotten it."

Jack gave the console a quick once-over before turning to his best friend and confidant of over thirty years, his face drawn and as colorless as the cloud of fog swallowing them whole from all sides.

"It's better that way, Clark. Believe me. It's better she…forgets." "What?" Clark replied with an open-mouthed glare, cocking his head in comical confusion.

Lowering his head as if deeply shamed, Jack's entire frame seemed to shrink in utter fatigue.

"Go down below and get the wives, Clark. Bring 'em up here. I've…got something to tell them. Something to tell…you all."

***

"My lord, Jack, I can't see anything in…in this."

"We're pretty well…flying blind, Jess. It'll break soon, right Jack-O?" "Eventually," Jack replied stoically, peering out with unblinking eyes into the milky murk as if visualizing a distant object the others were unable to detect, "It'll fade soon…transform…mutate. Soon, we'll all see things much, much clearer"

"Uh…yeah, great Rod Serling impersonation there, um, Jack-O," Clark stammered, pulling Sonja close and essentially pinning her to his side, "...now cut the psychobabble bullshit and tell us this deep, dark secret that only you seem privy to."

Lowering his chin, Jack turned slowly before locking eyes with his childhood friend.

Clark audibly gasped, feeling Sonya hug him ever tighter. The shadows engulfing the dimly lit bridge seemed to have aged Jack a full decade, his complexion shockingly pale.

"You saw it too, buddy-boy," he replied curtly, peering straight ahead through unblinking eyes, "you saw what I saw. What...the children saw."

"Damn it, Clark!" Sonya bellowed, struggling to pull free from her husband's steely grip, "what the hell is going on? What did the children see?"

Jessica soon joined her on opposite sides from the men. "I...we...it w-was offshore, just past those j-jagged rocks on overlook...overlook hill," Clark stammered, his voice growing increasingly shrill, "shit! I...I can't...it was like a d-dream..."

"I'll take it from here, old buddy," Jack interrupted calmly, allowing the wheel to swing loosely as he turned to face them, "it's only fair. What you and the children witnessed only makes sense to me anyhow."

"My god, Jack, stop talking in riddles! Why did you force us to leave the island?"

Lowering his gaze to the bridge's slickly waxed surface, Jack's voice seemed strangely hollow and utterly without emotion.

"A pipe dream, my dear, sweet Jess, but like all dreams, there has to be an awakening.

Do...any of you recall when we landed on one

of the Berry islands to replenish the water supply?"

Clark shrugged knowingly.

"Sure, that was only about three weeks after we'd left port in Myrtle Beach."

"That's right," Sonya added between intense sessions of fingernail gnawing, "we were down to three or four gallon jugs."

"What about it, Jack?' Jess inquired angrily while staring past her husband and into the dense clouds beyond, 'Jesus, don't do this. Don't draw this out like a damned stage play. Just cut to the chase."

"If you'll recall, Chad wondered off as we'd entered that first tourist villa." The trio instantly displayed similar expressions of pained bewilderment. Clark: "Chad? I don't..."

Sonya: "Wondered off...where? I can't remember..."

Jessica: "Jack honey, are you...okay? I mean, you really don't look well at all, and what you're saying just doesn't make sense."

"We split up and eventually found him-I found him- talking to an old man sitting outside a closed down strip club. Before I could get to them, the old man had reached over and stroked Chad's head with the back of his hand. A hand encrusted in sores. Red flaming...leaking...sores."

Clark: "When the hell did this happen?" Sonya: "Jack, you must've dreamed this..."

Jessica: "Strange. I...recall reaching the Berry islands but...nothing after we'd docked..."

Spinning about to retake the wheel, Jack ignored the comments and continued to drone away in the same eerie, dry monotone. As his rambling monologue proceeded, he gradually turned his head away from them until only the back of his sweat-moistened skull was visible.

"If I had done what...what we had all vowed to do in such a situation, things could've been different. But he was...he's my son, damn it! I couldn't just...*abandon* him...leave him there to rot on that damn island with the rest..."

Clark: "Jack...buddy...maybe you need to let me take the wheel..." Sonya: "Maybe he hit his head or something..."

Jessica: "Lord...lord, look at his...his hands!"

Gripping the wheel in a double-fisted vise, the flesh of each hand seemed to glow and pulsate, resembling some alien, translucent fiber.

"I...know I shouldn't have brought him back aboard. I...I knew better. I'd just hoped...prayed that...he hadn't contracted..."

Clark (backing slowly away with his hands held up in a blocking pose): "Oh god...oh dear god...he's...."

Wild-eyed with fear, Sonya sprinted to her husband's side, barely avoiding sliding on her knees in the process.

"By the time we...passed Freeport, we were all...infected...full blown. The children were...I mean, they fought it tooth and nail. A couple of...real troopers...but, their immune systems were....so weak..."

Clark: "You're...crazy, man! If...I mean...we'd...all be..."

Sonya: "Clark, we've got to...hop on the inflatable and g-get out...dear lord...g-get out now

110

before he...gives it to us..."

Jessica (covering her ears and screeching): "Jack, stop it! Just STOP IT!"

They all grew silent in unison as the distinct sound of pattering feet originated from below deck.

At the same time, the fog bank seemed to dissipate dramatically as dawn's early light cracked the eastern horizon.

"You see...it wasn't until we reached Bermuda...the *triangle* that I...woke to find us in our...present states. I'd often found...group hypnosis a useful tool to...alter one's perception of reality. Wasn't that difficult really...just a matter of utilizing my own personal vision of paradise..."

The pattering grew louder just as a pair of tiny yet distinct shadows appeared on the narrow stairwell leading to the bridge-while only patches of smog remained as the yacht sailed rapidly towards a yet unidentifiable beachhead.

"What could be better, after all, in the midst of such worldwide chaos and death, than to share a peaceful, tropical isle with one's best friends? The ones...who mean the most? Not...sure why it has...had to end this way...damned shame, really..."

The children dashed up and forward like twin torpedoes, bounding ahead in a blur until they each joined Jack at the wheel and began playfully tugging at its grooved handle.

"Now, now children...leave the wheel be. Spinning it about won't...cannot change our destination I'm afraid...nothing *can* or...*ever* will. Not...now." Whirling about as one, the youngsters smiled broadly, their childish giggles weirdly muffled, as if originating from a far distance. Jack reached down with shrunken, skeletal hands and patted each of their equally fleshless skulls.

A garbling yelp escaped the back of Sonya's throat as she fell to one knee before collapsing in a spasm-racked heap.

Clark joined her mere seconds later, clutching his throat as if in the throngs of a particularly deadly chemical reaction.

Jessica lay back and flailed about like a banked fish, her breathing strained and shallow as her eyes lolled about like rolled marbles.

"Look kids…Jess….we're…we're home…" Jack exclaimed cheerily, his hollowed eye sockets growing wide with grade-school glee as the tiny island swam into view, its desolate, barren landscape illuminated by the early morning sun glistening off of eerily calm seas.

As the yacht grew ever nearer, its long-deceased crew stood at the side rails and soon spotted the images of two children standing atop an oval-shaped sand dune. Seconds later, the children, a boy of perhaps ten and a girl a bit younger, were joined by two adult men. The men quickly scooped up the children dashed away in a mad sprint, as if being chased by some dangerous, unseen enemy.

"Ah, yes…" Jack whispered in a dreary, melancholy voice, "we are most definitely home…once again…"

And the voyage of the eternally damned would repeat verbatim as minutes turned into hours and hours to days…days to years and years to decades...decades to centuries and centuries to infinity...sailing atop the haunted waters surrounding *Delusion Island*.

***

The cold-hearted fact of the matter was, good people, that there was no such hidden paradise to escape to. Eventually, the plague extended its diseased arms to every distant shore; it simply took longer to reach some places than others If there are no objections, I'll proceed with the next segment. A real 'eye- opener', you might say. Around the tenth year of the plague, certain... medical advancements had been made, however crude, that prolonged not only the lifespan of the deceased hordes, but also vastly improved their quality of life, so to speak. Thus, certain aspects of 'old' society experienced a brief, if not ultimately doomed, renaissance. Listen closely as I explain the rather gruesome, but undeniably fascinating details...

7 - Slug Trail

A *'Rutger Cavander-Zombie Hit-Man'* Mystery

Cavander casually tossed back the lapel of his ankle-length black leather duster and lifted the snub-nosed spear-gun to shoulder height, squinting through his one remaining eye while taking careful aim. The duster was coated in dried gore, and crunched sharply with each pronounced movement. His intended target continued to bob and weave like a drunken pugilist, all the while resembling one of those 'shrunken head' dolls that had been all the rage in the late 20th Century.

"Damn...boy," Cavander grumbled, lowering the guns sights just a hair, "why would *anyone*...be ...so hell bent...on eliminating...your pathetic ass?"

The skeletal corpse continued to dance a wobbly jig, its grapefruit-sized head bobbing atop a stick-thin neck. Its eyes had long since hollowed out, the pupils jiggling inside the blackened sockets like prune pits dangling from a string.

"Regardless..." Cavander concluded, re-focusing his aim as the corpses' spastic movements finally seemed to settle a bit, "...it ain't...like they...pay me...to...give...a...shit..."

As if suddenly realizing its impending fate, the corpse took off in a wobbly lurch down the trash-strewn alleyway, its lone remaining arm serving as a directional rudder as it flung about wildly.

Cavander groaned, tugging at the bill of his badly faded *'Oakland Raiders'* baseball cap and

114

dropping the gun to his side, then pausing to register an official complaint into the stale, dead air before taking off in a casual jog.

"...wonder..ful...*now* he ...gets it."

He ignored the sharp cracking noises reverberating from his knees as he drew to within a dozen yards of his emaciated target, who he watched duck down still another virtual maze of alleys.

Cavander grunted angrily, reaching back to reposition a small backpack balanced between his shoulder blades. After an additional few steps, he slowed just enough to reach down and pull a marble-handled machete from a leather holster strapped to his outer left thigh.

Always...hated this...part of...town. Damned neon and concrete...sewer.

Sure as...hell hasn't...aged well...through the...fallout.

Lumbering past a two-story pile of auto wreckage, to include a late model SUV sitting sideways atop a badly crushed Lincoln Continental, he temporarily lost sight of his mark as the relatively narrow alleyway grew increasingly dark.

If this bird...wasn't in such...sorry shape...I wouldn't ever consider this...crazy shit. Never did...trust a...blind alley.

Halting just to the left of a mass grouping of metal trash cans, Cavander holstered the machete, propping the spear gun on his left shoulder while reaching back to grasp the handle of still another weapon and pulling its blackened, slightly rusted nozzle forward. The M2A1-7 Australian built flame- thrower was not only a genuine combat antique, a fact made sadly insignificant in recent times, but a vital piece of weaponry within his vast arsenal.

Shouldering the spear gun, he quickly adjusted the thrower's knob settings, then primed the trigger with several test squeezes. After pausing to scan the surrounding shadows for movement, he re-attained the spear gun and pointed the barrels of both weapons straight out at chest-level.

Normally, he wouldn't have pulled the thrower so hastily while pursuing a single target, much less one that was far beyond posing any serious threat. That is, not unless something felt seriously out of kilter. Clients definitely preferred the cleanliness the spear gun provided, though most would accept a slightly singed skull over nothing at all. In the dozen or so times he'd been forced to utilize its rather destructive power, only a single client had argued the end result. Even then, he'd received the majority of his standard fee.

"Might…as well…show yourself there…*Skeletor*…," he stammered, side- stepping by the cans with his back practically scraping the concrete wall on the opposite side, "…I promise you…it'll be quick…and…relatively pain…less. Hell, for a second…you can imagine…you're the…guest of honor…at the company…barbecue."

He jerked back as one of the cans, one of those hundred-gallon, Rubbermaid plastic jobs with the foot-pedal lift, began to shake violently from side to side.

"If that's…a rat in there…I apologize

116

in...advance," he snarled, flicking the weapon's built-in striker and aiming the thrower's nozzle at the can's bloated midsection.

Just as the blue flame ignited and his trigger finger began to curl, the alleyway blazed to light like an exploding supernova, sending Cavander flailing back into the cold brick.

"Shiiiitttt..." he blurted, fumbling the thrower while falling onto this backside with a strained huff, "...happy fucking...New Year..."

"Just...stay where...you lay, tough guy," a voice rang out, obviously filtered through a hand-held bullhorn, "you...so much...as flick a booger or...cough up...a kidney and...parts of you...will litter every surrounding...block...like chimney...soot."

"Wonderful..." Cavander mumbled, carefully laying aside the machete, spear gun and flame thrower while bringing his knees to his chest, "...set up...like a...bowling pin. Should've known...this mark was...too damn...easy."

"Wellllll, dip me... in battery acid and... call me bleached," the mystery guest blurted in sarcastic glee, "if it isn't...the late...great...and soon to be...deceased once again...private dick turned...ass-sasssss.innnn... 'Slug Trail' Cavander himself, in the *peeling* flesh and *chalky* bone."

After pausing briefly as to properly identify the originator, Cavander nodded knowingly and flashed a weary smile before leaning his head back against the cool stone wall.

"Ahhh, hell. Mama...said...they'd be...days like...these."

I discovered the payoff sitting on the wooden deck of my hillside condo; a number six Jiffy bag with the word 'CAVANDER' hand-written in blue Sharpee across its middle. The jiffy was taped to an Igloo cooler and accompanied by a ten-gallon metal container filled with gasoline. As with the dozen or so previous times my mysterious client had come to call, I'd been supplied with exactly half the required fee, with the other half no doubt payable upon completion of the assigned task. On a single sheet of blank letterhead were neatly typed instructions, as well as photos of the intended target and applicable background info. Whoever my mystery client was, he or she was nothing if not predictable. The medium-sized cooler held several ice packs sitting atop at least a dozen separate cellophane bags, thus helping to maintain a semblance of freshness. Upon tearing away the cellophane in ragged strips as the maddening hunger pushed away all manner of self-control, I'd noted little in the way of actual bleeding, though the texture did hold just enough moistness to rule out complete coagulation. Got to admit, I was salivating like a starving mutt over a meaty plate of Alpo's finest.

The feeding had lasted less than five minutes, in which time I'd managed to scarf down ample portions of thigh, calf, and forearm, all meticulously clean shaven, though obviously taken from the male of the species.

As the blood lust had gradually subsided, I busied himself with the second element of payment, that being the TR injections. It had been six weeks since my last series, and I'd watched in awestruck wonder as the weathered flesh of my arms, chests, legs and groin reacted almost instantly. The shuffling masses call the stuff 'liquid gold', and it sells for quite the heady price on the street. The so-called 'Tissue Rejuvenator' medication worked best either on those whose passing was fairly recent (no longer than three years in duration) or those who'd managed to stash away a supply plentiful enough to allow for weekly injections.

Personally, I considered myself middle of the pack in terms of getting what I needed, juice- wise Definitely could've used more- who the hell couldn't? But I also realized just how damn lucky I was to be working steady enough to warrant at least semi-monthly injections.

The folder contained six photos of a man listed as a one-time auto mechanic and former CEO of 'Horizontal Smiles' Inc, a chain of 'specialty' porn/sex shops in and around the state that had long been reputed as delving into both prostitution and illegal gambling. Having kicked-off of plague-related symptoms approximately fourteen months earlier, the pictures provided displayed the man in gradual degrees of decay, from a 'live' shot to a more recent, whereas he'd lost the majority of both his body weight, hair, and flesh. Dude looked like your classic 'mixed breed' pimp; half cauc and half spic. Mid-to-late forties.

Greasy, slick-downed hair that had been about two shades too dark to be natural and a soft, sagging mid-section that screamed of too many late night stops at Taco Bell.

Nothing new or dramatic about the guy's decline. Happens to all of us, though some seem to hold it together better than others. Many think it's the family gene pool that decides the level of acceleration. I personally hold to the notion that it all depends on how many loaded TR syringes one can procure on at least a semi-regular basis. It's pretty damn simple, really; take away the magic juice and dead tissue does what's natural, only at warp speed.

The target file provided but a single address to use as a starting point, that being 'Lings Nookie Palace' on J.Jamison Avenue, a gentleman's club that had been quite the hot-spot in its late 20th and early 21st Century heyday. In addition, a lone name was scribbled alongside the address. Leah Kim. It was a name, however generically Asian in origin, that rang strangely familiar, though for the life of me, pardon the pun, I couldn't place it at the time. Clients instructions for successful task completion was simple and to the point. Extermination, disintegration, and skull retrieval as proof of said mission completion. In other words, SSDD.

***

It took nearly an hour to reach what had once been referred to as the 'Skin District' from my pad. In better days, when my reflexes were sharper and my eyesight unaffected by dead cells and decaying tissue, I could've made the same trek in half the time.

Before the plague, I'd been fortunate to avoid such areas as the 'Skin District' unless absolutely necessary. A once prosperous business strip, in later years it had deteriorated into a low-income shit-hole frequented by hordes of multi-cultural gang-bangers, strung-out junkies and teenaged runaways turning tricks for their daily fixes. As auto plants, printing shops and textile mills had given way to titty-bars, pawn shops and liquor stores, the crime rate soared and long-time residents fled for the suburbs.

I parked my freshly waxed Grand Prix, AKA 'the Slug Mobile' in an alley behind 'Ling's' , and side-stepped several panhandlers while turning a corner leading to the front entrance.

"Get...a job," I quipped, strolling by a bloated Hispanic female whose head had swollen to medicine-ball proportions. After I'd passed, her upturned palms slowly rotated about as the middle finger of each hand was briefly extended in my general direction.

"Same to you, sweets," I replied with a grin, picking up speed as I'd bypassed an African-American male squatting in a 'lotus style' pose while holding an empty coffee can airborne. Somewhere along the line, the dude's face had been mashed inward with great force, as his nose had collapsed deep inside the nasal cavity with his upper palate serving as a pulped tray-table of sorts. He had a sign hanging about his toothpick-thin neck that read 'ANIMAL PARTS ARE FINE: HOMELESS AND HUNGRY DON'T MEAN PICKY'.

"Sorry, Bud...if I owned a cat...you'd be...more than welcome to it."

Amazing as it seemed at first glance, the

panhandlers were merely acting on instinct, as most shufflers with limited resources were want to do. They were the same in death as they had been in life. Frequenting street corners in search of a handout was simply what they knew. Death and subsequent resurrection had done little to alter that particular fact. Difference was, they no longer plied their trade for loose change or paper currency, but any spare scrap of edible tissue that might serve to temporarily quell the incessant aching inside their putrefied, mucus-packed midsections. Dog eat dog world, indeed. Welcome to the new millennia.

Standing at the double-door entrance to 'Lings', I could hear the sounds of a familiar pop tune from the late eighties or early nineties echoing from inside. I paused, tucking my hands inside my duster's side pockets, trying to recall both title and artist. Had a true knack for rock and pop trivia, especially the fascinating category of 'one-hit wonders'.

"Wang Chung...Everybody... Wang Chung Tonight. Redundant as hell but...not without its toe-tapping...qualities. Definitely...a guilty pleasure," I finally blurted just before shoving the entrance door ajar and stepping inside a virtual fog bank of stage and cigarette smoke.

Place was pretty damned roomy compared to the other skin shops on the strip. From what I'd heard, it had always been a money maker. There were four separate 'runways' in which the girls plaid their trade, and a circular bar that must've measured twenty-five yards in length.

"Take ...your hat, big... boy?" a tall, brunette

hostess inquired as seductively as possible for a woman missing the majority of her lower jaw.

"Think I'll...just keep it...for now, darlin'," I'd responded, scanning the smog-filled room with a raised hand shielding my functioning eye, "nice crowd."

"Nah, not really. Same old... peeling faces," she'd sighed, chewing loudly and popping her gum every few seconds, "something to wet the whistle, then?"

"What do you suggest?"

"Bloody Mary's are ...the house favorite. Just food coloring, but it....does have a nice little sugar kick."

"Anything...solid on the menu?"

"Just some...rawhide chews...most of 'em expired. I'd...suggest you...stick with the liquid...variety."

"Sounds like...a winner," I replied, eyeing a pole dancer a few dozen or so feet to the left.

The woman paused, her upper plate exposed in a permanent grimace. I couldn't help but ponder how she managed to keep the flies from congregating or the rats from nesting when she slept.

"Prepay, please. House rules."

I pulled a small plastic baggie from my inner vest and slapped it in her palm. "That's a Vita-pack; four Biotin, three C's and two E's." "Expiry dates?"

"Toddlers from the factory, darlin'. Late two-thousand twelve. So, how much does that buy me these days?"

She pulled the bag to her face, tilted her head to the left and studied the contents, rolling the pills about for a few seconds like a trained chemist studying his wares.

"Hmm, I'd say...two hours of voyeuristic pleasure and three to four drinks. Fair enough?"

Damn. Club prices had sure skyrocketed since my last excursion. Time was when a pocket full of barely expired vitamins or a carton of semi-fresh smokes would buy you a boat-load of sugar pop and a full evening of ogling decayed flesh.

"No complaints here, babe."

"One house special coming right up. Sit back and enjoy the show, one-eye."

The woman strolled away on long, luxurious legs that once had no doubt been her best feature, but were now little more than fleshless stilts that looked on the verge of snapping from even the slightest outside pressure.

"You got it, stork-legs," I whispered not nearly loud enough for the woman to hear, my eye locked on the dancer; a drop-dead gorgeous Asian who was gyrating madly while stroking the oily-slick metal bar in a seductive double- fisted massage. I tilted my head to the left and rested my chin atop a clinched fist, suddenly in no hurry to rush things.

(Leah Kim. Leah...Kim. Why was that name so damned familiar?)

It hit me just as she completed her set and hopped from the circular stage with a fluidity and grace that I'd found equally surprising and arousing.

(Leah Kim, AKA 'Jade Fever'. Got'cha. I could

124

never forget such a beautiful face...or ass for that matter)

I watched her slip on a bright orange robe and sashay through the sparse crowd, vanishing into a narrow hallway that obviously led to a rear dressing room.

The waitress reappeared just as a new dancer took center runway, this one Caucasian and noticeably less attractive. Woman had large sections of flesh missing from her back, and a pretty nasty looking infection coating her rump. Girl was practically spewing pus from her butt-cheeks.

"Here... you go, Patch."

"You're...a real lifesaver...sweets," I said with a playful wink as a glass goblet was placed at the table's center, its blackish content resembling overused motor oil.

"Uh-huh. Need anything else, you... just let me... know."

"As a... matter of fact, can you relay... a message for me?"

"Sure," she said, snapping her gum louder than ever, "if... I can. Shoot."

"Could you... tell Jade Fever that her... number one fan wants to buy her... a drink."

The waitress rolled her eyes, only one of which rotated back into proper position as she'd moved away.

"Jade..? That's a new... one on me."

I motioned toward the dancer and the woman nodded through widened eyes, one of which held a dull, chalky color.

"Oh...you mean Leah?"

"Leah...Jade...whichever she answers to these days. Tell her I've got something for her."

"Yeah, sure. You... and every other pud-puller... in this joint, pal. Hijack a... truckload of Viagra, did... we?"

"Tell ya what, sweets, just tell... her The Skin King ... sends his... regards," I added, freezing her in her tracks until she damned near spilled her tray once those Pelican gams of hers locked up.

"Su-sure...I'll...let her know," the waitress said, her dap-like complexion having turned a shape paler. Always amazes me that walking corpses are capable. Even saw a target blush once. Again, it's all about TR injections and the frequency thereof. I do believe if that waitress' lower jaw had been intact, it most assuredly would've slipped off track like a rusty hinge as soon as I'd mentioned Ramirez by name. Obviously, either one popular SOB in his time, or a damn feared one.

As it was, it took less than three minutes for my little Jade honey to make a personal appearance. In the meantime, I'd ogled the 'alligator lady' on stage while taking a sip or three of the house's best WD-40.

"What's the... deal, Snake Plisken? I know you?" she asked with just a tint of sarcasm, her fists propped seductively on each hip. Got to admit, I was a bit disappointed at the complete lack of accent. Obviously she had been a pretty good actress after all, because she'd sounded grade-A, one-hundred percent Korean in the skin flicks I'd seen. Hell, in person she sounded more 'California Valley Girl' than of Asian descent. Another fantasy

falls by the wayside.

Bummer.

Her smile was slight but still sexy enough to set this boy's groin to tingling. It was damned amazing. Here was a chick that actually looked better up close than at a distance. I instantly placed her 'DASR' (Death and Subsequent Resurrection) date at no more than six months previous-eight at the outset. Her flesh still retained a glowing smoothness; her muscle tone as yet unaffected by wilting tissue No ifs, ands, or buts; this exotic little babe had a sugar-daddy who cared enough to supply only the very best in 'juvie' juice.

"Never had... the pleasure, babe, 'least not on... an up close and personal level," I replied, pulling a fresh fag from my duster, "smoke?"

She raised a hand palms-up while continuing to stare a hole through me. "Never... touch 'em. Who needs... it with the... twenty-four hour bonfire going on in here? Now, what's your... game, Cyclops?"

Definitely a recent casualty; even her speech pattern was smooth and almost void of the 'stutter and hesitate' symptoms that get us all eventually. It's maddening as hell to be able to think at normal speed but only speak said thoughts a full three gears slower.

"Game? I don't... follow, babe."

She rolled her exquisitely slanted eyes and began tapping the tabletop with the fingernails of both hands. Painted dark red and manicured to fine, serrated edges, I had no doubt those particular skin-peelers could do some serious damage if their owner were properly provoked. Still, just the sight of 'em increased my level of lust two-fold. Shit, she even smelled good-almost life-like.

"Smart-ass. Nobody... saunters in this joint by accident and spits out the name Jorge 'The Prince of Flesh' Ramirez without... an ulterior motive. If its trouble you're looking for, look... somewhere else."

I took another sip of sludge, then a long, lengthy draw from the Winston before replying, pleasantly surprised she hadn't given me the finger and walked off.

"Okay, you... got me. Sharp... as a tack, you are."

She snarled, revealing a polished set of choppers that were easily the whitest I'd seen on a corpse. Matter of fact, her gums looked pretty damned healthy as well.

"Speak... your piece, asshole. I've got another... session in five."

"Chill out, sweets. Jorge's an... old friend. Just... trying to locate him... is all," I said, raising both palms high in surrender.

Leah leaned in close, and I got an eyeful of those perky little tits. Once again, my groin was all a-tremor.

"Greasy Spic motherfucker didn't have... any friends, Cyclops, just deadly enemies. This I know... without a doubt. Allow me to repeat, what's your game?"

"He was... what, your... manager? Agent?"

"What the fuck do you... really want, man?" she growled, raking those exquisite nails over the tabletop like straight razors, "a lap dance? Or you... want me to reach over and massage those *grape-sized nuts before they shrivel... up and blow away for good? Well, kiss off. Go nab yourself a street...whore..."*

"Testy, testy...reel... in those claws, kitty-cat. I was... told you knew where to find... the man, that's all. Drink?" I replied with a wink and a nod, fighting the urge to further grill her just to see the flames shoot from those pretty little nostrils. Damn, she was a fire-plug.

"No time, Jack. This girl's got... to boogie." "No idea... where to find... him, then?" "Even if I did, why... should I tell you?"

"Well, there... is the need to find 'im before... I wax 'im, ya know."

She leaned back up, feigning shock. Don't ask me how I knew. I hadn't known the woman for five minutes. I just did. It's a knack I developed in my PI days. A knack that was rarely proved wrong.

"What...did you say?"

Lighting another smoke, I casually lifted my eye-patch and allowed a few puffs to shoot from the empty socket. Never fails to wow the chicks.

"I said...I'm going to...whack the...greasy Spic motherfucker."

"Tell you... what, Slick..." she said, obviously holding back a glee-fueled grin while leaning back and crossing thin yet nicely toned legs, "this last session's my last... for the night, then we'll...discuss things."

"You know...where to...find me," I said before draining the mug and mashing out the remains of my smoke.

I managed to finish off a second round of

reddish sludge and two more smokes while watching her expertly ply her trade, all the while feeling an altogether not unpleasant aching in my chest. True, my sexual tastes had always leaned toward the exotic, specifically those females of the Asian persuasion.

Two-plus years spent tooling about South Korea, Thailand and the Philippines leaves a young man wide open for a serious bout of Yellow Fever. That said, there was something more here; something that went infinitely deeper than simple lust. The mystery didn't begin to clear until hours later, after she'd agreed to accompany me to the condo and we'd concluded a brief but intense love-making session on my living room couch. Though the girl wasn't quite the spitting image of my first ex, there were certain features that were damned near identical.

Her eyes held the same sparkling, greenish hue as Mia's had, just as her pug-shaped nose, pouting lips and chiseled cheekbones held a similar shape.

While Leah's hair hugged her face and was barely shoulder-length, Mia had maintained ultra-lengthy locks that hung between her shoulder blades and past the curvature of her waist. At five-eight, Mia had been considered tall for a Korean female, while Leah appeared no more than five-one or two.

Wasn't sure why it had taken me so long to associate her with my one- time partner of just over five years. Maybe subconsciously I was trying like hell to separate the two while simultaneously being drawn in like steel to a magnet. Mia had been both the best and worst thing I'd ever experienced; half-

130

Asian goddess and half psychopathic demon, with little gray area in-between. Divorcing that woman was equal parts relief and anguish. It both saved my life and extinguished an inner fire I've never seen rekindled. The other two wives that followed were hollow shells by comparison, like pitting a box of soggy firecrackers against a truckload of nitro glycerin. Leah seemed to possess a similar explosive, though a bit more subdued.

Either way, I wasn't complaining about the carnal outcome, which had caught me completely off guard. She certainly hadn't given a clue on the drive up, staying pretty tight-lipped for the duration. I'd offered her a week's worth of TR injections for the info on her former boss, although she later confessed that she would've happily supplied said info for free.

After a quick tour of the 'Slug Pad', we'd shared a slab of my best semi- frozen tenderloin from the utility freezer, during which time I'd innocently (?) leaned over to lick a bloodied tatter from her chin. Long story short, the freak was soon very much 'on'.

Zombie sex, as a rule, can be a tricky affair, not to mention a bit frustrating when compared to its living counterpart. There's more...preparation involved. Additional...precautions are taken. Translation: 'Rough Sex' is definitely out, unless those involved are carelessly indifferent about keeping precious body parts intact. The TR juice, along with a monthly injection of selected hormonal boosters, allow for the occasional working erection on the male side, while similar chemical bombardment works its magic on the female side. I'd even heard the periodic orgasm is possible for the ladies, given the right persuasion. We males can only dream of the 'good old days' in terms of climax, being that the internal 'pipes' are essentially bone dry, pardon the pun. Confidentially, it had been quite a spell since I'd partaken in the practice of 'bumping uglies', being that finding a suitable partner is damned near impossible in a World where such a term has been drastically altered to 'bumping lifeless uglies' or perhaps 'bumping brittle uglies'. In Leah's case, however, the partner was so breathtakingly well-preserved that such trivialities meant little. To put it in the vernacular; that little girl rocked my world, and then some. Needless to say, the many and varied talents she'd acquired in the Porn business had carried over both to real life and the afterlife as well. This old boy was putty in her hands from minute number one, and she damn well knew it.

"You never... did tell... me," I said as we'd dug into a plate of dripping, barbecued fatback I had saved for just such a special occasion.

"Tell you... what?"

"What the man... did to you to... warrant such hatred."

"You mean... 'The Skin King', the 'Prince of Flesh'?" she sighed, pressing her head firmly against my chest as we lay naked across the wide leather sectional, "shiiiiit, where... do I begin?"

"At the beginning?"

"Why do they... call you Slug-Trail, anyway? Sounds nasty..."

132

"You're close. Since the majority of my...intended targets are....let's just say...on the slimy side....all I gotta do...is follow...the trail...get it?"

"Check. Well...Jorge definitely...qualifies..."
"He was your... manager, right?"

"Me and just about... every other chick... under contract with Blue Streak Films, Inc."

"I thought... Horizontal Smiles... was his lone empire." "HS was the poppa company... to Blue Streak."

"Oh. Got'cha. Jorge was...branching... out."

"Oh yeah, that was one south-of-the-border beaner with... big dreams and... sky-high aspirations. Saw himself... as the poor man's Hugh Hefner. Thing is, ol' Hef wasn't... saddled with a three G a day coke habit. I can't recall many... occasions not seeing that Jackass stoned out... of his gourd. Then again, that's not exactly a unique problem... in the porn business. Can't say I didn't partake on several... occasions myself. Tricks of the trade...to keep one...happily diverted from reality's icy chill.

"Anyhow, one day he just... closed up shop without... warning and poof!

Vanished without a trace... owing a lot of people a shit-load of cash, including yours truly."

"How much?"

"Right at fifteen grand. As it turned out, I did my... last three flicks for free. I know dead presidents don't... mean shit these days, but it still pisses me off."

I nodded, reaching down to gently stroke her

133

breasts, which I found to be amazingly pliable for one in our...condition. Again, the power of the TR injection on full display.

"I hear... you. I've seen people... waxed for much, much less."

"Wasn't just the money. Asshole... loved to slap us around when he was nice and coked up. Treated... us like street whores. Didn't exactly break my heart to hear the virus... took his ass out of the game fairly early."

"Why didn't... you just quit?"

"Two reasons; the man always owed... us just enough money to keep us around, and the crooked... contract we were all stupid enough to sign legally bound us to 'perform.' If you walked, you ended up owing him, and... he wasn't one to forget a debt. Man had mob affiliates that would ensure... you lived up to your side of the bargain."

I hugged her tight, leaning down to kiss her forehead.

"Well, obviously... somebody besides you still... holds a similar ...grudge, babe. That's... where I come in..."

Following another intense groping session, she provided a single lead that I hoped would pan out. Early the next morning we exchanged TR injections and she crashed while I left to check the lead. Weird is as weird does, I guess. I'd known the lady for less than twelve hours, and already felt like we'd been shacking for years. Again, it might've just been the Mia factor. Hell, even their love-making moans were similar. Regardless, after all those months of living alone, I wasn't fighting it. Might've been jumping the gun in a colossal way, but I was even planning on asking her to move in once I got back. I had to laugh at my own behavior-like a virgin teen after his first piece of ass.

Amid a flurry of outlandish rumors she'd immediately blown off as fiction, Leah had heard through her post-porn contacts that Jorge had been holed up with a mob contact of his following the fiasco at Blue Streak, and had sold the rights to Horizontal Smiles Inc. to a competing pornographer for around two point-five mil. She'd heard the mob flunkies name was Joseph Garluche, also known as 'Joey G.' Dude supposedly had a well-secured, eight-thousand square foot condo in the Millstone Hills area. Seems he and Jorge had been 'unofficial' partners in the local cocaine trade, wherein Mister Ramirez had first developed an insatiable love for the product.

It took just under two hours and damn near a half-tank of fuel to cover the sixty-eight mile trek to Millstone, an area infamous for its high-profile inhabitants, most of whom had obtained their wealth in highly illegal ways. With its remote location, majestic hills and scenic mountains, such an area was tailor- made for all lowlifes to lay low, so to speak.

Most of the homes I'd passed along the twisting, turning highways appeared long-deserted, the lawns having grown shoulder-high in some cases, while several others had extensive fire damage.

I arrived at 245 Stoneridge Court around noon, and it was damned obvious right from the get-go that Leah's tip was a lemon.

Found several fossilized husks near the pool area and three more inside the house, none of which had fit Jorge's description and more than likely had been former members of 'Joey G's' house staff, or possibly family even members. While the home itself was as spacious as advertised, the grounds reminded me of a college campus. All told, it took me two full hours just to search the house, and another two to cover the five-plus acres surrounding it. Along the wooded perimeter at the rear of the grounds, I found the occasional hollowed-out husk, several of which had decayed to piles of blackened ash in human guise. The ones that were still partially recognizable all seemed to share the same grisly fate. All had been executed gangland style with their hands bound at their backs and quarter-sized holes blown through their skulls. My guess; 'Joey G' had made them an offer they 'couldn't refuse'. Once again, none had even remotely resembled my intended mark, though the aforementioned ashes were always a possibility. Instincts told me otherwise, and the search continued unabated.

Back at the house, I did find several framed photos of both 'Joey G' and Ramirez, some posed with various family members and a few 'out on the town' shots of the two of them sharing space with various celebrities, most of whom I recognized from the Porn-industry. Even spotted a woman who bore a strong resemblance to Leah in the background of one, along with at least a dozen other of the more popular video 'starlets' of the day. No doubt on a

PR junket of some kind. Might sound ludicrous, but I have to confess feeling just a twinge of jealousy. Ludicrous hell...downright stupefying. I mean, the woman had been a b-list porn star for several years, credited with at least three dozen films and countless internet 'photo shoots'. What exactly did I think I had fallen into in the past day and a half? Had I really been that damned lonely? Guess the answer is obvious.

Got to say, 'Joey G' made Jorge 'The Skin King' Ramirez look positively GQ by comparison. Talk about your stereotypical Italian crime boss, that boy looked like a walking TV ad for 'The Sopranos'. I'm talking slick enough to slide off flypaper like an oily glob of snot.

After resigning myself to the fact that a useable clue was not to be found, I was walking back toward my ride when a growing chorus of growls forced me to turn on my heels. A quick glance at my watch revealed that I'd basically pissed away four and a half hours for absolute nada.

Now, I'd seen the occasional feral dog wandering about the city and even in the general proximity of the 'Slug Pad'. I'd also heard tales of wild packs roaming the outskirts in search of edible scraps; the word 'scraps' defined by anything and everything that had once held a pulse. In my personal estimation, a 'pack' would mean from three to perhaps....twelve or fifteen animals.

Case in point; using such numbers as a barometer, this wasn't merely a pack sprinting my way in furry droves from the west end of Joey G's estate...no siree...it was a fucking armored division.

137

I spotted everything from ankle-high Chihuahua's to knee-high Terriers to a chest high Irish Wolf-hound; a true canine melting pot, all with a burning desire to turn yours truly into two-dozen separate chew toys. Speaking of toys, saw a 'toy' poodle decked out in red ribbons and what looked like a diamond-studded collar, sprinting between a well-groomed Griffon and a collie right off the set of 'Lassie'.

Being that I was still a good twenty-five yards from my ride and the pack was closing in at warp speed, I knew there wasn't a chance in hell I'd make the driver's door before being swarmed over.

Before getting into the inevitable blood 'n guts, allow me to inject a note of humanity here. Rutger James Cavander was a tried and true dog lover in the living years-owned everything from bassets to Jack Russell's to miniature Dobermans; all of which were saved from the brink of termination via the gas chamber at local animal shelters. No doubt about it, this man was a trusted friend and master to all God's furry little creatures. Watched 'Animal Planet' on a regular basis. Took the wives and girlfriends to the zoo at least twice a year.

Donated money to local animal shelters without a thought. Hell, I even owned a ferret once, though it was given to me by an appreciate client. Damned thing shit all over everything, ate my clothes and chewed my furniture to kindling, but I still fed and cared for it.

That was the good news. Here comes the bad:

The first shot from my nine-mil Glock was a warning; sparking off of the paved driveway a good ten to fifteen yards in front of the charging pack. More bad news: they completely ignored its implications. I didn't normally use revolvers or live fire on marks, as most clients desired a complete desecration of the body via my specially designed flame-thrower. That being said, my aim was a bit off considering the lack of recent practice. Plus which, unlike the Glock, I was just breaking in a 22 caliber Beretta Neo semi-automatic that was jerking my wrist around like a fag waiving down a cab on Hollywood & Vine.

Crouching down onto one knee, I assumed a straight-armed pose and fired both revolvers in an 'outside-in' sweep-type rotation in an attempt to fell the front row of attackers while hopefully enticing the remaining formation to flee.

In a few scant ticks, I watched a pit-bull's snout torn from its face; a coon- dog's right ear sheered away, and the aforementioned collie's skull explode into a crimson mist of fur, blood and bone.

Despite the booming intrusion and their mauled, fallen comrades, the swarm continued forward in the same frantic dash, seemingly oblivious to the potential danger in doing so. To state the very least, I was disheartened by their calm, unaffected reaction. To state the very obvious, I was scared shitless as they continued on a b-line directly toward my dead ass.

I fired a total of ten additional rounds before leaping up, twisting about, and darting towards the Slug Mobile as fast as my wobbly gams would allow.

Saw the Chihuahua split in half like chopped

fruit, its tiny little back legs pumping madly even as its front half veered off into a nearby shrub.

Saw the Wolf-Hound's front left paw blown clean off at the midway point, though the damn thing just kept on progressing at a slightly skewed angle.

Saw a Saint Bernard's muzzle turn to pulped mush right before it rolled over and onto a Boston terrier, popping the poor little fella like a ripe zit.

I holstered the gats as I got to within a dozen or so steps from the driver's door, filling each palm with razor-sharp serrated steel pulled from inside my duster, where a Velcro patch had been sewn in for just such an occasion.

As I slammed on the brakes and reached for the handle, I literally felt the pavement shimmy and shake at my feet.

At least three separate bodies slammed me simultaneously, effectively pinning my back to the still-closed driver's door.

I heard something crunch as teeth clamped my left wrist, and I was able to focus on the miniature Doberman hanging from my arm like a tree ornament. I slung him loose, tossing him over the car hood, and instinctively began slashing in a wide, looping arc with both blades. Most of what transpired in the next thirty seconds or so is a frenzied blur, thankfully, as by the time I was finally able to slip behind the wheel of my ride, there wasn't a quarter inch of my ankle-length duster that wasn't coated in blood, gore, or matted dog fur. Even my chin had grown a multi-colored beard, as brown, black and white hairs had stuck to my flesh in moistened clumps.

I peeled out and gave the estate grounds a final glance in the rearview, where an estimated twenty to twenty-five animals lay dead while the survivors continued the chase.Not ashamed to admit, if I'd still owned a set of functional tear ducts, or 'duct' in my case, those bad boys would've spurted and spewed forth like Old Faithful.

It wasn't until I'd reached the main highway that I realized my combat knives were missing, and that I'd more than likely left them submerged in animal flesh One fact I know to be certain, in this life or any other: battlefield rage is one hell of an amnesia inducer, and that's definitely a good thing.

***

I arrived back inside city limits around six, just as dusk had started to settle over the distant mountain ranges. On an admittedly lunk-headed hunch, and with nothing else to go on, I cruised by the Horizontal Smiles Inc. location on Wilbery Avenue. It was more out of boredom that instinctual 'gut feeling' that I figured he might well be treading the old stomping grounds. Following a half-hour stroll in and around the dilapidated structure, stepping over and around all manner of sexual paraphernalia that lay scattered like confetti from a ticker-tape parade, I departed the area without a single clue as to what move to make next.

Driving past what had once been referred to as 'clunker street', due to a plethora of auto repair shops frequenting a four block area, it hit me like a lead pipe across the kisser. The client file had stated that Ramirez had been an auto mechanic before his meteoric rise in the smut industry. Hadn't I eyed a Firestone Repair Shop sitting right across the street from Horizontal Smiles? Damn straight I had. Crazy as it sounded, I had a premonition as stout as a jug of aged Kentucky White Lightning that 'The Skin King' was indeed stalking his old haunts, just not the most obvious one.

Took me less than five minutes to backtrack to the corner of Wilbery and 22nd Avenue North I parked the Slug Mobile in an alley behind CC's Sex Mall, which sat catty-corner from Horizontal Smiles Inc, then pulled my spear-gun and flamethrower from the trunk and strapped 'em on.

Movement was minimal, as was normally the case once the sun set in the 'old' downtown area. I saw a few latter-stage shufflers roaming about, the majority of which had no doubt taken up residence in one of the many deserted buildings nearby, if not within the maze of alleyways dominating the area. Such beings were long past posing a threat to anyone or thing; walking, moaning skeletal frames that held little flesh and zilch in the way of logical thought. Call me a snobby asshole, but the bottom feeders disgust me to no end. Maybe deep down it's because I realize I'm viewing a preview of my own future. Sad thing is, in many ways society's 'new' existence mirrored the old in that it was the elders who suffered the most, while the young dreaded the day when they too began to slip into a state of perpetual decomposition of both mind and body. I personally did my dead-letter best, pardon the pun once again, to not dwell on such depressing matters. It was hard enough just making it through each day as a functioning cadaver. The pressures of the old world, fueled by such self- important issues as love, money, and faith, had been unceremoniously voided from the menu, replaced by only the purest of physical necessities; food, supplemental boosts, and loaded syringes filled not with the nectar of life, but of prolonged death. Hell of a thing, really. It was like being on the set of your own warped Sci-Fi reality series, where one served as their own producer, director, writer and star, but with absolutely no 'creative control' as to what transpires in the way of plot.

I'd learned long ago not to psychoanalyze such madness. There was simply no upside to it. Go with the flow. Take it day by day- minute by minute. Most importantly, never underestimate the effectiveness of a good cliché when lying to one's self. Shaking dried bits of doggy gore from my duster, I made my way down a series of alleys to the back door of the Firestone shop. The lone entrance, a wooden door with no handle and a single key lock, was tightly secured. Could've easily walked around front, but instinct warned me otherwise.

Rusty as I was at such old school tactics, it still took less than a full minute to pick the lock. Reflexes just ain't what they used to be. Fingers are getting stiffer every day, like fossilized sausages.

I followed my mini-lights narrow beam through the back room, some type of storage area for boxed parts, and then into the open garages, being careful not to dive head-first into one of about a dozen open oil pits. Despite being deserted for the better part of five years, the place still reeked of gas and oil.

Good to know a few of the old sinus membranes still were still alive and sniffing. Magic juice does it again.

There were a few scattered vehicles parked inside or hoisted onto racks. Couldn't help but wonder the fate of the owners. Poor SOB's hadn't had a clue when they dropped their ride off that they'd never drive 'em again.

I rounded a man-made corner of stacked truck tires and almost stuck my noggin into and through an office door window. 'J. Potts – MANAGER' it proclaimed beneath a thick coating of cob webs. A hand-written cardboard sign hung near the knob; 'If you're knocking, it damn well better be good!' it read in dark black lettering.

Reaching for the knob, my left hand froze. I heard a faint scampering noise reverberate from inside, followed by a low moaning sound.

Backing up several steps, I clicked off the spear-gun's safety and checked to ensure the load was set.

I was in the process of bracing my feet when the office door slung open from the inside out, catching the very tip of the spear and causing the gun to lurch dramatically to the left.

The figured whisked by just as I slung the gun back around, forcing me to side step directly into a tire display. I watched it dart toward an open bay door as I was picking myself up from the oil-slick concrete. Gave serious consideration to pulling out the Glock Nine and plugging it right then and there, but didn't want to chance a head shot that might result in my sweeping up skull fragments for proof of mission completion. Besides, there was a damn good chance it wasn't even my mark, and I hated wasting good ammo. Nine mil slugs don't come cheap in an overly strapped universe such as this.

On the other hand, why would a wasted husk behave like a fugitive without a valid reason to do so?

Even with a minute's head start, I easily caught up with the figure Most shufflers in the latter stages of decomp fall pathetically short of Olympic sprinter status. They can surprise in short bursts, as this one had just proven, but long distance jaunts slow 'em to a crawl.

By the time I'd backed it into a narrow alley overflowing with a graveyard of metal dumpsters and trashcans, the figure had all but ran out of fuel.

I got my first clear look at its face as it whirled about. Though its horribly emaciated legs, arms and torso brought to mind a bag of bones held together by string, the facial features were still familiar enough to ID.

"Just hold still... and don't... flinch, Jorge. I'll make this as painless...as inhumanly possible."

***

Two hulking, hooded figures attired in matching black three-piece suits approached from between two dumpsters. The first bent down and retrieved the thrower and the machete; the second the spear-gun, while neither bothered to shoot even the most casual glance Cavander's way. After a quick pat-down, during which Cavander's face was pinned roughly to the wall, his twin revolvers were pulled from the dusters Velcro holsters and tossed

145

into a nearby dumpster. The two figures then lumbered back into the darkness as Cavander collapsed back onto the cracked concrete.

"You...are truly...without a doubt...the best at what you...do, Rutger," the voice continued to drone in electronically boosted waves, "damn! What skill...dedication...doggedly stubborn... and with the... instincts of a freakin' mutant! As the saying goes... in the trades ...Slug-Trail *always* gets... his husk..."

"Might as ...well show yourself, Bowen. It... ain't like I can't recognize... that certain girlish lilt in... your voice," Cavander finally countered, leaning against the cool concrete with his arms balanced atop his knees. Various swarms of assorted flying insects began to periodically dive-bomb his personal space, no doubt drawn by the caked-on canine gore coating his duster.

The plot...definitely...thickens. What's Mister Queer Eye for the Inmate's Eyes doing here? He ought to still be rotting in an eight-by-ten upstate. Must've blown the warden for extra time off.

"So how was the lock-up, dude? Sweet... and cuddly as you are, bet it didn't take... long for somebody to... make you their bride. Gotta say, I'm a little miffed... at not getting a wedding invite."

"Same old... smart-ass Cavander. I must confess, it's gonna be both an honor and... privilege to watch you get... segmented like a jigsaw puzzle."

Whoops. Fairy boy ain't playing around, no sir. Sounds sincerely pissed off.

Cavander bowed his head, tipping the Raiders cap ever further over his brow. His mind raced at the implications of Bowen's presence, though he doubted there was little if any coincidence involved.

The man appeared from the shadows as if he'd been magically transported, resembling a caped ghoul from some cheesy, twentieth century horror flick.

"Rutger, it's truly… been too long."

Tilting his head only slightly upward, Cavander peered out from between the cap's rounded bill and his own crossed forearms.

"Gerald. Six…maybe… seven years, at least."

"Try nine and… a half, fuck-face."

Yep, he's pissed. Well, better to be pissed off than…

"How time flys, wellll, 'cept maybe for those… incarcerated via their… own stupidity. What brings you… to the neighborhood, Bowen…slumming?"

His face shaded in a dark red felt hat that looked to have been confiscated from the prop room of a fifties crime noir film, the man stepped forward with a decidedly feminine sashay. He wore a brownish silk shirt and matching vest, meticulously creased dress slacks and black alligator boots, while around his neck was tied a red cape with a bright yellow backing.

"Surely you…know better, Rutger. Why, we've been…tailing you since the Nookie Palace."

Tailing? This shit is getting stranger by the millisecond…

"I owe you… money, girlfriend?" Cavander quipped, looking past Bowen to the two flunkies, who were standing on either side of the husk after pulling it from a nearby dumpster.

"Enjoy the… jocularity while you… still have a tongue, shitheel."

"My sincerest apologies. What's the…deal then, Lucille? Don't… tell me this is just about… revenge. Talk about… cliché, that's downright cornball, man."

Bowen lunged forward, planting a size eleven alligator boot directly into Cavander's breastbone before shoving him flush with the stone wall.

"Cliché or… not, it's an R&R double-header on… this special night, Rutger. Revenge and …retribution, *two-fold*."

"Better… spell it out…for me, Gerald. You…know I'm not…that quick…on the uptake," Cavander grunted, fighting the urge to scream out as the sharp- tipped boot seemed to penetrate his chest cavity.

"Why Rutger, your part in this… little drama should… be painfully obvious," Bowen replied, backing away with a graceful spin as Cavander collapsed forward onto his elbows and knees, "you did help put me away all those years ago, yes?"

"Just doing my…job, Gerald. Loan-sharking and racketeering were ….widely known….as illegal activities. You do…the crime…expect to…lose some time."

"Ohhh, Rutger. Talk about…cliché…quoting *Baretta*, for cripes sake…"

Rising onto his knees, Cavander reached up with both hands to inspect the newly concave crease just beneath his breastbone.

Another shot like that and I'll be a walking wind tunnel. "Touché. Please…proceed."

148

"I'll have you...know I... got turned in that fucking penitentiary, tough guy.

The whole...cellblock was...coming down with the...virus. They said...the informatory was...burning bodies in pairs. Had even...built their own....incinerator. I...had somehow managed...to avoid it. That is...'til I passed out from...the heat...the stress...and woke up to find some fucking....deadhead had gnawed half my...left calf away...along with...a sizeable portion of my ankle and all of my goddamned...toes!"

"That's...too bad, Gerald. I...there were better ways...to contract, for sure. Probably had a...hell of a time...finding shoes that...fit, I'd bet...." Cavander replied, maintaining eye contact while having casually positioned his hands on either side of his boots.

Clapping his hands briskly together as to snap himself from a self-imposed daze, Bowen began dancing a wild, impromptu jig that couldn't help but remind Cavander of an ancient '*Three Stooges*' skit.

"Actually, you being ...a part of this is... just icing on the cake, Rutger. Its Jorge here... that's the real...the *grand* prize. Least, I thought so...until I saw his hopelessly...hollowed frame."

Bowen halted just a few feet to the left from where his two henchmen held the trembling husk, whose bony neck seemed just a gentle jerk away from snapping free from its spindly host.

"You met his... partner up in the Millstone Hills, although... I doubt you were able to properly ID ...Mister Garluche as the scattered pile of ashes we left behind. You seeeee..." he continued,

149

gesturing with an extended thumb toward the rapidly wilting husk of a ruthless hood and pornographer once known as the 'The Skin King', "Jorge here …and the Italian Stallion had agreed to… distribute hijacked TR injections on… my behalf. The deal… was simple; I'd provide the goods and… they'd do all the deal making and subsequent selling, then …we'd split the profits evenly."

Leaning up until balanced on the heels of his feet, Cavander kept his hands tucked near both ankles. "Get to the …point, will ya Gerald? This is… turning into a… really lame Magnum P.I. Episode, *without* the …waves, palm trees, and cool ocean breezes."

"They stole… from me, Rutger. Can you… believe it? A wanna-be mobster with… shit for brains and the… spic smut-meister here ripped me off. One …year out of stir and they treat me… with monumental disrespect. Sold …over eight gallons worth …of TR and then took it upon themselves… to simply not pay …the supplier. Oh, they came up with some…. pathetic tale involving… an accidental explosion that supposedly destroyed the merchandise, but never… even volunteered to… show yours truly the… accident site. Oh, how the wicked must pay…and pay dearly."

"Why the hell… involve me, Gerald? You couldn't find… this ragged bird yourself?"

Bowen floated forward, whipping his waist-length cape forward in true 'Bela Lugosi' style.

"Oh, but… we tried, dear Rutger. For weeks… upon weeks, we've tried. Of course we… pleaded with Joey G. to confess his sins and tell us the... true whereabouts of the TR stash, along with the location of his flesh-peddling partner in... crime. I'll give the low-life, scum-sucking greaser this; he was... stubbornly loyal right to the end, even as my crew inserted a... Molotov cocktail into his anal... cavity and lit it ablaze.

" I had just about... given up when a local stoolie informed a trusted associate of mine about... a local professional type who specialized in finding ...the un-findable. A man... who would, for a rather steep price, also perform terminations. Imagine my shock...and utter...delight when that...professional turned out...to be none other...than...Rutger 'The Slug-King" Cavander....the man...most responsible...for the...walking...pile...of rotted viscera I...am today. Pity all your...fine efforts...were wasted on...such a pathetically...lost cause."

"You sent...me the...package? The info...on Ramirez? But...how the hell did you...find out...my..." Cavander marveled, now bouncing lightly on the heels of his boots. "The location of the secret 'Bat-cave?' Or should I say 'Slug-Cave?' Let's just say... I gave your regular client... an offer he simply couldn't refuse, may... he rest in...pieces."

"No skin off my...ass, Gerald, didn't...even...know...the man."

Ignoring the comment, Bowen casually lifted his gloved left hand and snapped his fingers girlishly.

As if on cue, the larger of the twin stoolies

151

jogged forward carrying a tri- colored gym bag.

"So the death of a… trusted client doesn't twinge …even a single steely nerve? Well, then…perhaps this just…might do the…trick."

Bowen unzipped the bag and carefully flipped it over, hopping away as a circular object fell to the concrete with a muffled thud. The object rolled unevenly before sliding to a halt mere feet from Cavander's boot tips.

"Ahhhh, this is indeed special…" Bowen cooed sarcastically, tossing the gym bag aside and wiping his hands across his vest in disgust, "there is simply…nothing that touches…this old…softies' heart…like seeing…lovers…reunited."

"Oh, sh-shit…n-no…not…" Cavander croaked through a single, widened eye. He felt a sudden, fiery rush; a burning sensation deep inside the lifeless confines of his chest cavity. Since being reincarnated into the realm of the dead, true anguish had eluded him until that very moment. He fell back against the wall, having already reached into his boots and filled each palm.

Her severed head lying sideways, Leah's mouth fell open and her lips trembled and squirmed; her eyes blinking rapidly as if the alleyway's dimly lit airspace was akin to a probing searchlight.

Bowen danced forward and lifted his left shoe, which hovered mere inches above Leah's right ear.

"Quality digs you… got there, Cavander. All nice… and secluded. Have to admit, I seriously considered… taking your ass out right then and… there. If I'd… known 'The Skin King' over there was… in such a sorry state, I most… definitely

152

would... have.Oh well...at least...I had...the pleasure...of making...your...girlfriend's acquaintance. We...got along...swimmingly...that is, until I broke out...the bone saw."

Releasing a warrior's shriek, Cavander's left arm whipped forward in a Frisbee tossing motion, after which he executed a combination flip/combat roll that sent him sprawling behind a nearby dumpster.

Bowen had time but to flinch as his left leg was severed just below the knee cap, the calf and foot falling away like chopped cordwood Before toppling over like a felled tree, he had just enough time to look down at his felled appendage and perform a comical double-take.

"Oh, you miserable...*fuck*. SHIT! You'll...pay...SHIIIIT!"

Crouching behind the dumpster, Cavander flipped the second five-pointed star from his left palm to the right. It had been the first time he'd found a use for them, having strapped them inside his boots on a whim after watching an old *Jet Li* movie a few weeks earlier. Grinning with malicious glee, he couldn't help but be pleasantly surprised at his own accuracy, especially considering he'd spent no more than a few hours on target practice.

He peeked over the top edge of the dumpster and watched the two hooded goons lumbering over to aid their fallen boss.

"Forget... about me, damn it!" Bowen cried, slapping their hands away as he balanced on his lone remaining knee, "Get that... bastard and sushi him... into about two-dozen portions! When you finish...bring me...the head! Cavander and... his whore will make...fine bookends..."

The hooded goons reached back over their heads in almost perfect unison and pulled twin long-swords from between their shoulder blades before advancing purposely forward.

Aw...hell. Just my...luck. Z-Ninjas. No doubt multiple black belts and armed with fucking pendulum blades. Somehow, someway I've got to get my mitts on that flamethrower.

This is gonna be dicey. Just hope it isn't yours truly that ends up diced.

Positioning the gleaming pointed star snugly between his thumb and forefinger, Cavander inhaled as if he still possessed a pair of working lungs. *Oh well, here goes nothing. Look at the bright side. What're they gonna do, kill you? Been there, done that.*

Leaping out from behind the dumpster in a semi-crotch, Cavander flung the star towards the advancing goons in an overhead motion. The goon to his left paused, stopping abruptly and twisting his head silently about as to address the other. He dropped his sword just as a large slab of his skull peeled away in a neatly sliced, rectangle-shaped segment.

Cavander rushed forward, leading with the heels of his boots as he sailed airborne.

The remaining goon, distracted by his partner's sudden, grisly demise, was unable to compensate in time as Cavander's hard-soled boots landed with a loud thud against his chin and upper chest. The sword flew from his grip as he played human

154

bowling ball to a congregation of metal trash cans.

Cavander scooped up the marble-handled sword without missing a step, cocking it back as he rushed toward the fallen goon, who was scrambling to his feet while howling with rage.

Kicking away several trash cans from underneath him, the goon was able to lift a forearm airborne just as Cavander drew near, as if to block an impending blow.

The blade whipped forward in a blurred, silver-tainted vapor trail, effortlessly slicing through the goon's thick forearm and beheading him just below the chin.

Wasting no time as he side-stepped the still-twitching torso, Cavander leapt over and impaled the severed head with a single thrust.

"Don't make...bad-ass ninjas like they...used to, I guess," he smirked, giving the spasmodic corpse a final glance.

"Pssst...hey...tough guy..." a teasing voice echoed from his left.

Cavander whirled about just as his left arm was sliced cleanly away at the elbow. He brought the sword around with his right, stumbling back a few steps as Bowen lurched forward brandishing the other goon's blade.

"Look at the...bright side, Slug. Now you've got the... same number of arms as... you do eyes..."

They slapped blades, the force of which almost forced Cavander to his knees. He glanced over and saw his dismembered appendage lying atop a trash can lid, the fingers still curling and uncurling in reflex.

Bowen danced a jig around him, thrusting playfully every few seconds, like a cat toying with its prey. Cavander continued to back deeper into the alley, barely avoiding tripping over something that had wrapped around his right ankle in snake-like fashion.

"....you fight pretty...good for a...girl..." he babbled, dashing between two dumpsters as Bowen followed close behind.

"...oh, you'll find... I'm quite the swordsman, Rutger. Comes from spending three years... in an eight by ten cell with Yakori Yakamoto, a three-time grand... master in several forms of... martial arts. The man taught me...much...about...survival..."

"And I'll bet you...paid him back in...sexual favors...right, Twinkle-Toes?"

Lunging forward, Bowen's double-handed thrust shattered Cavander's blade at the mid-point, bouncing the fractured steel off a nearby wall.

"....time to die, Rutger...once and for all."

Tossing the broken weapon aside, Cavander dived between two dumpsters, the mysterious cord still tangled around his ankle. Crawling forward on his knees and one remaining arm through a maze constructed of metal and plastic trash cans, wooden crates and various-sized dumpsters, he eventually backed against a stack of pallets and began untangling the cord.

"...oh, how embarrassing. Crawling about...like a...whipped...canine. I would...have never dreamed ...such cowardice from...a

156

living...legend such...yourself," Bowen scowled, "Come now...Rutger Face your demise...with some...semblance of...self-respect, what say? Why, even your...little...Asian whore displayed more...guts."

There was a series of low clicking sounds, and Bowen titled his head as to pinpoint the origin.

"Something...up your sleeve after...all, Rutger? Well then, by...all means...lets you...and I...dance."

"You...got it, Ace," came the reply from what seemed like an impossibly far distance, "...only...I lead."

Bowen took a single step back, gripping the sword in a double-fisted stance as its gore-smeared blade floated only inches from his face.

Cavander emerged from the shadows in a slow jog, the flamethrower's narrow barrel spitting blue flames in short, billowy waves.

Lowering the blade like a slowly falling curtain, Bowen's eyes grew huge with fear.

"Oh...oh fuck...."

"...You can...say that again, Gerald," Cavander said, priming the switch as he drew to within a dozen feet of his target, "then again...

...maybe you can't..."

The flame initially shot from the barrel in pencil-thin fashion, growing as thick as a phone-pole midway, then mutating to mushroom-cloud proportions as it swallowed its hapless victim whole.

Cavander pressed the trigger only once more, the second wave serving only to turn what hadn't already been transformed to ash into smoldering soot.

The alleyway lit ablaze beyond Bowen's fiery remains, and Cavander was forced to sprint through a narrow opening to avoid being trapped by the building flames.

He reclaimed the spear-gun near the same area where the thrower's cord had so miraculously found his ankle, then zig-zagged his way through the trashcan maze to where Leah's head had been so unceremoniously dumped.

Leaning down, he gently cradled her head to his chest with his lone remaining arm.

"Gonna...be okay, babe...you'll see..."

Cupping the jagged remains of her neck in his palm, Cavander held the disembodied skull straight out from his own face.

"Looks like...we both...require some...serious assembly line...upgrades," he grinned, shooting her a wink, "luckily, I know just... the place. Best damn... *chop-shop* in town. In my case, arms ain't a... problem. Got to say, though...gonna be... damn hard pressed to... find a body as fine as the last... one you owned, girl. Damn... hard pressed."

Leah returned the gesture, the toothy grin she displayed as brightly lit as the rising flames shading the background.

Cavander tucked her inside the thick folds of his duster, then turned to depart just as a figure dashed past in a frenzied blur.

The shambling thing that had once been Jorge 'The Skin King' Ramirez streaked down the alley toward the main street, losing several toes and a dislodged hip bone in the process. Somewhere along the line, he'd also misplaced his right arm.

Pulling the spear-gun forward as he tucked Leah beneath his half-arm, Cavander aimed at the skeletal pit that remained of the man's upper back...then paused.

After a moment's hesitation, he lowered the weapon as the fleshless husk vanished around a distant street corner.

"Nope. That would be...too easy, you bastard. Ain't gonna...do you any favors."

Several steps later, he discarded the weapon altogether.

Reaching his ride, Cavander placed his lovers head on the passenger seat and carefully strapped it in.

"What say we go get patched up, babe?" he beamed, "you just ain't the same without that sexy voice."

Seconds later, the 'Slug Mobile' peeled out onto the dark, deserted street, its physically challenged passengers nonetheless as mentally stable as they'd ever been.

***

It took damn near two full days and three tanks of fuel covering a four- hundred mile radius, but we eventually found just the right chop-shop for our separate ills. Leah's adjustment period was predictably longer and harder than my own, though my new arm hasn't yet 'grown on me' one-hundred percent, so to speak. My girl's a bit taller, nearly five-six, and the body isn't quite as well- toned and trim, but she's working on it. Besides, it was the best

159

match we could find for the price, which turned out to be a butt-load of TR juice. No big deal really, considering we still have enough on hand to last both of us several more years, even at the rate of two injections each per day.

As fate would have it, Leah knew more about Joey G. and Jorge's little 'hijacked stash' than she'd let on. Jorge had spilled the beans to her a few days after the caper, though she initially took this as simply more of his macho BS posturing to impress her into returning to his good graces.

Once I relayed Bowen's story to her about the TR theft, she knew just the place to check. It seems that the two masterminds had a Top Secret hiding place for such goods, and the rip-off from Bowen had been just the tip of the iceberg.

I'd spent the better part of six hours loading well-cushioned boxes of TR vials into a 'borrowed' van from the Joey G. estate. Hey, it sure as hell wasn't doing anybody any good there, right? Besides, we did our good deed for the millennium once our 'medical procedures' were paid for in full, dropping off over two-hundred six-ounce vials to the local Goodwill downtown.

That was just a few days before me and my gal left the city for good.

We've been holing up on this remote strip of sandy beachfront for just over eight months now, and life (or in this case, death) couldn't possibly be better. Got the love of my life (or, in the case...ah, never mind) by my side. Nothing is guaranteed, even with the plethora of available chemicals and a daily diet rich with proteins and iron, but we're bound to

160

enjoy each other's company as long as it's allowed. Neither of us talk about the past very often, but when it does come up, it's completely without shame. We simply did what all living, and un-living creatures do when faced with the direst of circumstances on a daily basis:

We survived, damn it.

We....survived to...live...die...or decay, as the case may be...another day.

***

The next tale, ladies and gentlemen, delves even further into the theme of 'body part replacement'.

As with the previous section covered, this is not for the faint of mind nor heart. It concerns a particular business practice that was, at least for a short time, all the rage in our post-plague world. Fortunately, such cruel, inhumane, and downright evil practices have long since been banished. Taking this story at face value, however, it gives serious credence to the argument that man's eventual fate was not only preordained by a higher power, but viewed as fully justified as far as punishments go. The practice itself may sound faintly familiar, though the 'parts' in question might well provide quite an emotional 'jolt' to the senses.

8 - CHOP-SHOP

Champing on an unlit stogie the size of a bowling pin, Marv 'The Scrounger' Maxwell balanced a clipboard atop his bony knees and flipped through a succession of newly typed invoices.

"Got an order for a left arm. Caucasian, at least eighteen inches in diameter. All the fingers have to be intact and at least partially flexible."

"Believe we got just the thing in one of the lower level bins in warehouse two. Husk used to be a pro wrestler," Bart 'The Part-meister'" Greene shot back in the husky growl that was his trademark, "Fairly new addition. Cadaver's got cannons the size of my thigh."

"Okie-doke. Need that one delivered by no later than Friday noon." "What else, Marv? I've still got the boys in the lab pulling a rib cage for that rich prick up in the 'burbs."

"Let's see…got a client on the East side requesting a penal upgrade. Says here he 'requires' no less than eight inches long by three in diameter. Prefers African-American but says it isn't mandatory."

"Holy Guacamole," Bart said, nodding wearily, "I'll never understand it, Marv. Why the hell order parts you can't possibly use? Damn things gonna shrivel up like a limp linguine noodle a few weeks after being attached."

Marv shrugged, having already flipped to a separate invoice.

"You got me. Must be for the grieving wife. Lot

of kinky crap going on out there these days."

Rolling his eyes in disgust, Bart then reached up and wiped away a flaky thread of dead flesh from his left cheek.

"Damned body soil. You ever stop and think how crazy all this is, Marv? I mean, what's the point in these folks having new body parts stitched onto a corpse?"

"From what I've heard, it's all about keeping their loved ones' memory alive, as well as their loved ones' husk. Some folks just can't let go, Bart." "Guess so, even when they gotta keep their so-called 'loved ones' chained to the garage door to keep it from eating the family cat. Well, job security is job security, 'specially these days. What else you got?"

"Whoaaaa.." Marv replied, pulling the clipboard closer to his face as to confirm the content, "...oh, you're gonna love this one. Talk about your tall orders."

"Not another damned specialty order?"

"Aw, you might say that," Marv continued with mock cheer.

"Came in via fax just this morning. Full torso, Asian or islander female, with all limbs intact and workable. Muscular, toned frame. Cannot be over five- three or body weight in excess of one-hundred ten pounds. Also, no partial or damaged breasts."

"Oh, for shits sake…!" Bart groaned, pacing the warehouse floor while waving his arms wildly. As was usually the case, Marv leaned back quietly and enjoyed the show, his toothy grin never wavering. It never ceased to amaze him how much his right-hand man resembled *Moe* from 'Three Stoogies' fame whenever a particularly animated rant ensued.

"Full tor-...Asian *or* islander? Five-three with...undamaged brea-? What kinda lame-brained, half-assed bullshit is that? This ain't no Sachs First Avenue, for Pete's sake! What am I supposed to do, Marv? Bend over and crap it out all gift-wrapped and ready to deliver? SHIT! I'm low-manned in the warehouse as it is, what with Myers and Kendrick hiring on with Johanssen's shop over on the East side and Poindexter losing an eye last week over in warehouse three.

Haven't had a chance to inventory shit in weeks...got parts scattered all over the lower bins...and now this ridiculous horse hockey? No partial or damaged tits my EYE!"

Pausing until the other man's outburst had completely subsided, Marv then casually leaned up from a stack of wooden pallets and raised a single hand airborne, exposing the palm.

"Don't birth a kidney, Bart. Night shift just happened to corral the perfect specimen last night down on the strip."

The Part-meister practically beamed, displaying a mostly toothless maw and blackened gums that appeared horribly swollen.

"No shit? Where did ol' no-neck Boykins and the Nocturnal twins store the little beauty?"

Marv paused to scan the invoice.

"Uh, says here warehouse four, bin A-three. Tell you what, Barty, I'll put Desmond and Jenkins on these other pulls. You go ahead and round up The Hulkster and take care of this one."

Having calmed somewhat, Bart ceased his pacing and took a seat at a comically cluttered desk adorned with a metal plaque reading *'WORK ZONE – Move it or lose it'*.

"You got it, boss. Should I take *Slice 'n Dice* along or is this a job for the surgical team?"

Balancing his spindly arms atop an ample midsection, Marv paused with a strained expression.

"Just to be on the safe side, you might consult with the Doc. Decap's are a might risky in these full-body transfers. From what I hear, if you sever the wrong tendon or crack a vital piece of vertebra, the head won't ever set quite right on the transplantee."

"What about the Dice-man?"

"Yeah, take him along too. Might help keep the crazy bastard out of trouble."

"Affirmative, boss," Bart replied, pushing himself up and stepping briskly toward the main warehouse's open dock door, "I'll keep you updated."

"Tell Hulkster not to get cocky with this one, Bart. Boykin lost two men to this hellcat last night. She's a scrapper. Real Asian killer to boot, and virtually damage-free, I'm hearing. Korean or Vietnamese or something similar. "

"Not to worry, boss. Nothing we can't handle, even if it's with kid gloves." "I have no doubt, Bart. You package her up pretty now. Client's paying in petrol, useable vitamins and a truckload of fresh veggies." Marv watched his long-time subordinate vanish into the early morning darkness before reaching into his coverall pocket and retrieving a small lighter. He sucked greedily while burning the tip of an oversized Cuban cigar, thinking back to a much simpler time, when he and Bart dealt in fan belts, distributor caps and car body frames instead of knee caps, spleens, and lower spines.

***

"Am I usin' the garrote brace or what, Bart?"

"Hold your damned horses, Dice. Gotta check with Doc Miller first.

Client's paying top dollar, so this one has to be handled with extreme care." "Ah, shiiit. I can already feel the thrill leaving this particular assignment."

At just over six feet six inches tall and weighing in at a less than robust one-hundred sixty-five pounds, Adam 'Dice-Man' McClintock was the definition of human 'walking stick'. A former shooting guard who'd spent several seasons in the CBA, he'd always appeared painfully underweight. That said, the noted limitations of his present diet had done little to alter that fact.

"Don't sweat it, shin bone. Either way it'll be you and Hulkster on the pin.

Where is that big SOB anyhow?"

"I radioed 'im. Should be lurkin' outside warehouse four by now." "You two finish up that lower leg order?"

"Yep. Hulkster's used his new toy to perfection."

Trudging slowly, they exited a small shack marked 'The Tool Shed', stepped over a short concrete walk, then entered an open breezeway leading to a one-story brick building fronted by a

166

sign reading '*MEDICAL SERVICES - Waste Disposal at REAR of BUILDING*'.

"Don't tell me. What is it this time, glue-on razor nails?"

"Some kinda spring-loaded contraption he straps to his wrists. Got marble handles and blades he cut from a bone saw."

"Man is a seriously sick pup."

"Shiiit, the Hulkster might be a racist, inbred cracker and A-one asshole, but even I'll admit the man is a master craftsman, Bart. A true professional in the fine art of husk dismemberment. Best corpse slicer in the whole damn shootin' match."

Bart snorted in mock disagreement as they entered an empty foyer, made a quick right, then descended down a short flight of concrete steps.

The two men strode down a narrow hallway, passing several closed, unmarked doors. The blood-stained walls reeked of human spoilage; a pungent mix of perforated gut and wet pennies.

Moments later, they entered a room filled with empty gurneys cloaked in crimson-splattered sheets. A small-framed man wearing an equally spattered white smock stood with his back to them. He was hunched over an examination table. A pair of pale, bare feet was visible from one end, though the rest of the body was hidden behind the man's bulk.

"Well, well, if it isn't the Mister *Good-wrench* and *Lord Torquemada* of the undead set," the man blurted as they grew closer, never bothering to turn about. "Sorry to interrupt, doc. Marv sent us down," Bart replied, openly cringing while side-stepping a steaming pile of viscera which trailed behind the

167

doctor like rubber tubing. Dice-man noted his boss's comically disgusted expression and used the back of a gloved hand to cover his building smile.

"We, uh, got a head extraction scheduled in warehouse four." "Somebody requesting a whole new package, eh?' the doctor inquired with mock interest, his voice a high-pitched irritant that never ceased to annoy any and *all* that knew him, "just give me a moment, gentleman. Almost...done. Want to... take a peek?"

The doctor backed away several steps, spreading his gore-drenched arms like a stage actor at the conclusion of a particularly dramatic scene.

Wriggling like a hooked fish trapped in wire netting, the cadaver twisted and contorted but was unable to budge the leather straps at its neck, wrists and ankles.

"Shit, doc,' Dice-man croaked in apparent revulsion, though his tone was clearly awe-stricken, "what the fuck you doin' to it?"

It might have once been a middle-aged Caucasian male, though the combination of its horribly deteriorated state and the doctor's recent facial alterations made it impossible to be sure.

Its midsection had been flayed open from chest to groin, leaving flaps of brownish skin peeled back and held in place by a half-dozen surgical clamps.

Similarly, its skull had been halved just past the bridge of its nose, giving the initial impression that the top portion was magically transparent.

"Poor chap had a tumor the size of grapefruit in his colon and another almost as large near the base of his brain. I was hoping to at least salvage enough useable tissue for cryogenic purposes. As it is, looks like just another candidate for the incinerators."

"Yeah, damn shame alright," Bart murmured, his eyes darting about the room as to avoid the mutilated monstrosity lying less than a dozen feet away, "Listen, doc...we gotta get this done paste haste. This client is supposedly paying in petrol, fresh veggies, and a butt-load of vitamin supplements that have yet to expire."

Shaking his head from side to side, the doctor continued unabated. "It's frightening, gentleman. I'm seeing much more of these type specimens in the past several weeks. I'm afraid it won't be long before the population of useable husks are completely extinct. Truly, truly frightening prospect."

"Um, yeah doc. We do...need to boogie," Dice-man added, though unable to pull his eyes from the same train-wreck of carnage that had his boss fighting off a gag reflex.

The doctor nodded, sighing deeply as he pulled the gore-drenched rubber gloves from each hand and tossed them into a nearby hamper.

"Understood. Give me a moment to clean up and I'll be...right with you."

As the doctor limped away with slumped shoulders, a pair of similarly dressed lab technicians entered the room and wheeled the squirming corpse away.

"Where to, doc?" one of them asked wearily while stepping on and squishing the moistened pile of intestine Bart had so stringently avoided.

Slowing his gait a bit to reply before departing

the room, all signs of jocularity had left the good doctor's tone.

"Pull the limbs and the spine and then light him up. He's no good to us otherwise."

Left alone under the lab's searing fluorescent lighting, the Part-meister and the Dice-man exchanged a wry glance.

"Ghouls, D-man…that's what we are. No better than grave robbers of old."

"Hey, what choice we got, Bart? Man does what he has to do to survive in these dark, dark days, am I right?"

"Maybe," Bart answered after an additional moment of strained silence, "then again, maybe there are things man isn't *meant* to survive."

Five minutes later, the eccentric trio departed the medical facility building in single-file formation, each quietly contemplating why their lives, and the planet as a whole, had so utterly turned to absolute shit.

***

"Been waiting long, Hulkster?"

"Long enough for a smoke is all. Had time to pull a few orders in the meantime; leg out of bin A-five; right arm from C-three"

Brian 'The Hulkster' McRae was rarely queried concerning the origin of his nickname. It simply wasn't necessary if even a tint of common sense was present. Standing six-eight and weighing just under two-hundred seventy-five pounds, he was a former wrestler and 'ultimate fighter', who, much like the Dice- man, had spent a large portion of his life involved in athletics. A connoisseur of illegal anabolic steroids since high school, his body weight had actually fallen from nearly three-forty since his salad days in the UFA (*Ultimate Fighting Association*). As with the majority of such 'luxury' items no longer produced for a mass market, muscle enhancers had gone the way of workout videos, diet pills and anti-aging lotions and creams.

"Damn, H, don't wear out those lungs. That was one hell of a speech, boy," Dice-man quipped, playfully elbowing the larger man on his tree-trunk sized right bicep.

The Hulkster wiped his arm as if he'd been shat on while eyeing the Dice-man with a menacing glare.

"Touch me again, *bro,* and I'll snap your spine like a dry leaf."

According to local scuttlebutt, McRae had once been a high-ranking officer within the Aryan nation's northeastern branch.

"Sure, Uncle Adolf. Got'cha. Won't happen again, massah," Dice-man replied with a wink, dancing away several steps. All the while, the doctor watched the pair with the same fascinated expression one might expect from a zoologist studying a rare, exotic species of animal.

"Cut the shit, you two. Let's get this done," Bart growled, leading the way as they crowded through the warehouse entrance.

"Damn, lotta empty bin spaces, boss," Dice-man said, propping a wooden-handled garrote neck-brace over one shoulder as the four men walked past a series of eight by ten wire cages on either side,

171

"looks like the doc wasn't bullshittin'. Job security ain't what it used to be. Too damn many vacancies."

"You're not kidding," Bart mumbled, though not nearly loud enough to be heard over the cluttering of their collective boots.

What few cages that were occupied held little in terms of valuable parts, mostly disembodied heads and torsos that had long-since been stripped of all useable limbs and organs.

"Why the hell we even keep most of this shit? One of those skulls even had the eyes pulled out and its nose sawed off. Wasn't nothin' left but a scalp and a pair'a lips."

"You know the routine, Dice," Bart replied scornfully as they turned a sharp curve and passed into a new block of mostly bare cages, "Have to wait for the incineration order."

"Worthless scraps, man. Ain't worth puttin' a match to."

"Pipe down, Slick," The Hulkster grumbled, wrapping a thick chain with wrist and ankle cuff attachments around his bloated left bicep, "just focus on the job at hand." "Hoo boy! Check it out! White-*bread* supremacist is stainin' his drawers over a little girl!"

Bart immediately turned on his heels, coming to an abrupt halt and forcing the trio to juke and dodge on opposite sides just to avoid collusion. Though the Dice-man dwarfed him by at least a foot in height, Bart nonetheless stood his ground and peered up and into the other man's eyes with fiery intensity.

"Fair warning, Dice. Don't underestimate this particular *little girl'*, or you're liable to depart that

172

cage minus a vital organ."

"Damn, boss, chink ain't but five feet tall and maybe eighty-five pounds soakin' wet."

"Maybe so, Slinky, but according to Boykin's filed report from last night, she managed to dislodge one of her own ribcage bones and stick it clean through Chester Masterson's forearm, while simultaneously sending 'Bad-Ass' Atkins to the infirmary with a shattered kneecap. Do...not...get careless in there. She's the only match we got that even comes close, and we can't afford to botch this order."

Leaning in, The Hulkster whispered just inches from Dice-man's left ear, from which hung a sizeable gold earring in the shape of a basketball.

"Get the picture, Ace?"

"Gentleman, we really need to procee..." the doctor injected weakly. "Not to worry, boss," Dice-man exclaimed with his usual overabundance of cockiness while purposely ignoring his hulking cohorts taunts, "ain't no thang. When the chips are down, the Dice-man never, ever craps out."

"Gentleman, I am on a very tight schedule here," the doctor repeated timidly.

The Hulkster tossed his massive noggin back and laughed aloud, hislengthy blondish locks flowing like a lion's mane. "Dice-man, Jackass truly be thy name."

"Bart, could we please dispense with these damned *grade school* antics?" the doctor barked a bit more sternly, though cautiously backing away a step as he did so. "Enough, you two," Bart grumbled, turning the doctor about and directing him onward.

The Foursome neared a center-block bin marked A-three, walking single file until all turned about in perfect unison to view the entity imprisoned inside. Individual reactions were wildly varied, from the doctor's stoic nonchalance, Dice-man's bug-eyed stare and The Hulkster's comic double take.

"Gentleman, there is our husk," Bart announced matter-of-factly, having pulled the invoice from his shirt pocket as for final confirmation.

Dice-man released a piercing whistle between pursed lips. "Dammmmmn, that husk is fine! If I was into nac-ro-delpia, I'd be on that like white on rice!"

"That's necrophilia, Einstein," the Hulkster countered, tilting his head from side to side while stepping closer to the cage's wire-mesh netting.

"I swear she looks…familiar somehow."

Leaning back with his mouth hanging agape, Dice-man's gold-coated front teeth shone like mirrors struck by a noonday sun.

"No shit, Blockhead? Maybe you and your Neo-Nazi butt-buddies burnt down her house or hung her parents or some similar hate-crime shit."

"I'm serious, dick-weed. I've seen the gook somewhere before. Back in the day, our paths crossed somewhere."

"Probably recognize her from a porn flick," Dice-man grinned mischievously, "she's got…*had* the looks for it, no doubt. Prime *dragon-lady with a horse-whip* material, dog."

Shrugging his shoulders impatiently, Bart

174

pulled a stale Marlboro from his rolled shirt-sleeve, lit it and took a lengthy drag before blowing a perfectly formed smoke-ring into the dimly lit airspace.

"Whatever...hell...*fire*...enough with the pre-game chit-chat already Forget her looks *and* her past. Just another piece of jerky as far as we're concerned.

Let's get this show on the road. I believe you both know the drill by heart. Sure wish you lab boys could come up with some kind of sedative to use on these things, doc. Make our lives a hell of a lot easier." The doctor considered Bart briefly but remained silent while retrieving a small scalpel from his smock's front pocket.

"Speak for yourself there, boss-man. I just love this shit! Think I missed my callin' back in the day. Dice-man would've made one hell of an assassin. Ninja Warrior D, that's me!"

Bracing himself at the cage entrance, the Hulkster's massively muscled frame visibly tensed.

"Sew those lip flaps, Dice, and get your bony ass over here."

"Key that mother whenever you're ready, Freddy," Dice-man countered, holding the garrote brace perfectly horizontal by its six foot wooden handle while resembling a flag bearer in a military formation.

Reaching forward with a skeleton key that fit all cages within block A, Bart maintained eye contact with the incarcerated occupant in case of a mad dash.

The Hulkster bent down until his left shoulder

pressed lightly against the cage door.

"Alright Dice, on my count…three…two…"

"Watch your asses, you two," Bart blurted, pulling the key from the lock before backing almost flush against the opposite cage door.

"One!"

The cage door swung outward with a loud screech, then shut with a resounding clang after the two men had leapt inside.

Almost immediately upon the door slamming shut, their intended target had fallen into a combination combat/meditation crouch, assuming a textbook 'lotus' pose with her chin lowered to her chest.

"What the fuck, over?" Dice-man asked nervously, now holding the brace like an oversized butterfly net. The two stood side by side with their legs spread, leaving precious little space between them and the cage door.

"Keep your guard up, slim," The Hulkster replied gruffly, taking a half-step forward with the thick chain pulled gaunt across his chest in a blocking stance, "this husk definitely has something up her sleeve."

"Careful with the limbs and torso, guys Contract clearly states the client won't pay for overly damaged goods," Bart announced, pinning the clipboard against his chest with folded arms. Though he remained intensely focused on the chosen target squatting less than five feet away, Dice-man nonetheless flashed a hurtful look.

"Boss…have we *ever* disappointed?"

"Make your move already, shin-bone. Secure

176

those choppers so I attach the binds," The Hulkster barked angrily.

"Chill, Lumpy, *chill*...I'm on my way," Diceman replied, half-stepping forward in virtual slow motion.

The woman rose from her stance just as Diceman had shuffled forward an additional six inches, gradually unfolding her sleek, toned physique like a skilled ballerina concluding a complicated dance routine.

"Careful! Careful! Try to secure the garrote at the lowest possible point," the doctor chimed in suddenly, practically pressing his gaunt, leathery face flush against the cage door, "do not tighten above the center point of the neck under *any* circumstances, understand? Those middle vertebra must not be severed!"

"Shit, doc...it ain't like I'm treadin' virgin territory here. Zip up and let me do my job!" Diceman shot back irately, instinctively backing up a half step as the woman remained frozen in her segmented pose.

Standing approximately five-feet two and possessing the lithe, tightly muscled form of a highly trained athlete, the woman had obviously been a fairly recent casualty. Her complexion still held a ruddy hue; her dark, lengthy locks a luxurious glow that had only begun to lose a fragment of its original luster.

Though her eyes held the cold, soulless stare associated with all similarly deceased brethren, her yellow-tinted flesh was seemingly without even the first hint of decomposition. Her small, naked breasts appeared healthy and pert, and thus far without the tale-tell signs of sagging that normally followed rigor mortis.

"Goin' in," Dice mumbled, cautiously reclaiming the space he'd lost. Gripping the garrote brace's lengthy handle at the specially grooved end,

Dice-man stretched his arms just enough in order to balance the wire noose directly over the woman's skull. "That's it, babe, don't move a pretty little hair. Stay reaaallll still for the Dice-man…"

The woman tilted her head just slightly to the left, as if straining to comprehend the Dice-man's words.

"Now, now, sweet-thang…don't be that way. Straighten up so Dice-man can collar your gorgeous ass proper-like."

Side-stepping to the right, The Hulkster wound the chains ever tighter around his massive fists.

"If she rushes forward, I'll make the tackle. You just be ready to *pull* that noose over her head if you have to."

"I hear ya, beefcake. Let's hope *that* drastic shit ain't necess--"

The woman seemed to magically levitate forward in a time-warped blur, gripping the garrote handle just past the wired end with her left hand and jerking down as her cocked right elbow met it halfway, splintering the solid oak handle like dry, brittle kindling.

"Wha-?" Dice-man managed, ogling what remained of his portion of the handle with wide-eyed awe.

Twisting about like a human top, the woman

178

executed a full three-sixty while balanced solely on her left heel, sliding to an abrupt halt only after slinging the jagged handle forward like an Olympic javelin.

Caught hopelessly flat-footed by the woman's sleek, lightning-quick maneuver, Dice-man never caught even the slightest glimpse of the streaking object that subsequently pierced his throat just below the Adam's apple and hurled him back, essentially pinning his bony frame to the cage door like a speared fish.

"Holy...shiiiit," The Hulkster shrieked, the brutish, fearless façade he normally displayed temporarily downgraded to something more akin to squeamish and fear-stricken.

Following the toss, the woman had instantly struck a semi-crouching martial arts pose, with her bare feet spread wide and her tightly clinched fists rotating ever-so-gracefully from chin to waist level. "My...God," Bart whimpered, tip-toeing ahead as if walking on egg shells while pulling a set of keys from his belt, "back towards the door, Hulk...I'm fixing to open her up."

With that, the doctor spun awkwardly around and scurried down the cellblock with his arms pin-wheeling and his head bobbing from side to side. He soon vanished, a feminine cry trailing his path as he disappeared beyond the same steep curve they'd previously covered upon entry.

"Back out my ass," The Hulkster spewed with renewed machismo as his former partner hung mere feet away, his arms, legs and feet enduring a final series of jerky death-spasms.

"Chink husk is gonna pay…and pay dearly."

Bart inserted the key but hesitated, his hands shaking wildly. "I said get your big butt outta there, man!"

Discarding the thick chain and attached cuffs, which he casually flipped over his left shoulder, The Hulkster slung his arms forward, pointing his hands straight out as if he'd just pulled a set of revolvers from a transparent holster. Two sharp, distinct clicking noises filled the cage as twin spring-loaded combat knives filled each of his colossal palms.

"No way, boss. Bitch is all mine…"

"Don't even think about it, Brian. That damn husk isn't worth a monkey's hide if it's all cut up. Now get the hell out-…!"

Ignoring his superiors ranting pleas, The Hulkster took a substantial stride forward just as an echoing screech filtered through the warehouse like a malfunctioning car alarm.

"What the hell?" Bart inquired, accidentally twisting the key until the tumbler caught, resulting in the cage door being pulled slightly ajar.

"Sounded like…like the doc."

Turning towards the direction of the scream, Bart unconsciously re- secured the cell door, leaving the key protruding from the lock as he backed into the middle of the hall.

"You…you hear that, Hulk?" he mumbled through visibly trembling lips, "sounds like a goddamned…stampede."

A faint rumbling sound echoed through the narrow corridor, accompanied by a low moaning that grew increasingly distinct as seconds passed.

Reaching back with his left hand, The Hulkster stuck the serrated blade through the bars and tugged lightly at the cage door.

"Awww hell...I do believe we've got ourselves a major breech in the compound, boss. Do me a favor and open this fucker up, will you?"

"I...it can't be...I didn't hear any alarms or...or *anything* to indicate...Marv wouldn't gotten word to us...Marv would've..." Bart stammered, his eyes slowly glazing over as he stumbled towards the source of the commotion.

The woman remained utterly still save her constantly rotating arms as The Hulkster tugged on the door with ever-increasing force.

"Fuck, Bart...unlock the door before they get here! NOW DAMN IT!!!"

Pulling a small handgun from his vest pocket, Bart's breathing had turned labored and shallow. The clipboard fell uselessly from his other hand, clanging onto the concrete as several loose invoices sailed airborne.

"Bart, SHIT! Come back here, you BASTARD!" The Hulkster bellowed, banging his bulky back and shoulders against the cage to little effect.

Seemingly entranced, Bart ignored the giant's rants and instead concentrated on holding the twenty-two steady while pointing it straight out at shoulder level.

The new arrival turned the curve leading into the block, barely breaking stride even after spotting Bart standing less than twenty yards away in a classic shooter's pose.

Donned in camouflage fatigues, spit-polished combat boots and a black beret complete with a skull and crossbones embalm sewn in, the stranger had an automatic rifle slung over one shoulder while grasping what resembled some sort of grenade launcher.

Short and stocky, the man wore a neatly trimmed beard and matching mustache; his movements precise and just a bit robotic, much like those associated with a professional soldier. "Better save all the rounds you've got in that little pop shooter, buddy- boy," he blurted harshly in a tone laced with cockiness.

"Ho-hold it right there, mister…or I'll…sho-.." Bart whined, trying frantically to halt the shaking of his cupped hands as the pistols short barrel weaved in a spastic semi-circle.

Shrugging, the man trudged ahead undaunted.

"Your call, pal, but it's only fair to warn you, there's a wave of inhumanity headed this way, and you're gonna need every round and about five-hundred more in about three minutes."

"H-hey, don't I…know you?" The Hulkster queried, his head rotating sporadically toward the new arrival before again refocusing on the woman.

Bart watched haplessly as the man strode up and then past him, the twenty-two having dropped to his side as he leaned weakly against the opposite cage door.

"Sorry. No time for amenities, asshole. Besides, looks to me like you've got a full plate of issues to deal with at the moment."

The stranger balanced the launcher against his

left thigh and peered into the cage, flashing a wide, toothy grin as he looked past the Hulkster toward the woman, whose stance had remained wholly unchanged.

"Hiya, babe. You sincerely would not *believe* how hard it's been to track you down. Placed orders with four similar chop-shops who said they had '*just the husk*' that matched your description to a tee."

Cocking her head just slightly to the right, the woman seemed to react to the man's voice with a brief shudder, though her overall stance remained unaltered.

"Yeah...YEAH! You're a...used to be some hotshot martial arts instructor.

Saw your ads on billboards all over town...Kahn or Crane, right?' The Hulkster gushed as if meeting a long-admired celebrity, 'and *that's* where I knew the chink from. She's your partner. Saw her mug on the internet and those billboards right alongside yours."

"Guilty as charged, muscles. Bart L. Crane, Tae Kwon Do grand master, at your disservice," the stranger replied with a weak bow.

"Thought so. Never forget a face. Now...h-how about seeing clear to busting me out of he-..."

"Got to give you boys credit for first snagging and then successfully holding onto Miko. I would've bet good money against such a feat. I'll make damn certain not to let her out of my sight again.

"Well, come now, sweetie. No time to waste. Chop chop, er...no pun intended. Take care of your business and let's motivate. I busted the dam walls on the way in and this is gonna be slaughterhouse central any minute now."

As if cued by the man's verbal command, the woman danced gracefully forward, her fluid movements again bringing to mind a professional skater or dancer.

Though he stood at least a foot and a half taller and outweighed the female husk by at least a hundred and fifty pounds, Brian 'The Hulkster' McRae nonetheless openly cringed at the mere sight of her graceful advance.

"Shit! Bart! Where the hell you at, man? Open the FUCKING CAGE DOOR! You miserable fucking COWARD! Get over here and let me OUT!"

Wedging the pistol into his belt, Bart stumbled forward, holding the key ring practically flush with his rapidly blinking eyes as to rediscover the magic skeleton key before recalling he'd left it hanging in the door lock.

He whipped his head about every few seconds to check his back, as the shuffling/groaning noises reverberated to a fever pitch.

"Hang…hang on, Brian. I'm…I'm…coming…just h-hang on."

"Not so fast, Buck-O," the stranger snapped, grasping Bart's right arm in a vice as the key flew from his palm and rattled against the opposite cage door, "employees of this immoral and *extremely* illegal establishment do not qualify for today's '*escape to breath another day*' special…"

The Stranger pinned Bart to the cage just long enough to slip a set of titanium handcuffs over his right wrist while securing the other cuff onto a thick metal brace at the top edge of the cage.

Bart stood flat footed as the uniformed man stepped back, eyeing his cuffed wrist with comic befuddlement.

"In other words, gents, just lay back and take your medicine. Lord knows you got it coming."

The Hulkster began slashing the cage doors inner mesh with the bone- saw blades as the woman continued to wriggle and gyrate mere feet from where he stood.

Whirling about like the caged animal he assuredly was, The Hulkster then rambled forward at full bore, swinging the nine-inch blades like twin pendulums.

The woman side-stepped his woefully telegraphed onslaught with frightening ease, even landing a fairly solid but unsubstantial side kick to his upper left thigh in the process.

"No time for this cat and mouse horseshit, Miko," the stranger scolded, balancing his hands atop his hips, "the natives are growing restless...and nearer. End this...now."

After regaining his balance by bounding from the rear cage wall, The Hulksters' eyes grew suddenly wide with newfound shock.

"Miko? Shit, you *can't* mean it," The Hulkster bellowed wide-eyed, "that's the chink that....no fucking way, man. She was like...ten-time World champ...No...fucking...way that can possibly be."

The stranger's silent smirk told The Hulkster all he didn't want to know about his own outlandish hunch.

"Whatever you say, Chief. Believe me, she was stouter than most of my male students to begin with, with natural skills like I'd never seen. It damned near killed me once the disease took her. She'd been…my greatest achievement as a teacher. The ultimate warrior. Hard to believe to look at her, but she passed almost a year ago to the day.

"Amazing what daily steroid treatments have done to enhance what was already one of the modern wonders of the martial arts world, isn't it? Simply astonishing. You boys sure picked the wrong chick to abduct to strip for parts. Really couldn't have asked for shittier luck. Oh well…" A simple nod from the stranger sent the woman flying forward in a flurry of jabs, kicks, and roundhouse punches, the majority of which landed at precise pressure points until the giant fell weakly to one knee, the first of his blades shattered at the midway point while the second hung limp and useless from his left wrist.

Both the *Parts-Meister* and *The Hulkster* released mournful moans at precisely the same moment, though for entirely different reasons.

Bart's anguish-filled wail had been fueled by the sight of a cramped, dimly lit corridor overflowing with approaching husks, at least one of which licked and gnawed on a bloodied, disembodied skull that for all the World resembled one Marv *'The Scrounger'* Maxwell.

The Hulksters cry, on the other hand, had originated purely from physical suffering, as the woman had taken his left arm and literally twisted it into a quivering mass of compound fractures and

186

shredded tendon. She had then shoved the attached blade into and through his chest cavity with such force that her own fist was clearly visible protruding from between his shoulder blades, clutching a portion of his severed spine.

Tossing the dead giant's spasm-racked carcass aside with no more effort than an infant discarding a tiresome toy, the woman then slowly turned at the sound of the cage door swinging outward and stood stiffly as if called to attention.

Blank-faced and unmoving, she displayed nary a sign of resistance as her former lover and mentor attached a metal face-plate that covered her nose and mouth like a horses bridal.

"You haven't lost a step, girl. Not a single blessed step. The naturally skilled adapt...overcome, *no matter* the odds.

"Some things even dying can't alter," he whispered proudly, leading her from the cage as the lumbering masses drew to within a dozen feet.

"You always make poppa so very proud."

Bart squirmed and squealed, even attempting to bite through his own wrist as the stinking horde drew a collective bead on the throbbing pulse beating at his throat. The stranger led the woman to the end of the hall, then turned to witness the starving masses fall upon the 'Part-Meister' and pull him asunder, leaving only a cuffed hand and severed arm hanging from dripping steel mesh.

Balancing the launcher on his right shoulder, he pulled the retractable stock free and fired a single shot. The east wing of warehouse four went up like a matchbox in an inferno. Less than ten minutes later, a modified Harley Davidson Sportster, complete with handle-bar mounted Uzi's and unbreakable glass shields welded onto on all sides, cruised through an open gate labeled '*MAXWELL'S PARTS & ACCESSORIES*', having managed to bob and weave through a building crowd of rotted husks who had roamed inside the once blockaded, electrified walls for their own warped version of an '*Open House*'.

***

The woman clung to the man's back like an infant to its mother's bosom, occasionally attempting to sniff the warm flesh beneath the clothing but finding it irritatingly futile. Despite the form-fitting mouthpiece that prevented her from acting on impulse, a thick line of drool would soon coat her chin, neck and bare bosom.

After traveling an endless array of narrow back streets and rubble-strewn alleys, the cycle pulled into an underground garage, where the woman would be returned to a safe haven both familiar and foreign within the foggy recesses of her fragmented mind.

"You can relax now, Miko," the man would say, sighing with obvious relief as he lifted her from the bike's convex seat and carried her inside the back entrance to what had once been the family business, "you're home…back where you belong."

The neon sign out front had long-since dimmed, though the painted letters were still perfectly legible if the moonlight shone bright;

'*MASTER KRANE'S SELF-DEFENSE & COMBAT ACADEMY*' as did the smaller notice beneath it, which proclaimed simply '*Featuring MIKO KRANE, Six Time World Champion, Tae kwon do, Kung Fu and Judo*'. The man reached down and kissed the cool, pasty flesh of the woman's exposed forehead.

"This time, I'm not letting you out of my sight for a minute."

The woman cooed seductively in response, all the while drooling like Pavlov's dogs.

***

Just for the record, the mass practice of limb and organ 'replacements' for the diseased ended approximately eight years after the plague's initial sweep, though it is possible a few underground shops still exist to this very day. Sad to say, at one time the city of Chicago alone possessed a dozen such facilities, while the posh community of Beverly Hills was reputed to be home for at least twice that many.

Pardon me, people. Jeremy is waiving like a madman, which means the transport bus might well be ready to load. Back in a moment.

(FOUR MINUTES LATER)
The green light has indeed been given, people. Staff members will now assist in loading you onto the transport. I'll see you once we've boarded to continue the briefing. The aforementioned drawing of blood will take place approximately mid-way through the trip.

Happy trails, folks. (EIGHTEEN MINUTES LATER)
Before we depart, did everyone get a chance to

use the lavatory? Yes, Misses Jackson?

As mentioned earlier, the duration of our trip normally takes approximately an hour or so, though it has taken up to two I must say, everyone certainly appears refreshed. Your color is much improved, and you all seem to possess a bit more 'spring' in your step. By tomorrow or the next day, the effects should fade altogether. It really depends on your individual metabolisms. Don't be surprised, however, if it takes your kidneys and bowels a bit longer to adjust. A few of the chemical agents used in cryogenics have a profound effect on bodily waste. Don't be alarmed...this too shall pass.

In a few moments, the staff will be passing out sugar cubes and an iron supplement for you to ingest. This is simply a part of the treatment that will speed your recovery.

Question, Mister Caldwell?

Ah yes, the windows. I was wondering how long it would take before someone's curiosity would overtake their timid nature. The reason the transport bus windows are tinted to prevent your viewing the outside world is two-fold.

Number one, the sun's rays have a tendency to cause medical complications with the corneas of folks coming out of cryogenic sleep. It usually takes three to four days for you to properly adjust to daylight. Coincidentally, everyone will all be given specially designed reflective-lens goggles to wear once we arrive at the in-processing station.

Number two, we simply don't think you're ready to emotionally handle what this...what your planet has evolved into in the past several decades.

Over the years, we have learned that a gradual breaking in is handled much easier.

You will attend various classes during the in-processing phase that will prepare you farther. My lecture is just the initial session of many you'll be subjected to in the next forty-eight to seventy-two hours. I suggest you all lay back and enjoy the ride, and refrain from obsessing about what lies beyond your present field of vision. In good time, you'll understand our rather firm stance on this.

Meanwhile, I will commence with still another saga. Before I proceed, however, let me state for the record that if there is one particular segment of this briefing I could skip without repercussion, this is... most definitely it.

You see, just a few years following the plague's initial sweep, there were those in the 'entertainment' business that simply refused to bow in the face of global tragedy, forcing their sick, twisted wares on what little portion of the viewing public still remained. The following is just a sample of a trend that was happily short-lived...

9 - You Are WHO You Eat

The announcer stares into the camera's lens with his one remaining eye, his jagged, yellow-colored teeth revealed in all their gruesome glory. A red light flashes within the dimly lit studio, and his pupil instantly dilates.

"Good evening and welcome to Arcade arena, just West of Non-Shuffle Central in the heart of downtown Deadwood Falls, formerly known as Englewood, California. We hope all you good folks in the Semi-Live Zone, as well as those of you in 'Scraps-Town' who still possess the twin senses are receiving this broadcast loud and clear over the WMEAT-TV networks.

"This is Vince McCauley along with my play by play guru, Levon Crutchfield, here to bring you what we believe will be the pinnacle sports event of calendar year D-4, the '*2018 Choice Cuts Gluttony Finals*'."

The camera pans slightly to the left, and Vince 'the Voice' McCauley, one-time Golden Boy of CBS's NFL and NBA coverage, turns to greet his booth cohort, Levon 'The Clutch' Crutchfield, a four-time NBA All-Star turned sports analyst. Levon's ebony features are somewhat enhanced by thick layers of dark- tinted pancake make-up. As always, he greets the audience with a toothy, broad smile and a gleam in his eyes. As is the norm when Levon is featured on camera, the lens purposely avoids displaying anything below his shoulders and upper chest, as his missing arms below the elbow have been deemed 'less than audience friendly' by the powers that be.

"Glad to be here, partner. Like you said, this outta be one heckuva contest between undoubtedly the most competitive line-up of heavyweight munchers ever to share the same buffet table."

"No doubt about it, Von, this is one formidable group of scarfers. As the man once said, this contest ain't gonna be for the faint of heart, timid of mind or weak of gut," Vince beams, the black patch covering his left eye hanging a bit crookedly from the effects of his equally warped grin. "Looks like another sellout crowd to boot, Vinnie."

"Right you are, Von. Upwards of twenty-five thousand at least. There've been nothing but packed houses since the playoff rounds ensued three weeks ago."

"*Dead-World* loves nothin' better than a kick-ass eat-off, Vinnie, and there is no better setting for such a colossal match-up than right here in Deadwood Falls; just a hop, limp and shuffle away from where the beloved LA Lakers once laced up the old B-Ball sneakers."

The arena's overhead lights activate a moment later, and both men openly cringe at the abrupt change. Camera's pan the cheering crowd, the majority of which are shockingly pale and missing at least one limb, a fact that cuts down dramatically on the two-handed applause that was once so commonplace within the nations vast sports arenas.

"Looks like it's almost time for introductions, Levon. I see the curtained- off area containing tonight's Top Secret buffet is still drawn, no doubt still being prepped with last minute additions,"

Vince blurts with a lustful enthusiasm once associated with grade-school children chasing down the neighborhood ice cream truck.

"Almost makes me wish I was down there with a fork and spoon myself, Vinnie," Levon adds cheerily as the camera focuses on a dark brown silk curtain encircling what was once the half-court area of a regulation basketball court.

"Know what you mean, Von, but I wouldn't advise it. With the line-up of Super-Eaters we've got scheduled tonight, they'll be gulping down everything in sight; bystanders included."

"True 'nuff, V-Man. Once those jaws get to movin', they ain't too choosy on what they clamp down on."

"Let's get to the introductions of tonight's Mega-Superstar line-up, Levon," Vince says as the monitors display a drop-down menu of personal information and stats on contestant number one.

A head-shot is displayed of a white male whose whitish face is horribly pock-marked. He has a crater the size and circumference of a Ping-Pong ball just beneath his left eye, and a thin stream of yellowish liquid seeps slowly onto his jaw-line. Completely bald except for a clump of matted, reddish hair above his right ear, his expression is one of comical shock, as if the camera's flash had provided a mild electric shock.

"First up is a guy whose legendary status within the elite of competitive eaters has been well-earned in both the dead and pre-dead eras. Just thirty-two years of age at the time of his demise, *Ricky 'The Pit' Garrison* won several prestigious titles in the early 21ˢᵗ Century, including the Long Island Sausage Contest two years running, where he once consumed fourteen and a half eight- ounce sausages in less than ten minutes. At six-two and two-hundred eighty pounds, Big Rick's favorite dead-era dish is listed as boiled kidneys.

"Gobbled down forty-two of those bad boys in less than five minutes during last week's semi-finals, Vinnie. That boy is an organ-grindin' machine," Levon weighs in as the monitor flashes the next contestant.

A chubby-cheeked Asian female is shown from the waist up, her pitch- black hair tied into a pony-tail that is slung over her left shoulder like knotted rope. Her thick, pouting lips crusted in crimson; tattered shreds of gore hanging from her open mouth like bloodied confetti. Her bared forehead is a map of deeply grooved scars, several of which encase circular bubbles that resemble large, greenish boils.

"Ah, the Dragon Lady of Gorging herself, Ms. *Tammy 'Mighty Bite' Tamura*, a former twenty-six year old legal secretary for a Tokyo law firm who won several eating competitions both abroad and in the U.S."

"Right you are, V-man. Back in the day, Tiny Tammy once ate five feet, three inches of a giant Sushi roll in just under fifteen minutes. Damn, Vin, where does she put it all? Little Jade Honey can't weigh more than eighty-five pounds tops, 'specially with that caved-in rib cage."

"Good question, Levon. The Asians were masters at the art of gorging during the last half of the twentieth century, and now 'Mighty Bite' has continued her legacy even in death. Just two weeks ago in a regional match, she gulped down six feet, six inches of packed intestine in eight minutes flat. I personally believe that medicine-ball sized hole in her gut provides a distinct advantage in the 'storage extraction' department."

"Who's next, Vinnie? So far, this line-up is truly Hall-of-Fame caliber." A moon-faced black male is displayed next, his meaty jowls and triple-chin giving the illusion that he literally is without a neck. Other than a patch or two of jagged stubble, his skull is slick and hairless, a fist-sized chunk missing from the right side just above the temple. His slug-like lips are grotesquely bloated, like ebony maggots on the verge of explosion.

Gasping aloud, Vince's voice cracks with excitement.

"Folks, we are indeed in for an awesome show this evening. None other than *Lester 'Hollow Legs' Carter* is gracing our presence At the time of his death at age forty-two, Carter had won more North American sponsored eating competitions than anyone in the history of the sport. This living legend tallied seventy-eight regional, state and nationwide titles. At five-seven and almost four- hundred pounds, he was blessed with ample space to work with, and was known more for quantity consumed rather than overall speed of consumption."

"As my dear departed and yet to be resurrected mama used to say, Vin, some folks don't eat to live, but live to eat. My man Lester definitely belongs in the latter of those categories."

"No doubt, Von. Carter once ate two fifty-four

ounce steaks in one sitting, along with three pounds of mashed potatoes, six ears of corn, and eight buttered country rolls. Legend has it he traveled the highways and byways of the South and Southeast, showing off his eating prowess and winning substantial bets along the way. To quality for tonight's showdown, Lester Carter gnawed his way through the astonishing amount of twenty-one boiled hearts in ten minutes flat."

"The man was...*is* a monster, Vinnie. Can't wait to see those big ol' jaws do their thang..."

Next in line came a ghastly thin male of Hispanic descent. Shown in a full body shot, the man is wearing only a pair of dark-smeared cut off shorts, his collarbones and ribs protruding from his badly peeling flesh as if the slightest of movements might tear it asunder. His legs are hardly more than pogo-sticks, the kneecaps of which stick out like skeletal ball-bearings. His left foot is nothing more than a gnarled nub, and his missing right ear looks as though it's been chewed off.

"Our next to last contestant built his reputation in Southern California, Nevada, and Arizona back in the late '90's. *Roberto 'Tamale King' Garcia* ruled what was referred to as the 'South of the Border Eating Circuit', winning a half dozen titles in a six-month span, then abruptly retiring without fanfare. Standing five-seven and weighing in at a shockingly miniscule one-hundred twenty pounds, Roberto's performances against the 'heavyweights' of the business quickly established him as somewhat of a local legend. His greatest claim to fame before passing at the tender age of thirty-four: eating an entire Mexican buffet, all thirty-two items worth, in less than forty-five minutes. This awesome display supposedly occurred in an El Paso eatery in late 2005, and has since been dismissed by many as myth."

"I tell ya what, Vin, looking at that little dude, that particular story *is* hard to swallow, so to speak," Levon adds with a chuckle just as the curtain begins a slow ascent and the crowd noise rises several decibels in growing anticipation.

"Folks, we're just moments away from what might be the single greatest eating contest the world has ever witnessed. We've been told that a yet to be announced contestant will be added to the already lethal mix, but thus far the sponsors have seen fit to keep this mystery guest's identity a guarded secret. And speaking of sponsors, Levon, let's hear from the people responsible for this unprecedented event, shall we?"

The camera departs the still-rising curtain and shifts to a studio shot of a young, blonde woman wearing a two-piece swim suit posing in front of an easel display. The girl's face carries several layers of thick, dark-tinted makeup in a failed attempt to cover the pale, lifeless flesh beneath. Her features are otherwise flawless, less the slightly warped shape of her right cheekbone. As Levon begins a dramatic voiceover, she grins happily while backing away a step, waiving her hand over the product display as if gripping a magic wand.

"Got'cha, Vince. This event is proudly sponsored by FRESHMEAT DAILY Incorporated, the elite meat producer for West Coast Shuffle-Free

Zones since 2015, providing only the choicest cuts from North America, Europe, and the Pacific Rim Remember, FRESHMEAT DAILY is deliciously filling with absolutely no fillers. Pick up a freezer full today"

"Thanks, 'Von my man. My mouth is watering already," Vince exclaims as the monitors quickly switch focus to the center stage, where a series of four lengthy metallic conference tables swim clearly into view. The Red Checker- clothed tables are filled to overflowing with large ceramic bowls that are equally burdened. Each table is separated by an eight-foot high, see-through glass wall on either side, and hold exactly fifteen of the serving bowls from end to end. A close-in camera shot slowly pans lovingly over each entree to be served as the crowd grows increasingly raucous.

"Behold the King's buffet, Levon, prepped and readied for five of the most revered eaters of our time. The glass walls were put in place in order to prevent the contestants from straying from their assigned table.

"No doubt about it, we are about to witness engorgement history, my friend," Vince announces, his voice crackling with emotion.

"Right you are, compadre. I can honestly say I ain't seen a spread like that since the living years and Thanksgiving's at my dear old granny's house. If I still owned a pair of workin' taste buds, Vin my friend, they'd be juicin' up like a wet sponge 'bout now."

As the arena lights dim, a carefully aimed spotlight blankets the stage. Lumbering onto the stage from four separate doors built just to the left of the center stage, the contestants are halted by a wire-meshed fence that fronts each serving table. They are utterly oblivious to the nearby cameras and crowd noise, their mouths dripping gruel in glutinous masses. All four are dressed in multicolored, skin-tight spandex costumes and calf-high black boots. Yellow lettering adorns the backs of these costumes, the words 'Gluttony.com' showcased briefly before the lens pans back out to reveal all four biting and clawing madly at the mesh blockade.

"Oh, they're fit be tied, Vinnie. Wouldn't be surprised if they gnaw their way through any minute now," Levon blurts happily, "Take a look at Big Lester. They don't ring the dinner bell soon, he's apt to whirl around and gulp down little Tammy Tamura like a California Roll."

"Looks like the wait is almost over, Levon. Let's turn our attention to the fifth door, where our surprise contestant of the evening is set to make a dramatic appearance," Vince replies as the spotlight falls on door five, and an immediate hush falls over the crowd in a sweeping wave. Cheers transform into gasps, claps and whistles into choked coughs and whiny sobs.

"I...is that who I think it is, Vince? Ho-leeeee sheeeeeiiit..." Levon mumbles, temporarily falling out of character, "...man's even bigger and uglier in person."

"R-right you are, Levon, and I see that, thankfully, he's not alone..."

Shambling to the stage, the echoes of the man's

heavy boots smacking the hard oak flooring easily drowns out the muffled whispers filling the area. He is flanked by uniformed handlers on either side, both of whom clasp the heavy chains which bind the man's legs, neck, and tree-sized arms, while still another trails a few steps behind, pointing a Taser Bazooka at the man's lower back.

"I've just been handed the official stat sheet, 'Von, allow me to cover the highlights while our home audience reads along.

"Ronald 'Man-Eater' Masterson was put to death by lethal injection by the Colorado Department of Criminal Justice in June of the year 2013 at the age of thirty-seven, following convictions in thirty-six cases of first degree murder that took place between the years 2002 and 2009. Standing seven-feet three and weighing four-hundred seventy pounds, he was buried in a specially constructed coffin in his hometown of Blacksburg, Wyoming.

"Ronald had been working as a laborer at various dude ranches in Wyoming and Arizona, where numerous disappearances began to take place in the late 90's. Upon investigation, it was discovered that Ronald had been abducting his victims and taking them to his desert cabin near Jacksboro, Arizona.

"Authorities subsequently discovered the skeletal remains of over forty-five separate bodies, only the aforementioned thirty-six of which were properly identified. Quite the craftsman, Ronald had utilized his victim's rib cages, femurs and spines to construct a back room made of nothing but bones;

lamp stands, chairs, even a bed frame. When asked why he had perpetrated such ghastly crimes, Ronald "Man-Eater" Masterson's only response was that he was a 'misunderstood craftsman who would some day be viewed as a true Renaissance man'.

"Having risen in the summer 2014, he's been kept at a top secret, maximum security lock up since it was discovered his little cannibalism problem hadn't completed abated since death. Reported just last year, Ronald attacked and, um…consumed a pair of correctional guards and a unit Warden before being subdued by no less than an entire armed division near the Scraps-Town border crossing.

"To this day, four years-plus into what has been termed the 'Renaissance Rising', Ronald Masterson is the sole individual proven to have willingly devoured dead flesh.Deemed the 'cannibal of cannibals', his name is whispered in stark fear within most circles, but with dumbstruck awe in still others, most of which reside deep within Scraps-Town. Tonight, we shall see if the legend can truly walk the walk, 'Von."

"I'll tell ya what, Vinnie, I don't envy those guards. Big freak would have to wear an iron-plated muzzle 'fore I'd share space with 'im." Levon cracks, although his valiant effort to levy humor is laced with anxiety.

The other four contestants are oblivious to the giant's presence just a scant few feet away, their faces pressed tightly against the wire mesh coated in whitish froth that seeps from their squirming lips.

"I've just been told the green light is just moments away, Levon. Once given, the blockade

202

will be lifted and all five contestants will be free to begin consumption. The rules are as simple as our competitors are single-minded; first eater to completely clear his or her table is declared the victor. Entrees vary from boiled livers and fried kidneys to large intestine stuffed with spleen-rolls. The total serving weight of each table is exactly one-hundred sixty-five pounds, or basically the body weight of your average male specimen, and we both know these five have had plenty of practice on the real-scale model, right, Von?"

"Affirmative, Vince. I heard tale that in the first year of the Renaissance, ol' Big Lester there finished off a bus load of Japanese tourists near Disneyland all by his lonesome, not stopping 'til he had swallowed a dozen or so Nikon cameras to boot. I would venture to guess that table-load ain't gonna last the victor more than ten to twelve minutes tops."

"Green light just flashed, Von, and the 2018 Choice Cuts Gluttony Challenge...begins!" Vince exclaims as the mesh fencing rises like a stage curtain, drawing a huge cheer from the live crowd.

The competitors charge forward in a clumsy, lumbering gait, as if shoved forcefully from the rear. All, that is, save one. Ronald Masterson stares over and down at the others with a comically exaggerated look of utter dismay as his neck and hand restraints are loosened with extreme caution. In another time, such an expression could have easily been interpreted as conveying a social upper-class snootiness; translated to mean, '*what the HELL is wrong with you people*?"

By the time he reaches the outer edge of his assigned table a full ninety seconds later:

Ricky 'The Pit' is into his ninth stir-fried butt-cheek patty. Tammy 'Mighty Bite' bites into her third foot of stuffed intestine.

Lester 'Hollow Legs' is finishing off the final of eight boiled hearts.

Roberto 'Tamale King' is in the process of shoveling in the last of five brain-stuffed burritos.

As Masterson bends low to survey the mission ahead, the announcing team describes the frenzied action at break-neck speed:

Levon: "Looks like the jolly Gangrene giant is gonna have to kick it into high gear if he's gonna catch up, Vinnie."

Vince: "Right you are, Levon. The others are setting an incredible pace. 'The Pit' is now diving head first into a steaming pile of breaded entrails, while 'Mighty Bite' is sucking down the last foot of intestine while greedily eye-balling a bowl of barbecued calf-muscle." Levon (giggling): "Check out my man "Hollow Legs". He's dipped his entire head into a bowl of pancreatic soup and is slurpin' and suckin' so loud it's drowning out the stage-side crowd."

Vince: "Levon, I have to admit at being completely dumbstruck by the performance of 'The Tamale King' The man is literally a walking pile of bones, yet having just finished off a fifteen pound helping of brain-wraps, he's face first into a bowl of shoulder loin. Where does he put it all?"

Levon: "You could ask the same of Tammy Tamura, V. 'Course, in her case, I can see the majority of what she inhales leakin' out that gut crater on her right side."

Vince: "She's leaving behind quite the slug trail, all right.

Three minutes in, Levon, and thus far the most surprising thing to me is the lack of productivity of one 'Man-Eater' Masterson, who many would consider the heavy favorite coming in."

Levon: "I'm right with ya, V Man looks downright bored. Are we sure he didn't chomp on a security guard or two before the match?"

Vince laughs a bit nervously but doesn't verbally reply.

FIVE MINUTES LATER:

Vince: "We're witnessing a humdinger of an upset, Mr. Crutchfield. So much for those sure-fire Vegas odds, am I right?"

Levon: "Correct-e-mundo, Mr. McCauley. Under the Old World cash system, I know who my hard-earned green-backs would have been on. But as one of my ESPN commentator idols used to say, 'that's why they play the game."

Vince: "While Masterson plays Mr. Nonchalant, having barely freed his table of a third of its contents, Tammy 'Mighty Bite' Tamura, all seventy five pounds of dead tissue and dry bones, is less than a minute away from a clean sweep. From the camera angle we're privy to, I see only one full bowl of baked lung remaining, and she's reaching for a handful as we speak."

Levon: "Ricky 'The Pit' Garrison is a distant

205

second, Vin, but he seems to be struggling to force down the breaded livers. Looks like he's 'bout to heave up his own in the process." Vince: "Same with Big Lester, Levon. He's gumming a bowl of sweet 'n sour collarbone soup, but is spitting roughly half the content back onto the table 'Tamale King' Garcia is still gnawing on a pile of grilled neck bones, but his decaying heart doesn't really seem to be in it at this point. Those two have nearly a half-table left to clear, and seem to be running out of gas at this point."

Levon: "I got to say I'm both shocked and disappointed with Mr. High 'n Mighty 'Man-Eater', Vin. Boy's been gnawin' on that same slab of rib meat for the past two minutes. Some legend…"

Vince: "Have to agree, Levon. Have you noticed how he continues to eyeball his competitors, as if studying their individual techniques? I did get a clear shot of the man's bared teeth a moment ago. Reminded me of a picture I once saw of a forty-foot Great White captured off the Florida coast back in the nineties. Thing had a set of choppers the size of rail spikes Masterson has a similarly impressive set, but it's a damned shame he doesn't seem motivated enough to use them to their maximum potential."

TWO MINUTES LATER:

Vince: "Looks like we have a winner, Levon! The judges have indicated that Tammy 'Mighty Bite' Tamura has indeed cleared her table, all one-hundred sixty-five pounds of it, and has been officially declared the 2018 Choice Cuts Glutton

Champion!"

Levon: "She kicked some undead booty, no doubt. But you gotta wonder, Vince, just how much that continuous cargo dump helped her cause. I mean, she didn't retain but maybe twenty percent of what she swallowed. The majority passed through her 'side-pocket' like kidney stones."

Vince: "Good point, my friend. Regardless, she earned the crown with a ferocity I've rarely seen outside a Scrap-Town ambush.

Point of note, Levon. The other contestants are being allowed to finish off their respective tables, after which the award ceremony will commence."

Levon: "Crowd has certainly grown calm. I think most of 'em are still in shock from Masterson's shameful showing."

Vince: "It was indeed a shocker, Levon. Folks, my partner and I are headed down from the booth for the award presentation, which will be MC'ed by the CEO of 'CHOICE CUTS Inc,' Mr. Michael P. Henry.

We'll be right back after this quick word from 'CHOICE CUTS', the best damn freeze-dried meat cutlets in the business."

Approximately ELEVEN minutes later:

Vince (his face seemingly pressed against the camera lens, screaming in a shrill, barely intelligible tone): "Shit...shit...shit...somebody n-needs to c-call somebody....he's...he's...Masterson is...is...."

Levon (enters the frame in a streaky blur): "Get your ass in gear, Vince!

The son of a bitch has taken out all the fuckin' guards, man! I just saw that crazy fucker turn the 'Tamale King' into a shredded taco!"

Vince (gesturing wildly for the camera to be pointed to his left): "F-folks, I'm hoping you can at least get a b-brief glimpse at the m-mass destruction being perpetrated by "Man-Eater" Masterson just a few dozen feet from where I…w-we stand."

Shaking erratically, first from side to side then up and down, the lens briefly manages to focus on center-stage, where 'The Man-Eater' is in the gruesome process of earning said nickname. Coated in green and yellow gore from neck to feet, his colossal form is encircled by a ring of severed body parts, some of which still twitch and gyrate as if attempting escape.

He holds the upper body of Ricky 'The Pit' Garrison airborne in his right hand as the man's intestines swing to and fro from his frayed waistline like detached electrical lines. His left grasps a petite female form minus the head, seen hanging from between his gritted teeth by a thin coil of black hair. The bludgeoned head swings around and faces the lens for a single split-second, revealing the horrendously pulped face of the newly ordained eating champion. Panning slightly to the right, the camera momentarily freezes on a fallen guard lying face up, the barrel end of a Taser Bazooka having pierced his chest like a giant javelin. The camera swings around once again to focus on the gaunt, pasty- white face of Vince McCauley, whose flesh seems to be melting as thick gobs of make-up fly free in concentrated chunks. Vince: "We…o-obviously the contest organizers didn't…c-couldn't have expected such…such insanity to transpire, but my…m-my god, to hire only a handful of security armed with T-Taser's was a mistake many p-present have paid dearly for…Levon…Levon! Can we make the side exit?"

Levon (yelling from a distance): "We're fucked this way, man. Panic city…they're piled up like cord wood in front of the fuckin' door! Turn back…haul ass towards the east exit!"

(The camera shakes and jumbles, displaying jerky, discombobulated shots of concrete flooring, empty stadium seating, and the occasional disembodied organ lying free from its host, eventually fading to black)

Four minutes later:

Vince (shrieking feline-like while apparently holding the camera himself, the view given bleared and unfocused): "Je-EEEE-Sussss..it's…h-h-he just..just p-pulled Levon's left leg from his bo-body like a fucking m-mosquito w-wing. I s- saw the crazy s-son of a b-bitch take a single bite from the c-calf then toss the damned thing away right…right before he…he mashed Von's skull like a fu…mashed it like a deflated…s-s-basketball…b-brains and b-b-bones popped across the damned floor..and…and splashed my p-pants and s-shirt…a-and s- shoes…a-and..s-shit…. (the camera refocuses and clears somewhat, capturing a grisly kaleidoscope of fleshy puree that coats the surrounding floors and walls in a crimson/yellow webbing, dripping and oozing from varied piles of raw muscle, tendon and decayed skin. An impossibly large shadow looms near, as if a 727 Jet had suddenly passed overhead *inside* the coliseum)...oh shiiiiiitttt...he's c- coming t-this way...a-and...h-he's got the C...the CE...O...ohhhhhhhhh!"

Ninety-seconds later:

The camera lens points downward at a sharp, titled angle. Vince McCauley lays prone, the left side of his head sheared away as a wide, toothy imprint is apparent at the ripped edges that remain. The left side of his skull resembles a hairy Big Mac minus a single humongous bite. His left eye dangles from the ruined socket like a loose marble. The camera pans to his chest and abdomen, which have been torn asunder and lain open; the organs tinted gray with the gradual rotting that is eventual in a state of perpetual dead. His legs are crushed, the shins of which are flipped forward and tucked tightly against his outer thighs. His ashen lips tremble and twitch.

"...p-point   t-t-taken......j-just   f-fin...finish.. me...you...s-s-sick b-bastard.."

A boot roughly the size of a manhole cover lumbers forward and quickly transforms Vince 'Silver Tongue' McCauley's face and head to pulped mush, popping his noggin like an oversized tick.

The camera swings around and apparently handed to an unseen party, who instantly tilts the lens at an upturned angle.

210

Ronald 'Man-Eater' Masterson positions his mountainous form dead center within the lens' still eye a split-second later.

"Hold it…steady…Mister C..E.O," the giant mumbles.

He tucks a Gold-Plated trophy (which he comically dwarfs) tightly against his enormous chest. A trophy with the words 'CHOICE CUTS Glutton Champion - 2018' engraved at its oval-shaped center. A trophy from which hangs a severed wrist and hand, a shiny silver watch still attached that reads 'CEO - CHOICE CUTS INC.' inside its titanium steel band.

Masterson, a man hardly considered a 'conversationalist' during the living years, leans down a bit and cradles the award like his first-born.

His words are soft-spoken, almost child-like in both tone and delivery.

His smile is hideous, the inch-long spaces between his piano-key sized teeth impacted with gluts of mangled gore.

"Winner…*eats*…the…spoils…" he whispers gleefully, tossing the trophy aside and leaping forward with a fierce growl.

Just before impact, the man forced to hold the camera is briefly heard whimpering like a spooked five-year old.

A virtual wall of darkness floods the lens, followed by set of chattering teeth that seem to engulf the landscape in a dark, maroon mist.

ONE HOUR LATER:

The one true champion steps unceremoniously forward to receive his crown. A crown constructed from the bones of those who would dare to challenge his greatness.

The champion bows to a nonexistent crowd, then proceeds to search through the scattered remains for only the 'choice cuts'.

***

According to legend, 'Man-Eater' Masterson was never re-captured and quite possibly still remains at large amongst the lumbering masses, though by now it's quite possible he's long since passed the 'expired' stage.

Does anyone require a break? Ah, several raised hands indicate so.

Let's take five, people.

(SIX MINUTES LATER)

Everyone back in their seats? Fine. Before I begin my next segment, two of our staff are going to come around and take a small vile of blood from each of you. A brief finger-prick is all that is required. After which, you'll all be provided a small snack. I do apologize for not being allowed to feed you all a more substantial meal, but potential medical complications prevent it. A friendly reminder, however, that once we arrive at the station, you'll be allowed to consume until your hearts, and bellies, are content. Now to the next segment: it is very similar in theme to the last, in that it concerns a rather sadistic form of post-plague entertainment, this time sports-related. Once again, society quickly shunned such outlandishly cruel events, eventually relegating them meaningless and thus, no longer viable.

10 - THE ZBA

God...I'm so tired...so damned...weary. I...used to...love this game. I have such ...vivid...memories of all the great nights...but even those thoughts...fade over...time. The pain is...worse each day...that I'm above ground. I want nothing more...than to....lie down...and never again...wake up.

But...something won't let me. The curse...won't allow for such...an easy...escape.

Luther throws me a behind the back pass just as I cross into ...the lane. I execute my...patented spin move and it sends...Reggie flying by me...one of his teeth flies out and bounces off of my shoulder. I throw up a fade-away and it kisses off the glass. The backboard is still...dripping blood and...pus where Jamaal rammed his head...against it back in quarter one. One of Jamaal's ears is hangin' by a thin thread of skin. It looks like...fish bait danglin' on a line. As I run back down court, hell, let's face it, it's more like shamble down court, I see Jamaal. He's a real trooper, my brother J. The right... side of his face is mashed in...like somebody took a metal pipe to it...his remaining eye is hanging down... on the side of his nose...swingin' back and forth...like a marble on a...string.

Jamaal used to be a killer...with the ladies, man. That dude had one in every...port. Probably...had...three...four, sometimes five in every port. He is definitely losin' his looks, though, and most of his skin...to boot.

I front Willie, who is tryin' to muscle me

under...the boards. Willie's ribs are hangin' out like flag poles, and every time he brushes...against me...I lose another chunk of flesh. I bring back my elbow and it catches him...right under the chin. I hear him...grunt and when I look back, I see his lower teeth have planted themselves... deep in the skin under...his nose. He looks like he ain't got no top plate of choppers. Like an...old man...whose lost...his dentures. He finally pulls...it loose and his tongue lands on my right...sneaker. He gets...pissed and throws a short jab at me, which...I duck away from easily. I hear a plopping... sound and see poor old Willie's arm fly...away and land near mid-court, the ...fist still clenched tight. He looks down at the hole...at his shoulder and Willie does his best...to keep his dignity by...acting like nothing happened. His...famous hook-shot will...never be... the same.

I rebound a missed...jumper by, I believe...Julius, and toss the ball up- court to Brent, who fires...up a thirty-foot jumper...and swishes it. That white boy...was the best damn...shot in the league, I don't give a rat's behind what...anybody says. Before things...went to shit a few years...back, Brent was on his way...to being one of the highest...paid shooting guards in...the game. He wasn't...much of a...playmaker, but that boy could...nail those trays.

I stumble back down court just as...Coach Griggs signals for an injury time out. Seems...Mitch 'The Enforcer' Wiggins...has misplaced his left leg. He's laying....on the far foul...line stripe, pointing at some slug in the crowd that is... gnawing on his skin...bone.

The referee jogs over...and blows the guy's head into...the third row.

Crowd participation...ain't what it used to...be. The ref and a few...other of the working crew....drag the guy's headless....body out into the far....tunnel. Mitch is being...dragged over to the sidelines. The doc and his med crew...are gonna try to...re-attach his leg. Mitch's eyes beg...for them to put the ref's shotgun barrel to his throat and...end this farce. I know the feelin', Mitch old buddy. But. they won't do it. They won't let...sleeping dogs...or *games* die. They have to.....hold onto....what they know. What they.. enjoyed. We were. entertainment.

We were.. a diversion in their...everyday lives. It don't matter that we're all...fallin' apart at the fuckin' seams. They want...to cheer. They want to watch us jump and slam...dribble and 'showtime' like the...old days. Only problem is...when we jump, half the time we leave parts of ourselves on the court.

When we dunk, our...fingers and hands snap land crunch on the rim.

When we 'showtime', we usually end up limbless.

Mitch is reachin' for the ref's gun while the doc is trying to sew on his leg.

He almost...reaches the stock and the ref walks away. The doc is droolin' as he leans over Mitch's leg. I think old doc is day-dreamin' about a well-done rib-eye or maybe grilled pork chops. The nurse...her hair a bloody bird's nest, holds the ...instruments and stares ...straight ahead. She's droolin' too. Jesus, what...is this bullshit? Wouldn't

216

hell...itself be better? Or...maybe that's...that's where we are...already.

This is...like were being...tortured for the...good fortune we had before Armageddon day, or 'A-day' as we...think...of it now.

I sat on the bench...and snap my right wrist...back into position. The wrist bone had been...shattered like dry cordwood...when I elbowed Willie.

I hack...and spit up something solid..something dark brown like...chili sauce..only chunkier... I think it may....be my...liver. Crapped a kidney last...week. Won't be too...damn long and I'll be...the *Hollow* Man.

"Cool Dog" Converse is leaning...over beside me. One of the great...power forwards the...game ever saw Dog once had fourteen straight double-doubles. He had...thirty-one rebounds in one game. Averaged over twenty points a game...for eight or nine straight years. The man...could flat out....play. He glances...over at me...with his one good eye, the other socket being all empty and hollowed out like a...Halloween Jack 'O Lantern, and flashes his best...smile. Not an easy...task...bein' that Dog has no lower jaw. The skin...on his face stretches out and splits from his upper jaw...to his neck.

Yellow pus sprays out and splatters my...jersey. Hell, I try but...just can't manage...to get...pissed at Dog. We shared too many...beers, joints, and. groupies before...A-day.

I had been...in my..seventh year...in the league. I had made the...All- Star team...as a reserve...for the second time. Was totallin' seventeen points and nine boards a game…we had a chance to make the playoffs for. the first time in…four years. I was…in my prime. Things were. lookin' up. Then suddenly they were lookin' straight down into….the pits…of hell itself. Hell. right smack dab here on. earth.

Things. get more…foggy as…dead time…drags on, but…I can still…remember…the day things…went completely to…shit. We were. In Cleveland and noticed the crowd…only a couple of thousand, which…was kinda…weird to begin with, started exiting the gym…in a panic. We were in…the middle of…lay-up drills when…the coach…called us over…and told us to get back…in the dressing room, that we…were all headed to…the airport. Kenny had his boom-box on in the locker room and we…all sat there with open mouths and…listened to the news. I mean…we all thought we..were dreamin' or something. To hear them talk…about dead folks. comin' back to life and attackin' the living made. us think we were all sharing the same nightmare.

By the time our flight landed in…Charlotte…the airport was mostly…deserted. The folks that were…still there. had this crazy-ass look…like they just went through…some serious shock. therapy.

It took me…half an hour…to flag down a cab, when usually the airport lots are…overloaded with 'em.

I wish…I could somehow erase the memory of…what I found when I walked…into the townhouse my wife and I had shared for. over three years.

218

She had...already murdered our son...and was had...e-eaten part of him...by the time...I took the...kitchen knife...and. and...oh lord, let me die with no memory of...that. My son...had been only...three. Yvonne and I had. Been together for...damn near five years. She had...truly been my soul mate. Helped me kick...the dope...and...the groupie scene for good.

I'm not...sure if...the other guys. are going through the same mental torture. My memories are...pretty damn clear, but...I can't act...on anything...I want. Don't matter how...hard...I...try. The only thing my body answers to is this...damn..hunger. Man, I'm starvin' all...the time. I never...used. to be that much of a ...meat eater...when I was...alive. Now all I think about, day...and night...is blood red meat, all juicy and wet, smellin' all...pink and raw.

Dog just spit out...what looks like his spleen. I ain't no sawbones. But that can't...be good for one's overall...health. Don't really matter, though...we're all dead as...a hammer anyhow.

The coach comes over...and screams at Luther for the constant...walkin' calls he's getting. Luther looks...kinda pathetic and...points down at. His left leg. Fragmented bone sticks out from just under...the knee cap. I up, can...see some fat, throbbin' maggots fall from the bone as Luther leans almost...stickin' the leg bone in coach's face. Coach shrugs it off...'no Excuses', he says. Usin' injuries...as an...excuse just don't cut it...in this league anymore.

We hobble out...onto...mid-court and we win

219

the…jump. Pervis "The Traveling Highlight Reel" Wilkerson, as he was…known in…his healthier days…fast breaks down and….thunder slams one. Even with his ribs half- stickin' out his back like a broken bird cage…that man…can still bring it.

I shoot him…a wink as we come down court…together and he tries to…return it, then recalls he ain't got no eye lids. Hey…we're all playin' with…handicaps these…days.

We can…see…the 'shirts' sitting in the dark up in the third level…of the Coliseum. They…never…show their…faces. They are…some…sick mo-fo's to…force us to do this…bullshit. I hear…the..warm bodies that…survived…pay big…bucks to watch the…games. Even have…their own…form of cable TV. Pay…per view…all the way. Only, ain't no…cash passin' hands these days…ain't about the fame, the women…the mountains of blow. Just the necessities, baby…shit paper, burnin' oil and fresh meats and vegetables.

But as …look around…at mostly empty seats…why the…hell even bother?

I guess times change…needs change. Greed will…never…go away…as long….as onewarm….body still…walks upright.

I toss up a one…handed jumper that banks in…and I hear 'em cheer. I want so bad…to turn around and shoot the dirty…bastards a double-barreled bird, but…again….my body won't…respond…it wants only one thing. I see the large. blue coolers sitting at the far end…of the court. Our…reward awaits. Don't know…where they...get the fresh meat. Don't care. Just....wanna chow. down.

We will put on...their sick sideshow. of what...used to be a ...great sport. We will run, stumble, crawl if we have to, down court...as long. as the reward is callin' to us. As long as we can...curb this damn craving...even if...for only a few minutes.

I block Jerome "The Postman" Jefferson's lay up attempt, which was...kinda weak on my part...since Jerome has this...problem of...telegraphin' his shot since he lost an arm...a month or so back.

Brent nails a couple of twenty-five foot...trays and we're up 42-29 at half.

Scores are kinda low these days. Lack of body parts means...lack of offensive weapons. The less fingers...and arms...ya have, the less...effective your shot...is gonna be, period.

At half-time, the coach throws us all a slab. I suck mine...down as quick as it hits my lips. I tell myself...I'm gonna slow down and savior it, but..it never works that way. I spotted some hairs on it..just before...I startin' chewin'. Most likely a...leg. Might be some hairy guy's back meat. Not that...we're picky. Mitch left...his leg in the middle....of the locker room floor. I...pick it up...and hand it to him. His eyes meet mine...and the sticky drool pours off...his chin...like spilled...molasses. He nods...and tries to stick the leg back into...place. The Doc slurps down...his snack and wobbles over...to assist Mitch. I think Mitch is damn near...done as far as being...on 'active duty'. I

221

think a permanent...trip...to 'injured reserve' might be in his near future. None...of the messy paperwork of the...old days. Just a shotgun to the...temple and your playin' 'Zone Defense on The Clouds' while blowin' on a harp. We all...dream of that day. At least I know I..do. Funny, we all used...to dread retirement. Now...we pray for it.

My body...is a pulpy mess...but seems to be holdin' its own, at least for now. The suits are...havin' a hard time...replacin' all the bodies, though. Most of the big names...the endorsement kings of old, are...already rotting away in the...bone yard. I...will personally...invite Mr. Grim Reaper in...with open arms and...a big,broad smile.

Horn sounds....third quarter kicks in. I feel newly...energized and hit my...first three shots right...out of the gate. There are times...the feelin' I used to get when I was in the 'Zone' sweeps over me. It don't last...but...a second, but damn, it feels good.

Ref calls time before...quarter ends to...clean up the court. I lost part of my...right pinkie. Mitch is comin' apart like...a ripped up rag doll out ...there. Both his..legs keep comin' unhinged and he looks like...a puppet with half its ...strings cut. He keeps grinnin' though. Grinnin' and glarin' at those coolers. After all, the feast is less than...thirteen minutes away.

Fourth quarter and I hear Coach Griggs screamin' at...Luther again. He had thrown...up an...air ball that cleared...the backboard by half a dozen feet. I think Luther is doin' it on purpose...to grab some pine. The poor dude's head is...hanging on by a few...ragged tendons. He looks kinda...like those plastic dolls with...the bobbin' heads you used to see hangin' from rear view mirrors.

Midway through the fourth, we're up 65-47, and we all...pause and wait at half court as...Coach Martin brings out...his 'secret weapon'. I can hear...the sparse crowd...and the suits sittin' in the dark whoopin' and hollerin'. This...shit...never fails to nauseate me, and that's damn hard...to do...these days.

He comes...joggin' out of the visitor's locker room like....the conquerin' hero. His fists are pumpin' in the air, and his toothless grin is...as wide as...the hole suckin' wind at my lower gut.

I never personally...liked...the asshole when...we were warm bodies. Bein' dead hasn't...exactly cured his...ego problem. At the time...of...A- day, he...was supposedly bringin' in forty mil a year...just in endorsements. When people....talked about the...league...his name came first...always. Every shot the...ball hoggin' Jackass hit seemed to be simulcast on...worldwide TV. ESPN licked his...monogrammed shoes...at every...opportunity.

They never...seemed to dwell on the...twenty-five shots...he missed every night, or the fact that his D was beyond weak and he...just about...led the league in...turnovers every year. The players, even some of his...teammates, called him 'ML', which...stood...for "Media Leech", and...he lived up to...it every night.

Now they call...him out...in the fourth quarter of every game...like some miracle worker. They don't want...him...fallin' apart like the rest of us...before his time, so his...playin' time is seriously limited.

Yeah, the arrogant shit...won four straight...MVP's and...three straight championships, but...everybody around the game...knows...that without the surroundin' cast he had...mostly to rebound his missed shots...he was just...another glorified show-boater.

I was...on the All-Star squad with him two years back...and the asshole never...said word one to me. I did my best...to keep the brick away...from him whenever I was in there. Of course, he hit...eight out of twenty-three from...the floor and won game MVP. When your own...teammates can't stand your ass...which I heard...was the case with him, you are one hurtin' dude, ego- wise, cause the man...in this league that had the...biggest ego is like the billionaire with the most...ships in his personal fleet. You are *King* Prick...amongst very stiff....competition.

Mr. MVP...practically steals the damn...ball from...Julius and fires up a twenty-five footer that clangs off the top of...the backboard...and nails...the ref in the side...of the noggin, then strolls on...down court with a shit- eatin' grin on his...face, like he swished it or...something. I pass the ball to Dog and he rips a...beautiful one-handed, not much choice in his case...fade-away from...about fifteen feet. I high...five him at mid-court and...he smiles, his tongue hangin' out the side of his mouth like the fattest... slug you ever saw.

MVP double-dribbles at least...three times but

the ref...doesn't whistle. I think they've been...instructed not to. He...banks in a lay up and starts...dancin' and muggin' like he's preppin' for SportsCenter. I see...out of the..corner of my one good eye...that Brent is lookin' mighty pissed. MVP elbowed Brent...in our last game with 'em and Brent has had a hard time..keepin' his intestines from floppin' loose ever since. I'm still eye-ballin' those bright blue coolers every...second or two. I try...to control my slobberin' and droolin', but it's one of those...things completely outta my control these days. I miss laughin'. I miss sleepin'. I miss real...emotions not driven by...hunger. I miss sex. I miss drivin' my Porsche at one-twenty on the...interstate at midnight...with a lit joint hangin' from my lip and a cold Malt liquor between...my legs. Lord, I miss...my family. I miss the crowd when...you go on a run, or when...you're in the zone and...everything you throw up there finds...the mark. I miss it all, but I...don't ...crave it. I only crave...the meat. It's all about. the *meat*.

Coach Griggs calls a TO. He's yellin' at Luther again, something about 'puttin' some D on MVP'. Luther puts his finger in his nostril...and begins to dig and...grind away like he's tryin' to pull out...a boulder made outta solid...gold.

The coaches...must be getting hot meals...clean water...gas allowances for their...cars, somethin' like that, for puttin' up with this crap. Every now and then I see...the frustration on Grigg's face. He knows this...ain't right. It ain't what God intended to...come from A- day. None...of us. are...supposed to...even try...to make

225

things..the way they were in the old world. They all. see in our...eyes that...we only do what they want...because of the meat. It's like...those dogs...at the track. racin' and chasin' the meal that hangs...only a few feet in front ..of 'em.

Doc and his crew are...lookin' over Dog. His collar...bone is...stickin' up into the...side of his neck...like a spear. Every time...he tries to. yank it loose...it rips a bigger hole...in his throat. The nurse is leanin' over lickin' up whatever falls out of the...wound. Sounds sick, I know...but watchin' her. is makin' my cravin' worse. I'm smackin' my lips...like a man...lookin' at burgers ...grill over an open flame.

Brent...is wavin' his arms and gruntin'...like he's rabid. We don't...understand the...words, but...he's pointin' at MVP across the court...and we all get his meanin'. This is...liable to get real...ugly.

MVP gets the ball and...starts his...one man show...routine. He gets...just over...half court and Brent meets him there...his right arm stuck...straight out from his body like a limbo-line batterin' ram.

He clothes-lines...MVP just...under the chin as he runs by. I hear two loud cracks...go off like grenades. Next...thing I see is Julius...leaning down over...MVP and...giggling like a three year old who just heard his...first fart joke. I swear...it was...the closest thing...to...a genuine laugh...I've seen or heard since before A- day. We all...make a circle around MVP laying on....the court and begin carefully...analyzing him. He's...lying on...his back, his...long skinny arms reachin' up and wavin' like...crazy. It...takes me..a second or two to realize...the man's head is gone. Well, not really...gone, just kinda 'tucked underneath his body. Brent's shot had...broken his neck...and his head... was lodged between. his own shoulder blades.

Non-contact sport. my black ass.

Brent's busted arm is...swingin' free by his side, only a...couple'a strands of skin holdin' it on, but I swear. he's so full of pride that...he don't mind losin' an appendage.

Coach Martin is...freakin'...rantin' and ravin'. he shoves us out of the way and rolls MVP...over on his side, pullin'...his head...free. MVP's mouth is movin', although I see. he's lost a gold tooth or two, and his eyes...are wipe open.

The coach is...practically...cryin' as he yells. for the Doc to get out there and...re-attach MVP's head. I don't think..Mr. MVP is gonna. be givin' anybody his famous... 'head fake' anytime soon.

Game...finally ends. We win... 77-61. I end up with...twelve points and eight boards. My usual...solid performance. None of us...give a rat's ass...about our stats anymore. That was a different era. A totally different...dimension, in fact.Stats meant...status. Stats meant...contract leverage. Now...stats mean shit. We...all eat..the same meal for reward of...performance or. non-performance. We all...get what's. comin' to us.

As they lead. us towards the coolers...I hear a shotgun blast in the..background. I look around and notice. I don't see Mitch...stumbling around...anywhere. I guess he...got his walkin' papers. Lucky…son of a bitch.

We dive into the moist, fresh meat like…men dyin' of…thirst jumpin' into a…cool lake. The…hunger will not. go away…not completely, no…matter how much…I feed. At least. this…slows it down a little. Not sure if…I even…taste it anymore, or if I ever did. Like everything else…that was. the old way of life…it don't seem to matter one way or…another…anymore.

One of the….suits has come down…from his…hiding place. in the dark and is…yellin' at Coach Griggs. Coach Martin is standin' there. too. Martin even …takes a swing at Griggs. Next thing we…see is all three of 'em…wrestling on the floor just…a few feet away from…where we…feast.

A few more…well-dressed and…very *tasty*…looking suits jump down…from the stands…and try to…break up..the fight I truly realize how damned…I am…when a man is…attractive to me…in any way, much ..less as…a possible meal.

Coach Martin rolls…a little too close into the designated feeding area…and Lord does he…pay the price for…such carelessness.

They…know…how dangerous we….become when we…are feedin'. I guess…seein' his MVP get…handed his head, so to speak….allowed the coach to forget this…little fact. Before any of us…know what is happenin', Luther and Dog have…Martin pinned between 'em. One is munchin' on his scalp, while the other….pulls his chest…apart with three or four quick …tugs. One of…Coach Martin's shirt buttons…hits me in the forehead, then sails off onto…the court, along with

228

a portion of his...spine.

Within seconds...it was like one of those...damn food fights we used...to have...in college. Coach Griggs...was shown no mercy...either. He had...rolled into the fray with those two suits...punchin' and gougin' at him.

Willie, Brent, and....Kenyon Miller are takin' turns bitin' chunks out of both the suits, while Dog and Juluis are now...in the middle of Coach Grigg's midsection, both...their heads buried...neck deep inside...his tubby. gut.

Before I know it, and as it always does, my appetite overwhelms my initial...nausea and...my own mouth gets busy.

We hear the sirens comin' outside. We know the ref's called in...the marksmen. He blew away...a few...but must have. ran outta ammo.

Everybody is havin' such...a good time, we...are beyond carin'.

They'll bring in. the guns in a few and...scatter the insides of our rotted, ecayed brains all...over the court. We invite it. Looks. like the league is...gonna have a ...personnel shortage. Two less...teams to count on for...attendance and...revenue. On well, life's a bitch...and then you die...and resurrect...and die again...

***

I bounce the object...once or twice before passing it...up court to Dog, who...dunks it happily through the now...crimson stained net. We...all stop and begin clapping. For just a moment...we feel like...Pro's again. Role models...millionaires fortunate enough...to play a kid's game for...a living. Brent scoops up the ball...Coach Grigg's badly...mutilated head...and throws it up court to me.

I only pause to take a quick bite, then I sail a tray from...the top of the key The net swishes just as the...first shotgun blast is heard.

I raise my hands in...final victory I spit out...part of an earlobe. I turn to the crowd...and wait for that *final* buzzer to sound.

***

I see most of you shaking your heads in disbelief. Well, believe it, folks. There are senior staff members at the in-processing center who witnessed these 'undead' sports leagues in all their unholy gruesomeness. Again, this bears witness to the shocking vileness only the human species seems capable of cultivating.

Before I delve into the next chapter, I want to thank you folks for your kind cooperation in allowing the staff their bloodletting jollies. Now, the colas and peanuts are on us...enjoy. For the record, barring any unforeseen roadblocks or mechanical delays, we are now less than forty-five minutes from the in- processing center.

This next segment centers around a rare breed of man who actually seemed to revel in the plague's fatal aftermath. Apocalyptic 'Road Warriors' of a sort, this strange sort traveled the deserted roadways like modern day nomads, the 'wandering gypsies' of the undead plains. Unfortunately, such men and woman had an extremely brief life expectancy, and the demise they suffered was hardly ever pleasant in nature. Witness such a case...

11 - Dawn of the SENTINEL

"You sure 'bout this, Earl? I mean, D.C. must be one overrun som'bitch by now, y'know?"

Earl Kramer burst out laughing, his knee accidentally turning the steering wheel of the Ford F150 to the left, sending the large truck squealing towards the guardrail.

With a grace and fluidity that only an experienced drunken driver could manage, he passed his open Budweiser from his right hand to his left and snagged the wheel, straightening the vehicle's trajectory until it centered the white line.

Earl scowled as thick strands of beer foam hung in his bushy beard like frothy soap suds.

"Damn it, Todd! Do you wanna be Vice-President or not? I thought we already cleared this shit up 'fore we left T-Town."

Todd Wain, who at twenty-two years of age was the larger man's junior by eighteen winters, leaned back wearing a horribly insincere grin.

"S-sure, Earl. I just meant that all those stinkin' sons of bitches must be roaming the streets in packs in a city the size of DC. You don't think we'd be walkin' into a hornets nest up there?"

Earl kept his bloodshot eyes glued to the abandoned roadway while reaching underneath the truck's seat for a fresh brew. A second later he popped the can open and took a healthy swig, then belched loudly, sending droplets of malt and barley splashing onto the already filthy windshield.

"Listen up, son, we've got all we need in the back of this rig to take care'a whatever we run into along the way. We've got forty-fives, thirty-eights, forty- fours, thirty-gauges, twelve gauges-even a couple of M-sixteen's. Hell, we got enough ammo to hold 'em off at the White House for a year if we had to."

Burping softly after a lengthy sip of his own, Todd braced himself as they topped a steep hill doing at least eighty-five.

"Yeah, but there's only two of us, Earl. I mean to say, if…if they surround the truck or back us into an alleyway or somethin', we might end up bein' the main course at a Zombie buffet, right?"

The truck flew through a steep curve and Earl abruptly slammed on the brakes, sending the truck skidding hard to the left and Todd sprawling onto the driver's lap. Beer suds flew onto the dash and windshield as Todd's brew took flight, and Earl laughed crazily as they finally rolled to a complete stop. Earl playfully shoved Todd back into the passenger's side seat, simultaneously grabbing a twelve-gauge from the gun-rack hanging behind his head.

"I don't like ya that much, Todd-O, even if ya are gonna be my running mate. Right now, I need to chew the fat with some potential voters…pardon me, son."

Exiting the truck more gracefully than his bulky, two-hundred fifty pound frame should have allowed, Earl gave Todd a cheery wink just before strolling to the front of the pick-up.

Todd leaned back with a yawn once he spotted the origin of his partner's excitement.

"Man just loves makin' sport of 'em. Earl…you

232

are one seriously sick puppy," he mumbled to himself, casually propping his hands behind his head.

Three of them shambled drunkenly down the center of the highway, their eyes glazed, their mouths agape and drooling. They had obviously smelled fresh meat in the general vicinity and were drawn to it like flies to a picnic. With the exuberant glee of a young boy firing his BB pistol at a live target for the first time, Earl shouldered the rifle and fired off three quick shots.

The first nailed the larger of the three, a white male who looked to be in his mid-forties at the time of his first death, or *'DEFCON 1'* as Earl had so amusingly labeled it. The top of the man's skull was sheered away just above the bridge of his nose, his wobbling torso taking several shaky steps forward before collapsing in a heap at the feet of target number two.

She was a heavy set, middle-aged woman of Hispanic descent whose coal-black hair was rolled into a tight bun at the tip of her scalp. She sauntered forward without benefit of a left foot, leaving a moistened slug trail in her wake. The shot blew off the upper left side of her head, the bun amazingly hanging on for dear life although half its base had vanished into the misty night air.

The woman fell almost directly on top of the man as a series of convulsions ensued, ending with a final, violent death-tremor that sent her rolling into a nearby ditch.

Target number three was a young black male of perhaps sixteen or seventeen at the time of his untimely passing.

Todd could have sworn he saw various acne related rashes still running rampant on the kid's forehead and chin. Earl bellowed out a raucous '*Ye-haaaa*' just before sending the kid's head screaming across the asphalt like a gore- coated bowling ball.

Earl hopped over and booted the ruined corpses a few times before returning to the truck, giggling maniacally as he turned the ignition.

"Talk about your multi-cultural family, I guess they were just out searchin' for a good take-out joint. Call me warped, Todd-O, but blowin' those dead-head bastards back to hell never fails to give me a mental boner."

As Earl pulled back onto the highway, Todd frowned while opening each of them a fresh brew.

"Wish I felt the same way, Earl ol' buddy. Just makes me wanna hurl my cookies."

His massive belly jiggling like a tub of soft tofu, Earl howled with laughter until the tears sprang from the corners of his eyes in thick streams.

"You kill, me Todd-O! Your gonna make a fine Vice Prez! A true credit to your species, yes sir."

Feeling fortunate that they hadn't run into a roadblock of any kind since departing Tupelo, Earl sipped his beer while Todd chewed on a stick of beef jerky. The vehicle cut through the murky dimness of the dusk at a dramatically reduced speed when compared to daylight hours. Todd offered Earl a piece of jerky, to which Earl passed on with a wave of one massive hand and a resounding belch.

"Bet you miss Regina pretty bad, huh boy?" Earl inquired in a casual, insincere tone that seemed to originate more from boredom than true interest.

Todd chewed noisily, staring into the passing darkness outside the passenger side window while scanning his inner-mind's picture files for just the right mental image of his former co-worker and sometime girlfriend.

"Damn straight I miss her, Earl. I mean, it just ain't fair that the dead- head's got to her 'fore I did. Just think, I'd be getting me some prime leg every night instead a' hangin' out with your gnarly ass."

Earl slowed the truck to near thirty and swung by an abandoned Chrysler Cordoba that had been left half parked onto the highway. He took note of a stiff, fleshless hand protruding from the car's driver's side as they'd cruised by.

"You nail her much, Todd-O? That pretty little thing polish your knob on a regular basis?"

Throwing an empty out the passenger's window, Todd leaned toward the dash and turned to stare at the larger man, his expression suddenly grim and comically serious.

"Earl, that girl wasn't the easiest to warm up, but once she got there you could just lay back and enjoy the ride. It was more than just the humpin' though. We had a lot in common, you know? She had the night shift stockin' at the warehouse and I was on days. We used to see each other for coffee in the mornings, her comin' off and me comin' on. We used to go out to the Plex and watch flicks. Truth be told, Regina could drink Jack Black like a man. She even used to laugh whenever I ate too much Beanie Weanie and got on one of my fartin' binges. Yep, special woman, she was."

235

Playfully fanning his right hand in front of his nose, Earl scowled sourly. "Brewskie does bring out the gas jockey in you, don't it? You release the hounds?"

As if on cue, Todd raised his left leg, grimacing as if in extreme pain, and released a long, shrieking fart. He then fell back against the cushioned upholstery, laughing so violently it soon transformed into a coughing fit. "Geez, you're a pig, son, I can't believe she ever let ya touch her."

As dawn began to lighten the freeway, Earl spotted a fenced-in farmhouse at the bottom of a wide, grassy valley. He braked and slowly turned onto a gravel drive leading to its front entrance. He'd been searching for such a structure for several hours, his eyelids drooping heavily and his shoulders slumped from exhaustion, both aftereffects from the eleven hours he'd driven and the sixteen beers that had been consumed along the way.

Todd awoke with a start as the truck first sank into and then bounced out of a deep, jagged pothole.

"Wha- where the hell are we, boss?" he croaked, reaching up with the forefingers of both hands to rub his eyes.

Earl instantly brightened as the homestead swam into view.

"Home sweet home, son. We have arrived at the Earl and Todd ranch, just in time for a warm plate of grub and some much needed shuteye."

"What… time is it anyhow?" Todd managed before yawning.

Earl glanced at the shiny Rolex attached to his

right wrist. He'd picked up that particular jewel a few weeks back in Jackson at an abandoned mall that had been dead-head free.

"Five-eighteen, Todd-O. We've made almost eleven hours since T-Town.

I figure another days drive should put us in is the middle of good ol' Virginny, then it's just a hop, skip and boot scoot boogie down the road to our new permanent digs. How's that hit ya?"

Scratching the stubble atop his pointy chin, Todd fought off another yawn. "Sounds like a plan, Big E. How long I been out anyhow?"

Pulling up and parking on the left side of the house, Earl cut off the ignition and set the emergency brake.

"Two or three hours, tops. I saw a couple of pale skins sittin' on the porch of a run-down trailer just outside Memphis. They were both suckin' on femur bones. I thought about stoppin' for a little target practice, but you was out like a light and I didn't want to interrupt your beauty nap. Lord knows ya need it, Todd- O." Todd managed a warped smile and practically fell from the truck's passenger side as he exited.

Each posed a few feet from the front porch and took in the surroundings It was a red brick, ranch style home that looked no older than ten or fifteen years. The mailbox out at the highway had read '*Dr. Robert Waxley, MD*'. There were no vehicles parked in the drive or underneath the covered carport. Thick scrubs that hadn't seen clippers since '*D day*' grew wildly at the corners of the house, and dozens of thick, ropey vines, known commonly in the southeast as 'kudzu', were overtaking the screen door at the house's entrance.

Earl stretched leisurely, then reached underneath the bed cover at the truck's rear and pulled out a tightly packed Army regulation duffel bag. He armed himself with a forty-four magnum revolver, ensured it was indeed loaded, then waited on his slower partner to follow suit. A moment later, Todd joined him in leaning on the grille of the truck while loading a thirty-thirty he'd retrieved from the bed.

"I'll police up the inside, old buddy, you patrol the surroundin' grounds.

Meet ya inside."

Todd nodded, struggling to stifle yet another yawn.

"Check. If I hear a shot, I'llbe in quicker than white on rice to back ya up." Earl patted him gently on the back.

"Same here, Todd-O. Just like that time at the Post Office back home. If you hadn't been there to torch ol' Zeke, I'd surely be a dead-head myself. I still have nightmares 'bout him chasin' me around my back yard, tryin' to have me for Sunday Brunch. Man had delivered our mail since I was knee high to a blue tick hound.

"Gotta admit, just the thought gives me the Willies."

Strolling away toward the back of the house, Todd dropped his duffel on the outside of the wooden porch.

"Yeah, Earl. The more I think about it, I believe it was one helluva good idea to get away from the hometown when we did. I don't think I could handle blowin' away members of my own family or any of the old gang from high school."

Earl took the first two steps of the porch cautiously, then paused.

"I hear ya, Todd. Choppin' off my Grandpa's head with a mower blade soured my ass real quick on hangin' out with the relatives."

Approximately an hour later, Earl lay spread eagle on a spacious leather couch, his pasty bare feet protruding off one end and his thick arms suspended from the sides. He resembled someone attempting to create a 'snow angel' without benefit of snow. His snorting, high-pitched snores echoed through the living room and into the kitchen, where Todd sat and slowly consumed a box of slightly stale crackers with a can of unheated chili. Todd so wished he could sleep as peacefully and carefree as his partner. He figured he hadn't had more than three hours at one sitting since 'D-Day'. It was simple logic to pin the blame for his chronic insomnia on simple paranoia. The thought of waking up to a dead- head gnawing on your ankle or sucking the intestines out of your gut like linguine noodles was enough to ensure sleep deprivation became just another part of daily living.

As he sat and munched with the freight train huffs of his partner ringing in his ears, Todd glanced at the nearest wall and noticed a 'Far Side' Calendar hanging just above the microwave. As with most he had come across since 'D- Day', it was frozen on the month of May He found it almost unfathomable to believe it had been just over five months since the

239

insanity had begun. Earl had been the one to suggest they get out of Springville and find out '*if the rest of the States had become one big-ass Shoney's breakfast buffet*'.

They had held up in the city's water department building for the previous three months, only venturing out when supplies ran low. The water department facility possessed concrete walls that were three feet thick, and offices that were underground. Todd had felt slightly claustrophobic at times during their stay, a condition Earl had labeled 'sardine syndrome', but at the same time, knew it was the safest place to be to avoid the starving masses and their seemingly insatiable appetites. True, he was glad they'd left that stinking, rotted town behind, though the open road had thus far provided little proof that things were much better anywhere else.

The two had been attacked numerous times in the three days spent on various two-lane highways heading northeast, avoiding the interstates since Earl figured they might well run into a roadblock littered with wrecked cars and ripe bodies. Without a doubt, the worst of many dicey situations had gone down at a gas station just outside Birmingham.

***

They had set up a procedure that when fuel was needed, one would pump while the other stood guard at the wheel, weapon in hand. After numerous attempts at finding a station with working pumps, they finally pulled into a BP just on the outskirts of the city and prepared to fill up both the tank and a trio of five- gallon jugs they'd brought along for back up. Earl had topped off the tank and was in the process of filling the second jug when Todd had spotted them.

The first had shambled from the shadows of the open garage, an old man missing half his left leg and dragging it around in his right hand as if searching for someone to properly reattach it. Todd's first shot blew the old man's left ear onto a far garage wall, pinning it there like a Velcro rag. The second had blown a half- dollar sized hole into and completely through his skeletal chest. By then, Earl had retrieved a twelve gauge from the truck bed and fired at will, casually depositing the old man's head against a nearby gas pump, which was drenched in strips of gore and blackened bodily fluids.

Todd had been leaning against the driver's door, cursing his pathetic aim, and had not seen the grotesquely bloated corpse sneak slowly toward him with its maggot-ridden mouth agape, eyeballing the soft, fleshy region between his neck and shoulder. Earl leaped up from where he'd been crouched while fueling, and half-tackled Todd just to get him out of the creature's path. Todd's left forearm had swung back as he was being hit, connecting with a loud crunch against the thing's crisp, dry-rotted nose. The thing, which in happy, healthier times might have once been a rather plump black female, staggered back with a look of comical shock on its watermelon-sized face as the majority of its nose landed with a soft plop onto the greasy pavement. Seconds later, his face beat red with rage, Todd practically stuck the barrel of his thirty-eight flush against the thing's right temple and fired. The rotund corpse spiraled back against a large display filled with spare tires, the close range of the shot literally blowing the face apart in torn, ripped sections of pus, blood and bone. Afterwards, it had taken a moment for Todd to realize that Earl was screaming something at him from the other side of the truck. Todd glanced around quickly as the origin of his partner's panic became readily apparent. A grouping of at least a dozen or more undead were piling out from the inside of the garage's oil pits, and were slowly making their way toward the truck. Earl had already thrown the gas jugs into the bed and was sitting in the driver's seat, bellowing at Todd to join him or soon they'd find themselves getting 'lubed and oiled' by the hungry masses. Todd snapped out of his self-imposed daze just as the first few bodies squirmed outside beyond the open garage doors As Earl pulled out, he got off a single shot that opened up the abdomen of the largest of the walking corpses, sending its blackened intestines sprawling onto the concrete like a nest of bloated snakes. To state the obvious, nary a tear was shed as they'd departed the bright lights of Birmingham.

***

Todd ate the last of the crackers, then poured himself a glass of warm bottled apple juice, the contents of which had been found in a large wooden cabinet filled with canned and bottled juices. It seems the good doctor had been stocking up on canned goods before either being chased off by roving bands of deadheads or, worst of all, had the unfortunate experience of joining their ranks. Either way, both Earl and Todd rejoiced over the ample supply of canned soups, potted meats, and juices they had discovered stocked neatly inside the kitchen cabinets.

Walking silently upstairs while the snorting and snoring of his partner only seemed to increase in both frequency and volume, Todd decided to execute a more thorough walk-through of the good doctor's spacious abode.

The master bedroom held nothing of interest save a large oak dresser sporting a line of framed photos indicating the doctor had been married and had a young son and teenaged daughter. The photos appeared recent, while the couple on display looked to be in their early to mid-forties. The son was perhaps ten at the outset, with bucked teeth and 'jumbo' sized ears.

Poor kid. Bet he caught hell for those elephant sails.

The daughter was pretty in a down home sort of way, with long blonde hair hanging from her thin shoulders, her tiny bosoms obviously still in the 'blooming' stage. She had deep, piercing blue eyes that reminded Todd of Regina.

Damn shame Girl might'a been a real knockout in five or six years.

Heartbreaker all the way.

He collapsed onto a neatly made King -sized bed and threw his hands behind his head, sighing loudly.

Lot of bright futures snuffed out that day, for sure. Yours truly included, truth be told.

'D-Day' was what the media had labeled it as newsrooms across the country were bombarded with reports of the rising and recently dead attacking the living. CNN had labeled it simply "*Day of The Dead*", while each network had created their own catchy headline to describe the primal madness that had overtaken the country in what seemed like record time. Todd had been stocking cycling equipment when he was told to 'go home and lock the doors' by his immediate supervisor, a grotesquely overweight individual with horrible ache named Lane Wilkes. He recalled Lane's sickly, panic-stricken expression, as if the man had just swallowed a Twinkie smothered in castor oil. Lane had only been perhaps five to six years older than Todd, but that morning had appeared to have aged a full decade within the scant span of a few precious hours. Todd had first heard of the wide-spread madness while driving home in a daze, lamenting the loss of income that comes with 'getting off early' from a job that barely paid him enough to support his half of the rent on a rat-trap apartment.

Various scientists and behavioral experts were already spouting their overblown theories of why the recently dead were suddenly back in circulation, and with a serious 'Jones' for human meat. Prime suspects ranged from the Ozone Layer to contaminated drinking water to the shifting of planets in the Solar System, with one particular government-employed egghead calling it an 'overblown case of mass hysteria'.

Within twelve hours, both CNN and MSNBC were off the air, soon to be joined by the networks and all other form of mass communication, to include internet and radio transmissions. Todd's roomie, a guy he'd met on the job six months earlier named Carl Fratner (everybody had called him *'Fart-ner'*, though he never seemed to find that particular nugget the least bit amusing) had driven up to Ohio to visit his parents a few days before. Todd had sat on a cheap imitation leather couch the two purchased together and clicked the TV remote in- between fixing a ham sandwich and some Chicken Noodle soup. After an hour of random flipping from channel to channel in dumbfounded awe, he'd ultimately paused to check on Regina He figured she was probably asleep after working the midnight shift, but felt she needed to be made aware of all the craziness going on.

It was around noon when he'd called, meaning she'd probably only slept a few hours at best; a fact her overly perturbed tone had born out. Todd had instructed her to turn on the news, ignoring her initial crankiness. She'd said (in a groggy, less irritable manner) that she'd check it out after a stout cup of Joe, then call him back a bit later. Todd would never hear her voice again.

Oh, he *had* seen a rather unappealing latter version of Regina stumble toward him with cold, carnivorous eyes, her scalp peeled clean and the majority of her fingers eaten away. He'd driven away from her house as fast as his ragged Honda Civic would allow, a little surprised and disappointed that the strongest emotion he'd felt was not sorrow, but pure *disgust*. In truth, though they had been close friends *and* sexual partners, neither had actually loved the other. In fact, Todd had never loved anyone save his parents, both long deceased from a car accident during his junior year in high school. He'd been on his own for almost five years, and had developed a relatively thick skin from early tragedies and traumas. A younger sister had died of leukemia at age five, while his grandparents had all passed in his early to late teens. He'd met Earl once he went full time at the store, and they had hit it off right away. Both were born pessimists, and the living hell the world had become came as no real surprise to either.

Earl had more ex-wives than dollar bills in the bank, had drank like a fish since his Navy days (late teens to early twenties) and had lived alone in a small trailer on the outskirts of Springville for the previous three years, cultivating a tiny but very lucrative pot crop. During their stay in the 'Four Walls Plaza' as Earl had nicknamed the Water Department's downstairs offices, Earl had revealed to Todd (over a few dozen brews) that he didn't shed nary a tear for the world and the ungodly mess it found itself in. Earl would giggle at the thought of never paying another dollar of child support for kids he'd never known (and wasn't totally convinced were his anyhow) and wives he had never truly loved (only lusted after).

Todd and Earl were the *Batman* and *Robin* of the Armageddon, and proud to answer to such eccentric titles.

Todd dozed as the bed became more comfortable, but deep sleep never seemed to find him. He couldn't help but be fitfully amused at the 'master plan' Earl had dreamed up, tickled to no end by the sheer ridiculousness of it.

Earl figured that most of the population, give or take a few thousand, were either walking worm dirt or undigested deadhead buffet. This meant everyone, from the Commander in Chief of the good old USA to the Russian Premier to the cart pushing, homeless bums taking up space on street corners in every mid-sized city in the country. Earl's plan was simplistic, pointless, imbecilic, and was just the sort of spontaneous lunacy Todd had been hoping would snap him out of his 'why bother living at all at this point' haze.

They would hang the Confederate flag's *Stars and Bars* over the capitol in D.C. and proclaim themselves President and Vice-president of the New "United States of the Immoral and Politically Incorrect". Todd had belched up that particular nugget as they'd shared a bottle of Jim Beam inside the basement of the Water Department. Earl had loved it, so much so he'd spit a thick stream of J. Beam out of his nose in a fit of howling laughter.

And so a plan had sprung from their alcohol-fevered minds. A plan that was completely without logic or common sense. Translation: a plan whose time had definitely come.

Thus, they had emerged from their underground prison and hit the back roads on a journey literally without meaning or just cause, but born from boredom and an ample amount of dementia laced insanity.

Todd awoke from his doze at the sound of a beer tab being pulled. He trudged slowly down the stairs and met Earl in the kitchen. His partner in crime was eating unheated Chili straight from the can, his beard suspending a few of the beans in mid-air like fresh catch in a fisherman's net.

"Breakfast of champions. You been snoozin' upstairs?" Earl mumbled between bites.

Todd began half-heartedly nibbling on a stale donut.

"Tried to anyhow. I think my shut eye button has been permanently placed in the off position."

Earl snorted amiably.

"Ya mean those 'ludes we picked up at that pharmacy ain't helped any?" "Nah. Just gives me a headache."

"Well, shotgun a cold Bud or three right before ya hit the sack. That'll put ya in La-La land, for sure. That's Doctor Earl's prescription, anyhow."

Throwing the uneaten portion of the powdered donut into the trash, Todd stood and stretched his arms, yawning loudly through chapped lips.

"Lots of grade-A canned supplies here. Good old Doc must have seen it coming."

Sighing loudly, Earl leaned back and rubbed his massive stomach. "Yep. Flat lot'a good it did him There probably ain't enough left of Mr.

Sawbones and his family to put in a cigar box. Let's stock up and get the hell outta dodge. We can make Lynchburg by nightfall."

An hour later, the truck backed out of the graveled drive and toward an open, eerily dead highway, various canned foods and soft drinks, along with a case of Busch beer found in a side closet, stocked tightly inside the bed.

248

As they crossed into Virginia nearly two hours later, both were secretly relieved that no dead-heads had been spotted along the way. For Todd, the thrill of hunting them down like in-season deer had passed soon after the gas station incident outside Birmingham.

About the time dusk had begun to fall, they spotted a large ranch home sitting on a distant cliff. By that time, each had consumed a healthy snoot full of hops and barley, and figured the Cliffside mansion might just be ticket for a good night's collapse.

Todd sincerely hoped the house grounds were free of roaming cadavers, as he doubted his aim when he was sober, much less when seeing double from the effects of a half case of beer.

The paved drive they had exited onto eventually led to a forked dirt path a mile or so up a steep mountain range, and Earl cut sharply to the left as just the very tip of the house's tiled roof came into view through a thick wall of foliage.

"Beautiful countryside here," Earl slurred, beautiful pronounced "Boo-ti- ful." Todd managed to nod in agreement, though an actual worded reply escaped his foggy mind.

As they parked in front of a thigh-high, rod-iron gate fronting the property, there was just enough light remaining to allow a full, majestic view of the spacious surrounding grounds.

Todd instantly thought of an old TV show he'd once watched called "*Houses of the Rich*", or possibly "*Homes of the Very Fortunate*", which had featured documentaries of celebrity homes.

Their chosen refuge was a two-story brick with wide glass living room windows and a solid oak front door that was at least twelve feet high. At first glance, Todd thought it resembled the entrance to an old English castle. The black rod-iron gate surrounding the house looked as if it had just been recently erected, or perhaps received a fresh coat of paint.

Both men exited the truck and stood silent for a moment, listening for anything other than the familiar noises *normally* associated with wooded, remote areas. Earl then limped over to the truck's bed and pulled a pearl-handled revolver from underneath the cover. He tossed Todd a rifle and small flashlight. Todd caught both items shakily, coming dangerously close to tripping over a small hedge before regaining what was left of his balance.

"You want inside or out, my man?" Earl asked while stuffing a large wad of Red Man chewing tobacco into his left jaw. In his severely inebriated state, it took Todd several moments to properly decipher the meaning of his partner's query. Finally, he stumbled forward towards the paved walkway leading to the colossal front door.

"Got the house, dude," he slurred.

Earl nodded sheepishly and strolled toward the left side of the home in a comically slumped pose. Even in his brew induced stupor, Todd was mildly taken back to find the door locked tight. All the other homes they'd 'borrowed' along the way had been as open as a twenty-four hour liquor store, some with doors standing wide open as if the owners had been advertising the fact that the days of

250

deeds, mortgages and rent paying were a thing of the past.

Two vicious, if not a bit off target, kicks to the doors solid oak midsection sent it flying back, the lock's metal hinge tearing off and sailing inside the darkened foyer within. His flashlight held out like a crucifix warding off unseen evil forces, Todd went from room to room, discovering along the way that the house was actually larger on the inside than it looked from the front drive.

Each bedroom room was filled with top of the line furnishings, including solid oak dressers and king-sized beds with lace covered canopies, while the spacious living room held a pair of matching genuine leather chairs and twin plasma TVs complete with matching DVD/VCR combination units and a home theater/stereo system. As was the case in most modern households, seemingly every room contained both a computer and TV of some variation.

Todd couldn't help but note, even in his present state of inebriation, just how meticulously clean and neat the place had remained, despite its abandoned state No evidence of even the thinnest layer of dust present on any of the furniture, nor a single dangling cobweb. He entered a roomy kitchen that held what seemed like enough pantry space to house a small army's worth of canned goods. He strolled past a mammoth refrigerator and glanced out a wall-sized window located at the rear of the room. There he spotted Earl standing on the back patio, his revolver hanging loosely at his side. His partner appeared comically perplexed while reaching up with a free hand to scratch his bushy noggin. He truly resembled a man frozen at a fork in the road, trying desperately to figure the correct path to take.

After a moments pause, Todd unfastened the chain lock on the back door and joined him on the wide, wooden deck.

Earl turned to him and grinned, then simply pointed toward the back yard without speaking. Todd leaned over the deck's crisscross railing and gasped aloud.

"Shit, Big E…what was this place…a used car lot?"

At least a dozen automobiles of various makes, models and ages were parked in a perfectly horizontal line atop the grassy grounds, as if they'd been purposely positioned for scheduled maintenance In the background stood a large, perhaps twenty by thirty feet, metal utility building.

Earl made his way clumsily down the wooden steps leading to the vehicles, while Todd remained on the deck, his bleary eyes now attempting to focus on the metal structure looming in the distance. It looked like one of those 'build it yourself' storage units, only a bit larger, and surrounded on all sides by tall shrubs that looked recently pruned.

"Well, what do ya know, Todd-O! We got a brand spankin' new Expedition down here with a grand total of eight thousand miles on 'er! I just may trade in the old 'pick 'em up' truck after all."

Seconds later, Todd joined him in the yard, his attention still trained on the storage building. He noticed it had three separate Master locks hanging from its only door, and that all three were presently engaged.

"What do ya think is in *there*, Earl? Somebody has it locked up like Fort Friggin' Knox," he said, following Earl around as the larger man checked out the mileage on an older model Monte Carlo. Earl turned and gave the building a quick, token glance.

"Who knows? Rich guys keep their garages full of tools, work benches and shit like that. Name brand *shit* more than likely, and hardly ever used.

"Hey, what do ya think about that Dodge Ram over there? I believe she's a two-thousand eight model, but she's only got fifty thousand miles under her belt. I know I said I'd never trade in old faithful, but man, it sure is tempting."

Todd shrugged, giving the same fleeting attention to the vehicles as Earl had the storage building.

"Can't blame ya, Earl. The new President of these here United States deserves a slick ride. Hey, I'm gonna slurp me one final beer and crash.

"Gotta tell ya, the inside of the mansion there is something to behold, brother. Fancy smancy..."

Earl giggled, slapping the badly oxidized hood of a Ford Mustang that had seen better years.

"I hear ya, Todd-O. I'll go check the kitchen for some eats, then probably hit the sack myself. Ya know, this place might warrant stickin' around a few days, just for a rest from the rigors of the road, am I right?"

Nodding wearily as he stepped back towards the deck, Todd tossed the barrel of his rifle across his shoulder.

"Sounds like a plan, Big E. It ain't like we have

253

some kinda appointment to meet anywheres else, right-O?"

"No truer words have ever been uttered, little buddy."

As potential cure for his insomnia, Todd chose the master bedroom. The room held a dresser almost as large as the truck they'd arrived in, with mirrored walls and a large screen TV that took up an entire corner. As he stripped down and lay across the soft, thickly blanketed mattress, he could have sworn he smelled freshly sprayed disinfectant emanating from the small bathroom just outside the bedroom door. In the pitch-black darkness of the powerless mansion, he eventually drifted off, never noticing that he'd been treading on recently waxed floors.

**

His head pounding painfully from the virtual boatload of beer consumed the day *and* night before, Todd stumbled out of bed just as the morning light illuminated the pulled curtains.

Through badly bloodshot eyes, he glanced at his watch while propped over a near spotless toilet, casually noting that it read 5:46 AM. Satisfied that he had actually slept almost five full hours without waking, he changed into a semi- clean T-shirt and stumbled haphazardly towards the kitchen.

As he made his way down a lengthy, curved hall leading to the living room and subsequently the kitchen, Todd's gait abruptly slowed as he studied the framed pictures lining the surrounding walls. Each picture looked to have been taken on the grounds of the home, yet each differed in the people they displayed save one inexplicably strange similarity.

An older man dressed in what appeared to be an identical pair of faded overalls was present in each shot, a toothy, somewhat grotesque smile covering his weathered, darkly tanned face. In photo number one, he grasped a shovel in liver-spot ravaged hands while encased on all sides by three children that looked to be in their early teens. In the next shot, he was holding a rake and flanking a gray-haired man wearing a black suit and a middle-aged woman sporting a light blue sundress. In still another, the old man wore gardening gloves and held a pair of oversized pruning shears as a pretty young girl of perhaps sixteen leaned against his left shoulder. There was something about the man's wide, predatory grin that caused Todd to openly cringe. It was a smile that seemed totally identical in each photo, as if someone had pasted his face into each frame.

"Huh. Must be the groundskeeper. Creepy looking dude."

The kitchen table was layered in empty cracker wrappers and a pair of stained soup bowls.

"Looks like Big E had the midnight munchies last AM," Todd muttered, wishing he had a handful of Extra-Strength Tylenol to wash down with the bottle of lukewarm grape-juice he was nursing.

After deducing that a house of such mammoth proportions must hold at least three or four full bathrooms, Todd decided to check out the medicine cabinets in each for some much needed hangover relief.

He knew they probably had some type of pain

reliever in the truck, but didn't feel like disorganizing the *organized* mess that their traveling HQ had become since leaving Springville.

About the time that Todd ran across a half-empty bottle of Excedrin in a bathroom discovered on the West side of the house, it suddenly hit him that the house was completely silent, eerily so, save for the faint sounds of birds chirping outside the paned windows. The familiar freight train-like blaring of his partner's snoring should have been cutting a crease through the morning quiet, as was generally the case. Figuring that Earl might be outside searching through the truck, Todd dry swallowed three Excedrin and then headed for the front of the house. He noticed the front door standing slightly ajar as he neared, but quickly disregarded that as just another sign of Earl's presence outside.

He pulled the heavy oak door open and stepped through, then abruptly froze in his tracks while still hanging halfway inside the house.

The truck was gone. The paved area where it had sat held a small circular stain of leaking oil as the only proof it had ever been parked there. Leaving the front door open, Todd half-jogged toward the back of the house.

He cruised through the kitchen, almost slipping on a puddle of unidentified liquid as he paused to exit onto the deck. He leaned over the railing, breathing hard as his eyes scanned the parked vehicles they'd inspected the night before. The truck sat parked next to a red Honda Accord that had a large, circular dent on its hood.

Frowning deeply, Todd couldn't understand why Earl would've moved the truck from the front of the house He stepped back into the kitchen and reached into a nearby cabinet for a bag of unopened potato chips. A moment later, a warped smile cracked his unshaven face; his baggy, bloodshot eyes lighting up as much as his hangover would allow.

"Of course. That's it. He was probably movin' the supplies from old faithful there to the new vehicle he picked out for the rest of the trip. Whew, I gotta lay off the suds for a few days. Gonna kill off all the brain cells I got left, and Lord knows I ain't got a surplus to spare."

After chugging down the rest of the grape juice and eating a handful of chips, Todd rose groggily from the kitchen table with the intention of finding his missing partner. He walked purposely through the house, pausing at the threshold of each room to yell Earl's name in a grasping croak that was the definition of bone-weary.

Todd felt the first pangs of worry begin to build as no response was forthcoming from inside the house, then felt the worry grow into a barely restrained panic as he realized he hadn't seen hide nor hair of his friend outdoors either.

He walked back to the front of the house, pausing only to pull open the front door, then stopped.

"Waitaminnit. Wait one damn minute here. Didn't I leave this heavy sombitch open just a few minutes ago? Who the hell closed it back, the tooth fairy? I'm either losin' my marbles, or Big E is playin' some seriously sick mind games. Let's just hope it ain't the former, old buddy."

He pulled the door open with a single jerk, gasping from the effort, then lurched forward through the open space. He'd managed to complete only one full step before impact, his arms flailing wildly as he fell back onto his backside with a resounding thump.

The figure wore faded blue jean overalls literally coated from the shoulder straps to the leg hems in a reeking mix of dried and moistened gore. The figure's wide, aware eyes were fiery red, while in complete contrast, its complexion was waxy and ghostly white, as if coated in cooking flour. It possessed no ears, just jagged, crimson holes seeping orange-shaded pus. The corners of its mouth shook and its slug-lips trembled. Its front teeth were broken and jagged, as if shattered by the pointed edge of a chip hammer.

Todd yelped as if physically goosed, scooting backwards while using his hands and feet to shoot across the living rooms thick, shag carpet like a scampering spider. Crashing head first into a marble nightstand, Todd rolled onto his back just as the figure's leering face leaned over his own. He felt strong, icy cold fingers clamp around the whole of his neck and begin to squeeze, increasing the pressure until his lungs caught fire and his vision faded to streaking shadow. Gagging from the stench of rancid, decomposing meat, Todd soon slipped into a realm of numbing tranquility that was as strangely soothing as it was terrifying.

***

258

Blinking rapidly, Todd's double-vision gradually cleared as blurred images slowly drifted into focus. His hands had been tied over his head with tightly coiled rope. He could feel the coolness of the metallic table on the naked flesh of his back. His feet felt similarly bound at the rear of the table, and what might have been duct tape held his neck and head stiffly against the flat surface. He managed to turn his head just enough to the left to see his captor standing only a few feet away.

The figure was slumped over a table similar to the one Todd was strapped to, its face hidden in shadows that managed to elude the sunlight breaking through the storage building's open door.

The stifling air within the confined space was rancid, like spoiled meat wrapped within a cocoon of equally rotten vegetables, and Todd struggled to refrain from heaving.

The flesh of his neck burned and ached from the earlier throttling, and his left shoulder felt weirdly disconnected, as if it had been separated and subsequently popped back into place at an awkward angle. He briefly strained against his bonds but felt nary an inch of give.

Cocking his eyes to the right, he locked onto several disjointed shapes that, at least initially, held no familiarity whatsoever. However, upon looking away momentarily and then back to said images, Todd felt the air lock in his throat as his mouth fell open in a silent gasp. Never one for practicing religion, Todd nonetheless prayed to whatever God might exist that he be immediately awakened from the hellish dreamscape that had chosen *him* as its leading man. Much like the infamous '*train wreck*' scenario, he found the simple act of turning away a virtual impossibility.

Image number one: The man who'd been one of the hallway photos, decked out in the neatly pressed suit, now hanging by a steel hook on the far Eastern wall. Armless and with only a portion of his right leg intact below the knee, the top of the man's head looked to have been sheared off by a power tool, his right eye dangling onto his lower jaw like an unfurled yo-yo.

Image number two: The middle-aged lady who'd been featured in the same aforementioned photo wearing a lovely blue sundress, now hanging beside the man who had accompanied her in that particular Kodak moment, also via a thick steel hook. The woman's lower body had vanished below the waist. Thick coils of intestine swung freely a few feet below her torn midsection as an army of bloated flies circled the dark cavity that had once been her torso's midway point.

Image number three was a kaleidoscope of various horrors Bits, pieces and whole sections of severed and dismembered body parts hung from the wall like hunting trophies. Arms (with or *without* the connecting hands), legs, ears, feet (with or *without* the connecting ankles) and rib cages all mounted like spare parts marked for sale at a ghoulish flea market; some from hooks and others secured to the wall with twenty-penny nails. There was even a cadaver lying spread eagle on the concrete floor a few feet to Todd's right, though proper identification was made impossible by a blood-splattered wool blanket that covered it from head to toe.

By the time his mysterious captor whirled around to face him, Todd had already began screaming. The piercing shrieks were soon downgraded to gasping moans by the time he realized it was human fingers protruding from his captor's mouth like gnawed breadsticks. The figure leaned down and groaned, accidentally dropping a severed finger onto Todd's exposed chest.

It then reached over and playfully tugged at Todd's right ear, all the while humming a familiar ditty Todd struggled to properly ID. Seconds later, Todd screeched in anguish as the figure tore the lobe free with a violent jerk before casually popping it into his open maw like a piece of hard candy. Todd could feel the warm wetness running down his neck as his continuing struggles against the binds grew increasingly futile. His breathing harsh and labored, he released a mournful sigh, closing his eyes tightly as if expecting a final, fatal assault that never materialized.

He opened his eyes in tiny segments, only to discover the figure was nowhere in sight. Todd's ear stung and pulsated from the loss of its lower half, but he quickly dismissed it as a mere inconvenience compared to what might befall him if an escape route wasn't soon found. Sucking in several deep breaths, he began assaulting his binds with renewed fervor. Following several minutes of intense struggles, he found the rope pinning his right hand and wrist to the table loosening somewhat, and concentrated all his remaining strength on that specific bind. Realizing it might be mere seconds before the figure returned, he gave the rope a final, brutal twist that tore it apart at the forearm.

Todd was peeling the masking tape from his neck when he noticed that the form lying beneath the blanket to his right had shifted. As he worked on the ropes binding his legs and ankles, he saw the body openly twitch and gyrate in a jerky spasm. Pulling the ropes free from his calves, he sat up with a muffled huff, then was barely able to refrain from howling in terrified shock as the mutilated bodies, as well as the dozen or more detached parts, all began to shimmy and shake as if electrified.

An audible click escaped the back of his parched throat as he leapt from the metal table, a naked man spattered in tiny, crimson splotches from his feet to his scalp. Just as he'd spun from the tabletop and landed with bare feet onto the cool stone flooring, he noticed the figure's still shadow parked just over his left shoulder.

Todd managed to duck just as the figure's arm whooshed over the top of his head, barely connecting with the tip of his skull. He quickly dropped to the floor, rolling onto his left side and then back to his feet, his hands balled into fists. He felt something moist and clammy brush across his left ankle, and glanced down for only a split second as not to lose focus on his assailant.

Todd's mouth fell open to scream, only to discover that particular function was temporarily out of service. His internal 'shriek meter' was pegged out and no longer able to comply with mental commands. For at least the third time in the previous hour, he felt the air choke off in his throat as a bolt of stark fear stabbed his midsection like an icy spear.

Earl crawled from beneath the wool blanket, dragging himself along with his lone remaining arm. Todd's partner and former running mate was missing most of the right side of his face, while the left side was embellished by deep- grooved tooth marks and torn flaps of shredded flesh that hung free in thick flaps. Todd brought his left food down heel first, crushing Earl's skull against the concrete floor with a loud crunch. Todd backed away as gray matter spurted and oozed from the massive hole like runny oatmeal. Earl leaned up from the massive puddle of gore the kick had created, grinning devilishly at his young protégé with what few remaining teeth he owned before collapsing in a heap.

Todd whirled about, searching frantically for a weapon, and eventually found a long wooden handle that had once had a hoe or perhaps a shovel blade attached to it, holding it out from his chest in a decidedly defensive posture.

The figure lumbered towards him in a clumsy gait, its arms held straight out from its chest as if sleepwalking. Todd began swinging the handle back and forth like a man attempting to strike a fluttering butterfly in mid-flight.

Todd could see the body parts wriggling and squirming in the background like beached fish, a few of which had fallen from the wall and seemed to be actively pursuing him. He noticed that the chained hooks that had previously held them now swung free like kite strings in a stiff breeze.

Backing against a far wall, the force of his swings becoming less and less aggressive, Todd came to a rather abrupt and horrific realization as to precisely what his part was in this particularly gruesome stage play. In verbally stating his case, though utterly unaware he was doing so, Todd repeated the identical refrain continuously even as the only potential escape route was being systematically blockaded by a virtual swarm of detached organs and severed limbs.

"Nooooowwww I understand," he cackled gleefully, frothy spittle flying from his chapped, shriveled lips, 'the *Sentinel* here rang the dinner bell, and I'm gonna be the main course! Am I right? That's it, right? The *Sentinel* is cook, gardener, housekeeper…just one multi-talented som'bitch, is he not? Talk to me people…TALK TO MEEEEEEE!!!!!!"

It was painfully simple, really, if one possessed the required amount of common sense. All those who had come before he and Earl, the ones who'd owned the deserted vehicles parked in the back yard, had been similarly duped and then utilized in the same manner. Drawn in by the majestic beauty of the home and its tranquil surroundings, they had all let their guard down, temporarily forgetting the potentially fatal consequences that might derive from doing so.

They had thought the home a temporary safe haven from the ungodly carnage; the insanity; the unbearable madness. In turn, they had all paid an equally ungodly price.

He and Earl, the self-proclaimed '*Kings of the Road-Kill*', had indeed fallen for the same simplistic trap. They had delivered themselves like Chinese takeout to a ruthless, merciless Sentinel whose lone duty was to protect and feed those he had for so long dedicated his entire existence to. Without active brain waves, it acted purely on instinct; habit; memory. Simply put, The Sentinel continued to perform his sworn duty to the best of his capability. Death could slow, but not halt his one-minded, three-tiered mission. *Maintain* the grounds; *protect* the family; *feed* the family. The Sentinel would do as it had always done; adapt…overcome…succeed.

Todd threw the handle at the caretaker, who watched in puzzlement as it bounced off his fleshless noggin and clanged uselessly to the floor. Todd used the brief diversion to dart for the open door, but was tripped up after only a few short steps.

He flew headfirst into the same metal table that just minutes ago he had been tied to, striking his left temple and setting off a fireworks display in both pupils. Shaking off the blows effect by sheer will and a heavy dose of adrenalin, Todd slid blindly beneath the table and rose onto his hands and knees, only to be hauled out by the ankles and wrists and then pinned onto his back by what felt like two dozen separate hands.

"G-get get…off me…you d-deadhead… son…s-som…b-bit…ches…!" he croaked as greedy fingers reached into his mouth and gripped his tongue.

His left arm broke free and swung around in a wide, looping arc, connecting with something pliable and moist. Before he could even attempt another punch, his arm was pulled back to the stone floor. Todd felt warm, sticky fluids fill his eyes like poured honey, then coat his face, lips, neck and chest in a gooey cascade. Unable to control his own bodily functions as his struggles grew weaker, he began vomiting from the overwhelming stench of decayed flesh.

He felt the first bite near his left ankle; a sharp, piercing pain shooting up his spine, though there was little time to dwell on such virgin agony before the next set of teeth bore into his right thigh.

Todd's eyes opened periodically but were unable to focus on anything other than a frenzied series of rapidly shifting blurs. He did manage to catch a brief glimpse of the Sentinel, standing erect and perfectly still in the background like some dime-store wooden Indian.

The majority of Todd's nose was ripped free just moments later, cartilage snapping like brittle twigs under the force of the ravenous bite. The skin was pulled free from his right elbow with a loud flapping noise, like a bed sheet hanging in a stiff wind, and Todd felt the initial stages of merciful unconsciousness finally begin to settle over his battered senses.

Something or someone was tearing at his jeans near the crotch area as the blood from his ruined nose poured onto his face in a cloudburst of crimson.

All things faded mercifully to black just as he felt a dull gnawing sensation at his groin.

***

He awoke with a gasp, a hacking cough almost

266

spilling him from the bed as he pulled his knees to his chest in the textbook 'fetal' position.

His face and forehead were coated in warm, sour-smelling sweat, which he wiped away with a naked forearm while slowly rolling his legs over the side of the mattress. The coughing fit having finally subsided, he tiled his head back and inhaled long and deep, holding his breath for a full ten seconds before exhaling wearily.

"Lord, what a nightmare. Trip city, dude. I do believe that's the third such mind bender just this week."

Wobbling into the bathroom, he splashed his face with cool tap water and gradually began to feel the fog lift at least somewhat. A half hour later, as he sipped his second cup of steaming black coffee, the return to normalcy was near complete save the inexplicable weakness in his muscles and joints.

"Might be coming down with a virus. Lot of sick pups roamin' around the plant lately,' he mumbled, finishing off the cup with a final swallow, 'can't have that, no sir. Gotta bring home the full paycheck or something's getting hocked or repossessed."

Twenty minutes later, he pulled into a large, fenced in gravel lot marked 'Employees Only', grinning sheepishly as a mud-splattered Ford F150 swam into view from his left. He parked his Honda next to Earl's ride and stifled a yawn, stretching as he exited the vehicle's cramped confines.

He entered the well-lit warehouse with a wobbly gait, strolling past several rows of pilled wooden pallets and through a chained-link fence to a small gathering of familiar individuals congregating just outside the supervisor's office. As was normally the case just before first shift officially began, the group was loud and raucous.

Todd reached for his time card, barely noticing that the gang had fallen deadly silent since his arrival. After swiping his card through the narrow slot, he turned about and instantly locked on Big Earl, who sat facing away from him at the end of a long conference table. Grinning despite the bone-weariness that refused to subside, he pocketed his time card and strolled forward, braking after only a few steps.

"What the hell, over?" he muttered, reaching up to scratch his head beneath his 'Atlanta *BRAVES*' cap.

The entire group either sat or stood with their backs to him. He recognized several just from their profiles. There was Sally K. from records; Jimmy Hemstrot from Shipping; Mac Desmond from Fulfillment.

They sat or stood in utter silence, nary a single twitch of movement between them.

Moving ahead with baby steps, Todd ignored every logical instinct and proceeded to reach cautiously forward, tapping Big E on his massive right shoulder.

"H-hey dude, you ain't gonna believe the... nightmare I had. Seriously, we gotta lay off the zombie flicks, pal."

Earl neither budged nor verbally responded, and Todd suddenly became aware of an awful stench; like raw, bloody meat on the verge of turning permanently rank.

Frozen in place, Todd's mind wavered, and he felt his knees grow ever weaker. He heard wet, slurping noises. Suddenly his body aches seemed to intensify ten-fold.

He glanced down at the hand he had placed on Earl's shirt. It was coated to the wrist in crimson-shaded slime. He glanced back up and his breath caught in his throat like a man trapped in an underwater tomb gasping for nonexistent oxygen.

Though Earl's body was still facing the opposite direction, the big man's head had twisted a full one-hundred eighty degrees; his cold, shark-like eyes locking on Todd's with predatory intensity.

A large chunk of Big E's skull looked to have been sheared off with a chainsaw, leaving it weirdly octagon-shaped. The big man sized up his former partner and giggled hysterically, revealing a mouthful of bloody teeth as thin as syringe needles.

Regina then appeared as if magically teleported, standing beside Earl with ragged, dark holes in the place where her ample breasts had been. Her lower jaw had been ripped away; the upper plate trembling madly as though trying to speak or possibly chew without benefit of a bottom row of teeth.

Behind them both suddenly appeared the *Sentinel*, his overalls meticulously cleaned and pressed. The smile he displayed was the warm, jovial sort one might expect from a long-missing relative, though there was an obvious undercurrent of malevolence lurking just below the surface.

The Sentinel held a trio of large serving plates in his hands He passed one to Regina and the other to Earl, who regarded Todd with an amiable nod before speaking through cracked, peeling lips the color of ash.

"About time ya got here, Todd-O…we've been waitin', ya know. Can't start a shift on an empty stomach, and since the breakfast truck took the day off…I guess we'll just have to make due…"

Earl's grin grew to grotesque proportions, and Todd clearly saw a bloated roach briefly emerge onto the tip of the big man's tongue and extract its lengthy feelers before scuttling back inside.

"Ya see, we drew straws, little buddy…

…and you lost. Come to Big E now, Todd-O…man my size needs his nourishment, and ya know what they say…breakfast is the most important meal of the day."

Todd turned to run, but discovered his lower extremities were no longer adhering to mental commands. His arms were lead and hung useless at his sides; his feet submerged in fast-drying cement.

Their cold, lifeless hands gripped him in a dozen separate vices, lifting him airborne and tossing him onto the conference table as the air filled with bloodthirsty, guttural growls. Although closing his eyes allowed him to elude their predatory stares, Todd was unable to block out the rancid air slapping his face in putrid waves. He fell into an uneasy, fitful realm of numbing unconsciousness, wherein he dreamed of literally being stripped alive.

***

Waking as his head shakes violently, Todd discovers the searing pain has mercifully passed, as

270

if he were trapped within the powerful throngs of an extremely strong pain-killer. He initially believes he has gone blind before his eyes slowly adjust to the darkness and the items around him begin to gradually take shape.

He feels a sense of unbridled relief flood his battered mind, and attempts to exhale but finds he cannot. He hears a hinge creak as a door opens slowly to his right.

Just enough light illuminates the room to allow Todd a clear picture of his present situation.

He wriggles madly, but discovers the hook is imbedded too deeply into the pit of his back. He peers to his left and stares directly into the hollowed eye sockets of a severed head hanging from a similar hook wedged into its jagged neck.

The head is Big Earl's, the corners of his mouth turned up in his familiar 'good ol' boy' grin.

Todd watches The Sentinel grasp a large meat cleaver, swing it overhead, and begin systematically chopping a set of bare, severed legs until the femur bones glow white in the swirling shadows.

Purely from instinct, Todd glances downward. He thought those particular legs looked familiar.

All those damn *zombie* movies had it all wrong after all, Todd muses as his fragile mind finally snaps like a rubber band stretched to the breaking point.

The Dead do indeed feel pain…

…The Dead also feel a sense of loss….

… and despite an obvious lack of oxygen…

…The Dead can also *scream*….

***

I'm sure there were a small minority of such wonton travelers who did manage to discover permanent asylum along the vast highways of the World, though the odds were obviously stacked against them. Overmatched and hopelessly outmanned, most would eventually fall victim to their own carelessness, done in by a false sense of security that no longer existed in such a mad, chaotic realm. This concludes the initial in-brief, people. You can all now breathe a collective sigh of relief. As I advise all newcomers to this strange and dangerous new era, the main thing to keep in mind is to never, and I mean ever, let your guard down. Such old-World terms as 'watch your back', or 'cover your ass' still apply, no matter the situation or location. That isn't to say trust no one. The colony is packed with good-hearted, caring individuals, many of which have been in your shoes.

We have become a close-knit society by necessity. All the unwarranted strife, racial injustice and bitter hatred of one's fellow man are no longer issues. All that said, there are still those amongst our rank and file who put their own selfish needs above the needs of all others. Be wary of those who would put you in harm's way.

In the society you are about to enter and become a part of, we have but one single-minded mission; survival. It's a daily struggle, and one that consumes every waking minute of every new day. I wish you luck in your new lives, and sincerely hope you are able to find a fraction of usefulness from this briefing.

Yes, it was gruesome, graphic, and might have

even seemed a bit over the top, but it isn't our intention to shock or revolt. We pull no punches for a reason, people. Soon, you'll understand why.

Well, well...the incessant buzzing in my left ear must mean we have arrived at our destination, folks. Please excuse me one final time.

(THREE MINUTES LATER)

Okay group, we have indeed arrived at the 'Welcome Mat Hotel'. I've been told a steaming buffet supper awaits, as are separate rooms complete with a fresh change of clothes, clean linen, and hot shower capability.

You have a question, Mister Vincent?

Yes, sir...the buffet is indeed priority one (laughs). Fourteen main courses, as I understand. I can see that ravenous look in everyone's eyes. Well then, by all means let us go quench it.

Why yes, Miss Jackson, it will indeed be a relief to remove this cursed chemical suit and officially greet all of you 'face to face'. I sincerely look forward to sitting down to a good meal with a new group of friends. You just don't know how invigorating it is for us old-timers whenever new blood arrives within the colony.

(FIVE MINUTES LATER)

That's it, Miss Oldham, step easy. It's only natural that your equilibrium is a bit off. Food and proper rest will assist in rectifying that particular malady.

Why yes, Mister Caldwell, as I understand it, this particular Grand Hotel was indeed the site of several Miss USA pageants in the late 20th Century, as well as one of the last Democratic Political Conventions ever held. Thirty stories containing two-hundred twenty five rooms and three separate convention halls. I wholeheartedly agree, Mister C. 'Majestic' is truly the only word that does it justice.

No, Misses Jackson, you are at least the fourth such group we've rescued in the past several years. The last was near the city of Denver...a class of sixteen if I recall correctly.

Step carefully now...I understand your hunger, but it isn't worth a trip to the infirmary. Interns Gordon and Cronenberg will lead you through the vast lobby to the equally colossal dining area. Enjoy the meal, folks. I'll see you soon...in the meantime, bon appetite...

(THIRTEEN MINUTES LATER)

Quiet down, everyone! Quiet down, please! Let us raise our glass and toast the new arrivals! Ah...good wine, good food, and dare I say...the best of company.

Folks, in just a few moments you'll be formally introduced to the Colony's duly elected President, currently serving his third full term as our Command in Chief.

Once again, let me apologize for the temporary power outage and delay in serving the scheduled dinner. There were...complications with the main generator that were unavoidable. For now, enjoy the wine while I do my best ad- lib and attempt to keep you at least semi-entertained.

The following is normally the introduction to the second lecture you would receive upon arrival, and usually isn't given until the following morning. Be that as it may, allow me to 'jump the gun' as it were, while we await the president's arrival. I think you'll find it quite...intriguing.

In the twenty-one years the fourteen of you have been...let's just say 'away', the nature of the enemy has gone through a rather dramatic transformation.

While the plague originally birthed a mindless army of ravenous ghouls utterly without the powers of reason or logical thought, a gradual metamorphosis began to transpire under the watchful eye of Doctor Williem G. Dermitzen, a German-born pathologist and plague survivor who put together a crack staff of physicians and scientists. Scientists whose radical experimentation, however controversial, eventually led to the subspecies that now dominates the landscape in a manner their more savage, less intelligent brethren could never have possibly done.

Much like the plague itself, this sweeping change, once given life, saw the landscape beyond altered dramatically within a relatively short span. This dominant species has now ruled the land for almost two full decades, spreading its infectious wings over five continents. When broken down in scientific terms, it is truly an amaz-...why, I do believe I see a raised hand piercing the shadows....yes, Mister Caldwell, is it?

Drowsy did you say? Well, I'd have to check

with a member of the medical staff, but it's more than likely just the effects of the wine on an empty stomach. Miss Jackson, you're feeling the same? Oh, I'm seeing a show of hands now. Maybe the wine idea was a mistake. Um, everyone please refrain from further consumption and maybe the feeling will fade once you begin eating.

Now, to continue…ah, the commotion to the left of the stage can only mean one thing, folks. The main man, our trusted leader and the founding father of our colony, has arrived!

Ladies and gentleman, it is my pleasure to introduce, the honorable Doctor William G. Dermitzen!!!

(A light spattering of applause from the rear of the hall) "Thank you, Phillip, and good evening, dear guests. Let me reiterate our regret at the lack of lighting. I've been told it's only a matter of minutes.

Alas, as a trained medical professional, I must say, the lot of you appear to be suffering from extreme exhaustion. (long pause) Excellent. The sedative is working its magic. Now, now…don't be alarmed. Believe me, there is a method to our madness.

Oh dear. Phillip, we may have underestimated the fatigue factor with this particular group. Even through this murky dimness, I see some of them have that 'about to keel over' appearance. I must 'cut to the chase' to use the vernacular,. that is before consciousness is completely lost. You see, an explanation is in order, I believe. In all honestly, it is the least I can do.

276

While you were indeed brought here to join our thriving little colony, you will first serve a much more vital role...that of life giver. I know, I know...I hear your confused mumblings...please, let me finish. The blood taken from you earlier wasn't for testing, you see, but for future cloning cycles. Simply put, it is how our...race maintains and replenishes.

Again, although I cannot view your faces clearly, I can almost feel your befuddlement.

To save precious time, let me state this as bluntly as I know how. The fourteen of you were indeed rescued, revived, and transported here for a promised feast, and a feast we shall have! Unfortunately, it shall be at great, albeit temporary, expense to you.

Lights on, Phillip...it's SH-SH-SHOWIME!!

(bright fluorescent lights flash overhead as muffled gasps fill the spacious chamber)

Oh, I was afraid of this. Happens every time without fail.

Sadly, our pale, pasty, openly frightening appearance is but one of many reasons we are forced to retain anonymity until the sedative takes full effect, thus the bulky chemical suits my loyal staff are forced to endure.

(Gasping, choking sounds)

Folks, folks, please don't embarrass yourselves....all this screaming, shrieking and whining serves no purpose, nor will it alter the inevitable outcome.

Yours is a noble, if not somewhat forced, sacrifice. Don't ruin it with all this childish negativity. True, we are admittedly deceiving in our methods, but over the years we've found the practice of honesty to be less than effective in terms of convincing folks such as you that this is truly an honorable act. The main reason for the charade we so expertly perpetrate is, however, medically motivated. To use laymen's terms, the chemical agents used to effectively utilize Cryogenics require a three to four hour block to be successfully 'purged' from the human waste system. This self-cleansing of the inner organs is mandatory for...what is next on the agenda.

Phillip did not prevaricate when explaining that we truly have evolved as a race.

Though we do still depend somewhat heavily on raw, unprocessed meat as our primary source of energy and growth, alternate food sources are currently being developed to slowly wean us off said dependency. By the close of this decade, the term 'Ghoul' will hopefully, and happily, no longer apply!

Mister Caldwell, please put down the cutlery and submit without further incident! There is no need to suffer needlessly, people! Our preparers are trained to sever only the major arteries, thus limiting any physical discomfort to a minimum! My god, we are not the simplistic savages of old. I can promise you, no one will be 'eaten alive' under this man's administration. Consumed YES, but never while alert or aware. I am, after all, first and foremost, a man of medicine!

Now, as I alluded to earlier, your DNA samples will ensure a glorious rebirth for each of you.

Additionally, you will be celebrated as such, adorned with specially engraved birthmarks that label each of you as 'Replicas of the Renaissance,' wherein special privileges are automatically awarded.

To conclude (pauses)...excellent job retrieving the steak knife, Warren. At least Mister Caldwell wasn't able to cut into an artery. I cannot help but cringe whenever they resort to self-mutilation in the name of suicide.

As I was saying (clears throat), to conclude...

Yes, dear friends, soon you will join us as trusted allies...this I can promise as I will personally oversee the cloning as it pertains to each and every one of you...

But...as for today... This minute...

This historic moment in time...

You provide my colony with something equally essential...

...nourishment!

Sleep well, my flock...

I will see you on resurrection day! (long pause)

Phillip, they seem adequately sedated... Let us begin with the Termination Phase... My minions...

Let us begin... to feed...

(The hall fills with a chorus of weak, pathetic cries which quickly subside, to first be replaced by the sounds of flesh, muscle and sinew being flayed, ripped, and torn asunder, and finally by moist, sucking noises as bones are licked dry and gnawed into minute fragments)

***

As we take our final, gasping breath and our

bodies are reduced to pulse- less husks, there lies the daunting task of assigning the disembodied soul to its final destination. As the following tale attests, such a decision isn't nearly as cut and dry as one might think.

12 - SOUL EVALUATOR

DATE: 2006Y March 24th D
TIME: 1835 Hours/Eastern Daylight Time
LOCATION: Undetermined

"Files are uploaded whenever you're ready. If I may be permitted, sir, it's quite the eccentric bunch today. Truly one extreme to the other."

"Par for the course of late, Aaron, par for the course. Numbers please" "Three subjects for placement."

"Fine, fine (sighs wearily)."

"Deadline for final decisions is 6 AM eastern daylight time, sir. Celestial Judge Cantrel will be in contact to record your findings."

"Understood, Aaron. Goodnight."

"Goodnight, sir, and um…good luck on your new position. It's been…an honor and pleasure working with you. The department will surely miss one of your considerable talent…and um…professionalism."

"Appreciate the kind words, Aaron. You've been a worthy assistant. I will recommend you for promotion without hesitation."

"Thank you, sir. Goodbye." "Goodbye, Aaron."

(Connector inserted into brain stem port; files instantaneously downloaded. File one visuals fade in; series of three photos at top of screen, typed text (on bottom)

First photo (far left-hand corner) displays subject at age eighteen (legal age)

Second photo (middle) displays subject at age thirty-five.

Third photo (far right corner) displays subject at age fifty-seven (two days before expiration).

SUBJECT BIOGRAPHICAL INFO:

CASE #2006Y – March 24D-41,245
NAME: Brenda Gale Wainwright
AGE AT TIME OF EXPIRATION (Years/Months/Days): 57Y-8M-4D
RACE: Caucasian
SEX: Female
COUNTRY/CITY OF BIRTH: Louisville, KY (UNITED STATES) **RESIDENCE AT TIME OF EXPIRATION:** Fort Wayne,Indiana (USA) **EXPIRATION DATE ASSIGNED (Y/D/T):** 2006Y-January 20D-1345H
HEIGHT/WEIGHT AT TIME OF EXPIRATION: 5 Feet, three inches – one- hundred ninety-three pounds.
CAUSE OF DEATH: Coronary Failure (Heart Attack) **MARTIAL STATUS:** Widow (Spouse expired 2001Y-3M-21st D) **SURVIVING OFFSPRING:** Milton (son). Age: 28Y-2M-19D **NON-SURVIVING OFFSPRING**: None.
OCCUPATION: Medical records clerk (administrative).
RELIGIOUS BELIEFS: Conservative Christian. ACTIVE at time of expiration.
PERSONALITY TYPE (Three descriptive words or phrases): Loud, opinionated, kind hearted.

MEDICAL HISTORY (Pertinent ailments only. Excludes minor cases such as colds, flu, etc):

YR/DATE: 1979/August 12th
AILMENT: Stomach pains
TREATMENT: surgical - gall bladder removed
RESULT: full recovery

YR/DATE: 1985/Dec 14th **AILMENT:**Broken ankle **TREATMENT:** surgical **RESULT:** full recovery

YR/DATE: 1991/Nov 10th **AILMENT:** Chest pains **TREATMENT:** non-surgical
RESULT: on-going treatment of chronic heart disease

PERTINENT PERSONAL STATS (Starting at legal age (18): CRIMINAL FELONIES COMMITED (Y/D/T): None.
CRIMINAL MISDEMEANORS COMMITED (Y/D/T):
Traffic citations only.
CRIMES AGAINST HUMANITY (UNDETECTED):
ASSAULTS (Simple): 1
ASSAULTS (Aggravated): 0
ASSAULTS (Sexual): 0
THEFTS: 1 (shoplifting charge at age 19 – Not detained or charged)

PROFANITIES USED (Since age 13): 63,121 (38% below average for thirty-nine year span)

UNTRUTHS (vernacular: LIES) TOLD since age 18: 2,255 (45% below average for thirty-nine year span)

MASTURBATION **FREQUENCY** (Beginning Age: 13): 561 total – approximately 44 occurrences per year (45 % below average)

INITIAL CASE EVALUATION (recorded under case CASE #2006Y – March 24D-41,245): *"Sooooo, what we have here is your basic housewife and homemaker with a malfunctioning ticker whose sole vice was not being able to push away from the dinner table. Thus, carrying that extra eighty pounds of body weight proved to be her undoing. As far as placement, nothing complicated about this one. On to case number two..."* File two visuals fade in; series of three photos at top of screen (typed text at bottom)

First photo (far left-hand corner) displays subject at age eighteen (legal age).

Second photo (middle) displays subject at age twenty-five.

Third photo (far right corner) displays subject at age thirty-four (three days before expiration).

CASE #2006Y-March 24D-41,246:

NAME: Juan Rivera Gonzales

AGE AT TIME OF EXPIRATION: 34D-11M-13D

RACE: Hispanic

SEX: Male

COUNTRY/CITY OF BIRTH: Mendio (Mexico)

RESIDENCE AT TIME OF EXPIRATION:
Pharr, Texas (USA)

EXPIRATION DATE ASSIGNED (Y/D/T):
2006Y-Feb 23D-1523H

HEIGHT/WEIGHT AT TIME OF EXPIRATION: 5 Feet, eight inches – one- hundred sixty-five pounds.

CAUSE OF DEATH: Homicide (gunshots to head, neck, and abdomen).

Shot to death by wife (Lucinda) of fifteen years.

MARTIAL STATUS: Married.

SURVIVING OFFSPRING: Juan Jr (son) age: 11Y-4M-2D; Maria (daughter) age: 9Y-3M-13D; Julio (son) age: 6Y-3M-19D; Manny (son) age:4Y- 10M-14D; Stephanie (daughter) age: 3Y-3M-4D.

NON-SURVIVING OFFSPRING: None.

OCCUPATION: Construction worker.

RELIGIOUS BELIEFS: Atheist (non-practicing)

PERSONALITY TYPE (Three descriptive words or phrases): Gentle (when sober), caring (when sober), maniacal (when inebriated)

MEDICAL HISTORY (Pertinent ailments only. Excludes minor cases such as colds, flu, etc):

YR/DATEAILMENT TREATMENTRESULT
None.

PERTINENT PERSONAL STATS (Starting at LEGAL AGE (18): CRIMINAL FELONIES COMMITED (Y/D/T): None.

CRIMINAL   MISDEMEANORS COMMITED (Y/D/T):

1991Y-Oct 5th D-1845 hours.

Charge: Spousal abuse. Alcohol related. Outcome: Charges dropped.

1991Y-Nov 9th-D-2153 hours.

Charge: Spousal abuse; drunk & disorderly. Outcome: Three days in country jail. Probation. 1992Y-May 2nd-D-0124 hours.

Charge: Spousal abuse. Alcohol related. Outcome: Charges dropped.

EIGHT SIMILAR CHARGES LISTED (Last in 2005Y-March 9th-D-1625)

CRIMES AGAINST HUMANITY (Not DETECTED):

ASSAULTS (Simple): 87

ASSAULTS (Aggravated): 1 (Resulted in Homicide – see *NOTE* below)

NOTE: Was involved in an altercation outside a Hidalgo, Texas bar at age nineteen. Subsequently, Juan Rivera Gonzales (inebriated at time of incident) stabbed another subject in the stomach with pocketknife, ultimately resulting in the subject's death.

ASSAULTS (Sexual): 1 (fondle only; no penetration)

THEFTS: 1 (gas drive-off at age twenty).

PROFANITIES USED (From age 13): 4,921,202 (35% over average for twenty-one year span)

UNTRUTHS (vernacular: LIES) TOLD since age 18: 3,562 (6 % below average for sixteen year span)

MASTURBATION   FREQUENCY

(Beginning age: 13) 1,237 total – (approximately 60 occurrences per year - 8 % above average) **INITIAL CASE EVALUATION** (recorded under case CASE #2006Y – March 24D-41,246): "*A real rarity Alcoholic wife beater with a relatively clean record otherwise. Reputed to be a hard worker, caring father and steady provider for his family. Yes, A rare bird indeed. Wife had suffered a broken nose, several shattered ribs and numerous contusions the night she shot him down in self-defense. Man had consumed thirteen Budweiser long-necks and half a pint of Tequila the evening of the incident (sighs). As was normally the case, he began to accuse her of infidelities. Ahh yes, the devil's brew is a mighty instigator of mayhem. Cut and dry, this isn't, especially considering the listed lack of faith. Onto to case number three:*

File three visuals fade in; series of three photos at top of screen (typed text at bottom).

First photo (far left-hand corner) displays subject at age eighteen (legal age).

Second photo (middle) displays subject at age thirty-two.

Third photo (far right corner) displays subject at age forty-four (two days before expiration).

CASE #2006Y-March 24D-41,247:
NAME: Rutger Grimrich
AGE AT TIME OF EXPIRATION: 44Y-10M-22nd D
RACE: White
SEX: Male

COUNTRY/CITY OF BIRTH: Stuttgart, Germany

RESIDENCE AT TIME OF EXPIRATION: Stuttgart, Germany

EXPIRATION DATE ASSIGNED (Y/D/T): 2006Y-May 14D-1122H

HEIGHT/WEIGHT AT TIME OF EXPIRATION: 6 Feet, two inches – two- hundred forty-two pounds.

CAUSE OF DEATH: Drug overdose.

MARTIAL STATUS: Single.

SURVIVING OFFSPRING: None legally listed; sired five illegitimate children from four different women, ages 14 to 59, two via rape

NON-SURVIVING OFFSPRING: None.

OCCUPATION: Sold illegal narcotics.

RELIGIOUS BELIEFS: Raised in Christian faith; abandoned during teen years.

PERSONALITY TYPE (Three descriptive words or phrases): Mean; vicious; unmerciful.

MEDICAL HISTORY (Pertinent ailments only. Excludes minor cases such as colds, flu, etc):

YR/DATE: 1992/Dec 11th **AILMENT:** Drug Overdose **TREATMENT:** Detox
RESULT: Refused full treatment

YR/DATE: 1994/Nov 9th **AILMENT:** Drug Overdose **TREATMENT:** Detox
RESULT: Refused full treatment

YR/DATE: 1996/Mar 24th

AILMENT: Gunshot wound

TREATMENT: Clinical Released following two surgeries

RESULT: full recovery

YR/DATE: 1997/Jan 4th

AILMENT: Stab wounds

TREATMENT: Clinical Released following surgery

RESULT: full recovery

YR/DATE: 2002/Aug 29th

AILMENT: Concussion/Abrasions

TREATMENT: Clinical Released following three-day hospital stay

RESULT: full recovery

YR/DATE: 2004/June 10th

AILMENT: Gunshot wound

TREATMENT: Clinical Released following surgery,two week hospital stay

RESULT: Lost use of right arm, partially paralyzed

PERTINENT PERSONAL STATS (Starting at LEGAL AGE (18): CRIMINAL FELONIES COMMITED (Y/D/T):

1985Y-Jul 8th D-2144 hours.

Charge: Breaking & Entering; theft. Possession of marijuana and other drug-related paraphernalia.

Outcome: Conviction. Placed on three years' probation. 1989Y-Feb 21st D-0456 hours.

Charge: Possession of cocaine with the intent to

distribute. Outcome: Freed on technicality.

1994Y-Sep 3rdD-0714 hours.

Charge: Possession of prescription narcotics with the intent to distribute Outcome: Convicted. Sentenced to four—six years in state penitentiary.

Paroled after serving twenty-two months. Placed on two years' probation 2000Y-April 2ndD-2043 hours.

Charge: Possession of stolen handgun. Possession of crack cocaine.

Possession of marijuana.

Outcome: Convicted. Sentenced to five years in state penitentiary.

Paroled after serving eighteen months. Placed on two years' probation.

(NOTE: At time of expiration, was found to possess heroin, cocaine, and LSD on person. A coroner's report proved conclusively that overdose was due to all of the above)

CRIMINAL MISDEMEANORS COMMITED (Y/D/T):

Fourteen items shown from 1983Y-Jan 5th D to 2005Y-Oct 20thD to include all traffic violations (six) and simple assaults (5).

CRIMES AGAINST HUMANITY (Not DETECTED):

ASSAULTS (Simple): 46

ASSAULTS (Aggravated): 3

ASSAULTS (Sexual): 11 (to include forced sodomy on a minor) **THEFTS:** 22 (to include shoplifting and pickpocket activities) **PROFANITIES USED** (Since age 13): 242 (89% below average for thirty-one year span)

UNTRUTHS (vernacular: LIES) TOLD since age 18: 19,240 (26 % above average for twenty-six year span)

MASTURBATION   **FREQUENCY** (Beginning age: 13) 5,856 total – (approximately 208 occurrences per year - 58 % above average) **INITIAL CASE EVALUATION** (recorded under case CASE #2006Y –

March 24D-41,247): *"What we have here is the textbook definition of 'sexual deviant'. Rapist; compulsive masturbation; various sexual assaults, to include victimization of minors. Inexplicably, the man virtually never cursed. Strange for one prone with such undeniably violent tendencies. Toss in drug-dealing, drug using, drug abusing thief, and we have what is termed in baseball jargon as a 'five tool threat'. To dismiss as 'purely evil' is, as always, a bit on the trite side. Doling out a justifiable afterlife for such individuals is never quite as easy as outlined in the Evaluator manuals.*

As Aaron mentioned earlier, this is truly an eccentric trio. Sometimes it is hard to fathom how members of the same species can stand at such opposite ends of the behavioral spectrum.

I must admit, such quandaries do add to both the curiosity and fascination factors within my chosen field. Although I sincerely look forward to my new assignment in alterations, there is no doubt my tour in evaluations has been the most satisfying in the afterlife section.

Ah, decisions...decisions. Well, as the man said, let's get to cranking.

***

DATE: 2006YMarch 25ᵗʰ D **TIME**: 0559 Hours AM Eastern Daylight Time

"Have you come to a definite conclusion in each of the three cases presented?"

"Yes, sir, Celestial Judge."

"Confirmation complete. This verbal exchange will later be transcribed as an official documentation of those decisions."

"Understood, sir." "Please proceed."

"In the case of Brenda Gail Wainwright, case number 2006Y – March 24D- 41,245, I recommend placement at the fourth level of the higher plain."

"Reservations or notations?"

"No, sir. A kind, good soul, Miss Wainwright. If not for a fiery temper and a flare for stubbornness that bordered on the extreme, I could have easily recommended a level five placement."

"Duly noted Proceed to next case."

"Yes, sir. In the case of Juan Rivera Gonzales, case number 2006Y, March 24ᵗʰ D-41,246, I have no choice by regulation but banishment into the lower realm. The aforementioned homicide strictly forbids my deciding otherwise, thus eliminating all but level placement. Thus, I recommend the subject be placed at level four of the lower realm."

"The least harsh of all levels?"

"Yes, sir. The homicide in question, if tried in a court of law, could have easily been labeled self-defense."

"Duly noted Proceed to next case."

"Yes, sir. In the case of Rutger Grimrich, case number 2006Y-March 24ᵗʰ D-41,247, I highly recommend 'RR' status be granted."

"Per celestial law, Please explain your reasoning for recommending Rebirth Reincarnation."

"Yes, sir. As you well know, I am a staunch supporter in soul rehabilitation."

"Um, yes, well documented. Go on..." "Mister Grimrich was, no doubt, a rather despicable individual. The proof is well documented. He was both a rapist and pedophile, and seemed to take wicked pleasure in the harming of others, both physically and psychologically.

Not only a dealer in deadly, mind-altering drugs, but also an addict to same, he spent a forty-four year existence literally caring for no one but himself. That said, all indications are that this blackened soul is indeed repairable."

"I take it your research is complete on this matter"

"Yes sir. All indications are that Grimrich, once reborn as a young Filipino girl, will eventually be sold into prostitution and slavery. Through her childhood and teenaged years, she will be beaten and brutalized by her captors, as well as by the multitudes of sadistic men and women who pay handsomely to do so.

Given time, indications are that the girl will enter the nun-hood and positively influence many lives, thus having suffered the retribution due. Grimrich's dark legacy, she will have allowed for the rehabilitation of same."

"Research noted, as well as the requested recommendation. Records for the aforementioned cases are now officially closed pending Celestial

Board approval."

(short pause) "Fine job, Josef."

"Thank you, Judge Cantrel."

"You'll be sorely missed within the department, but I wish you well in alterations. I have no doubt you are up to the challenge."

"Thank you again, Thomas. Off the record, do you think the recommendation for reincarnation for Grimrich will stick?"

"Hard to say, Josef You know the rules. Its nigh impossible to acquire the ninety percent vote required from the board."

"Oh yes, sir. Things certainly have changed over the years in that regard, haven't they?"

"Quite. Times are different, the species easier to hold accountable than decades past.

Honesty, Josef, among all other evaluators, you alone still carry the torch for the 'RR' program."

"I…know, sir That may well be why I've chosen to leave the field." "Your prejudice is understandable, after all, you were held up as the prime example of why the reincarnation program worked. You were the prototype."

"Yes, sir. I have you to thank for it. For…*everything*, sir."

"Thank yourself, Josef. But, you made it happen, after all. The countless lives you saved as young Doctor Stanley M. Bryant more than justified our decision to give your damned soul a second chance. I was but a fraction of the voting board."

"Regardless, I will always be in your debt, as well as all those past board members. I wouldn't be speaking to you now if not for your wisdom and foresight."

"I am truly regretful that your...second life as Doctor Bryant was cut so tragically short, but those in higher places saw a need for your intellect within our ranks. Still, you were doing such wonderful work with the starving masses in South America Their decision must have been a difficult one."

"I guess I felt an obligation to those poor, pathetic people, Thomas." "Naturally. During your initial incarnation, you did live among them while hiding from authorities and droves of bounty hunters."

"True. I don't think...I could ever do enough to make up for...well, you understand."

"Certainly. I've always wondered though..." "What's that, Thomas?"

"Well, why you choose to take back your original birth name? I mean, wouldn't you rather...forget?"

"It's a reminder, sir. A painful reminder of what I was, and never, *ever* could possibly expire to be again. It's as simple as that."

"No need to elaborate farther then, Josef. Needless to say, you have always made those responsible for your rebirth proud. Again, I wish you luck on your newest endeavor." "Thank you, sir."

"No...thank you, *Doctor Mengele.*"

***

People ponder why often times the good die young and horribly, while the truly evil amongst us are allowed a free ride into their golden years only to pass peacefully in the night. Witness a case to the extreme opposite side of said spectrum in this next chilling saga, wherein the vilest of all get their just due, and *then some*, from the most unlikely of sources...

13 - THE REAL MONSTERS

Multiple announcements reverberated in true assembly-line fashion from a plethora of wall and ceiling mounted speakers.

"Z-881, please proceed to assignment booth forty-eight. Z-eight-eight one to assignment booth four-eight."

"V-321, please proceed to assignment booth fifty-six. V, three- two-one to assignment booth five-six."

"G-444, please proceed to assignment booth seventy-nine. G, four-forty four to assignment booth seventy-nine."

From various locations within the colossal, cathedral-style hall, they rose to obey whichever verbal command pertained in relentless waves of undead inhumanity.

"WW-248, please proceed to assignment booth one-sixty. W, two-four- eight to assignment booth one-sixty.'

"M-23, please proceed to retirements branch, room seventy-eight. M, twenty-three to retirements branch, room seventy-eight."

A spattering of applause filled one corner of the hall as the potential retiree is shown a level of respect deserving one who had served so tirelessly through the decades (or perhaps *centuries*, depending on the individual addressed).

In the front center section of rows sat a diverse grouping of job hunters of varying skills and experiences, each calmly awaiting a droned voice to direct them to one of a possible seven-hundred fifty assignment booths. Booths that rotated in three to four minute intervals on a twenty-hour, seven-day-a-week schedule like revolving doors caught in a permanent spin.

Occupying an aisle seat lounged *Z-198*, an 'old school' warrior from the undead legions of the late nineteen sixties. Having perished following a Haitian political riot, he was then revived and reanimated (via family request) just days later by one of the island's most noted Voodoo doctors. Despite decades of wear, tear and natural decomposition, he has fed well and thereby maintained the gist of his body parts, save a missing left arm at the elbow and a gaping hole below his rib cage. Like all those within the workforce designated under the '*Z-FE* (Zombie –FLESH EATER)' classification, he was required to wear thick metallic mouth and neck braces until physically arriving within the assigned task perimeter. Due to the 'Z' workers penchant for attacking on instinct, the razor- wire mouth guard disallowed random biting of innocents, just as the cylinder- styled neck restraint limited neck movement.

"AP-133, please proceed to assignment booth two-eleven. AP, three-thirty three to assignment booth two-eleven"

Sitting two seats over was *W-486*, who eyed Z-198 with obvious anxiety.

A pudgy, middle-aged man with a balding plate and puffy jowls, he had once been revered as a skilled hunter of big game, that is until a dark, foggy night on the English moors saw him forced into the role of hunted. As his turning was fairly recent

(October of nineteen ninety-six), his blatant inexperience in dealing with those not of his kind was readily apparent. He wore his fear like a shiny gold badge, like so many of the '*WWL* (Werewolf-LUPINE) designation whose courage only surfaced within the fiery glow of a full moon.

"V-516, please proceed to assignment booth ninety-six. V, five-one-six to assignment booth ninety-six."

Wearing an expression of casual indifference, *V-132* (officially designated *V-BS* – Vampiric/BLOOD SUCKER) filled a chair just three spots to the right. Cocking her head to the right, she brushed back her lengthy locks (pitch black with streaks of silver) with spidery fingers that sported three-inch nails painted blood red. Her complexion was best described as pasty; though her lips (frozen in a permanent 'pout') were full and shaded in dark crimson. Having been turned at the tender age of seventeen within a tiny, remote Danish village, she has done ample time within the frenzied, chaotic atmosphere the hall provided.

"First time?" She droned seductively, her accent thick but easily comprehensible.WW-486's eyes widened momentarily at the sudden, unexpected inquiry. He quickly narrowed them and puffed out his woefully concave chest, apparently executing his best 'Clint Eastwood' impersonation to offset the stark fear clasping his undead soul.

"Naw. Not this boy. Been here…done that...," he crowed through a shaky, warped grin as a thick bead of sweat formed directly between his bushy eyebrows, "…and you?"

"Might be wise to monitor your back, young man," she replied, having leaned over to whisper into an outstretched palm, then gesturing with a thumb towards the rows directly behind them.

"...that *GL* a few seats back is drooling over you like a freshly sliced slab of prize bovine meat."

Whipping his head around at break-neck speed, WW-486 cringed back as if ducking an incoming aerial assault.

Two rows back and directly behind him, GL-779 leaned forward and sniffed the air aggressively, thick threads of drool coating the underside of the 'Iron Maiden' styled mask that all assigned *GL-FE* (Ghouls- FLESH EATER) were forced to don while in pre-task mode. As with all GL's, the creature is assigned a 'Guardian'; a lifelong 'S*entinel*' of sorts who is supplied with behavioral modification drugs administered solely for preventive measures. Long heralded as the 'loose cannon' of the undead, those designated as 'GL's are generally labeled the '*Tasmanian Devils* of the underworld', prone to attacks on both the living and undead with similar frequency and ferociousness. To the majority of GL's, flesh is *flesh* and meat is *meat*, regardless of whether or not the host is with or *without* pulse.

"WW-219, please proceed to assignment booth one-fifty-three. WW, two- one-nine to assignment booth one-five-three."

"Tsk...tsk...and not a single ray of precious moonlight in sight," V-132 crooned, parting her lips to reveal inch-long incisors and waiving a skeletal forefinger from side to side like a ticking pendulum blade, "...ah, the perilous non- life of a shape-

300

shifter. So potentially dangerous yet so very vulnerable."

"How right you are, Elvita," spat an unidentified *V (Vampirc)* designate from several rows over. Tall and gaunt, his slick-backed, grayish-brown hair was wound into a ponytail that hung over his rounded shoulder like a pet snake. His accent was slight and virtually impossible to properly identify, though there were hints of either a watered-down Romanian or Ukrainian dialect.

"Damn fur-balls don't even belong here in their human guises. Like frightened rabbits, one and all. Hiring standards have most certainly taken a severe turn for the worst in recent decades.

Such a pathetic sight that never ceases to sour my gut."

V-132 turned to acknowledge her distant kin with a slight nod and a subsequent roll of her sparkling hazel eyes.

"Greetings, Williem. Discontented as usual, I take it. Ah, *youngsters* You must all learn to harness such futile frustrations for the mission to come. Besides, questioning the *W.H.A's* policies aloud isn't very wise, you know. Big brother is indeed everywhere."

The male bloodsucker frowned, grunting sarcastically without verbal response. WW-486 watched in silent relief as the GL's muscle-bound, leather-clad Sentinel tugged at one end of a heavy chain that essentially forced the creature back into its seat. Before turning to again face-front, WW-486 spotted an entity positioned a row back, several seats over from the ghoul and his one-man

301

entourage.

With its scaly, bloated, multi-colored torso, tentacle-like appendages and a trio of pumpkin shaped skulls propped atop a narrow, translucent neck, even a novice like himself knew it was undoubtedly an '*AP*' designate. AP's ('*Alien Predators*') were not only the new kid on the planet's predatory block, with an earthbound ancestry of less than fifty years, but also the fastest *growing* minority, with a current 'listed employee' population of just over four hundred. This of course, paled considerably to such veteran entities as The *Living Dead*, the roster of which included:

ZOMBIES (2005 census count of just under eleven thousand world-wide, mostly within The Virgin Islands, Haiti and the Caribbean islands), and GHOULS (seventy-six hundred, centered mostly in South America)

Plus other familiar stalwarts of the 'societal purging' trade, such as:

VAMPIRIC PARASITES (nine thousand registered; though the overall population was estimated at near double that total if counting Eastern Europe's age-old 'purist' masses, which had long since refused to 'stoop' to what they considered 'manual slave labor')

WEREWOLVES (sixty-five hundred; with North America, Europe and Southeast Asia housing the main 'vein')

And of course, the grandfather of the underworld, the MUMMY (less than two-hundred active employees, almost all located in either Egypt or Saudi Arabia).

"AP-294, please report to CORRECTIONS unit six. AP, two-nine-four, proceed to CORRECTIONS unit six."

With that, the bloated alien of psychedelic colors slithered from its seat with multiple legs pumping, leaving behind a thick trail of glutinous goo as several 'Z' and 'V' designates dived out of its lumbering path. *"Security Units Three and four, report to employee lounge. Security Units three and four to employee lounge. Please escort AP-294 to corrections unit six. Escort AP two-nine-four to corrections unit six. Utilize whatever force necessary. Repeat...utilize whatever force is deemed necessary."*

Within seconds, five heavily armored sentries teleported onto the scene and pinned the AP designate to the carpeted floor via hand-held 'shock wands', narrow electrical rods capable of emitting electrical charges of up to two- hundred-fifty thousand volts.

With the precision of a veteran pit crew, the sentries took less than a full minute to fit circular steel bands over each set of the Alien's snapping teeth while effectively shackling its tentacles. Seconds later, they dragged it past the gathering crowd towards a large, neon-lit overhang reading '*W.H.A CORRECTIONS DEPARTMENT* – 2 LEVELS UP', where a wide, double-door elevator awaited.

"What...what will they do to...it? Incarceration perhaps?" WW-486 asked aloud without addressing anyone in particular.

The male vampire howled with sardonic glee.

303

"Incar-….? My word, you are indeed as green as freshly lain Kentucky blue grass, aren't you?"

"There are no prison cells within the corrections unit, my dear Lupine hybrid,' V-132 interjected between yawns, 'it is more a matter of *disintegration.* Within the stringent rules and regulations set to and enforced by the powers that be, transformation into a pile of smoldering ash is akin to being handed what humans refer to as a '*pink slip.'*

"Oh…oh yeah. I remember now. It's…in the contract," WW-486 mumbled, swallowing nervously.

"W.H.A Operating Instruction A-nineteen. Page four, line seven, if I recall correctly," V-132 replied matter-of-factly, "Any deviation from assigned mission for personal gain shall result in severe reprimand. Three such incidents shall result in termination with *extreme prejudice.*

Three strikes and you're *ash* (she sighed). Makes one long for the carefree days of freelance slaughter, does it not?"

"Z-1,233, please proceed to assignment booth five-twenty-seven. Z one two three-three, proceed to assignment booth five-twenty-seven."

As the crowd slowly settled back down from the previous commotion, WW-486 turned and faced front, weary of further conversation.

A trio of new arrivals sat side by side just two rows ahead, the hand- weapons each brandished instantly setting them apart from the rest of the gathered crowd.

WW-486's chair squeaked loudly as he leaned

forward with both nostrils flaring. From the corner of both eyes, he detected a mass of movement. Whirling about, he saw several Z designates shamble forward from various directions, followed by a spattering of G's (dragging their respective Sentinels along for the ride) and a fellow W-rep, all of which tilted their heads to one side and displayed wide, flaring nostrils. Within moments, the newly arrived trio was literally surrounded on all sides. The female V rep identified earlier as 'Elvita' faced down the man occupying the center chair, the ankle-length maroon cape she donned flowing gracefully over her petite frame as if possessing a life all its own.

"Are we lost, gentleman?" she cooed softly, licking her ruby lips. "Why do you ask, madam?" the middle man replied apprehensively, scanning the building crowd while clutching a mini-grenade launcher tightly against his slim midsection. The man's exposed skin was the color of baked clay; his hair dark and oily, his eyes coal black pits. He was donned in nothing more elaborate than blue jeans, black boots and a white, cotton Tee-shirt, and spoke broken English with a distinct Middle-Eastern accent.

By dramatic contrast, his cohort on the right was shaved bald, his complexion fish-belly white. A huge specimen with wide-shoulders, thickly muscled arms (he wore a muscle tee with the words '*TO KILL IS TO TRULY LIVE*' stenciled across the back) and a barrel-shaped chest, he gripped a nine-millimeter handgun in each palm, crossing his arms across his chest in an 'X' shape. His accent was

North American in nature, possibly the United States Midwest. "What the hell's going on, Omar? Ya know I don't like crowds, man."

The third of the group was a medium-sized African-American male decked out in camouflaged fatigues with a black beret pulled low onto his squared forehead. A thickly roped ammo/utility belt hung across his left shoulder, and was filled to capacity with various weapons of destruction, to include grenades, several serrated combat knives, and at least three revolvers of various sizes and makes. His deep, brutish accent seemed a hybrid of perhaps South Africa and a native of the West Indies.

"My god, what manner of devils are these? Omar, where have you led us, you imbecile!"

"I...I came where I am told to report, that's all...report here, they say...I do as told," Omar shrieked with the discovery that he could not pull away from Elvita's mesmerizing stare.

"Identify yourselves, gentleman....please," she asked while seemingly holding the bludgeoning crowd at bay with a mental command that they alone were privy to.

"Why, we are liberators of the New World Order," Omar blurted, his expression growing increasingly trance-like; the words spoken in a robotic monotone, "I serve as the Chief Coordinator...North American Sector...for the *Global Coalition*.

We...fight...we *kill* for all the oppressed...for justice. I am Omar...once a high ranking officer within Al Qaeda, I branched out...for the greater

306

good of...my people..."

Elvita's searing gaze quickly shifted to the large man on Omar's right. "I'm Jake M-Myers...." he began to prattle in the same mechanical tone, his moon-shaped face slowly turning a bright shade of red, "...Codename *'Master Blaster'* Explosives and hand-to-hand...mayhem's my...specialty. Plied my trade with both the KKK and Aryan Brotherhood for just over twelve years...before...becomin' a foundin'...member of...The Global Coalition."

Lastly, she trained her sights on the third, who openly winced before falling victim to her steely, hypnotic   glare. "Benjamin...Jerome...McCafee...former member in good standing with...several high level Black Separatists Groups, to include...the Ebony Warriors and the...Dark Shields of Hope. Was...recruited by...Global Coalition for my....strategic experience...and peerless...combat record..."

"Why, color me impressed. A true melting pot of evil, you are," Elvita exclaimed in mock glee, bowing slightly as all three men seemed to snap from their collective trances at precisely the same moment, "unfortunately, it seems a rather...*fatal* mistake has been made. Quite irreversible, I'm afraid, at this point."

The hall's PA system wailed in true Klaxon-horn fashion before she was allowed to properly elaborate.

"Attention...attention...will Terrorists delegates 290, 291, and 292 please report to HR Assignments, main control desk, LEVEL 1. Repeat: Terrorist delegates two-nine-oh, two-nine-one, and two-nine-

two please report to Human Resource Assignments, main control desk, LEVEL ONE."

The three men eyed each other momentarily, each donning masks of comical befuddlement, before turning back to Elvita.

"Get it, fellas? *Human* Resource Assignments?" she cackled, her cape swooning and swaying as never before, "doesn't happen very often, I'll grant you. Amazing how one could 'accidentally' bypass such carefully guarded security measures at Level One. Actually, damned *astonishing* is a better term."

"I do not...under-..." Omar blubbered, slowly lifting the grenade launcher towards his left shoulder.

"So we're on the wrong damn floor, lady. Who gives a rat's ass? C'mon guys, let's blow this freak show. *Lilly Munster* and her travelin' geek revue are startin' to creep me out," Jake interrupted gruffly, allowing the twin revolvers to rest in his lap even as his massive shoulders began to bulge and contract from building tension.

"Omar, I told you floor *one.* Those badges we were given outside the hall were meant for someone else," McCafee shouted, reaching over to slap the smaller man across the back of his scalp.

The male vampire suddenly appeared as from nowhere and posed next to Elvita. Rail thin, the creature stood at least seven feet tall He and Elvita exchanged knowing nods.

"It is possible?" he inquired with a hideous grin.

"Why, I do believe so, dear Williem. Fringe

308

benefits from the company.

How very thoughtful of upper management."

"And here I thought they no longer cared," he concluded, studying the terrorists with a baleful stare.

"Don't get us wrong, gentleman," he continued in a polite yet somehow menacing tone, "it isn't as though we were not at least *somewhat* sympathetic to the vile, cowardly acts individuals such as yourselves specialize in. Crude but effective, I must confess. It's just that...hidden bombs and suicide missions that serve for martyrdom purposes alone hold little value within our little fraternity."

WW-486 elbowed his way towards the front of the surging mass, his breathing huffy and labored.

"Did I hear right? These...assholes are nothing but ordinary, everyday terrorists?"

"Correct, greenhorn," the male vampire spat disdainfully, "idols of yours?" "Not quite, Slinky. It was yellow bastards just like these that were responsible for the murder of my niece several years ago...September eleven, two-thousand one to be exact. The Twin tower bombings."

Positioning her right arm across the lower portion of the male vampire's narrow waist, Elvita levitated the entire group as one, essentially backing up the swelling horde several feet without benefit of taking an actual step. "I'd heard the World Horror Association's recruitment of human associates had fallen so severely that they were scraping the bottom of the barrel, but this is *truly* disheartening."

Glancing up, she noticed a pair of security hovercraft floating above, each containing at least four armed guards. Gesturing silently to the lead guard with a 'what now?' expression, she calmly awaited an answer. To her left, a masked Sentinel reached up to remove his assigned Ghoul's iron mask. A similar scene played out less than five feet to her right, as several Zombies were assisted in removing both mouth and neck guards. Seconds later, the head security officer nodded solemnly beneath his dark faceplate and the hovers slowly distanced themselves from the maddening crowd.

"Now then," Elvita purred seductively, floating back down until she centered the three seated men, "I believe there is the matter of a reprimand to be doled out. Talk about the wrong place at the wrong time...."

"Kiss my ass, freak," Jake snarled, pointing the revolvers up and out in a single, fluid movement that paid loving homage to Wild West gunslingers of old, "now you and your travelin' Carny act back the hell off or I start decoratin' the place with body parts."

"Well then, by all means, tough guy," Elvita replied with a fearsome scowl, spreading her arms wide while levitating slowly forward, "allow me to be the first to volunteer for such a drastic make-over."

The eight shots that followed were executed at a range of less than two full feet, a fact that would normally have left the intended victim a twitching pile of unidentifiable mush. As it was, Jake remained frozen in a classic shooters pose; his arms fully extended as misty tendrils of smoke rose from both barrels of the twin nine millimeters. Similarly,

Elvita's bare feet still hovered airborne, both her wingspan and ghoulish expression wholly unchanged. Her midsection and upper chest were riddled with dark, quarter-sized holes that sporadically leaked perfectly circular smoke rings. As she floated several inches higher, the wounds began to refill before vanishing altogether.

Standing directly behind her, a female zombie (sans the mouth and neck guards) studied the half-dozen baseball-sized craters torn into her own torso with comical bemusement.

"Uh-oh Hope you fellas took the time to map out a 'Plan B'," Elvita quipped through a hideously wide, toothy grin that literally seemed to stretch from ear to ear. Rising over the pulsating crowd, she then levitated slowly back while waiving a single arm forward, much like a softball pitcher tossing an underhanded offering to home plate.

"Bon appetite, dear comrades! Enjoy this rare treat your employers have been so kind to offer!" she shrieked, watching the crowd rush forward as if a transparent force field had been lifted.

After leaping two full rows of seats, *Omar Shakif Mohammad*, who once took pride in the death of an extended family member via a carefully hidden car bomb, had time but to lift the launcher onto his shoulder before it was torn from his grip.

Hoisted airborne, his girlish screams were quickly cut off as he was effectively drawn and quartered in mid-air, though not before his terror-filled eyes temporarily locked onto the black-pitted orbs of the ancient *Mummy* who ripped him into separate halves with frightening ease.

Pinned to his seat before he could do little but grasp the marble handle of a Colt Ranger Bowie knife strapped to his belt, *Benjamin Jerome McCafee,* widely known in terrorist circles as 'the decapitator' of political enemies, had his own skull torn from his shoulders by a single swipe of a clawed hand. As geysers of maroon mist spewed forth from the ravaged stump of his neck, 'The Decapitators' headless torso continued its shaky death-spasm even as dozens of greedy hands and gnashing teeth lunged forward for the spoils.

Using the butt-end of both revolvers to pound away at the head and face of the giant male vampire holding him airborne, *Jake 'Master Blaster' Myers,* an 'equal opportunity' killer of both small children and senior citizens alike, had his arms torn from their respective sockets moments before his neck was snapped like a rotted plank.

Raising his head from the frenzied hordes encircling the fresh kill, the male vampire spat out a sizeable chunk of scalp in order to verbally address Elvita, who stood a dozen feet away, surveying the carnage with casual aplomb.

"Sure you won't indulge, my dear?" he asked as strands of moistened gore hung from his pointed chin like seaweed from a ship's hull, "the flesh is a bit rank, but the warm nectar beneath is quite refreshing still."

"I'll pass, dear Williem. Just save me a drumstick if at all possible," she replied with a sly nod.

The male vampire returned the gesture and dipped his head back into the shredded mush that had once been one of the more feared terrorists on the planet.

"Damn. Is such a thing…actually permitted without consequences?" WW- 486 asked, having taken up position directly to the female vampire's right, "not that the wholesale slaughter of such scum bothers me in the least, but…I mean…*damn*…"

"Permitted? More like *sanctioned*," she replied curtly, "It was no *accident* they were given the wrong security badges or allowed past Level One. The company…recruits such men every blue moon or so, simply as a gift to *our* kind. They toss us the occasional bone, so to speak, usually a serial killer or mass murderer, if memory serves."

"Gift? I don't…" he began, frowning in disgust as a veritable monkey-pile of bodies grew atop each victim's sparse remains like feeding maggots.

"Look at it this way…um, what's your name again?" "Jack…Jack Jenkins. New York City…formerly."

"Well, *Wolfman Jack* of New York City, look at it this way. Our kind, and the company as a whole, view men of such ilk, *terrorists* in particular, in the same vein as incarcerated humans do your basic child molester."

"I…see. But…why exactly? I mean, we 're all *here* for generally the same purpose…"

She turned on him wearing a fierce sneer, her incisors dripping frothy drool.

"I cannot disagree more fervently, Sir Jack. In most people's minds, we are nothing more than mythical creatures, kept alive by hokey Hollywood films and the occasional killing spree that goes unsolved. A select few within the Super Powers are privy to our existence, and deem us a necessary evil; as much a vital cog in the World's eco-system as Great White Sharks, Vultures and intestinal parasites. A vital part of the food chain, yes, but also a secret, stringently guarded one.

The *World Horror Association* was created in order to…keep our killing sprees in check, therefore maintaining our anonymity while also providing an extra layer of security for the human race."

"Have to confess," he sighed wearily, "once I found out what those men were, I wished with all my might I had the ability to shape-shift at will just to take a bite out of their asses myself."

Her anger having subsided, Elvita smiled warmly, pausing to give him a quick once-over.

"Guess we're not as different as one might think, you and I."

They watched in silence as the multitude of creatures slowly began to dissipate, leaving behind little more than a spattering of gnawed bone and a trio of wide blood smears.

"Guess not. Can't really say I feel an ounce of guilt at such a thought." "Don't sweat it, Wolfman Jack," she said, lightly patting his back as she began to slowly levitate away, "Thing is, you're baring witness to a fact known by few outside the supernatural community"

"What's that?" WW-486 inquired, studying the separate blood smears a final time before turning to saunter away.

"That even we so-called Monsters have our *standards*." After a moment, the task

314

announcements began anew....

***

Hospital waiting rooms have often been referred to as the 21st Century equivalent to *The Spanish Inquisition*. Perhaps a bit overstated, though not if one refers to the following terror tale, as all those unfortunate enough to be labeled 'patient' inhabit a nightmarish realm of infinite 'limbo' filled with unimaginable horrors...

14 - THE WAITING ROOM

The man peers cautiously over the top edge of the crinkled, sour smelling magazine (wondering what kind of diseased individual had his or her toilet- grippers on it earlier) and notices the kid still glaring at him.

The irritating ankle-biter looks to be around four or five. He's got his right index finger buried knuckle-deep into his left nostril.

Dear ol' dad used to call that 'Digging for Gold' or 'Scratching Your Brain', rest his demented soul.

"Hi!" the kid blurts out, a word the annoying squirt had repeated ad nauseam in the twenty minutes since the man's arrival in the perpetual 'Dead Zone' hospitals label as 'waiting rooms.'

He raises the magazine back up to cover his eyes, ignoring the snot- nosed cretin. In his less than humble opinion, kids should never be seen nor heard.

What kind of so-called parent drags his offspring with him to a doctor's office anyhow? Not just a doctor's office, but a Urologist, for cripes sake. Ever hear of a babysitter, you idiot? I doubt the kid suffers the throbbing, burning pain I have in and around my testicles. I doubt if the little nuisance has to drag himself from the comfort of his bed three or four times nightly to drain his bladder, as I do. Someday, kid, you and Mr. Pain will be formally introduced. Just give it a decade or three Let him first properly decide how best to torture you.

"Bobby, you close your mouth and be still," a

316

female voice whispers harshly. The kid, as most do in these modern days of 'time-outs' and 'verbal counseling', completely ignores her and begins to scream and whine, tossing magazines to the floor with obvious glee.

The gas that presently bloats the man's ever-expanding gut garbles loudly and he fears that despite the piped in elevator music overhead, it can be clearly heard by all; a virtual lower colon *concerto*. "Wah..wah WAH!" the kid screams.

"Be quiet, Bobby! You're gonna get it, boy!" the woman says without a hint of actual anger.

"Wah...Wah...DAH DAH! DOO DOO...Doo-Doo breath!" the kid replies defiantly.

The man feels his blood pressure rise like a thermometer struck by desert heat.

It's his initial visit to this particular doctor, and the apprehension begins to build. His groin feels like someone had poured a glass of gasoline on it and tossed on a lit match for good measure.

The article he scans without a thread of sincere interest speaks of 'Academy Award Picks, 2005! The date on the top of the page reads February of the same year, and he has to suppress a cynical giggle He recalls his dear departed Mother quipping 'You know you're in a second-rate doctor's office when the magazines are over two years old'. *Mom would have sprinted out of here screaming*, he deduces with a sour smirk.

"Mr. Humphries?" the receptionist bellows, her voice shrill and obviously a bit peeved. Another satisfied employee, it seems He had noticed her less-than- thrilled-to-be-here attitude upon his arrival. She had practically scowled at him after he had signed in and forgot to include the specific doctor's name that he'd come to see.

Uncrossing his legs, as he had felt his right foot begin to tingle and drift away into a deep slumber, the man puts the magazine down and leans back, suppressing a yawn.

"Hi! Who're you?" the kid yells as he takes a few steps forward and almost trips.

The man's knees pop like brittle kindling as he pushes himself from the narrow, foul-smelling chair and gingerly strolls towards the receptionist's desk.

The kid promptly jumps into the man's seat as he ambles away. The man would gladly find another if need be.

His groin burns and aches anew as he nears the windowed office, occupied solely by the heavy-set, perpetually frowning woman imprisoned within its stifling confines.

"Miss?" he whispers through gritted teeth, fighting off the urge to massage his privates right then and there.

She ignores him for a few moments, hands frozen on her computer keypad, then finally acknowledges him with an annoyed grunt.

"My...uh... appointment with Doctor Mills was set for one PM. It's almost two-thirty. Is there a problem I should know about?"

Her eyes roll. She is a middle-aged white woman carrying an extra hundred pounds on a frame far too small to accommodate such bulk.

"Mister...?"

"Jamison. Jerry Jamison," he replies curtly.

"Mister Jamison, I have no idea what the delay is. I would think the doctor will get to you as soon as he can. Please have a seat and be *patient*."

Temples pounding, his jaws sore from the constant pressure of the tightening and then releasing of facial muscles, he sighs and turns to find a new island of solitude to inhabit.

He finds a spot on the opposite side of where he'd been, seemingly a safe distance from the dead-end kid and his spineless parent.

A man who looks to be in his eighties or nineties sits a few seats to his left, a wadded newspaper in his lap. The old man's chin rests on his bony chest, a small line of drool making its way slowly from the right corner of his mouth towards his slumped shoulder. He figures the old guy's plumbing has probably gone south, big- time. The man can sympathize.

Poor old guy probably spends three hours a day straining over a urinal.

At least I'm not at that stage ...yet.

His watch now reads 2:41 PM. A woman sits three chairs over to his right, her head leaned back but her eyes wide open behind comically thick glasses that are partially fogged over. The actual size of her eyeballs are magnified ten-fold by the microscope-like lenses. Her hands are crossed over her purse; her mouth slightly agape. She could have been as young as thirty-five or as old as fifty, it was impossible to gauge. She has a huge band-aid positioned on each of her chubby kneecaps, and her right wrist is entombed in a small cast. She sits eerily still, her breathing virtually impossible to detect. She looks as if she had already croaked right there in the chair.

Might be a relief at that, the man muses.

He has a strange feeling that the woman was sizing him up somehow, studying him, although she remains rigidly still.

The sharp pains in his groin transform into a different kind of discomfort by the time his watch reads 3 PM It was as if someone has poured itching powder into his pubic hair. He wants desperately to scratch, but a young couple sitting across from him would surely witness the act, along with Ms. Coke bottle goggles. He thinks about exiting to the men's bathroom just outside in the hallway, but figures his name might be called just as he departs the room.

Grimacing, he feels the initial pangs of potential diarrhea tap at his lower stomach.

That would be the ultimate pisser, now wouldn't it? They'd probably 'reschedule me' out of pure spite.

The young couple whispers to one another and grin mischievously. They are in their twenties, ten years or more his junior.

The man frowns as if pinched.

They didn't know pain yet, either. It bides it's time when you're in your twenties, he deduced, waiting until the mid to late thirties point to rear its ugly head with a vengeance. When a person's health started to go, it was like a rotted plywood wall attempting to hold back raging flood waters. Everything seemed to collapse at once.

The man had visited a doctor's office exactly four times in his twenties, in each instance to be

320

treated for the flu or similar cold symptoms.

He couldn't tally such visits with a calculator since reaching the big three- oh. This was his fourth Urologist in the past year, and that didn't take into account all the family practice doctors and Proctologists that had taken turns poking and probing his lower extremities. His family and friends had written him off as a hopeless hypochondriac or pity-seeking '*drama king*', but he knew better. The problems that had arisen with his shoulders, legs, and now his groin were real, not some fictional figment of his imagination. He hopes with every pain-racked fiber in his body that this will finally be the miracle physician who can recognize and eliminate this latest malady.

The young couple begins to kiss lightly, shamelessly snuggling like they were at a drive-in movie.

The man's eyes grow unbearably heavy as he watches them grope. The younggirl has a zit the size of a marble on her chin, and the young man is sporting a deep scar that runs from the corner of his left eye down his jaw line, hooking underneath his ear lobe.

Closing his eyes to both avoid their display and to rest his anxiety-ridden mind, the man leans back and inhales deeply.

The shrill, bitter voice of the receptionist shakes him back to reality moments (*hours*?) later.

"Mr. Cobb? Mr. John Cobb?"

A large, middle-aged man wearing a work uniform of some type strolls by as the smell of petrol fills the air in sweeping waves.

A young, slim, rather attractive nurse greets the man at the entrance to the back offices, her smile kind yet strikingly insincere and a tad bit predatory. Her tiny, polished teeth seem overly pointed at the tips, like those of a piranha.

The man rubs his eyes vigorously and glances back up just in time to see the young girl *biting* the neck of the young man. The young man is lying back, only the whites of his eyes revealed, flashing an expression of pure ecstasy.

Small trickles of blood escape the punctures in his neck as faint slurping sounds become clearly audible.

Something catches the corner of the man's right eye and he turns quickly, the bones in his neck popping like blank rounds from a cap pistol.

The drooling old man is now sitting next to him, his eyes closed tightly and his breathing labored.

"You okay, old timer?" the man asks wearily. The old man doesn't respond except to lift his right arm and gesture towards the obviously ancient Timex watch attached to his frail-looking left wrist.

The minute hand is spinning wildly, the second hand a complete blur. The old man's lips tremble. His breath smells of mouth balls and moldy cloth.

"It's..the *waitin'*...that gets ya, son...it's..the waitin'..that does ya..in ," he mumbles, then keels over head first into the floor like an overstuffed laundry bag.

Looking around for help, the man suddenly discovers he is the only one remaining in the room save for the collapsed senior citizen and the

322

annoying kid, who is standing over the old man while chomping casually on a piece of gum.

"What's the matter with him, Mister? Was it the *wait*?" The kid asks in- between noisy smacks.

The man sees the receptionist office window is now closed, a cardboard sign reading '*CLOSED UNTIL FURTHER NOTICE*' hung with Scotch tape from the inside.

The kid is now standing on top of the old man's back, periodically stomping up and down forcefully, as if trying to revive him.

Reaching to grasp the kid's shoulder, the man cringes back a moment later as if electrically shocked.

The child's grating voice seems to penetrate his very flesh. "What's his problem? I was *born* here, and they still won't let me go home! I'm almost five! It's not fair! I want to go HOME, DAMMIT!" the child screams in a voice that is chillingly adult.

The child looks up at the man, pleading. The child's face is covered with skin that is leathery, like baked clay. His drooping, bloodshot eyes speak of infinite frustration, of precious youth eternally wasted.

"It isn't fair that he should get out of it this easily! I've been here much, much longer...*much, much, much, much..*,"

The words ring in the man's ears as he rushes towards the double glass door exit.

He hears his name called just as he shoves the doors outward. "Mr. Jamison? Mr. Jerry Jamison?" it blares in a monotone that is almost comically robotic. It is definitely *not* the receptionist's voice.

Whirling around and re-entering the waiting room in one smooth movement, he halts only when greeted by the announcement's originator.

A quick look at his watch reveals that it is now five-ten PM

The day reads Wednesday, April 13th. Didn't he arrive on the 11th? At least, that was his appointment date, he...thinks.

He is greeted by an older, white-haired gentleman who sports a long lab coat with a stethoscope looped around his narrow, horribly wrinkled neck. The instrument is cloaked in thick cobwebs. The man notices the black shoes the stranger wears are painted in white dust. The stranger holds a metal tray in both his liver-spot ravaged hands. The tray is covered by a wide cloth that is almost blinding in its snow-white cleanliness.

"Mr. Jamison, you almost left without these. Wouldn't want to live *without them,* no siree," the stranger whispers through a mouth void of teeth, his moist, exposed gums riddled with black, pit-like holes.

Somehow realizing he most definitely DID NOT want to know what lay underneath the cloth, the man tries to turn back towards the exit. Small but remarkably strong hands grip him at the elbows from the rear. It is the child, the cackling, giggling noises emitting from his shrill voice filled with maniacal ticks and choking gargles.

"Too soon, doctor. It isn't fair! Too soon for this one!" the child rants.

The man pulls back the cloth with a grace usually reserved for waiters in upscale restaurants

324

displaying a main course to the wealthiest of clients.

Although his eyes focus and then re-focus on the items spread across the tray, it takes a full minute (*hour?*) for the definition of each to become clear due to just how ridiculously out of place they are just lying there.

"You can re-attach them with a fine sewing needle, or even Super Glue if you prefer," the stranger says with a hint of humor, seemingly gumming back a chuckle. The stranger's breathe reeks of infinite decay, like rotted cabbage wilting inside a hot-house. The moist, displaced organs roll around on the metal tray like marbles on a slick concrete slab One of the them, possibly a testicle, rolls off of the edge, and as the stranger reaches down to retrieve it, the child jumps forward and playfully kicks it across the room.

"Wheeeee! Let's play soccer!" he yelps joyfully.

The man feels the pain of the disconnected organ even as it bounces off an adjoining wall like a tennis ball ricocheting from a swung racket.

Turning and stumbling forward, he feels a sudden urge to pee. He reaches down between his legs and discovers a smooth, completely bulge-free area of skin where his manhood had once occupied.

The man falls hard onto the carpeted floor of the outside hallway, sparking light filling his senses as he rolls over into a relieved state of oblivion.

Sweet darkness envelops him, and he welcomes it with a weak, somewhat pathetic smile. As his eyes mercifully close, the scent of antiseptic is overwhelming.

Glancing at the rusted watch that is practically embedded onto her wrist, she sees it reads two-forty-five PM.

Ignoring the bothersome child that is staring at her and making faces in the adjoining seat, she lifts herself gingerly to her shaky feet and walks (*wobbles*?) towards the receptionist area.

The woman ignores her at first, then glances slowly upward, wearing an expression of mild disgust.

"I told you just three weeks ago, Miss Cameron. You have to be *patient*. Doctor Mills will see you as soon as he possibly can," the woman blurts, the large brown spider that has nested just above her right temple frantically completing the most recent addition to the already impressive suite constructed there.

"But my appointment was weeks (*years? decades*?) ago. It's not fair...I'm in some *serious* discomfort here."

The receptionist doesn't respond, but instead resumes typing, a bloated cockroach crawling from the space her ample cleavage has provided.

The woman limps back to her chair, the sharp pains in her lower back aggravated more than ever from the short trek.

It itches like mad inside her arm cast, and she is tempted for the hundredth time that morning (*afternoon*?) to tear it off and chew into her wound like a rabid animal.

The scabs on her knees ache like rotted teeth. She adjusts her heavy- framed glasses and leans back awkwardly in the small, confining chair.

The young couple a few seats to her left continue to cuddle, both of their necks smeared with dried blood. Although their faces are youthful, the flesh of their arms and neck seem freeze-dried; grotesquely pockmarked and ravaged with age spots.

She picks up the magazine in front of her and pretends to read an article on some new movies scheduled for release. Depressingly, she realizes these same films were released on video nearly a decade before.

The child paces in front of her and babbles incoherently.

She doesn't listen to his words. She has heard them many times before, and somehow understands that she is bound to endure them for an eternity to come.

The man sitting across from her pretends to read a magazine. He grimaces noticeably with each moment of his hips. His face is set in a permanent scowl. Shockingly, he reaches down and openly massages his groin every three to five minutes, as if set on an eternal timer to do so.

The magazine dips momentarily, and she glimpses the hollowed-out emptiness of the eyes beyond the cracked lens of his glasses.

She will bide her time, for it is the one thing the waiting room provides in sickening abundance. Alas, it isn't as if she, or any of them, have a choice.

The child dances and rants, raves and dances. His voice is ancient, his hair ashen gray; the fingernails on his elongated digits grotesquely overgrown.

"Too soon for you, lady!" he sings between mad ramblings.

"Too soon for any of us. You have to be *patient*...we *all* have to patient." Time clicks away as the elevator music drones on endlessly.... A name is called somewhere in the far distance....

The smell of antiseptic is somehow sweetly intoxicating...

Outside the stained glass windows of the *waiting room*, yellow flames rise and descend from the fiery pits as the screams of the damned echo through endless corridors filled with eternal misery and infinite, searing pain...

***

Phantom spirits have but a precious few hours within each calendar year to roam and mingle among the living, and while the vast majority are harmless and non-malevolent, many seize the opportunity to evoke horrors that go way beyond simple Halloween 'pranks'....

15 - HALLOW'S EVE

"Mister, believe me when I tell ya, there ain't no time for explanations. It's eleven-fifty seven. You two got 'bout three minutes to get off the street or wish like hell that ya had."

The young couple exchanged a worrisome glance before scanning the street in both directions. If not for a single Styrofoam cup being tossed about by the occasional gust of wind, one would have thought the scene a still photograph or painting instead of a live picture.

"This is crazy, hon. I'm not about to dive into a sewer drain because some old lush..." the man began, yelping aloud as the woman drove her elbow firmly into his ribs.

"Shut up and do as the man says, Ed. I...I think he's...I don't know...something's just not right here, can't you feel it?"

Her cheeks had turned beet red, emphasizing the overall paleness of her freckle-ravaged complexion.

The old man's head stuck from the hole like a curious prairie dog. His bloodshot eyes darted wildly as he ran a gnarled hand through his thick gray beard.

"Ya got two minutes, folks. Good luck to ya...yer sure gonna need it," he slurred, ducking inside and gripping the manhole cover at its rounded edge as to pull it closed.

Whirling about as a sudden movement caught his eye, Ed watched the streets lone red light flicker, reset and eventually fade to black.

"Come on, Liz. There's gotta be an open gas station somewhere nea-.." "Wait!" the woman blurted, shoving the man aside as she backed onto the initial step and began to slowly descend.

Ed followed closely behind wearing a contorted scowl, giving the dark, desolate street a final glance before ducking his head inside and pulling the cover snugly into place.

"We'd better put some distance 'tween ourselves and the street. I usually go a few hundred feet or so...," the old man said, crouching slightly despite his diminutive height, which left a good foot to spare from the top of the concrete drain, "...just to be on the safe side. Nine years and they've never followed me down here yet. I think they're pretty much banned from leavin' the streets. That is, unless they're invited in. Kinda like Vampires in that regard, I reckon."

The flashlight he held warbled from side to side, bathing the circular pipe like a rotating strobe light.

"You've hid in the sewer for nine straight Halloween eves? Waiting for the *Great Pumpkin*, are we?" Ed blurted sarcastically while attempting to keep his dress shoes from submerging into the murky pool that cut a trail down the center of the pipe.

"Oh, clam up, Ed We wouldn't even be in this mess if you could follow simple directions," Liz replied angrily, keeping her sandals balanced on the outer edges to avoid the same slushy quagmire.

"You young folks just passin' through Hallows Eve, are ya?" the old man queried, clumsily side-stepping the bloated carcass of a dead rat.

"We're...we *were* on our way upstate when Mister 'lets take the scenic route back to campus' here took a few dozen wrong turns," Liz grumbled, pinching her nostrils as she passed over the same spot.

"Hey, it wasn't me complaining about the interstate traffic. Besides, I never have trusted Mapquest...wasn't my fault th-.."

The old man abruptly halted in his tracks as the drain neared a sharp right-hand curve.

"This outta do it. There's another manhole openin' a few dozen feet past this turn. Comes up at the intersection of Elm and Oak. I just don't wanna be visible from either direction."

Turning to face the couple with the light pointed into the tangled thickness of his chin growth, the old man could have passed for a B-movie ghoul from the black & white era of horror films. The couple froze in mid-step, the woman gasping aloud as the upturned light had transformed the old man's eyes into pearl-white pits; his unruly hair, hunched shoulders, and glowing yellow teeth serving to enhance the overall effect of repulsion.

"I...you mean this is our supposed safe haven? Mister, what could possibly be so horrible as to drive an entire town into hiding for...and another thing, how long are we going to be subjected to this foolishness?" Ed asked, cowering back a step as the light filled his eyes.

The old man ignored the question, shifting the beam to the pipe floor as to allow for more centralized visibility.

"Can't believe Sheriff MacReady allowed ya to slip through. He and that lame-brained deputy of his usually do a bang-up job of quarrantinin' the city limits on All Hell's Eve."

"All Hell's…is this some kind of joke?" Liz asked, kneeling down with her elbows balanced atop her knees, "…you're saying the entire town is effectively shut down and boarded up every-…?"

"Affirmative, missy. Pretty much since it's foundin' over a century back." Leaning next to Liz, Ed's knees popped like small arms fire.

"Pray tell, what exactly are we hiding from, Mister…um…what *is* your name, by the way?"

"Oh, sorry 'bout that. Pardon my rudeness. Names Myers. Frank Myers. To answer your first question there, young Eddie, I'm gonna hafta ask ya both to suspend disbelief…big time. We don't get many outsiders in Hallows Eve, specially this time'a year."

After a short pause, Myers joined the couple in a group squat, belching loudly while placing the light between them, wherein the dank sewer air became thick with the sickly scent of rot gut whiskey.

"Bein' that it's a few minutes past the Witchin' Hour, what were hidin' from is more than likely walkin' the streets above us as we speak."

"And that is…what exactly?" Liz injected a bit wearily.

"Specters, missy. Spirits from the supernatural. Not your' Casper the friendly ghost' types, neither. I'm talkin' bad to the bone malevolence with a capital 'M' Before ya ask, this ain't the booze

332

talkin'. I've seen 'em, up close and personal, on more than one occasion."

"Uh-huh. Where's the hidden camera mounted, old man?" Ed spat irritably, placing a hand on Liz's shoulder and tugging gently at her shirt collar.

"We're being played for fools, hon, can't you see that? Might even be one of those cable reality shows like *Fear Factor'*, or even th-.."

The old man's voice broke with anger as he raised a badly trembling hand and slowly curled it into a fist.

"This ain't no gag, son, believe you me. If ya truly think you're bein' duped, by all means crawl up the nearest ladder and pop your noggin topside. I promise you, it'll be the last thing you ever accomplish in this here world."

"Okay, okay...reel in the incisors, old man. Didn't mean to slice into a nerve," Ed replied, holding both hands up palms out.

There was a sharp retort as Liz reached around and slapped Ed across his bare forearm.

"Once and for all, put a sock in it, Ed. Please continue, Mister Myers. If nothing else, this sure fits the holiday mood."

"Appreciate it, missy, though there ain't no holiday cheer to be had, I'm afraid. Seems we got another forty five minutes or so to burn before all's clear, so I'll try my best to give ya the Reader's Digest version."

Leaning against the cool stone with his legs curled beneath him, the old man released a lengthy sigh born from pure exhaustion, equal parts physical and psychological.

"Nathan James Wendell, a strict puritan born and bred, was the leader of a substantial wagon train that settled into what is now known as Hallows Eve way back in the winter of eighteen seventy-nine. Over two-hundred folks assisted in clearin' the land in what was then referred to as the 'Wendell Colony'. As years passed and additional settlers arrived, the townships initial scandal surfaced with a vengeance. Several of the new arrivals were accused of spell-castin' and such, and instantly branded witches and warlocks by town council members, led by none other than Nathan Wendell himself. Man fancied hisself the southeastern Cotton Mather, I reckon.

Well, it's said that on October 31st, eighteen eighty-two, Wendell and several other prominent council members organized a lynch mob and held a town-square hangin' of at least fifteen named 'occultists'. Bodies were burned and the ashes dumped in the nearby Chamberland River Years later it was revealed that Nathan Wendell hisself had been quite the practitioner of black magic, this little tidbit comin' from the man's very own family.

Anyhow, the story concludes that just before he was ceremoniously hung in the town square that bore his name, ol' Nate placed a curse on the town. A curse that would manifest each Halloween 'tween midnight and one AM in the form of rovin' demons in search of warm, human flesh to render and souls to cast into eternal ruin."

A low huff parted Ed's tightly-pursed lips, and Liz released a muffled giggle she quickly stifled with an open hand.

"Hey, I don't write this stuff. Just passin' it on for what it's worth," the old man continued, "township was re-named Hallows Eve just weeks after Nathan's demise, and all the talk of curses and such was shrugged off as nothin' more than a dyin' lunatic's rant, that is, 'til the next October rolled around."

The old man paused to pull a glass pint bottle from his jacket pocket. "Pardon me, folks. Throat's a might parched."

After a quick sip, he resealed the bottle and placed it next to his left boot.

Several moments of strained silence followed, during which time the old man seemed to nod off. Scowling, Ed cleared his throat in obvious frustration.

"Oh, sorry 'bout that," the old man muttered, vigorously scratching his head with both hands, "I do have a tendency to drift."

Liz hugged herself as if suddenly chilled.

"I...we understand, Mr. Myers. Please continue."

"Oh yeah, I was just up to Black Tuesday, wasn't I? October 31, the Year of Our Lord Eighteen eighty-three. 'Tween the hours of midnight and one AM, it's said that thirty-four townspeople breathed their last. Seems a butt-load'a uninvited guests crashed their annual holiday wing-ding. Uninvited guests that bore a strikin' resemblance to former citizens once accused of witchcraft and long since buried away in the nearby Hallows Eve bone-yard.

The official town journal states that those that

didn't attend the midnight festivities awoke to find friends, neighbors and co-workers strung up all over main street with make-shift nooses, some of 'em gutted like hogs; others missin' a leg, arm, or even their head. It was hell on earth, stated the keeper of the journal; hell on earth right smack dab in America's heartland."

"My god. Was any of this…this story substantiated by the proper authorities?" Liz queried, her chin resting atop her kneecaps.

"Not a chance, missy. Never has been."

Ed stood stiffly, the pipe again filled with the ringing echo of his creaking knees.

"What exactly do you mean, '*never*' has been. There's been other such occurrences?"

Cocking his head to the right, the old man raised both hands in a 'shushing' gesture.

Despite an obvious lack of visibility within the pipe's cramped confines, the trio allstared upward at precisely the same time.

A series of muffled thumps became apparent, as if the synchronized footsteps of a silent marching band were passing over the street above. Less than thirty seconds later, deafening silence again staked its claim as sole proprietor of the surrounding airwaves.

"Ya hear 'em?" the old man asked, his voice crackling with fear, "…that ain't no founders day parade, folks. They're up there…and they're on the hunt"

Liz had a hand clamped tightly over her mouth, while Ed stood like a recently erected gargoyle, his eyes wide and his mouth hanging slightly ajar.

336

"To answer your question, son, yes, there have been…incidents over the decades, the last just ten years back. Halloween nineteen ninety-six. Outsider, kinda like yourselves, had the sad luck of passing through the limits when his motorcycle conked out on 'im. Just a kid, really, no more than twenty or twenty- one. Damned shame. Citizens know better, sure, but strangers never have a chance unless there's time to warn 'em off the streets. Obviously, this kid didn't have your luck. We found 'im…parts of 'im anyhow, scattered about Main, Elm, Maple, and Pine streets. Kerry Thrasher got back into town from a huntin' trip and found the kid's head stuffed inside his mailbox, still tucked inside the motorcycle helmet he'd wore into town.

The fifties and sixties were the worst, though. Lotta new folks movin' into town. Always took us as pranksters when we passed the tale on to 'em. Can't say I really blame 'em. Only those born and raised here truly understand…"

Breaking from a bout with suspended animation, Ed stepped past Liz until he practically loomed over the old man.

"You actually expect us to believe that the outside world knows nothing of these…multiple homicides? Man, you've got me confused with some other imbecile…"

"Ed, would you please SHUT UP? Let the man finish, for god's sake…" Liz scolded, reaching ahead to grasp Ed's blue jeans by the empty belt loops.

"Wasn't never an option, son. The elders of this town always made it priority number one to keep the curse of Hallows Eve contained within the city

337

limits. Media would'a turned this place into Amityville, only ten times worse.

These days, with the internet, cable news networks and all the other modern technologies floatin' about, why, the hard-working people of this town would be driven out by ghost-huntin' thrill-seekers and crack-pot reporters lookin' for their big break."

His shoulders slumped like a scolded child, Ed backed silently away and continued to stand as Liz hugged his left thigh.

"How much longer we have to play mole in this stinking tunnel then?" he finally snapped, although his bark had lost a considerable amount of bite.

Scooping up the light, the old man pointed the beam directly at his right wrist. Slipping from his hand, the flashlight rolled into the center of a deep, murky puddle, throwing the trio into complete darkness. Scrambling on his hands and knees, it took the old man a full two minutes to locate and reactive the fading light. As if the first result had been a fluke, he again aimed its dimming beam towards his shaking wrist.

"Well...I'm be damned. Looks like this Timex didn't have to take a lickin' 'fore it quit tickin' Hands froze up like a February icicle at...a-at.." his hand began to tremble as he fought to keep the narrow beam focused,

"eleven fifty-eigh...eleven..."

"Fifty-eight, mister Mayor? You mean your watch stopped at two minutes before midnight? Two measly, miserable minutes?" Liz mocked, obviously on the verge of giggling hysterically.

"Talk about your crappy luck. Old timer, you just rolled a lifetime's worth of snake eyes in a single stroke of misfortune," Ed chimed in through a wide, toothy grin Myers couldn't actually visualize but somehow knew was present.

Both spoke with dramatically altered tones, like stage actors reading from cue cards.

"Wha-what do you...Mayor? But...but how did you...do you? Your...your voices." he muttered, ever-so-gradually moving the badly shaking light towards the source. Backing against the cool stone until his backbone ached from the constant pressure, the old man could see the couple now stood side by side with their arms and legs extended, as if to barricade their end of the pipe.

"You really let that kid's death consume your very being, didn't you Mayor?" Liz inquired, taking a half step forward as the center of the light coated her legs and lower torso, "who could truly blame you for turning him away? True, he knocked on your door several times that night, pleading and sobbing as the gathering darkness formed a circle around his doomed, damned soul. But you knew...you *understood* the consequences if you'd allowed him entry into your home. Why allow such a baseless sacrifice for the sake of sentimental symbolism, am I right, Mayor Myers?"

The wavering beam bathed her lower torso, then her bosom. The old man's eyes were saucers. His purple-tinted lips squirmed and gyrated.

"Anyone in your position would surely have made the same choice, I believe. Then again, I'm hardly an expert on such matters of civility." He

339

ceased to breathe as her face filled the jittery spotlight, along with the shocking realization that her partner had seemingly vanished altogether.

"Ten years residing in the bottom of a whiskey bottle, only to have it end like this. Tsk tsk...how the mighty have fallen...from top city official to town lush in less than a decade. "

"My son! He was my son, d-damn it!" the old man howled as the flashlight fell from his grip and his arms toppled uselessly to his sides.

"I...I should have let...let him in. He..Justin..had rode his motorcy cycle all the way from...he...was going to surprise us. with an unannounced visit. Even as a ...child...he had never believed the stories. I...my...my wife never. she never f-forgave me for...n-not lettin' him.. in. For not savin'..our only son."

The old man collapsed onto his backside and covered his face with sludge-coated hands.

"Fear not, old man. We're here to relieve your misery, although I'm afraid our cleansing procedure of choice isn't the least bit pleasant," spoke the husky male voice, and the old man peeked through his fingers to see Ed's shadow poised on the opposite side of the pipe.

"W-who. who are y-you?" he managed, slowly dropping his splayed fingers.

As if on cue, their flesh began to glow and radiate, illuminating the tubular stone pillar in a bright green hue.

"The guise I choose is an oldie but goodie," Liz chortled, dancing an impromptu jig as her physical features grew increasingly distinct, "...see if you

340

recognize my personal theme song....

..Lizzy Borden took an axe...

..and gave her father forty whacks..

...when she saw what she had done...

...she gave her mother forty-one...

...need I sing more?"

Her build had thickened dramatically, her round, chubby face chalky pale.

Her hair no longer hung upon her shoulders but was streaked in gray and tied into a sizeable bun at the base of her skull. Her eyes were without pupils and the color of recently laid tar. She gripped a wooden-handled axe in both hands. An axe dripping glutinous, caramel-colored liquid from its finely honed twin-edges.

"Now, Frank, is such a foolish question truly necessary?"

The man was a noticeably shorter, with hunched shoulders and a squatty, stout build. As he stepped forward to reveal a hooked scythe curled into the palm of his right hand, the mostly toothless grin on display was malevolence personified.

"The names Gein, mayor. *Ed Gein*. Ring a bell? I'm gonna peel you like ripe fruit, old man, and sew a blanket from your leathery hide."

The old man shoved his feet into the sticky mire and forced himself upright, reaching back for balance as his boots repeatedly slipped.

"Y-you...you? But...that's not r-right. N-not f-fair. Y-you didn't. Your not...allowed d-down here...unless. "

The woman moved forward until the old man could practically taste her cool, bile-scented breath.

"Unless what, mayor? Someone personally *invited* us into this drain?"

Recall if you will, poor Frank, good Samaritan that you are, that you did ...precisely.that!

Really should have taken the time to double-check that watch battery, Mayor. Five minutes can make a world of difference you know, especially on this particular night."

The old man cringed back, then abruptly straightened, his stoic body posture the definition of stubborn defiance.

"What are you waitin' for then? An engraved invitation? Claim your prize, demons. I can only hope ya choke on my bones."

The couple exchanged a bemused glance, then reared back their respective weapons as if to simultaneously strike.

The old man winced, squeezing his eyes shut and bracing for a grisly finality that never materialized.

Instead, a barrage of raucous laughter filled the concrete catacomb as light faded to dark, followed by choking sobs that soon grew eerily silent.

***

"Did ya see his face? Man oh man, talk about priceless!" squealed the costumed 'Lizzy' while wiping thick gobs of bright greenish make up from her cheeks.

"What are you waiting for then, an *invitation*? *Grab your prize, demons*!" added the 'Ed Gein' subject before reaching up to remove a false row of 'blackened' teeth, "best damn bait and switch ever!...hook, line, and tracker-trailer sized sinker...it

342

surely doesn't get any better. How is such gullibility possible?"

"Only wish we had it on film," the regular guy Ed chimed in happily, "...that old man was as nuts as advertised, though I guess that story 'bout his son must have some truth to it. Hope the old geezer didn't keel over and croak down there."

"Hope ya *choke* on my bones!" concluded 'Liz', wrapping her arms around 'Ed Gein's' waist as he began wiping the same fluorescent gel from his face, neck and arms, "..you guys realize that nobody back at the frat house is gonna buy a word of this, right? I mean, would *you*?"

Standing beneath the lone functioning light that main street had to offer, the four individuals continued in unbridled revelry, growing increasingly vocal even as the rollicking laughter gradually subsided.

"Got most of the goop off anyhow,' quipped 'Ed Gein', having regained his youthful looks as the clever disguise had fallen away, 'how 'bout you, 'Lizzy'?

"Gonna take three hot showers to get it all, but it was worth every minute.

We leaving, troops? It's almost one in the AM..." she replied, tossing a pair of dark-shaded contact lenses aside, then playfully flipping the axe over her left shoulder.

Regular Ed shrugged.

"Yeah, it's a good forty-five minutes back to campus, and I don't wanna miss all of Larry's bash over at Sigma-phi. After all, I funded at least two of the kegs." They turned as one, casually strolling

343

down the center of Main street, the sounds of their pounding feet the lone filler amidst otherwise dead air.

As their SUV swam into view a few hundred feet ahead, parked around the corner of a long-closed BP station, Regular Liz broke the silence.

"Hard to believe an entire town could buy into some flaky urban legend.

Still, can't deny the 'ghost-town' spookiness, right?"

"Creep-show city, no doubt. Like Professor Canby said, even in the 21st century, superstition is still a universal force," the 'Ed Gein' subject added, digging into his jeans pocket.

The key chain accidentally flung from his fingers, landing atop a man-hole cover engulfed by fallen oak leaves.

Just as he knelt to retrieve them, the cover wobbled ever-so-slightly, then shifted a few inches to the left.

"What the h…" Ed Gein began, leaping back as if goosed. A moment later, soiled fingers rose from the narrow crack.

"Ohhh, don't even tell me..." regular Liz moaned as the four formed a circle around the cover.

"Gotta be the old man...but how did he get all the way over he-.." regular Ed stated just as the heavy iron cover shot skyward as if propelled by high explosives.

"Hollllly sheeeeeee..." he concluded, falling back with a resounding thump, thus joining his three accomplices lying atop the cool pavement.

The figure didn't crawl from the hole. Nor did it jump exactly. Moreover, it seemed to *levitate* as if pulled to the surface by invisible wires.

The shell-shocked foursome scrambled and crawled away as the figure landed softly between them.

"You play a good joke, I must say...acting so very entranced at my sad, sad tale...switching places in the dark...veeerrrrry clever, yes indeed..."it croaked in a raspy tone that seemed to originate from every direction at once, weirdly unaffected by the dull shaded, badly scarred motorcycle helmet concealing its identity. "..but one who dishes it out must also be prepared to take it, correct?

I do a pretty good imitation of my old man, wouldn't you agree? Right down to his grungy beard and rank BO, yes? Had you 'young folks' on the edge of your seat there for a while, ya gotta admit..."

As the figure's outer guise peeled away like parched confetti and the air thickened with the scent of rot and decay, the fallen foursome screeched as one.

"Before final sentencing commences, allow me a formal introduction," it bellowed cheerily, its long, skeletal fingers splayed wide to reveal speared tips, ".....the names Justin, *Justin Myers*", the helmet split down the center and fell away as shreds of blackened skin melted from its gore-slick skull in moist clumps, the faux facial hair having long since evaporated ". and it's gonna be great having kids my age to hang out with, if only for an hour every October! By the way, gang....

.....Nathan Wendell sends his regards, and wants to wish you and yours ...."

>From each of its bony, gnarled hands, it waived twin carving knifes from side to side with amazing quickness and expertise. Without benefit of either a running start or crouched leap, it took flight, then swept downward in a clock-wise arc...

'...a *Happy Halloween*'

..Four separate sets of howling screams ensued....

...and abruptly ended in a barrage of frenzied hacking....

...and slicing of flesh...

...and crunching of bones....

***

November 1st, 5 AM: The good citizens of Hallows Eve awake to discover four bodies, each minus a rather notable organ, hanging from a massive oak tree that corners Oak and Pine streets.

November 1st, 7:10 AM: The local caretaker of the Hallows Eve cemetery reports four severed heads lined atop a single grave site, the head stone of which reads;

HERE LIES THE HONORABLE FRANK J. MYERS 1942-2002

A FINE MAN, A FINE MAYOR...MAY HE FIND ETERNAL PIECE WITHIN THE WAITING ARMS OF HIS LOVING SON

The dawn's rising on November 2nd in Hallows Eve breeds the return of normalcy ...that is, at least for another 363 days...

346

Death is not limited solely to living, breathing organisms. Cultures can also perish, driven to extinction as generations pass and age-old traditions fade like mornings early fog into blazing sunlight. Bear witness to such a unique tragedy in the following futuristic saga, where computer 'Super-Viruses' will be utilized not for destruction, but as sophisticated learning tools....

16 - SOUTHERN EXTINCTION

"Settle down, class. We have one more series to get through before mid- day nutrition commences," the instructor announced, kneeling down a bit to insert a palm-sized disk into a nearby wall unit She heard the class groan in unison just as the virtual display hummed to life.

"Now, now…none of that. You cannot honestly tell me the series on the American Indian wasn't utterly fascinating, as was the history of immigration in the early to late 20th Century."

The majority of the twenty-six eighth graders before her nodded in mild agreement, although a few remained stubbornly defiant. There was little argument amongst the student body and faculty alike that '*Virtual American History*' was one of the more popular middle grade classes, surpassing '*The Basics of Pre-Teen Teleportation*', while admittedly running a close second to '*Sexual Awakenings: Your Bodies Initial Signal to Initiate Hormone Control Treatments*'.

"Yes, Simon-346?" the instructor asked somewhat wearily, eyeing the young man fronting the row nearest to her.

"Instructor Laura, how long before we cover the early 21st Century oil wars? My father told me that mass chemical warfare usage practically eliminated the Middle Eastern bloc, and that clouds of nerve gas killed thousands in the Midwestern US. He also sa..."

"Simon-346, we still have several personality biographies to cover before we delve into such grave matters,' the instructor interrupted sternly, leaving the boy slightly red-faced, 'I understand how subjects involving insane acts of uncontrolled violence and rage fascinate young men such as yourself, but you need to learn to control such...*morbid* curiosity, least an extra session of behavioral modification be in order."

"Yes, m'am," he whispered, lowering his head in shame. "Now, everyone insert a blank disc into your memory pads, as there will be a quiz given at day's end. Ensure you highlight as instructed by the visual aid, and please notify me immediately if you detect even the slightest pulse wave interference."

Stepping to the rear of the spacious classroom, she aimed a tiny remote device towards a far wall just as the children's cockpit-styled desk units whirled around in the direction of a circular glass stage.

The classroom lights dimmed and the flat stage lit up in synchronized unison, the children's foreheads now pressed firmly against the virtual reality headsets protruding from the front edge of their respective desk tops.

"The title of the visual aid presentation is '19/20th/21st Century Man Specific Region: Southeastern United States. A History of: Southern Heritage, Culture, and Tradition.' Downloading visual aid host circa the year two-thousand fifty-one."

The virtual setting appeared in segments, like an ancient puzzle whose pieces fell together in a fragmented frenzy of slow motion construction.

The visual host initially appeared as a middle

aged Caucasian male, perhaps between the ages of 40-50, sporting short-cropped hair which was graying at the temples and a lengthy growth of facial hair that was streaked in patches of ivory. He wore a gray uniform shirt with large black buttons, and had a long-barreled rifle balanced atop his right shoulder. Standing at the center of a wide, grassy pasture, an animal (identified to the students as a **'HORSE – Working Mammal- extinct 22nd century'** in a typed menu at the setting's top right hand corner) stood causally grazing in the background. In the far distance, tendrils of black smoke arose from a wooden shack that was practically hidden between a row of massive elm and oak trees (again listed in the menu as such).

The man spat a dark liquid from between pursed lips (quickly identified as **'TOBACCO PRODUCT – banned by government order in the year 2039'**), then stared straight ahead wearing a dazed expression and initiated the presentation prologue.

"The year is 1864; the place-the Southern United states The Civil War ran from 1861 to 1865; a tragic time in US History wherein brother fought brother over such issues as states rights and slavery. Until the South American Border wars of 2029, the Civil War was responsible for more combat related deaths than any skirmish fought within the borders of the United States It was during this span that the Southern region truly became a separate entity from their Northern and Western brethren, establishing a tangible state of mind, equal parts physical and psychological. Despite an

eventual surrender due to equipment and manpower shortages, the southern people held firm to certain beliefs that outsiders either viewed as stubborn and short-sided, or simply ignorant in nature. The Emancipation Proclamation (HIGHLIGHTED on student menu) abolished slavery once the war ended in Northern victory, but a vast majority of the southern region held firm to old beliefs, thus the issue of racial equality wasn't initially accepted without decades of continued strife and conflict."

The host gave a small nod even as the visuals around him gradually transformed; the surrounding rural landscape replaced by a three story plantation fronted by a trio of 20th century automobiles (the student menu labeled each by make and model, the newest constructed in 1954). The surrounding forest and overgrown foliage melted away to be quickly replaced by ancient maple and elm trees, manicured lawns and perfectly coifed shrubbery. The host no longer donned the uniform of the Confederacy, but a slick white suit and black bow tie, his hair as neatly combed as his meticulously trimmed beard.

"A minority of the southern population thrived during the agricultural age; riches spawned from such diverse crops as corn, cotton and wheat, while a larger majority in such industrially poor states such as Mississippi, Alabama, Arkansas and Tennessee lived in relative squalor. In the decades following World War II, businesses slowly began to migrate to the South, quick to take advantage of a population willing to work for less than their Northern counterparts. Farming was still the main economic source (HIGHLIGHTED), although

industrial and production type jobs were beginning to make a dent.

It was during this time, as Northerners slowly began to make their way South for fresh job opportunities, that such terms as 'Southern Pride', 'Southern Hospitality', and 'Southern Heritage' first came into play. Even as third and fourth generation Southerners dominated the work force, they were soon intermingled with immigrants from Europe and South America, as well as a growing population of Black Americans of African descent. Thus, what was referred to as 'social integration' quickly grew into a trouble source within the region.

Again, the host's head tilted just slightly as the scene altered to reveal a more urban background. The host sported a more casual look; his facial hair having vanished even as his thick, graying hair melted away to reveal lengthier, blondish locks tucked beneath a worn baseball cap (identified as **'Fashion Head Accessory'** in menu). He wore baggy plaid pants, a white T-shirt and a pair of well-worn, heavy-duty work boots. Small shops and street vendors selling various fruits and vegetables from wooden crates now dominated the background visual.

"As the sixth decade of the twentieth century came to pass, winds of change began to pick up intensity within the very Heart of Dixie (HIGHLIGHTED), a term meaning the very core of the Southland.

The equality movement was running rampant nationwide involving the female and black population, as well as the many immigrants from

Eastern Europe, all in search of a fair shake within the world of politics and overall social acceptance. Southerners in particular had a difficult adjustment period regarding such issues, with state and local politicians...a-a-g-g-g-reeing to d-dis-a-gree on m-m-m-ma-t-t-t-t-ers.o—o-o-o-...'

His movements comically mechanical, the host eventually froze in mid- word, his mouth agape and his right hand stuck airborne as the background scene began to flicker and flash without a single moment's coherence. Objects appeared and then vanished abruptly without ever truly taking permanent shape in a surreal kaleidoscope of unidentifiable colors. A new figure entered the screen just as all background movement halted, stepping into the frame as if magically transported from real-world time, like a man entering a TV screen from *outside* the set. Completely bald, his scalp and forehead were beet red and held just a tint of perspiration. He looked to be in his late thirties to early forties, stocky in build and wearing a bushy, walrus-type mustache that curled tightly at its pointed ends.

"Howdy, y'all. Pardon my abrupt and rather rude interruption, kids," the man announced in a thick southern drawl utterly void of the stiff, robotic tone used by the previous host, "but with my own eyelids growing increasingly heavy from this programs rather dry, mechanical delivery, I figured you, as a class, must be on the outer edge of passin' out altogether."

Wearing dark blue jeans, a white cotton T-shirt and brown work-boots ravaged with grooved scars near the circular toes, the man stood with his thick, muscular arms crossed across his barrel-shaped chest. As his monologue continued, the earlier host and accompanying scenery vanished in a misty, static- filled light, to be gradually replaced by a dark black, late 20th Century model Ford Pick-up truck (as listed in menu) parked atop a gravel drive in front of a modest two-story brick home.

*"Now that the programmed robot MC ('**Master of Ceremonies**', read a separate drop-down menu) has flown the coop, we can get down to some real history, minus most of the crap that just don't matter, like specific dates and locations. It's the personal aspect...the people and the changes they endured that needs to be covered, not these dry-ass factoids (defined as '**slang/profanity**' in menu), pardon my French."*

The ever-changing, rapidly merging landscape behind the man eventually fell completely into place, the truck now flanked by a spacious, hilly field engulfed in perfectly spaced rows of corn that stretched as far and wide as the image could project. The man leaned against the trucks shiny chrome grill, gently tapping his forehead with a white rag he'd pulled from his jeans' rear pocket.

*"I'm sure you've covered the American Civil War with its causes and aftermaths 'til your pretty much fed up with the particulars. Like I said, what I want you to focus on is the heritage and culture of the southern people...their way of life. First off, I guess formal intros are in order. Unlike old tight jaws before me, I ain't no computer programmed image or CGI design, no siree (**slang term**:*

*undefined). Instead, your peepers (**slang term:** defined as meaning 'eyes') are presently trained on a bon-I-fied 21st Century hologram designed to infiltrate computerized fields of study. In other words, boys and girls, an updated version of what used to be referred to in computer terms as a 'virus'. My physical appearance and mannerisms are not of a single man, but a virtual montage of the three men who created me. They are memorialized as follows:*

James Murray Hemstrout, white male, was born on March 9th, 1989 in Montgomery, Alabama A computer analyst until his retirement in the year 2056, he passed away at the ripe old age of eight-eight in Tucson, Arizona.

William Jay Henriksen, white male, was born on January 19th, 1991 in Tupelo, Mississippi. He worked as a systems administrator for the US Navy for twenty years, then retired after ten additional years with NASA/Asian Branch. He passed away at the age of ninety-four in Biloxi, Mississippi.

*Carl Lee Shots, black male, was born on May 10th, 1992 in Richmond, Virginia. Widely touted as one of the top ten 'systems hackers' of the 21st Century, his work in the field of 'Virus Busting' was instrumental in the cure of '**The Black Plague'** of 2023, wherein the entire Eastern seaboard of the United States and portions of Canada experienced a computer 'blackout' that lasted twenty-seven days due to the so-called 'Black Plague' worm. Carl worked the last seventeen years of his life in the Pentagon's Top Secret Underground Programming Division, where he established virus-detection and* *elimination hardware that is still in use eleven decades later. He died at his home inWheeling, West Virginia at the age of ninety.*

These three complex individuals saw fit to use me as their personal history teacher; creating me in their own image, a digital spokesman engraved inside this program in order to provide a fitting epitaph for the heritage they loved, admired and, sad to say, watched dissipate into just another footnote within a society that had become cold, mechanical, and woefully bland. A society that frowned on regional individualism until it was phased out altogether; replaced by what my creators would call 'personality cloning'. To put it in simple southern terms, what they're doin' today just plain ain't right."

The man paused to stare into the bright, clear sky overhead while reaching to retrieve a small, multi-colored box from the roll of his left shirt sleeve. Pulling a narrow white tube from the box, he placed it gently between his lips while tugging at his left jeans pocket.

He casually released a tiny flame from one end of a small, circular, blue colored object (Defined as: **Lighter. Outlawed nationwide in 2038 by The COMBUSTIBLE MATERIALS Ordinance**) and inhaled deeply as thin tendrils of smoke departed the narrow tube's (Defined as: **Cigarette TOBACCO PRODUCT: banned nationwide in 2039**) burnt end.

Leaning over with one elbow propped casually against the truck's shiny hood, he exhaled smoke from both nostrils.

*"My creators were fiercely proud of their southern heritage, even as they departed the Southland for distant territories, the Northern states and Southern California to be exact, to begin plying their trade in the booming IT markets of the early 21st Century. In many cases, they were greeted with initial skepticism from colleagues who doubted their abilities and even their intelligence once the twang of their southern accents became apparent. It was almost always an uphill battle for my creators to earn the respect they so richly deserved once their place of birth was made an issue. Don't get me wrong, it wasn't anywhere near the same type of treatment as Jackie Robinson (**SPORTS REFERENCE**: 'First African- American Major League Baseball Player) or Catherine Jamison (**POLITICAL REFERENCE: First female President of the United States**) endured, but there were those who simply would not easily accept a southerner within the higher ranks of the IT community due to their lineage."*

Tossing what little remained of the burnt tube onto the dirt road surface, he stamped it forcefully with his left boot, then walked slowly away from the truck up the gravelly path.

"Growing up in the South of the late 20th and early 21st Centuries, the creators were already residing in a rapidly changin' landscape within the region itself. The technological advances of earlier decades, most notably nineteen ninety to two-thousand-ten, had pretty much evened the playin' field nationwide. Cable TV and the Internet changed the way the world listened, learned, and lived. So, it

357

was mostly the stories told by their elders that instilled the sense of southern pride that became a permanent part of who they were as men. Codes to live by, so to speak, no matter where you laid your head outside the Mason/Dixon line.

Southerners, especially those raised in smaller townships, were taught to be courteous and kind, especially to strangers.

They got to know their neighbors and the people in their community, and would come to their aid without hesitation if the need arose. They invited said neighbors to supper, 'dinner' was for snobs, never once considerin' a possible shortage of food in the cupboard afterwards.

Sunday mornings at church were as mandatory as school attendance the following day.

Priorities were simple; cut and dry. God; family; country, PERIOD. Breach of said order was unthinkable, and in some communities, simply not tolerated.

They were taught to revel in the simple pleasures that country living had to offer. Harvestin' the rewards from gardens grown from countless hours of sweat was a privilege, not a chore.

*As **CHILDREN**, their elders grew up with black and white TV, and sometimes had but two local channels to view. During the summer, they cultivated a garden large enough to keep them well-stocked with fresh vegetables through the following Fall and Winter.*

Summer fun for the younger set was had without video or virtual reality games, cable television, live 'interactive' programming, palm digital readers, or the Internet.

They played baseball, football and basketball, sure, but also kick-the-can, kick-ball, and dodge-ball in July heat that would have literally melted their Northern counterparts.

They caught fireflies and placed them in jars as 'homemade' flashlights. They fished with bamboo poles and wire hooks.

They skipped rocks from creek banks.

They rode their bikes for hours on end, whether the trail be asphalt, gravel or dirt.

They didn't get their sports news from cable networks, sports-tickers, or 'wrist-flash' cams, but from battery-operated transistor radios hung from bike handlebars or hanging from their belts. Same with the music they listened to.

Along the same lines, the third most popular religious sect within the region, following hot on the trail of the Baptists and Methodists, was definitely the Southern FOOTBALL fanatic.

They 'borrowed' watermelons from neighboring farms. They 'camped out' in each other's yards in makeshift tents.

On Halloween, they soaped car windows and filled trees with toilet tissue, all the while roaming the countryside like carefree gnomes, unafraid of adult 'predators' that had yet to become the norm.

At Christmas, they didn't purchase their trees from 'tree lots' or Wal-Mart, but cut one down from their own property. The decorating of the tree was a family affair, and treated with great reverence.

They built clubhouses and forts from materials

found on their parent's land.

And, true enough, the majority of the summer months werespent barefoot. Southern ADULT MALES were ingrained with a work ethic that normally included dawn risings and sunset quitting times.

They were caring but stern fathers who didn't hesitate to use a belt or wooden 'switch' to get their point across to unruly offspring. Wasn't any 'time-outs' in those days. The fear they instilled in their children wasn't done out of cruelty, but love. It helped teach the young to respect those older and more knowledgeable, something direly lacking as the 20th Century closed and youth crime rates soared.

During the early 20th Century, the majority of southern men knew only two things; hard work and family. Feeding, clothing and providing a stable home was their role, and most passed away early with callused hands and weathered skin.

The southern FEMALE couldn't be so easily defined, as this was oft times a creature of mystery and not so easily pigeonholed. Of course, a lot depended on one's standing in the community. Homemakers all until their gradual infusion into the workforce during the 1960's, many performed double-duty as both homemaker and farm laborer. Raising the children was sometimes the sole responsibility of the mother, along with the cooking, cleaning, and shopping tasks. If raised among the wealthy, the female assumed the role of 'Dixie Debutante' at a very tender age. From there, she was expected to marry rich to maintain a status of elite standing within the community.

As a whole, to be raised in the Southland during the early to mid-twentieth Century meant living a hard but relatively simple life dominated by family issues. *These were basically good-hearted, hard-working, but undeniably stubborn people who took pride in their work and were fiercely protective of what was theirs.*

The bloodlines were rich even if the family wasn't, and steeped in a tradition built on sweat, tears, and old-fashioned values."

The man wiped his brow and sighed, frowning deeply.

"That said, to ignore the blatant racism that transpired in those times would be an unforgivable omission. African-Americans were, for the most part, still being treated as third-class citizens a full century after the Civil War had given them their freedom. I'm not gonna emphasize the particulars; you've all been tested on 'em since pre-grade school in the **'Equal but Separate: A Question of Color'** *forums. Let's call it what it was; cruel, heartless, ignorant, and utterly regrettable.*

Caucasian Southerners of the 21st Century spent a good portion of their lives apologizing for the horrid mistakes of their elders.

Many attempted to make sincere amends, while a tiny minority made it their simple-minded mission to carry on the campaign of hatred and bigotry, organizing so-called 'hate groups' to further persecute those they deemed 'unworthy' due to race, color, or ethnic background. By the year 2013, such groups had either disbanded voluntarily or been forced from the public eye by law enforcement. Fortunately, such erratic, deviant behavior isn't allowed in today's government regulated society.

As the 21st Century closed, several factors had teamed to all but eliminate the southern culture as a whole. The constant flow of immigration through the century, as well as technological advances in agriculture, was the main culprits. Even the distinct, trademark accent that had always separated southerners from their Northern and Western counterparts dissipated like mist in the morning sun as decades passed and generations passed on."

As the man faced forward, the cornfield behind him began to melt away, replaced by a frenzied montage of fragmented film clips, beaming forth like hundreds of ancient TV screens on display in an antique department store window, and all showing separate programs.

"To sum up, kids, the south and its people gave a lot to the country in terms of culture. Much more than most historical scholars will ever give them credit for."

One screen displayed an outdoor sports arena filled to overflowing (**NOTE:** such activities banned in 2079 due to UV Ray contamination once Ozone Layer collapsed) as the sun shone bright on the football (**NOTE:** Banned sport as of 2065) players frequenting the field below.

"...such as the great sports traditions..."

Another showcased a group of musicians, most of which wore large Cowboy (**NOTE:** circa 19th century farm-hand, gunfighter, etc.) hats, standing on a stage in front of a large, seated audience. The

362

crowd seemed to be singing along as the band performed, with clapping hands and stamping feet.

"...*country music (**NOTE**: banned in 2055, along with all music labeled 'popular', as it was defined by Government regulation as a NEGATIVE YOUTH INFLUENCE) had its rich roots here.*"

Still another flashed scene after majestic scene of wheat, cotton and barley fields, spread out over countless acres both hilly and flat. Surrounding screens were filled with farmhouses of all sizes and designs, most of which were backed by a large barn or similar structure.

"...*while the southern farmer was instrumental in feeding the nation as a whole...*"

The majority of the screens were dominated simply by faces; quick-hit profiles of smiling children and stern-faced adults of all colors and races; of aged grandfathers and grandmothers whose grave, unsmiling expressions were easily dismissed as clever disguises by the kindness behind their brightly lit eyes.

"...*and gave us a people whose dedication to family and country was unmatched in their time. Though the media and Entertainment industry of the late 20th and early 21st Century historically labeled or simply wrote off southerners as either uneducated hicks or ignorant buffoons, it was the visitors from other parts of the land who saw them for what they truly were. A proud people. A kind people. Folks who would literally give you 'the shirt off their backs', if need be.*

My creators endured the snide remarks concerning their heritage; the allegations that they

363

too 'must be racist' if born and raised in a region where such ideals flourished in the distant past. They adapted and overcame, all the while keeping a stiff upper lip, and never bothering to give those who ridiculed or accused the satisfaction of seeing them angered. They too, were proud, you see. Proud to be Americans first. Proud to be Southern Americans second. To them, the definition of the word 'Redneck' was far removed from the modern-day comedian's take of 'ignorant southerner', but instead simply meant 'hard working folk whose neck shone red from the sun'. When someone referred to one of the creators as such, he would nod his head amiably, thanking them for the compliment."

The man folded his arms across his chest and winked playfully as the background again began to alter, slowly melding back into its original text from whence he first appeared. A guitar-driver musical tune grew louder as this happened, and the man began to tap his feet to the rhythm even as his very form began to break away and vanish in miniscule chunks of static.

"remember the heritage, children, and the culture. You are all extensions of what came before you, despite this government's attempt to mechanize your lives; your very. personalities. The human race was a colossal tree with roots that stretched the length and width of the country itself. You are black...you are white...you are red...you are yellow...you are brown You are all these things in one. Your cells are rich in cultural diversity. And somewhere amongst those millions and millions of cells, you are also....

...Southern by the Grace of God."

The form bowed slightly before vanishing in a spattering of streaky blue flame. The virtual scene had returned to the space he had entered, the original host still frozen in mid-word, his right arm propped airborne.

Moments later, the classroom lights came up as the children's cockpit chairs whirled about as one, shifting around and down until they were back in their original position. The instructor shut down the virtual display with a single click, then moved swiftly to the podium as the students removed their headsets, their movements clumsily executed; their eyes weary and dazed, as if having just awakened from a deep slumber.

"The contaminated file you have just viewed should be ignored, thus instantly forgotten, class. Do you understand?" she barked angrily, her face beet red.

"Yes, Instructor Laura", the class droned as one.

"I must apologize for not being able to shut it down before its completion, but these aged viruses are known to carry a hypnotic agent of some type, and will now allow for conscious interruption. Needless to say, I will immediately have these disks removed and sent to Principal Instructor Prine for immediate destruction," she said loudly, tapping her fingers against the podium in obvious frustration.

"You are dismissed for nutrition intake until your next forum at one- twenty. Remember, class...information gathered from a purposely infected program is not to be taken literally. While

365

some of the content may indeed be fact, the majority, I'm afraid, is merely speculation...or simply a minority's opinion."

"Yes, instructor Laura," they repeated, filing out a row at a time. The twenty-six students exited the class for the dome-covered walkway, forming a three-file formation. As the march ensued in utter silence, Simon-346 fought to wipe the tight smile forming on his purple-shaded lips.

The lyrics refused to fade from his mind, mainly due to only a half- hearted effort to push them away. After a moment, he gave up the fight completely and allowed the song to play freely. After another moment, he decided it wasn't such a bad thing after all. In fact, he secretly hoped it would stay with him at least for the rest of the day.

And the song went:

'...*I wish I were in Dixie, Away, Away...*
...In Dixieland I'll make my stand...
...to live and die in Dixie...
...Away...Away...Away down south in Dixie..."

By the time the class regrouped for their next forum, similar tunes whose origins remained a mystery were filling their collective minds. Tunes rich with instrumental harmonies long-since banned: violins sang; banjos hummed, and guitars strummed. All the while, more than a few feet tapped happily in unison.

Over the next several days, many of the students who were exposed to what became known as the '*Southern Extinction*' virus were also reprimanded for the blatant misuse of such non-words as '*Y'all*' and '*Ain't*'.

366

One particular 'malcontent' was even expelled when a digital sketch drawing was discovered tucked inside one of his history excel-files. The drawing displayed a flag of sorts, with crossed bars in the shape of an X.

Drawn within the bars were stars.

Beneath the rough sketch was typed a single word:

'Rebel'.